Seven adventurers entered the Depths of Madness.

Davoren raised a fist, which crackled with spinning energy. "What's to keep me from smiting your leader right now and taking her place?"

Then he raised his other fist, and the energy arced between them.

"And a second—a corollary, if you will." He furrowed his brow, as though thoughtful. "What's to keep me from smiting all of you right now? It seems to me that none of us are armed, and I need no weapo—"

As the words snapped out of his mouth, Twilight exploded into motion. She dived into a roll, came up inside the circle of Davoren's arms, and whipped the metal shard, which she had concealed behind her arm, against his throat.

The warlock chuckled. "Meaningless," he said. "My powers are of the Nine Hells, and in my veins pumps the blood of demons—no mere metal can bite my skin."

"Yes, but I'm willing to wager that if you've a demon's blood, you've a demon's weakness," Twilight said. "And this, if you hadn't noticed, is cold-wrought iron."

Davoren did not move or blink, but the rage in his eyes said enough.

Unless they can work together, all seven will die.

THE DUNGEONS

DEPTHS OF MADNESS
Erik Scott de Bie

THE HOWLING DELVE
Jaleigh Johnson
July 2007

STARDEEP
Bruce R. Cordell
November 2007

CRYPT OF THE MOANING DIAMOND
Rosemary Jones
December 2007

Other books by Erik Scott de Bie
GHOSTWALKER

THE DUNGEONS

DEPTHS OF MADNESS

Erik Scott de Bie

The Dungeons

DEPTHS OF MADNESS

©2007 Wizards of the Coast, Inc.

Cover art by Erik Gist
Map by Robert Lazzaretti
First Printing: March 2007

9 8 7 6 5 4 3 2 1

ISBN: 978-0-7869-4314-2
620-95972740-001-EN

U.S., CANADA,
ASIA, PACIFIC, & LATIN AMERICA
Wizards of the Coast, Inc.
P.O. Box 707
Renton, WA 98057-0707
+1-800-324-6496

EUROPEAN HEADQUARTERS
Hasbro UK Ltd
Caswell Way
Newport, Gwent NP9 0YH
GREAT BRITAIN
Save this address for your records.

Visit our web site at www.wizards.com

Dedication

This one is for three special ladies.
For Nan, who told me I could make the descent.
For Donna, who kept the faith I'd find my way in the darkness.
And for Shelley, who walks with me through the depths.

Acknowledgments

Susan, my editor, for all her help in molding this one. Ed, Elaine, Bob, Steven, and Paul, for all their advice and their generous well-wishes. Andrew, for all the wit and support, and the excellent recommendations traded. Sean, for all that work down in Portland and for being such an excellent host. Erik, for the look. The scribes at Candlekeep: Sweet water and light laughter. And all the Young Dragons . . . RAR!

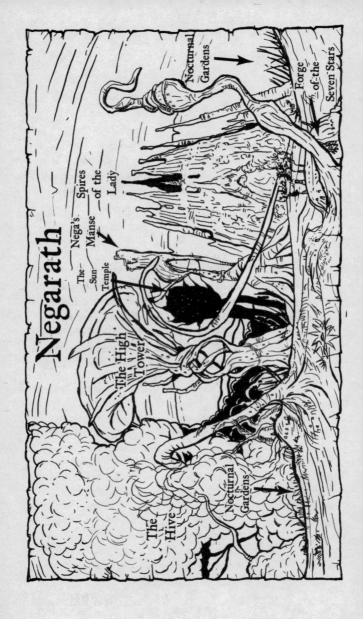

PROLOGUE

When Galandra fell, a spear piercing her throat, Arandon knew they would all die.

His arms had never felt so tired. The warrior swept at the onslaught as ineffectually as a child bats at a swarm of gnats, his axe cutting back and forth as fast as he could swing it. The steel knocked a spear aside, then buried itself in a lizardman's chest. Arandon let go and snatched a pair of handaxes from his belt just in time to trap a hurled spear between them. He twisted and the shaft spun through the air, driving back a dozen of the creatures.

More took their places.

Scores upon scores of the things poured out of openings all around the black chamber. Their crimson eyes gleamed, as did the obsidian that tipped their weapons. Cords of muscle, serrate scale ridges, and clawed wings spoke of a heritage far removed from the human realms. Caustic green foam dripped from their fangs.

Galandra screamed, then gurgled. Arandon looked just in time to see the priestess fall. Her shield dropped to her side, letting half a dozen spears jab into her body, piercing her crimson mail. Quelin leaped to her defense, his hammer smashing back and forth, but it was too late.

Arandon cursed. "Do something, Davoren!"

An arc of flame cut in front of him, searing scales and flesh to cinders. The warlock was helping, he supposed, but it wasn't enough. The chains of flame had kept them alive thus far, wedging the horde against the walls, but without healing magic. . . .

Arandon felt eyes watching him, but he knew no one was there.

"Lass?" he asked over his shoulder, not sparing the heartbeat it would take to look. A spear hit solidly and shattered on his buckler, numbing his arm.

The reply came in the form of an inhuman screech. Two lizardmen sank to the ground, clutching their throats. Arandon heard a contemptuous scoff meant for him. Despite his desperation, he smiled.

Five paces away, Telketh hacked with his sword, the blows driven home by raw strength. Arandon's axes skipped and slid off the lizardmen's slimy hides more often than they bit, but Quelin swung his hammer to good effect, dashing brains across the floor with every swipe.

"Forward!" Telketh shouted. Spears glanced off his shining armor, but he strode on, fearless. Arandon cut faster, courage burning in him.

Quelin smashed yet another lizardman, stepped forward to bat aside a spear that nearly struck Telketh's shoulder, and stepped back hard on a runic marking. A column of entropic energy flowed up and engulfed half the paladin's body, which writhed into dozens of forms at once. A heartbeat later, the man's scream became an agonized whistle, then a whining moan, then a wet gurgle as he fell, a quivering mass of flesh.

Arandon's heart sank. Now they were four: a sword, an axe, a caster, and a liar.

The scaly fiends were pushing them back toward a wall of black stone. The four fought hard, but without a priest or paladin, they were dead. He felt that invisible gaze again, focusing on him. Was he next?

"What's watching us?" he shouted as he hacked.

"Impossible," their captain said, fingering her sapphire amulet.

Then the lizardmen hesitated. Arandon and Telketh cut down two more. The lizardmen fell back, spears ready, and the four didn't pursue. Davoren let the fires die.

They heard a devil's bemused chuckle.

"What . . . ?" Arandon started.

"It comes," Davoren said wryly.

A great roar ripped through the cavern, and all eyes turned to its source.

The creature that loomed out of the shadows stood twice as tall as even the hulking Telketh. It sprouted limbs of mad distortion—one arm long and gangly, the other thick and clawed, while one leg pulsed with wiry muscle and the other stomped like a boulder. It ran at Twilight, who stared, shocked. The lizardmen fled down dark passages.

"Twilight!" Arandon stumbled. He looked to his bitter rival, standing at her side. "Telketh, aid her!"

Telketh leveled his sword. "Lass!" He shoved her aside, just in time for the huge claws to close around him and snap him into several pieces, giant sword and all.

With an avenging cry, Arandon threw himself at the creature's thicker leg, but his axes shattered against the mottled scales. The beast clubbed Arandon aside with Telketh's ragged torso. His body slammed against the wall like a discarded bone, and everything went red.

He'd lost his limbs; whether they were attached or not, he could not feel them. Blood dribbled down his chin. Spears punctured his body. He thought he saw fire. He heard the screams of the dying and the jeers of the living.

A shadow flickered across his vision. A familiar face looked into his with bright eyes that seemed white in the dimming light. He prayed that his lover, at least, might escape.

"Go," he tried to say. Nothing.

She understood.

Arandon watched the elf vanish into the shadows and rebuked himself. If anyone survived, it would be *her*.

Tymora, I'm coming, he thought.

Then a pair of eyes opened before him in his mind—cold eyes devoid of humanity or passion.

No, a quiet voice said in his head. *No, you aren't.*

Arandon tried to scream.

CHAPTER ONE

A dull, half-hearted light leaked in from the torches burning in the hallway. The woman opened her eyes a crack.

She awoke cold and mostly naked in muddy darkness. Her splitting headache made the world thrash as she tried to comprehend what had happened. Little sniffling sounds, like deep breathing or perhaps growling, came to her ears. Every bit of her ached, and her mind was as bleary as her eyes. She saw, dimly, a scar on her right hand, and contemplated it as she awakened.

"Typical," Twilight murmured.

She wondered, for a moment, which cheap dive she had awakened in this time. The mustiness and the water dripping on her forehead reminded her of the Curling Asp in Westgate. The vaguely disturbing sounds brought back a certain guest chamber she had occupied on her one and only visit to the unsightly bowels of Zhentil Keep. The salty foulness in the air—a blend of spit, rot, and dried excrement—brought to mind a certain Haggling Harpy in Athkatla, which was ostensibly named for a local legend. Its name actually came from the technique that one needed to ply in order to procure a decent room.

The Fox-at-Twilight realized, though, that her cheek was stuck to cold stone that was far too comfortable to be one of the pallets at the Harpy. She peeled herself off and blinked. She detected a certain mixture of damp fur, mildew, and useless tears mixed with human foulness. She could practically hear the unanswered prayers from decades of prisoners.

"A cell," Twilight said as she rose to a sitting position, grateful that she could move. She sniffed and scowled. "Not *as* typical."

She focused on the sole source of light—a murky, pink-red radiance in the corridor. She padded to it on thick soles quite accustomed to a lack of boots. Twilight felt oddly light on her feet, a sensation much like being slightly tipsy on Calishite wine.

Ignoring the feeling, Twilight examined the exit. A series of blades and rods folded and fit together like a genius child's puzzle to make up the cell door. A lever, when shifted, would cause it to open in what Twilight could only guess would be a scintillating wonder of engineering. This door was highly sophisticated, magically wrought, and definitely something Twilight wouldn't expect outside of a dwarf citadel, the mage towers of Evermeet, or the mystic kingdom of Halruaa.

The lock, on the other hand, was a simple padlock that held the lever in place.

"Now that's juxtaposition," she mused. "But no sense turning down the Lady's kiss before it becomes a bite." She reached for her belt, which was not there. She wore only the tattered remains of a once-white chemise. The musky air was chill on her skin.

Twilight groaned. Not that she objected to nudity out of principle—she had found it quite useful in a tight spot or three—but it meant that she had no picks when it mattered.

Her eyes scanned the hall. Shadows. Good. Twilight closed her eyes, relaxed her thoughts, and . . . instead of dancing into the shadows, nothing happened.

"By the Maid," she cursed. "A mage cell."

"You aren't going to find Tymora's favor with that portal."

Twilight whirled and slammed her back against the marvelous door. Again, her hand twitched toward her missing belt, this time to draw a nonexistent rapier.

How she'd failed to notice the young man in the shadows was

beyond her, but there he sat, on a crude, stained cot. She could see little about him but for his mismatched eyes—one green, one gray-blue—which shone dully in the dim torchlight.

Many thanks, strange lad who offers sage but perfectly obvious advice at crucial junctures, she thought, but she kept silent. Such a quip would be unnecessarily rude, and Twilight was never unnecessary.

"I wouldn't stand there," her companion added. "Tlork upsets easily."

"Tlork," she repeated.

Instinct sent her springing just before a mass of iron slammed into the door. The bars creaked and bent inward under the impact of a warhammer with a head the size of an ale keg. Even from half a pace away, the concussion sent her stumbling.

She ended up headfirst in the lad's lap.

"But, uh . . . we've yet to be properly introduced!" he protested.

Ignoring him, Twilight scurried to her feet and stared up at the twisted creature that loomed in the corridor, and blurry memories started coming back.

It was a troll—or at least, it had been, once.

Both its original arms had been severed at the shoulders and replaced. Its left—holding the hammer—was long and wiry with half a dozen digits, and its right was a muscled limb three times as thick that ended in a clawed hand. A stumpy, elephantlike leg rooted it to the floor alongside a ganglier limb. It was balanced by a segmented, prehensile tail that looked like a scorpion's. Because of the oddly imbalanced limbs, the creature walked with a drunken sway. Half its skin had been replaced with the mottled pelts of demons: vrock, babau, and several she didn't recognize.

"Pretty elfy—not pretty when Tlork crush." It—he—made a twisted face.

Twilight remained crouched in the shadows until the troll left. She remembered exactly how heavy that hammer was, and exactly how fast that distorted body could move. Now she remembered how she'd come to the cell.

"He's gone, methinks," said the man. The troll had not seemed to notice him.

"My thanks again," Twilight murmured under her breath.

Then the implications of her situation hit her, and her hand darted up to her breastbone. The youth might have thought her frightened, but in reality she was searching. Her hand fell.

It was gone.

Twilight's blood ran a touch colder. How long? How long had she lain visible?

The youth stood and walked into the light. He wore a coarse tunic, dirt, and sweat. "Well met, Lady. I am Liet—Liet Sagrin of Harrowdale."

Twilight took his hand. It bore sword calluses, but was otherwise soft and limber. By human age, Twilight guessed this Liet could not have seen thirty winters.

Twilight smiled . . . and drove her knee up between his legs.

Liet yelped like a wounded puppy, eyes bugging. He seemed as if he would remain standing, so she kneed him again, this time in the stomach. He sagged, only to catch her backhand with his nose. Then Liet's only resistance was a moan—a moan of surprisingly high pitch.

Within a breath, Tlork was back, drooling greenish spittle that sizzled when it struck the floor. "What you do? You—you shut yourself up in there!" The words came out together awkwardly— the troll put them together with effort, it seemed.

No, Twilight thought with a whimsical grin, *you* shut me-self up in here.

Aloud, she gave no response, but put a bare heel—hard—into Liet's stomach, eliciting a breathless groan.

The troll fumbled with a huge key and opened the lock. Then, for all of the portal's intricate engineering, the troll wrenched it open like any other door, almost tearing it from its hinges. Tlork roared and leaped inside.

Just as the troll's claws were about to close around her head, Twilight ducked, dived, rolled between the mismatched legs, and darted out the door. A flick of her wrist clicked the padlock shut behind her.

By its dull, confused grunt, the troll was almost as stunned as the groaning Liet.

------◆·◆·◆------

Twilight ran down the hall, her eyes darting back and forth for signs of an ambush. She felt unusually light on her feet and faster for it.

Good. Unarmed, she could not fight an attacker. Evasion, subtlety, and attention—her own, and not that of her enemies—were her three best allies for now. The shadows further comforted her, like the mother's caress she had long forsaken, or the arms of a loving god—if such a thing existed. Outside the confines of the mage cell, a brief shadowdance just might be possible.

The corridor, perhaps a spearcast in length, curved and snaked off to other cells. Some contained enough space for a dozen prisoners, some only enough for one or two.

For political prisoners, she guessed, or mages. She remembered the anti-magic field in her own cell. She hadn't been able to feel it, but that confirmed its presence.

Twilight had known many disciplinary facilities—what some called dungeons—in her day, but none shaped like this, with its twisting and curling corridors. What maniac had imagined such atrocious architecture? Most elves would have blamed a dwarf, but Twilight was not most elves. Who had built this place?

These questions made it easier—easier not to think about being alone, weaponless, and nearly naked in a dark prison, and when—*if* that troll caught her. . . .

Twilight saw no other guards. Four small cells were shut, all of them dark—she guessed they held prisoners. Twilight passed them by. She had her priorities.

At the end of the corridor, she came to a chamber whose smell told her, beyond a doubt, that she had discovered the fiendish troll's lair. It had once been a torture room, she decided upon seeing the rusty knives, moldy rack, and pitted cauldron meant for boiling oil. The withered devices seemed relics of an ancient age.

"Years pass," she murmured, "methods of conversation remain the same."

She noticed a creature of darkness and dived behind the cauldron. She listened, tense, but the only sounds she heard were of a furious troll bashing on cell bars.

After a heartbeat, Twilight sniffed. An onyx griffin crouched in the center of the room. Its features appeared mad, making it all the more frightening, but it was only stone.

"Interesting taste," Twilight said.

A stout chest lay nestled under the onyx griffin's claws—locked, of course. Casting about for tools, Twilight wrenched a rusty blade from an unpleasant looking harness. Crude, but she had worked with worse. And if her guess about the chest's contents was correct, this was the only lock she would be picking with an iron shard.

Though really, she thought, what are the chances?

It didn't matter. She *had* to have the Shroud.

Twilight bent to work on the chest and her delicate ears picked up the jangling of keys—telltale sound of a troll getting smart. If she lingered a heartbeat longer, she would be caught, and it would almost be worth it. But she wasn't certain about the chest, so she made the logical decision.

It was not easy, though—she wasn't sure she didn't prefer death.

With a wince and an oath, Twilight left the chest and dived into the shadows. She concealed the rusty spike along her forearm—it might prove useful.

As soon as she reentered the curving corridor, Twilight grimaced. She saw the troll fumbling with a thick key ring to get the padlock open. She couldn't dance back into a room that forbade magic, and she would never slip past a cautious troll.

Not without her other powers—powers *he* had taught her.

Though it twisted in her gut like a serrate blade, Twilight knew it was necessary. A creature of pragmatism, she could not let personal anger interfere with survival, no matter how much it vexed her.

But without the Shroud, it made her nervous.

"Chameleon watch my comings and my goings," she murmured. "Take my hand and guide me through the darkness."

With the words came a feeling the Fox-at-Twilight knew only too well. A cool mantle of power—like the shadows, but teasing her every nerve—settled over her. It would vanish in the anti-magic field, but she would make it in.

As always, a tiny, mocking laugh tickled the back of her consciousness, one she had long ago learned to ignore. It sounded too familiar to be real.

When she moved, Twilight may as well have vanished.

———◆———

Tlork threw the door open and lumbered into the hall, hefting his massive hammer. Wherever the elf had gone, he would find her and crush her. No one made a fool of Tlork Thunderhead.

The troll paused and winced. It was happening again. Tlork was, painfully, *thinking*. Like a paralyzing plague, rationality settled upon Tlork's scrambled mind and forced the troll to a grinding halt.

A dim memory associated with the moniker Tlork Thunderhead struggled to assert itself. The troll's mind chugged along: That's not what the master calls me, not quite *Th*-underhead.

The thought rumbled through Tlork's head and departed, and the troll breathed a sigh of relief.

Then Tlork heard the cell door bang closed. He whirled, only to find the elf lounging on one of the pallets in the cell, swinging her legs idly.

The troll furrowed his brow. If he had been confused before, now Tlork tumbled entirely off reason's cliff into a mad, upside-down sea. When he last checked, she had run *out,* not in, and no one could have gone past him. Tlork growled at her through the bars.

"What you do there?" Tlork growled.

"You'd know better than I," the elf said. "I don't know why you put me in here."

"Tlork put you?" Tlork said. "You prisoner. Tlork guard."

"And an excellent job you're doing with that." She spread her hands and laughed brightly. "I thought I could escape, but apparently I was wrong. Silly me, eh, *guard?*"

"What?" Tlork was confused—a sensation familiar to him. "Tlork guard."

"And a wonderful job you're doing with that," she said.

Tlork would not be undone so easily. "But you out."

"No, I'm in."

Tlork was lost.

Twilight stretched languidly on her stone pallet and rested her head on her hands. She would enjoy this immensely.

"You out," Tlork said.

"Oh," she said, feigning confusion. "You want me to come out?"

"No." Tlork paused. "But you out."

She shrugged, rose, and dusted herself. "Well, if you say so, but I was getting quite comfortable in here. It's rather nice, isn't it? Despite the misery and decrepitness—right, Lee, Late, Li . . . ?"

"Liet." The youth groaned from the corner in which he had curled into a ball.

"Right," said Twilight, not looking away from Tlork. "But since you're being so insistent, I might just pop out for a spell. I mean, not literally, you know." Unfortunately, Liet was a little too dazed and Tlork a little too dumb to appreciate that witticism. "At your insistence, of course."

Tlork's answer came in the form of an incoherent grunt.

"Eh? I think I missed that, handsome," Twilight said.

"You in."

"You said I should come out."

"No, you . . ." Tlork's head almost made an audible grinding sound as he fought for the right verbiage. "You *stay* in. But you . . . out. *Was* out."

The way he said it, one would think his use of the past tense a grand victory.

"I *was* out," Twilight said, slowly. "Oh! You must mean before you put me in."

"No. After."

"After we're speaking? Oh, don't jest! I *know* that hasn't happened yet."

"No. *Before*." Tlork's head visibly ached from the complex concepts.

"Before you put me in, yes?"

The troll finally gave up trying to make himself understood, gave an impotent snarl, and stamped off down the hall. Twilight imagined he was trying to make sense of a situation impossible to understand without a child's grasp of tense and grammar. She rubbed her hands together, stretched where she stood, and looked around.

Twilight was not surprised to find Liet still in the cell. In the brief moment in which she had formed an impression of him—before seriously compromising his fathering capabilities—the human had not struck her as particularly experienced or strong, overly courageous or bold, or for that matter, armed.

"Well . . . done," he managed from the corner. "Bold . . . and ruth . . . less . . ."

"I have plenty of ruth. I just know when to use it and when to ignore it."

"I . . . see. . . ."

She lay down again and contemplated the ceiling. "Really, trolls should all have tattoos that say, 'This one's stupid.' I guess whoever altered that one forgot to add a brain while he was mucking around with everything else."

A groan was the only reply forthcoming.

"Oh, come now," Twilight said. "You've had the count of at least three hundred to recover. Don't tell me you're still crippled."

"Only my pride," said Liet. "And the fact is, lass—"

"Don't call me that," said Twilight. "I'm five times your age."

"Maid—"

"Not a maid either. None too young or overly innocent."

Liet flushed. From his expression, he hadn't considered it. "Then lady—"

"Not that either. Neither that old nor that rich, lad-of-twenty-eight-winters-or-so."

"How do you know how old I am?"

"Trade secret."

Liet seemed hesitant to accept that answer, but since no other was coming, it would have to do. "Well. The fact is . . . you hit really hard."

Twilight rolled her eyes. She had to admit that bit.

She swung down—not complaining to be off the filthy pallet—and helped Liet up. He was handsome, with sandy, wavy hair. Other than the oddity of his mismatched eyes, she saw nothing remarkable about him. Not much in the way of muscle, even less grace, and a glass jaw—or, rather, groin. If he could've faced a goblin, fully armed and girded, and not soiled his breeches, Twilight would have been surprised.

She looked down at his hand clasping hers. Good grip, though.

"My thanks." Liet placed his hands protectively over his midsection. One of his sleeves slipped a finger's breadth and revealed gray, puckered flesh beneath. This one had been tortured, perhaps. He saw the gap, reddened, and covered the wrist.

Twilight yawned and returned to her pallet. There she flopped, letting one leg swing, and stared at the ceiling. The boy let out a breath and limped to his pallet.

A pause filled the space between them.

"So what do I call you, then?"

Twilight's pale eyes flicked in his direction. "Hmm?"

"Besides lass or lady, that is," said Liet with a shaky smile.

"The Fox-at-Twilight—princess of elves, seducer of kings, lover of gods. Shadowdancer and divine seeker." She made the titles suitably grandiose—convincing. Two of those were actually true. Then she yawned. "You can call me 'Light."

Liet blinked at her. "What kind of a *name*—"

"First rule, brightblade," she said, holding up a finger without looking at him. "No questions about me."

"But—"

"Second rule, jack: No questions about the rules."

"Well." Liet fidgeted, twisting his fingers in a way that looked almost like spellcasting. Twilight didn't feel the familiar resonance that would have meant use of the Art, though she supposed the aura of anti-magic would have spoiled it.

"Any other rules I should know about?" asked Liet. "I wouldn't want to break any of them accidentally—consequences, you know." He gave an unconvincing chuckle.

She examined the nails on her left hand. With her right, she held up three fingers.

"Aye?"

"No stabbing me in the back, and I won't return the favor." One finger uncurled.

"Simple enough." Liet shrugged. He pointed at her last raised finger. "And?"

A brief smile flickered across Twilight's face. "No falling in love with me."

Liet snorted. "Well, that's easy," he said. "I assure you, oh lovely hipskirts . . ."

He paused, perhaps to see if she had taken offense to that remark, which she hadn't. It was a somewhat more polite version of the phrase "pretty woman" than she was used to on the streets of Waterdeep or Westgate.

This was not, of course, to imply that she failed to address it.

"Oh, come now, lad," she said. "Longclaws, that's more appropriate, or slickhips, perhaps—as opposed to lickhips, which I don't recommend saying to anyone. Or, kisscloak, if you're feeling flirtatious. Or, if you feel witty—"

"Ahem!" Liet went even redder and hurriedly finished his thought, cutting her off there. "Oh, lovely hipskirts who shows little regard for my manhood—I shall have no difficulty with your rule the fourth." He thought he was being funny.

Twilight pursed her lips and nodded. "Oh, I have no *doubt.*"

"You don't believe me?"

"About as much as I believe any jack on thy side of the court with oiled and sharpened arms." This was as if to say *not at all.* "But I digress. You believe you can follow these rules?" Languidly, she put out a delicate hand.

"To be certain," said Liet as he took it. "But why?"

"Welcome aboard," said Twilight, "partner."

"Partner in what?"

"Our grand escape."

Now it was Liet's turn to look unconvinced. "Very well, then—excellent jest."

"You don't believe me?"

"Oh, I have no *doubt,*" Liet said, imitating her sarcastic tone.

"I see." Twilight drew out the shard of iron she had taken from the torture chamber and twirled it between her fingers. "Well, I shall simply have to disappoint."

"Did you see that mountain of a guard? With the big hammer, aye?"

Twilight shrugged noncommittally. "I've seen stranger things."

She lay back. Reverie would not come—she knew that, of course—and her mind was too active to permit sleep, but it didn't matter.

"So why'd you return?" Liet asked after a five-count. "You could've escaped."

"That was just scouting."

"Scouting." Liet laughed ruefully. "I don't think he'll fall for that again."

Twilight just smiled and closed her eyes.

Torchlight flickering, Gestal stared at her, eyes not a hand's breadth from her face. Lord Divergence knew she feigned sleep—her breath was soft and regular. She waited to enact her plan.

Rid of her troublesome amulet, he could watch the elf directly. He'd taken steps to ensure that would not change when she found it again, as well. For now, though, he could not reach into her mind—only cut through the webs she weaved so deftly.

"Your lies fail to impress," he mused.

Gestal considered how she had dealt with the boy—ruthlessly, brutally. The scarred hand hovered over her cheek, wondering at its softness.

Was this the one? he wondered.

He would soon find out.

CHAPTER TWO

L iet awoke with a yawn, opening his mouth almost as wide as the cell door.

He rubbed the sleep from his eyes, wishing he still dreamed—a welcome state, compared to this cell. Tragically, no gold dragons burst through the ceiling to rescue him, and no scantily clad warrior maidens manifested to resolve his . . . concerns. He sighed.

The door.

Liet blinked, wondering if he were still dreaming and the maidens were just playing coy. Sure enough, the portal stood wide open, admitting smoke from the guttering torches into the cell. He was suddenly afraid.

"Ah?" Liet rose unsteadily. "Uh—lady? Elf? Where—?"

A serious face appeared around the side of the door, a face that seemed familiar. The one who had pummeled him. "You're awake," the elf said.

He realized he should probably be angry, seeing how she had him so unfairly, but he kept calm. "Uh, I—I am. Awake. Yes. Aye."

"I was wondering if you'd need a kiss."

Liet blinked. "Wh-what?"

"Silence, lad," Twilight said. "Trolls are notoriously light sleepers."

"Truly?" Liet asked, freezing.

"No," she replied, "but silence anyway."

She vanished, but returned an instant later. Seeming to glide through the shadows, she clutched his arm, making him start, even though he had been watching for her.

"Is . . . is it safe?" His voice was meek.

"Safer than staying there," Twilight said. "You'd best stay by my side, boy." Her eyes narrowed. "Don't worry—I won't pounce on you any time soon."

"Pounce on me?"

She winked. "Keep up!"

Then she was gone.

Liet fumbled after her, groping his way into the darkness. "Wait!"

<hr />

Twilight abandoned the youth in the dank cell and returned to where she'd left the gigantic key ring in front of the door opposite her own. She knelt beside it and tested the twenty-second of the thirty or so keys. The cell was completely silent, though a small form huddled on the pallet across from her, watching her activities keenly.

After a time, a gasp came from behind her, and Twilight glanced back. Liet was standing there, hand on his chest. " 'Tis merely me." Twilight tried another key. It fit, but wouldn't turn. "Though I'm never 'merely,' as you shall discover."

"I'll take your word." He scurried to her side and knelt down. "Wh-where . . . ?"

"Asleep at the end of the hall," Twilight said. When Liet sucked in a breath, she rolled her eyes. "Easy—I've secured him."

"Secured him?"

"That's what I said." She tried the twenty-fourth key. No good. It might have been faster to pick this lock. "At least a candle's life, I think, before he comes after us."

"Then what?"

"I imagine we'd do well to escape by then, eh?" The padlock

clicked open finally, and the door shivered. She wondered why this prisoner was kept in silence.

Then a small form struck her in a flying tackle. "Oh, thank-you-thank-you-thank-you!" the prisoner said in a girlish voice. She squeezed Twilight as though to choke the air from her lungs. "Oh gods, it was dreadful! Dreadful! But now I'm free! Thank you, most divine mistress! Oh, thank Yondalla for you!"

"Well . . . met," Twilight managed, her words stifled. "I'm . . . Twilight . . ."

"Well met!" cried the prisoner, ignoring Liet entirely. "I'm Billfora Brightbrows, but my friends call me Slip, and you can, too, as it pleases you, Mistress Twilight!"

Liet chuckled—for which Twilight vowed to knee him again.

"Yes . . . just . . ." she choked. "Get . . . off."

Slip was off her with a bound, and blessed—albeit stagnant and putrid—air returned. "Yes, Mistress!" she said. "Thank the Mother! Thank all her daughters! They kept me in that silence for so long, but you freed me! Oh, what a great, joyous day!" She looked around. "Where are we?"

"That's Liet," Twilight said, pointing at the youth hesitantly, but the little woman was gazing all around, completely oblivious, her mouth running at fifty leagues a candle. Now Twilight understood why she'd been given the silent treatment.

"You're a halfling?" Liet asked.

"Halfling?" Slip asked without looking. "Half-human? Half-elf? Dwarf? Troll?"

"Ah," Liet said. "You know . . . like a . . . *halfling*. The wee folk."

"Oh." Slip finally looked at him, and blinked. She stared at him for a long time, as though struggling to recognize him—or his words. She shrugged. "Well, yes."

Now it was Twilight's turn to grin. "Do you know anything about picking locks?"

"Yes, yes!" Slip laughed. "Back in Crimel, I was the best lock-picker of the whole lock-picking bunch. We had contests!

Though . . ." She looked at the tattered robe she wore. "Usually I had my tools."

"I see." Twilight stuck her head in the cell and all sound vanished. She leaned into another universe, where only the spaces between objects existed. Unnerving.

She straightened and sound returned. "Anyone else in there?"

"Nope!" Slip said. "Just me!"

"Very well," Twilight said. "Come with us. We're organizing an escape. But quietly—our guard may be a light sleeper."

"Yes, Mistress!" Slip shouted. When the elf gave her an icy look, she lowered her voice. "Yes, Mistress. Whatever you command, I obey. My life and body are yours."

Liet reddened and Twilight rolled her eyes. What a child. "Good."

She handed Slip the key ring. "Open the other cells and gather all the prisoners. That"—she pointed down the main corridor, away from Tlork's chamber, toward a wide room that might once have been a guard station—"will do quite well."

The halfling gave her the widest of grins and scampered off.

"Just like that?" Liet blinked. "Why trust her?"

Twilight shrugged. "Why *not* trust her?" she asked. "After all, I own her life and body, as you noted in such *manly* fashion."

"N-nay." Liet's face went red. "I didn't—I meant, why'd you give her the keys?"

Twilight plucked up her shard of iron. "The Hells I'm going through *that* again."

———◆◆◆———

In wonder, Liet watched the black-haired elf work.

Eyes closed, she knelt before a heavy lock, fingers twisting and prying with the shard of iron. Every so often, she laid her fingers gently upon the lock's surface and paused. Then she would press her ear against the door, peering up at the lock from below.

He realized he hadn't looked at the elf closely, up until this moment. It was not necessarily a beautiful face, but a certain edge caught his mind as he looked upon her and her image bounced back and forth in his mind, unwilling to leave. She had skin like alabaster and features delicate as porcelain, and her hair seemed so black as to be almost blue. He found that he couldn't identify the color of her eyes—gray, blue, green . . . it depended upon the light.

She appeared calm—peaceful. If Liet hadn't breathed the stagnant air, felt the freezing stone under his feet, and heard the great snores filtering down the corridor, he would have forgotten where he was entirely. "Ah, Twilight? I—"

"Silence, please," she said.

"But you let that Slip talk as much as she wanted—about nothing."

"That was Slip." Twilight adjusted the iron, wedging it against something unseen in the lock. "You can be silent."

"But why?"

"Three reasons," Twilight said. "One, so you don't wake up the troll. Two, because this isn't a silent cell, like Slip's was." She focused on the lock.

After a pause, Liet coughed nervously. "And the third?"

"Because I hate you," she said brightly.

The lock clicked open. Twilight shifted and stood without using her arms, then put her hand to the oddly curved handle. She hesitated.

"On second thought," she said. "You do it."

"Me?" Liet put his hand on it without thought, brushing hers. "Why?" he asked.

Twilight merely smiled, stepped behind him, and allowed him to open the door.

An upright palm emerged and struck him full in the chin. He staggered, and his attacker followed, dashing him to the ground. A yellow knee settled on his throat, and green eyes with golden spots burned down at him. Liet gasped and squirmed.

An iron shard slipped around his attacker's throat. "Ah-ah," Twilight said. The eyes widened at its sound. "That one's mine."

Then Twilight hissed and wrenched herself aside just before a shaft of wood could fall on her skull. It merely clipped her temple as she rolled. She kicked out and knocked her attacker to the ground. He gasped raggedly.

"Asson!" The weight vanished from atop Liet, leaving him sputtering, and the woman—for so she was, a lithe, golden-skinned woman—leaped to her companion's side. The human man was old and weak, and he coughed as he settled into her protective arms.

"We . . ." Liet coughed into the floor. "We aren't your enemies . . ."

The golden woman looked at Twilight, who stared as though startled by her golden hair or perhaps just dazed. The features were different but just as delicate. An elf, Liet realized as he gazed, fascinated.

"We thought you were our captors, come to torture us." She narrowed her eyes, as though still uncertain, then glanced at the old man, concern in her eyes.

This broke her hold over them both.

Twilight got to her knees. Her fingers probed gently at the blood trickling down her cheek. "We're here to release you . . . unless you'd *prefer* torture." Liet's jaw dropped, until he saw her smile.

"We owe you amends, then," the golden elf said. "I am Taslin, and this is my husband, Asson." The old man waved weakly. "I am a priestess of Corellon Larethian, though my prayers could not reach him in that place." She gestured at the cell. "Asson is very sick. I would use my remaining strength to heal him rather than your wounds."

Liet stood stunned. Twilight merely waved with acceptance. "As you will." She pointed down the corridor. "We shall meet in that chamber, when you can."

The golden elf nodded and turned her eyes on Liet, where he sat, dumb. The youth mumbled something he hoped was agreement. Taslin began chanting tenderly.

Something nudged Liet in the ribs. There was Twilight, eyeing him in something like exasperation. He rose with the aid of her hand. "What's the matter?" he asked.

Twilight just rolled her eyes and pulled him away.

Liet knew he'd never understand yet always admire two things: elves and women.

<hr />

"How goes it, little one?"

In response, the lock clicked under Slip's delicate touch and the door to the fourth cell swung open. The halfling turned. "I don't like it here," she said. "It's dark."

"Yes," Twilight said. Her aching head was muddy. "You and Liet go . . ." She frowned at the boy. "Well, *take* Liet and go free the others."

"What?" Liet's face went ashen.

"Yes, Mistress!" Slip nodded, didn't look at Liet, and scampered toward the last door, the one farthest from Twilight's original cell.

"Wait," Twilight said. She bent her face to the door and inhaled a familiar scent. Through the small window, the darkness in the cell was impenetrable, and she sensed nothing within. It blocked her magical sight. Somehow, though, she sensed eyes—eyes that stared at her from a hair's breadth distant. Not pleasant.

She looked back. Liet was massaging his neck and Slip was staring up at him, as though trying to place him. Twilight shrugged that oddness away—the halfling did not seem exactly normal for her kind.

"No— *you* collect this one." She lifted the ring of keys. "I'll go free the last."

The halfling looked at her for a long breath, then silently pulled the door open.

"Come," Twilight said, pulling Liet across the corridor. She took out the shard.

"The last?" Liet asked.

"Six, including you, but not me. Choose one." She extended the keys.

Liet tapped one at random, dully. Twilight put it in the lock.

"You know of this place?" Liet pressed.

"No." The lock clicked open. "What an *amazing* guess."

Liet opened his mouth but Twilight grinned and slipped into the cell.

Twilight could see with greater acuity than any human when light was lacking, as it certainly was in the cell. Unlike others of her kind, however, she could see as well in the dark as any dwarf or orc. And what she saw took her by surprise.

A huge form huddling in the corner did not look up. At first glance, it might have been a massive man, towering seven feet in height, but the skin was leathery and thick. She could see no color, but did not expect that it would match any human shade. Tattered sackcloth covered its body. The chamber was silent, but not from any spell.

"Hail, good sir," she said aloud. Liet sucked in a breath at her side, surprised at the sudden noise. Twilight had forgotten—of course, the human couldn't see.

No response came from the creature. It might have been dead for all Twilight saw of it, but she could sense faint breath stirring its lips.

"A giant of some—" she started, but a viselike grip cut off the flow of air that powered her words. She tried to breathe or think, but couldn't manage either.

The creature had closed the distance between them faster than she had seen it move, and seized her up. Now Twilight's feet dangled six hands off the ground.

In the blackness, she could see it only too well. Its flesh was a mottled gray and its arms rippled with muscles. Red patches lay patterned across its skin, and bumps and protrusions like small pebbles spotted its flesh. Most of all, though, Twilight saw the creature's green eyes—pupilless orbs that drank her in even as its muscular body crushed the life from her.

"Let go of her!" Liet shouted from somewhere in the darkness.

He leaped upon the creature's left arm. It slapped him aside as easily as one swats a nagging insect. Liet crashed against the wall and slumped to the floor.

The attempt had given Twilight the distraction she needed. She swung her legs up to lock around the thick arm—one under, one over—so as to gain leverage, and twisted herself to the right, sliding the creature's rough hand off her throat and onto the back of her neck. As she had expected, the creature turned its attention back to her. She scissor-kicked it in the face as she leaped down.

The elf fell lightly onto her fingers, pushed off, and rolled away. As she went, Twilight whipped out her jagged shard of metal and made ready to slash.

The creature did not follow. It towered in the center of the room, facing Liet, who blinked dazedly at the behemoth. The giant rumbled something in a harsh but somehow musical tongue. The words were deeper than any human or dwarf could utter, low and strong like stones breaking upon one another. Then he spoke a word she understood.

"Quick," he said.

"Indeed," Twilight replied with a nod. "And you?"

"Strong."

She had to grin at that. "I am called Fox-at-Twilight," she said. She put a hand on her breast. Then she beckoned to him. "And you are called?"

The giant stepped into the light from the corridor. His skin was gray like stone, and tiny swells rose like warts along thick muscles. A design in red, like a birthmark or tattoo, spanned the creature's mostly bare chest and belly, covered only by a tattered tunic. Twilight stiffened and had to stop her fingers from straying to her lower back.

"Gargan Vathkelke Kaugathal," he said. "No . . . giant."

A keen intellect shone in the creature's emerald eyes—eyes that flickered with something like recognition. This creature was not simple-minded. More than that, an eerie wisdom burned there—an uncanny intuition. He seemed more than capable of understanding what was said, likely from body language and inflection. A rare talent.

Suddenly afraid, she forced a peaceable grin.

"If not a giant, then what," asked Liet, climbing to his feet shakily, "are you?"

The stone-skinned creature regarded him flatly, his eyes

judging, deciding, and dismissing. Twilight made a note of it. She had already guessed the answer.

"He's a goliath."

Gargan nodded and bowed his head slightly. *"Kuli gumatha goli kanakath."*

Twilight extended her hand, and the goliath looked down at it, curious.

"What was that?" Liet whispered.

"I've no idea," Twilight said through a clenched smile.

CHAPTER THREE

In less than a quarter bell, the prisoners were assembled in the guard chamber, as far from Tlork as they could manage. Each waited in his or her distinct fashion.

Gargan the goliath leaned against the back corner of the room, arms folded. He had spoken no more since being released, a fact that did not surprise Twilight. She had heard of the goliath race, but had never heard them called verbose. At his feet lay the locked chest, carried from Tlork's chamber through the application of stony muscles.

Liet paced, shivering and casting wary glances around. When he saw Twilight looking at him, he visibly relaxed, but she wouldn't give him that. She looked away, letting him grow progressively more nervous.

Taslin and Asson stood together in a different corner, the woman protectively in front of her companion. Taslin had enough strength for both of them. "How long?" she questioned.

"Soon," Twilight said. "I need all of us together."

No sooner had she spoken than Slip entered. The uneasy look on the halfling's face, even before Twilight saw the cowled figure that walked behind her, told her that she should reconsider gathering all the prisoners.

"I brought the one from the wizard cell." Slip bit her lip. "He's got himself a nasty streak, this one. Beware!"

Slowly, Twilight nodded. She'd sensed evil in that cell, and she'd been right.

"Spare me this runt's drivel," the man snapped. "Who among you speaks sense?"

Taslin stepped forward. "Who are you?" she asked, defiant, shoulders back.

Twilight cursed. That a champion of the Seldarine could sense what she herself had felt failed to surprise her. She was entirely too familiar with the devout.

The cowled man shot his dark eyes over them all and a glittering sneer of sharp teeth appeared in the depths of the cowl. The air around his hands shimmered, and ruby energy crackled to life in his palms. The prisoners stepped back, all but Twilight, who palmed the iron shard. Her eyes went to the locked chest—perhaps she should have opened it before releasing the others, but she couldn't have carried it without Gargan.

"I am the warlock Davoren Hellsheart," the cowled man said. "And from now on, you will speak only when I speak to you, yellow whore." He accentuated the point with a glare that promised swift, magical death. "You as well, whitebeard."

Taslin's face went white. "In Corellon's name—"

Twilight stopped her with a hand on her arm and a sharp look, at which Taslin frowned. She looked away. "Well met, Davoren," Twilight said pointedly.

The warlock's eyes flicked to her and he paused, cruel mouth twisted. His gaze was chill. "Indeed," he said. "You know my name, and I—"

"Fox-at-Twilight," she said, cutting him off. "And I say we waste no more time."

Davoren pulled back his hood, revealing surprisingly well-groomed, yellow-white hair and a brush of grayish stubble across his chin and throat. The features were not ugly in and of themselves, but the whole was hideous. His dusky skin was odd—as though it were made of something other than human flesh.

"What do you propose, Fox-at-Twilight?" Davoren said.

"Simple—we choose a leader for this band, then get the Hells out of this place."

"Band?" The warlock scoffed. He gestured at the other six. "All I see are huddled weaklings."

"None of us know what's beyond the troll," Twilight said. "And none of us can make it alone. We either work together to escape, or we stay here and rot." Though she didn't say it, she realized that second option would likely involve bloodshed.

"Right!" piped up Slip. "And in this here band, we should all rule over each other, and have equal voice, and . . . and be best companions!"

"Equal voice?" Davoren laughed. "Spare me."

Everyone but Slip glared at him. "Why not equal?" she asked, blinking.

"Equality is the crutch the weak impose on the strong." Though he spoke to Slip, Davoren's eyes remained on Twilight. "Thus do rabble rule where they have no business doing so. If you wish to indulge in such narcissistic tripe, leave my sight."

"*You* may be gone," said Taslin. "We have no need of arrog—"

Twilight spoke over her. "I'm not going to impose anything on you." She disdained the implications of those words; he'd twisted her into calling herself weak. "Ordinarily, I'd say every elf for herself, but we will die if we can't work together."

In the silence that followed, heads began to nod, and even Davoren's scowl gradually faded. Twilight felt she was right—none of them knew what they faced, but all of them knew they could not face it alone. Even the warlock.

To a point. "I see no reason why we should have equal voice. Our voice should be weighted based on our relevance, or whether we exist only for comedy and amusement."

Slip blinked. "Why's everyone looking at me?"

"And you are to judge this?" Taslin asked, stepping forward again.

"As though you would be better, spellbegger."

At that, Asson brought his hand up as though to shape a spell.

In response, Davoren clenched his fist and narrowed his eyes. "Suddenly grown a backbone, whitebeard?" Crimson eldritch energy swirled around his forearm. "Let us see who is stronger." He grinned. "Especially without your precious powders and trinkets."

"Enough!" snapped Twilight. She stepped between the two and stared Davoren in the eye. "We can stand here arguing until the Abyss gleams with holy light, or we can establish a leader and get out of here while that troll yet sleeps."

The warlock smiled cruelly. "Very well, she-elf," he said. "I knew you'd come around to my way of thinking. As my first command . . ."

A rumble vibrated the room. It took all the adventurers a full breath to realize that it had come from the mottled giant of a man who sat behind them. It was the second time Gargan had spoken. Though Twilight did not understand his words, she understood the meaning of his finger well enough, pointing at her. Taslin nodded, almost imperceptibly. Could she understand the goliath somehow?

Davoren's face contorted in indignation. "Speak a civil tongue," he snapped. "Then perhaps we might consider your input, monster."

"Twilight," said Liet. "It's got to be Twilight."

Silence fell. Davoren stared, dumbfounded and furious, at Liet. The youth receded, as though shrinking back into the shadows under that gaze. Twilight might have interposed herself, but she had a feeling that would anger the warlock more.

Finally, Taslin stepped toward Liet. "Say on, lad," she bid.

"Well . . ." Liet scratched the back of his head. "Slip's too loud of mouth, Gargan too soft. Asson's too old, and Taslin favors him too much. We need someone who represents us all." The priestess stiffened, but bowed in concession. "Davoren's too divisive"—Davoren scoffed at that—"and I . . . I'm too young." He spread his hands. "Who's left but Twilight?"

In the pause that followed, Twilight kept her silence and her eyes on Liet, weighing and watching.

"So it's Twilight," said Taslin. "Objections?"

"Indeed," said Davoren. "I've one." He raised a fist, which

crackled with spinning energy. "What's to keep me from smiting your leader right now and taking her place?"

Then he raised his other fist, and the energy arced between them.

"And a second—a corollary, if you will." He furrowed his brow, as though thoughtful. "What's to keep me from smiting all of you right now? It seems to me that none of us are armed, and I need no weapo—"

As the words snapped out of his mouth, Twilight exploded into motion. She dived into a roll, came up inside the circle of Davoren's arms, and whipped the metal shard, which she had concealed behind her arm, against his throat.

The warlock chuckled. "Meaningless," he said. "My powers are of the Nine Hells, and in my veins pumps the blood of demons—no mere metal can bite my skin."

"Yes, but I'm willing to wager that if you've a demon's blood, you've a demon's weakness," Twilight said. "And this, if you hadn't noticed, is cold-wrought iron."

Davoren did not move or blink, but the rage in his eyes said enough.

During the standoff, both poised to slay the other in a single flick of the wrist, the other prisoners watched, awestruck. No one spoke.

Then, of all assembled, Asson stepped forward. "Davoren, Twilight," he said, the trepidation clear in his voice. "This gets us nowhere. That troll won't sleep forever." Down the corridor, the room having gone silent, they could hear its snores.

Neither moved, but the tension slowly dissolved between them. Or, more appropriately, reality intruded and forced some of their rancor aside.

Some.

"Very well." Davoren lowered his hands. "I shall accept the *filliken*'s leadership." Taslin and Asson cringed at the words in Elvish for "skirt" and "open," combined with Davoren's tone. "For now."

The elf smiled only slightly and drew her blade away. "Very well," she said.

Slowly, hot anger subsided into cold anxiety. Torches flickered where they lit the chamber, and the troll's hacking snores did not reassure Twilight. Who knew what other dangers might be in the darkness?

But she wouldn't think about it. She picked at her damp chemise and eyed the frayed cloaks and robes they all wore. Then she looked at the chest and the ring of keys.

I hope this isn't a jest, she thought. I'm near dead for some decent clothes.

———◆———

Exactly three hundred heartbeats later, Davoren snarled for the sixth time, startling Liet. "I thought our waiting was for a purpose," he said. "Was I mistaken?"

"Patience is not your specialty, then," Taslin said. She kept watch at his side, gazing down the corridor and waiting for any sign of the troll, or other horror.

"No," Davoren said. "But rampant destruction . . . that I do quite well."

Liet knelt next to a wall, his arms around his knees. He tried not to think about the darkness, or the cold, or the troll he could still hear snoring, or . . . then he caught himself, stopped, and shivered. He felt awkward—alone, even surrounded by the others.

He glanced at Twilight. The elf had tried every key and was now working on that black chest with her shard of iron. She'd shushed him when he'd tried to talk to her. The intensity in her eyes when she focused on a task disturbed him.

"Here!" Slip shouted from where she perched atop Gargan's shoulder. Her loud voice caused half of them to jump and the others to hiss at her in warning.

If Slip noticed, she made no sign. Fingers traced a crease in the stone. "Found it!"

"Found what?" Liet asked, allowing himself to hope. "A way out?"

He looked, and sure enough, she pointed to a line in the stone, a crack like the edge of a trapdoor. Slip knocked on one side of the groove, which gave off a stony thump, then upon the other, which produced a metallic ring.

Setting the halfling down gently, eliciting a giggle from the little creature, Gargan put his hands to the ceiling, only a head above him. The goliath pushed, gently at first, then with greater effort. With a scrape, the metal plate rose a good thumb's breadth. A trace of dust filtered down. The goliath pushed—slowly, so as not to produce noise, and revealed a disk of metal, like a trapdoor, which he shifted out of the way.

"From the lack of dust, 'tis a well-used portal, by my estimation," Asson said near Liet's side, startling him. The old man was surprisingly quick and silent.

"Estimation? I'm surprised you can even see it, old one," Davoren said. Taslin glared, but the warlock merely shrugged. " 'Tis no great slight to call an old man old."

Taslin drew back, but Asson laid a gentle hand on her shoulder. The priestess looked away from Davoren and gave her husband a gentle smile.

Then the chest clicked, and Liet turned back to Twilight. The lithe elf perched over the strongbox, a wide smile on her face. "Happy Naming Day, all."

"Gold is meant to help us?" the warlock asked.

The elf snapped open the lock and flung back the cover, revealing weapons, armor, and gear. Eyes lit up around the room, and the adventurers fell upon it.

From the chest, Taslin claimed a mithral long sword. Liet chose a paired thrusting sword and dagger, and Gargan took a great battle-axe. Deep in the chest, Liet saw a dusky old rapier.

"Betrayal," Twilight whispered as she lifted it.

"What?" Liet started.

Twilight didn't seem to hear. Her eyes locked on a certain blue gem medallion wrapped around the blade's hilt. Unobtrusively, she untangled it and secured the chain around her throat, leaving the pendant to hang beneath her torn chemise. Liet stared at her, curious, until Twilight returned the gaze. He looked away, balancing his sword.

"You know how to use one of those, then?" Twilight asked

in his ear, and he whirled. He almost hit her in the face with the blade, and if she hadn't moved her rapier to parry, he would have slashed her. He thought he saw sparks.

"Well, uh, yes," Liet said. "The point, anyway."

"Well," Twilight said. She brought a hand up to her cheek and flicked the blade wide with a wink. "See that you mind it well."

Liet didn't know what she meant, but the way she said it made him flush.

Asson declined a weapon in favor of his staff. One item remained for Davoren and Slip to dispute—a small mace that would have been a weighty bludgeon in the halfling's hands.

"I care not," Davoren said. "My gifts are all the weapons I need." As if to reinforce the point, flames danced in his eyes. Liet shuddered.

Farther into the chest came further spoils, including a suit of golden mail fitted for Taslin, a pair of vambraces too large for any but Gargan, and a shield Liet himself claimed. Built of stout wood, with a sheath on its reverse for a dagger, the shield pleased him greatly.

Asson laid claim to a pouch seemingly of spellcasting ingredients. Twilight discovered a black belt holding lockpicks, tiny crossbow quarrels, and myriad small devices. Beneath these lay a pair of black gauntlets decorated with snarling devils that no one would claim except Davoren. The chest held a further collection of mixed equipment, including empty waterskins, rope, and a grappling hook. Slip seized a largely empty sack that seemed to contain scraps of cloth and a strand or two of rope. Taslin's eyes lit up when she removed a cloth-wrapped bundle, and she handed it to Asson reverently.

And beneath, folded, stacked, and reasonably clean, were— to Liet's weary eyes and filthy limbs—the greatest prizes of all.

Clearly, Twilight agreed. "Thanks be to Lady Doom," she whispered. Then, without a thought to modesty other than turning her back, she threw off her tattered shift.

Liet stared. As the elf's prisoner garb was tossed aside, and before her long, loose hair could fall down her back, Liet glimpsed a black tattoo of a many-pointed star at the base of her spine. He heard a sharp intake of breath and saw Taslin stiffen beside him.

He gaped, stunned by Twilight's abrupt lack of clothes, for a single breath before she spun back. Black trousers fit her slim legs snugly, while a white, billowing blouse lay light and loose around her soft curves. With a flourish, she added a deep scarlet half cape to the ensemble and pulled a leather glove onto her right hand.

She must have realized they were staring—the women in shock, the men in disbelief. "What?" she asked as she belted the sword around her slim waist.

A chorus of murmurs greeted her question.

The halfling grinned. "That's a nice sword!"

Twilight's hand flicked to her rapier hilt, fingers brushing the star set in its dusky steel. Liet realized that it matched her tattoo, which, in turn, led him to think about her mark's position, and he felt his face going hot.

Liet found an earthen-colored tunic of his size in the strong-box, and hugged it to his chest. He felt Twilight watching him, her eyes searching, and he wished he could turn invisible. He resolved to change in one of the open cells. Davoren and Slip had already left to do so. Taslin seemed to care about nudity as little as Twilight did, though she changed with a little more propriety—standing behind Asson.

Further rooting brought a new matter to light—only six sets of clothing.

"Not a difficulty," Asson said with a shiver. "My robe will be enough."

Taslin looked a question at him, but the old man just smiled. Twilight's appraising gaze went to him.

Then Gargan tossed a red robe he'd meant to use as a loin-cloth to Asson. The goliath ripped off his ragged tunic and wrapped it around his waist, girding himself snugly. His gray muscles gleamed, punctuated by odd gem-colored growths that sprouted like pebbles from his skin. With his heavy axe, Liet thought Gargan looked more dangerous divested of clothing than he would have in full plate.

"We are ready, then," Twilight said.

Davoren rolled his eyes. "So lead, *leader.*" He'd reappeared in tight dark leathers slashed through with red, like bloody cuts. His wrists were covered by black bracers with hideous, fiendlike faces melded into the leather. A black hooded cloak swirled around him to complete the ensemble. That they were his clothes was obvious—no one else would have worn such garments.

Twilight didn't address her reply to the warlock. "First, we escape." She pointed up at the trapdoor Gargan had wedged open. "Second, we look for food and water. That troll's alive, so there must be food—unless, of course, he just eats prisoners."

The warlock smirked.

"I can address our hunger," said Taslin. "The powers of the mighty Corellon—"

"Have peace." Twilight glared at Taslin dangerously, her eyebrows furrowed. The priestess returned the look, concerned, then nodded.

Asson unwrapped his parcel—a spellbook, Liet realized—and caressed its worn cover. "I look forward to reuniting with this little tome. And using it to our aid."

Davoren just scoffed.

"Good," Twilight said. "Now then. Slip?" She gestured toward the trapdoor.

"Aye, Mistress!" the halfling said cheerily.

There was a pause as they each stared at Slip—and she stared back.

Finally, Twilight coughed. "The rope," she said behind her hand.

"Oh," Slip said. She looked down at the rope and grappling hook she had been tying in many creative knots. "Right!"

With a shudder, Liet got the feeling that with Davoren's malevolence, Twilight's whimsy, and Slip's inability to focus, they were probably all going to die.

<hr />

Twilight waited until last, watching as they all climbed up. Liet lingered as well. She watched several times as he started for the rope, then turned back, too hesitant to make the climb.

He moved to help Asson, but Gargan lifted the frail old man himself. Even this seemed to weaken the wizard, and he sat in the upper room, coughing and sputtering while Taslin chanted another spell. The goliath exercised his huge muscles and hoisted his wide frame up after them. Liet retreated to the shadows, his hands flexing impotently.

When they were alone and Liet still stared at the rope, Twilight shook her head.

"I appreciate the vote of confidence," she said. "You must not know how many men Betrayal has led to their deaths."

"Oh," Liet said.

Between them, there came an awkward pause.

She clapped once, startling him. "You're confused."

He blushed. He did that often. "N-nay . . . er, aye, I s'pose. I . . . er . . ."

"Betrayal," she said.

Liet blinked and his mouth opened, but no words came out.

"What I said before," Twilight said. "The name of my sword. Betrayal."

"Oh." He fidgeted. "Charming."

"Are you going to climb, or is there something else?" Twilight's eyes narrowed and her lip curled suggestively. "You saw something you appreciated, eh?"

Turning away to hide an even rosier blush, Liet stuttered. "I-I d-didn't want to say it in front of the others . . ."

"I was *right*."

"Well," said Liet. "Even though I've had a little training—with swords, I mean—I'm . . . I'm not much of a warrior. 'Tis just that . . . uh . . ."

"You're afraid, and you want me to watch out for you," guessed Twilight.

Liet cleared his throat. "Uh . . . aye. Yes."

Twilight shrugged. "No."

"No?" Liet blinked. "Just like that? You won't even consider it?"

"No alliances, no favors," said Twilight. "Those breed jealousies. Maybe I could watch you and myself in kind, but what if someone else needs my protection? What if another of them also asks me for an extra eye? I have but two, and only a single blade." She tapped her fingers against her rapier's hilt. "It would be easy to turn down Davoren—as if he would ask for help—but Asson? The halfling? Taslin, one of . . . the People? Consider what you ask."

Liet's face fell. He rubbed his arms. "Sorry," he said. "I didn't think—"

"No." Twilight laid the back of her hand against his cheek. "No, you didn't."

Watching Liet freeze under her touch, she could, of course, understand why. "And I respect your honesty." Then she tapped his thin nose. "I will watch out for you as I may."

Liet opened his mouth, but Twilight put a finger to his lips.

"But do not count on it," she said. "My lord and I share many traits, and while I do not take it to such infuriating heights, unpredictability is one of them."

"Your lord?"

Twilight frowned a warning.

"I'll be careful," said Liet. "Y-you as well?"

She blinked at him, as though he had just lost his mind. Twilight waited until his back was turned and he was going up the rope before she flashed a grin.

---◆◆◆---

Taslin looked away as Gargan helped Liet up, pretending not to have heard his conversation with Twilight. Asson breathed heavily next to her, and she rocked him until the shuddering passed. Her thoughts did not lie with him. Instead, she wondered about the young moon elf.

The child's lord, she thought. Her mark—the star.

Her eyes went to Davoren, who leaned against the wall on the far side of the hole. Those red eyes met her look immediately. What did he know? What was he thinking?

Taslin held Asson a little tighter.

Tlork leaped up as though a hornet had stung his ear. He growled and spun about, massive warhammer in hand, but he couldn't see anyone.

The prisoners have slipped past you, came the master's thoughts.

"Wha?" Tlork stared down the corridor, and all the prison doors stood open. The chest that should have been at his feet was gone. Tlork's mind processed it slowly: Not only had the manlings escaped, but they'd found all their weapons, too.

Pursue, the master said in his mind. *Now*.

Tlork jumped to obey, tottered, and slammed to the floor, his wiry foot yanked out from under him. The clumsy action broke Tlork's neck, but it was a simple matter for the troll to twist his head and correct the problem. He looked down and saw a thick iron chain snaking from his ankle to the statue of the griffon. Tlork growled.

"Master?" asked Tlork aloud. He'd never understood communicating silently—it involved thought, which was not the troll's strength. "Master? How do I . . . ?"

Tlork waited a few breaths, just in case thought didn't travel fast, but heard nothing.

No matter. Tlork could do what Master commanded. He was smart enough, and more importantly, he was strong enough.

The statue gave a dull pop as the troll's massive warhammer fell upon it. The obsidian held, but a series of cracks spiderwebbed through it, each about the length of a thumbnail. Tlork swung again and again. Perhaps, after hitting it a few thousand times, the troll could reduce the lion-thing to rubble and break free.

At no point in the two days it took him to annihilate the statue did it occur to Tlork that a single mighty swing at the chain would have powdered the ancient iron.

CHAPTER FOUR

Liet scrambled up the rope, helped by Gargan. He looked at the trapdoor. It had not been designed as a trapdoor, but it was the pitted remains of a metal platform opening onto the foot of an old flight of stone steps. He didn't know the first thing to make of it.

He could see dimly from the torchlight below and Slip's own torch. Asson panted, leaning heavily on Taslin, but as Liet scrambled up, the old wizard revived. He whispered a word and the end of his staff lit with silvery flames. He examined the metal plate as Taslin, confident that she could stand without her aid, drew her sword and made for the steps. Edgy, Liet silently bid Twilight hurry.

Likely, Asson had seen him gazing down the hole and misapprehended his interest. "Perhaps it's a tool to lower prisoners," he hypothesized, indicating the platform.

"Where are the winches, then?" mused Davoren in his ear. Liet found the man almost at his back. He hadn't realized the warlock was so close, and that gave him chills.

"By magic," Taslin hissed back. "I am surprised you did not think of that, *mahri.*"

Liet did not speak Elvish, but Taslin's tone was enough. Davoren hardly seemed to hear—or to care. The Dalesman stared at Davoren, the warlock at Liet. The older man's red eyes glowed like fire. His face was shadowy—Asson's silver light diminished when it touched the man, seemingly absorbed—but Liet thought he could see a mirthless smile.

Then a hand grasped his sword belt, and Liet jumped. He froze in terror, sure he was about to be yanked into the darkness to a grisly fate. Instead, a certain pale elf swung up beside him, scrambling along the rope like a spider. He stared at her.

"My thanks for the hand," Twilight said, letting go of Liet's belt with a wink. For the third time in a hundred-count, his face went hot. Liet was glad of the darkness.

"Pardon me for overhearing," Twilight said. "I suppose magic—I've seen stranger things. Best leave curiosity behind—it's conducive to stumbling upon traps."

Slip reeled in her rope, and the companions drew weapons and ascended the stairs. The halfling and moon elf took the front, the powerful goliath moved to the rear, and the rest traveled in the middle, Taslin helping Asson to stagger along.

As they moved up the stairs, each step broken and cracked, Liet felt heavier, as though he were growing weary. Was it simple nausea, or was the darkness truly making him tired? Perhaps he should have stayed behind. He felt no safer here.

He tried speaking, quietly, to distract himself. He would address something Twilight had said. He liked the idea of talking to her, even if she didn't answer.

"Well, 'Light—we can't simply abandon curiosity, can we?"

No one answered. He wondered if they'd heard.

They reached a landing where the stairs turned to the left—west, perhaps, though of course they didn't know. At that realization, Liet's lip shook, and he looked around, desperate for some distraction.

"Mayhap all these things are connected? The locks, the platform, maybe . . . maybe this." He noted a symbol on the wall. It didn't look dangerous—much like Mystra's stars, arranged in an upside-down pyramid. "Maybe—"

Almost as quick as Twilight would have, Taslin caught his hand. "Do not," she warned, her green eyes bright and very serious.

Liet needed only half a breath to feel ashamed. He pulled his hand away.

"What's this do?" Slip asked aloud, scrutinizing the symbol.

The others hissed warnings or reached for her, but the halfling merely rolled her eyes and evaded their hands. "Aye, I'm not going to touch it. Just because I'm short doesn't mean I'm clueless." She wove her fingers through the air and murmured.

Liet saw Twilight stiffen. He opened his mouth, but magic interrupted him. A green radiance manifested in the corridor and spread along the wall. A rune, outlined by the magic in emerald, suddenly pulsed to life. It declaimed a phrase in a language Liet didn't come close to understanding, though the tone was none too gentle. Then the runelight increased in intensity.

"Aye, 'twas cute," Slip said. "What'd it say?"

"Something touching the matter of passwords," said Asson.

"Bother," the halfling said, and flung herself aside.

Liet blinked as the adventurers scattered. Twilight leaped and knocked him to the floor. His arms went reflexively around her and they rolled together down the stairs. His leg ground painfully. They skidded down three steps and stopped.

They cleared the landing not a second too soon, for a wave of emerald fire washed over them. It beat upon his back like heat from an oven into which the sun had misplaced itself. Liet felt his skin hissing in the heat, but was relieved when he didn't burn. He stared down, down into green fire that more than matched the rune's fury above.

Then, just as suddenly as it started, it ended. The storm of flame snuffed itself out in a matter of heartbeats. The corridor seemed darker and quieter in its absence.

Liet felt its cessation, but only distantly. His eyes were fixed downward, staring at Twilight's white face. Her wide eyes stared back, daring him to blink. The green went out of her eyes and they settled back into the silver of Asson's staff mingled with the firelight from Slip's torch and the ruby power tracing Davoren's fists. Liet's arms were around Twilight's shoulders, hers around his waist.

"Well, I think we've all learned a lesson this day," Slip said, breaking the awkward silence. "Best to ignore the scenery."

The others stared. Twilight's eyes flicked to the side, and Liet looked at the halfling, who beamed. "What?" Slip asked.

Liet looked back down at Twilight. The luminous eyes were upon him again.

"Well," she whispered. "Are you going to move?"

Liet scrambled to do just that. His hands skimmed a few parts of her body as he did so, for which he cursed himself even more.

That's the second time I've leaped on that boy, Twilight thought as Liet groped his way off her. Best not make a habit of it.

She rose, fluidly and gracefully. Gargan and Slip seemed indifferent. Taslin and Asson had politely turned their backs. Only Davoren stared. Twilight shot him a kiss, and he turned away.

She waved them on and they continued up the steps, avoiding the walls.

"What language was that?" she asked Asson, who had seemed to understand it.

"Netherese," the old wizard said. " 'Tis a difficult dialect, though." Taslin, Twilight noted, scratched at an earring she wore. "The words were . . . inverted, somehow. Curious. I shall ponder this."

"Well, keep pondering," said Davoren. "It's all you'll be good for."

Twilight hissed them to silence. The top of the steps opened into a new chamber.

Motioning Slip to join her, Twilight drew Betrayal and crept up the stairs, leaving the others a few paces behind. The dusky blade felt light and eager in her hand. Flames, alternating with a humming pulse of lightning, hissed up the blade out of the corner of her eye. Twilight was accustomed to the idiosyncrasies of the rapier, so much that they reassured her. They provided a kind of constancy in a world defined by change.

She and Slip crept to the opening, staying low to the floor.

"I can't see in the dark," whispered the halfling.

"I can," replied Twilight. She scanned the rough-hewn walls and the myriad runes inscribed on stone slabs that lay strewn about the room. "A crypt." She eyed the sarcophagi, many of which were upset or torn open. "A *disturbed* crypt."

"By the Matriarch," said Slip with a shudder. "A crypt? I hate crypts!"

"We're probably coming from the lowest point in these catacombs," said Twilight. "Why? Because that's always the way it is."

She could see no movement in the crypt, but that didn't mean nothing was there. Possessed of the silence and patience of the grave, undead could elude the most delicate eyes. Twilight saw red streaks that traced a path from this stair deeper into the chamber. She didn't have to smell or taste it to know what it was.

"Slip." Twilight turned to her companion, who was huddled against the wall beside her. She reached out and touched the halfling lightly on the shoulder, which evoked a gasp. "Does Yondalla grant you power over the dead?"

"Well, um, I, uh," said Slip. Some of her confusion might have come from shock at Twilight's guess—some from fear. "I'm not really, um, a priest, uh, exactly."

"Fair enough." She turned back and beckoned. "Taslin."

The elf moved up to Twilight's side. Clad in full armor, hand on her sword hilt, the eldritch priestess looked bold and strong compared to the hesitant halfling at her side. Slip crossed her arms and assumed a pout.

Twilight's eyes narrowed. "Do *you* have power over the walking dead?"

"The power of Corellon shall smite them if they dare rise against us," Taslin said.

"An 'aye' would do as well, *sun*—but onward. Conjure some light and let us go."

Twilight, Slip, and Taslin strode into the room. In her armor, the priestess made enough noise to wake the dead, but Twilight decided that was irrelevant. If anything objected to being roused, Taslin would give them a morning feast of Corellon's power. The Seldarine had their uses.

Slip, not to be completely undone, sent a flicker of magic into a stone that she held, lighting it.

The crypt was wide with a low ceiling. Compartments for the dead were carved in the walls. Decorating the walls were runes and crumbling mosaics. The former she could not read, and the latter depicted great battles between spellhurlers, dragons, and creatures she didn't recognize—strange worms shaped like cones, with arms that flung fire. The humans seemed to be winning, but Twilight knew appearances could be deceiving. A central mosaic on the ceiling depicted a number of casters—one crowned wizard in particular—surrounding a black creature in a cage of magical force.

She and Slip scanned the coffins but found nothing. Neither rat nor insect moved, and not a shadow stirred. They found no corpses, nor bones become half-dust—though the fresh stains were curious. In several of the compartments, Twilight also found teeth—broken and discarded—which she didn't reveal to the others. No sense worrying them.

Twilight waved forward the others. Gargan and Liet, blades at the ready, stood at the flanks of Davoren and Asson. The warlock sneered, uncertain whether to be insulted at the concern or pleased at the attention. Jaw set, Asson gripped his walking staff with its silver flame.

From the way Taslin, Asson, and Gargan moved, Twilight could tell they had delved into crypts before. Slip and Liet, not so much.

Several long breaths passed and nothing sprang from the darkness to attack. Each visibly relaxed, and even the nervous Slip breathed easier.

"Aye," she said, making them all jump. "Why do you suppose we're here?"

"Philosophy is a waste of schooling," Davoren said with a dismissive wave.

"No, silly," Slip said. "I mean here in this dungeon, of course."

That got a reaction. Twilight saw Davoren staring at her. His mouth opened, and she held up a hand to stop them all. "Perhaps later," Twilight said. "Keep your guard."

"Twilight is correct," Taslin said, though the words didn't seem to please her. "We cannot be too careful." She fell into a chant, then, beseeching Corellon's aid.

"A meaningless gesture," said Davoren. He leaned against an open sarcophagus and illuminated its interior with ruby fire. Empty. "There hasn't been anything alive in these catacombs for many years."

Twilight thought of a riposte, but Asson beat her to it. "Undead are, by definition, dead," he said.

Davoren spat on the floor.

Taslin finished her spell and laid a hand on Asson's shoulder. A golden aura surrounded him, then faded. "So *you* will need no aid," she said to Davoren.

The warlock scoffed. "As though I would accept your pathetic spells."

"As you say," said Taslin. "I can cast the spell once more." She looked at Gargan, but the goliath stepped away.

"No," said Twilight when Taslin turned to her. The sun elf didn't seem convinced, so Twilight added an explanation. "As much as I can avoid it."

Though her eyes remained suspicious, Taslin shrugged. She looked to Liet, who made no protest. Tenderly, she laid her hands on his cheeks, fostering the aura around him, and Twilight felt a twinge in her stomach. Suppressing a growl, Twilight broke away from the others.

It did not seem possible that they were alone. This tomb might have been carved a millennium past, but those bloody stains were fresh. Twilight kept her guard up as she headed toward the opening to another catacomb. Outside the aura of magelight, her attunement to the shadows took over, and she could see in the darkness.

The next room looked as empty as the first, devoid of bodies as if the interred dead had withered, been stolen, or—most unsettling—walked away. She didn't enter the room, but searched along the door for traps or magical wards.

A ten count yielded a series of scorch marks along the inside of the portal, as well as a series of sigils inscribed faintly along the stone doorframe. Twilight tentatively examined them with her fingers and concentrated, seeking the resonance within the lettering. She felt nothing. A magical ward had once bound this portal, but its power had been long exhausted.

Just behind her, Twilight sensed a presence.

She peered into the gloom, ostensibly planning their route, all the while observing her companion without her eyes. She could not hear breathing or feel a heartbeat. Then, on her own count of five, she spun and bent her knees for a lunge.

"Gah!" Liet stumbled back, startled. "My-my apologies!"

How he had kept so quiet, Twilight could only wonder. She supposed she must have been more intent upon the door than she thought.

"Sneak up on many lasses, do you?" Twilight reached to help Liet to his feet.

"Uh, no, not as such," he said, climbing up. When he had risen, he looked at her awkwardly. His face was red. "I wanted . . . to talk to you . . . about . . ."

"What?" she asked. And this boy was almost thirty years of age? She'd thought humans became adults before twenty. Well, no matter—she was sure no elf would call her mature for *her* age.

Liet's eyes widened. "Oh, ah, nothing, then . . ."

"I see," Twilight said, allowing a little danger in her voice.

He gave her a helpless grin, and shielded himself with his hands.

Twilight had to smile at that. He might have been immature, but he didn't suffer from stupidity—or plainness, for that matter.

She slapped Liet's cheek lightly. "Now pay attention, boy," she said. "Look with more than your eyes."

"Eh?" Liet asked.

"I'll show you." She took his hand and pointed him toward the chamber. They gazed into the darkness. Liet's grasp was tight, and Twilight found she enjoyed it.

Enjoyed it too much. She dropped his hand.

———◆◆◆———

Davoren grumbled something under his breath, too soft for Taslin to hear.

"What was that?" Slip asked brightly. She looked at her mace, then down at Gargan's bare foot, as though comparing the weapon and his toe.

"Why do we wait here?" the warlock asked. He nodded at Twilight and Liet. "Does she know something, or do they merely wish to be alone, I wonder?"

"Pettiness toward a boy, Lord Hellsheart?" Taslin asked. "Are you jealous of him?" She looked at Asson, who smiled at her. "Or of *her*, perhaps?"

The warlock whirled, outraged. Asson grinned, and Slip's mouth became an **O.**

"Jealous of her authority, that is," Taslin finished, to a chuckle and a snicker.

Davoren scowled. "She is a liar," he said. "Do not trust her."

"How do you know?" Slip asked, stealing what Taslin had been thinking.

The warlock's lips pressed into a line, and his blood red eyes narrowed at Twilight. "Look at the way she claims to represent the interests of all, yet obviously favors that one."

Taslin looked at them, standing close, looking into the darkness. As she and Asson watched, Twilight took Liet's hand for a breath, then dropped it, as though realizing she was being watched.

Slip looked back. "Nay," she said. "Not seeing it."

Davoren sighed. "She lies," he said. "She is hiding something. What of her mark? Her sword? That jewel she wears at her neck? Surely those, at least, mean something."

Taslin stared hard at him. "You know Twilight?"

"The golden goddess speaks!" Davoren said. "Very well. I shall—"

Then his words vanished, choked off. An unseen force lifted and hurled the warlock into Gargan, who staggered back, stunned.

CHAPTER FIVE

Twilight heard shouts and a crash as Davoren slammed into Gargan. She whirled.

A creature materialized where the warlock had stood. Desiccated flesh stretched tightly across the gaunt figure's bony ridges, and its eyes burned with rage and hatred. Its clothes were old and tattered, the fashion of a long-forgotten age. Tufts of inky black hair stood on its cracked and peeling scalp, and it grinned a mouthful of needlelike teeth.

"Wights!" Twilight shouted, thrusting Liet behind her and brandishing her rapier.

"By Corellon!" Taslin shouted, channeling Corellon's wrath. Her holy symbol, a golden crescent fused to her sword's hilt, burst with daylight.

The wight flew backward and shattered into thousands of pieces, all of which crumbled to dust before striking the opposite wall.

All around the creature's path, monsters just like it shimmered into being, shambling as though dazed. The display of Corellon's power had not destroyed them, like the first wight, but it had ruined their concealing magic.

"*Invisible* wights," corrected Twilight.

A score of the horrid creatures burst into view all around them, claws and fangs raking. Only Taslin's power kept them all from being overwhelmed in that first moment, foiling many attacks as the wights recoiled from the painful light.

Twilight shut her eyes, relying instead on her hearing and instinct, and lunged ahead. Sure enough, she impaled one of the invisible monsters as it prepared to leap at her. The thing, confused by her sudden, perfect strike, slumped to the ground, its animating essence lost. Flames flickered up and down Betrayal's hissing steel.

The shadowdancer had no time to gloat, for she sensed an attack coming from her right. She dived forward in a roll as blasts of energy scored the air where she had stood. Her success was short lived, however, as the bolts veered in the air to slam into Twilight's chest, blowing her to the floor. Through her agony, she saw a wight standing in a corner, weaving its hands in arcane gestures.

"Wizard wights?" she groaned.

" 'Light!" Liet shouted, leaping to the attack, but a half-visible wight slammed into him. Liet tumbled to the floor, grappling with the horror.

Weapons darting, the others formed a tight circle around the staggering Davoren and the coughing Asson. Gargan caused the most havoc to the wights, his battle-axe sending a creature whithering with every swing or two. Taslin continued to blast holy power to shatter the undead foes or drive them back. Davoren righted himself, his eyes blazing. Then he threw a deafening blast of crimson power that drove one of the monsters staggering back, burned by otherworldly fire in the shape of snarling devils.

"Help Twilight and Liet!" shouted Asson. The old mage could do little but shine the light of his staff wherever the creatures seemed thickest and direct the defense there.

"Leave them!" Davoren shouted. "Worry for yourself, whitebeard!" He cast out a forked blast of eldritch power, sending two of the gaunt monsters staggering back. The power sizzled outward to more wights, burning their flesh as well.

Thanks for the support, Twilight mused.

Without looking, she waited until a wight leaped for her

from behind, then snapped her blade up, spearing it through the throat. The blow was hardly enough to destroy an undead creature, but the beast paused. Twilight used the opportunity to roll between its legs to aid the struggling Liet.

The youth had lost his sword in the wight's rush and now bent his strength against the creature, merely to keep its claws from his face. Pus and yellowish ooze dripped from a dagger embedded in its eye, but it failed to distract the wight. As they wrestled, it hissed and slavered over Liet, snapping its fangs at his nose.

Twilight leaped to the youth's defense, putting her rapier clean through the wight's head. The wight turned its attention, and its claws, to the elf. Though the last thing Twilight wanted was to draw an attack, it gave Liet the instant's pause he needed to scrabble out from under the wight.

Liet climbed to his feet as Twilight danced away, her blade whipping back and forth to ward off the wight's claws. A strike caught her hand, ripping open her thick leather gauntlet, and she felt its cold power stealing away a bit of her vitality. Yet another reason not to let the wights strike her—their touch of the grave. Had Liet not known the protection of Taslin's spell, the wight would have slain him within heartbeats.

As it lunged, Twilight managed to parry the creature to the left and then riposte, carving a hole in its face. As the wight scrabbled away, screaming in fury and frustration, Twilight snatched the opportunity to glance at the others.

The tight circle of adventurers made up the center of a hive of clawing wights. Stacked two or three deep, the horrid creatures gouged and slashed from every angle, swarming the living beings with a violence born of incomprehensible hatred. Gargan's axe and Taslin's magic provided stout defense, but the goliath's swings came a little slower each time as the wights stole away his life little by little. Though his stoic face would never show it, Gargan was growing weary.

In the end, only Davoren kept the wights at bay, each of his blasts striking two or three monsters, pushing them back. And the warlock showed no signs of tiring. As long as the others could keep the circle around him, he could keep blasting.

Not counting the creature that Twilight dueled, only three of the wights stayed out of the battle. Two of them spat words of magic, and the other lay probing at its torn throat from Twilight's attack. The casters had focused on the circle of adventurers, but with so many fellows in the way, the two mage-wights turned on Twilight and Liet.

"Just my luck," Twilight muttered as she leaped back to avoid sweeping claws. "Thanks be to the Maid." Her riposte ran the creature through.

The monster clawed at her, not hesitating at the pain, but Twilight expected this. Instead of dodging back, she dived around the wight, dragging the sword with all her momentum and strength. The rapier was not made for cutting, but its magically hot blade could certainly stir up the inside of the creature. With a sickly plop, the wight's rotten lungs and heart came out with the sword, and its entrails slithered out onto the floor.

Though none of the wights died from blows that would have felled a man, Twilight hoped this one would have trouble fighting in so many pieces. When she pulled free, splashed with putrid blood, Twilight locked eyes with a casting wight. She had no hope of dodging more mystical darts.

But then Liet was there, shouting to distract the wight, thrusting his recovered sword in the way. Surprisingly, the creature flinched and recoiled, abandoning its spell.

Never one to pass up an opportunity, Twilight danced into the shadows. Darkness flickered across her pale eyes. In a heartbeat, she vanished, only to appear behind the mage-wight. She ran her rapier through its jaws.

Let it cast without a mouth, she decided.

The adventurers had almost turned the tide. They could not have destroyed so many wights by strength alone, but Taslin's priestly powers, exhausted as they almost were, had taken their toll, and Davoren's fire laid the wights to waste. The wights were slowly falling away, most to lie unmoving on the floor.

Twilight even saw Slip doing her part, with just her little

mace. A wight leaped on her, but she clubbed at it madly, taking out groin, fingers, and eye in quick succession. Twilight saw the wight she'd injured rushing at the distracted halfling, though, and angled a charge to intercept.

In her rush, Twilight stared down the wight—fresher than its fellows—and she skidded to a halt. "A-Aran . . ." she stammered, frozen.

It gave her a wicked, mad smile and hacked at Slip with a blood-smeared axe Twilight recognized all too well.

"Dav-rin!" it hissed. "Dav-rin!"

The halfling managed to elude the blow, but the wight ran right over her. Slip cried out and hit the ground. The creature lunged in, smashing Davoren to the floor. The warlock's aim faltered and ruby energy burned a trail along the floor. He turned to face his fomer companion, now his attacker, and earned a trio of black gashes across the face. Davoren could do little more than sputter and curse as the wight pummeled him into the floor. If the deathly touch ate away his life-force, he made no sign, but blood sprayed.

"No!" Twilight shouted.

With the warlock down, the rest of the wights redoubled their efforts, battering at the defensive ring of adventurers like an angry sea against a fortress sculpted of sand. Without Davoren's eldritch might to bolster them, the weakening warriors would fall.

Twilight stared. The others were fully occupied with their struggles—none could save the warlock, if any had the motivation—and yet she stood frozen. She stared at the wight who would destroy them—that familiar auburn hair, that smeared axe . . .

The other mage-wight, having apparently exhausted its spells, chose that moment to rush her. Liet jumped in the way, slashing at the beast, but it elbowed him aside, bearing down on its chosen foe.

Only instinct saved her. Twilight met the wight with a high stop thrust—a defensive stab the creature slapped aside. She danced back, weaving, parrying its dagger-sharp claws. She didn't care if it beat her defense. Without Davoren's magic, they were dead anyway.

And Arandon. . . .

Taslin knew they were lost. Her powers faded, and without the warlock, no matter how dangerous he was, they had no chance. They had been fools to follow Twilight's lead—they believed such a child could keep them safe?

Then Taslin heard a wheeze, and she knew what was happening. Asson—her weak Asson, though he had no spells or even a decent weapon—would save them. Perhaps he recognized the threat to them all if Davoren did not rise, perhaps it was instinct, or perhaps he felt compassion for the warlock.

Whatever the reason, the wizened mage took his staff in both hands. He smashed the glowing crystal into the wight's head as hard as his aged muscles could drive it. The hard oak did little damage, but the magelight seared the creature's eyes. The wight flinched back from its battered prey and Taslin's heart leaped.

It lunged for Asson instead, jabbing dagger claws deep into his belly. With a sputter, the old mage crumpled, and so did Taslin's heart. Corellon's aura might keep his soul, but his body could die just as easily as any man's. She watched, horrified, as the wight closed it jaws on his ankle, and he screamed.

"Asson!" screamed Taslin. She tried to summon up Corellon's power to smite the beast, but she felt not even a tingle. She had exhausted it all.

Then the mighty Gargan spun and hacked at the wight, yanking its shattered head from its withered body. Wights piled onto his back, clawing and scrabbling. Taslin couldn't reach Asson, so she plied her sword, trying to hack the beasts off the goliath.

The warlock rose shakily to his knees. Blood smeared his neat goatee, but the hate burning in his eyes did not allow him to look weakened. Davoren roared and flung his arms out wide.

A curtain of red and black flames screamed into being around the group, slicing open wights like a burning blade. Creatures fell in pieces and chunks, the ends of limbs cauterized black from dried blood. The ruby light burst in the darkness like an angry star, almost blinding Taslin. She looked at Davoren and saw his ruby eyes gleaming madly, caged in furrows of black blood. He laughed, hysterical. The wights screamed, burning.

The priestess could not tear her gaze away. Which was the real threat?

Blinking to clear the spots from her bleary eyes, Twilight missed a parry. The wight caught the blade over its arm, threw the rapier wide, and lunged for her throat.

Then a blade burst from the wight's chest, and the creature froze. Not knowing the source of her luck but not questioning it either, Twilight took a single step back, put her sword in line, and rammed it through the creature's heart and back out in one movement. Its chest seeping, the wight toppled, revealing Liet, smeared with its yellow fluid, panting.

She looked at her bloody blade. Davoren's fire died down and burned out. That ring of fire could have been used to save them before they'd even come to this place. All of them.

The band of seven coughed and wheezed in the dusty silence

Taslin was the first to break the quiet. "Asson!" she cried, falling to her knees beside the battered old man. His foot had become a pool of blood. She slipped into a healing chant, laying her hands upon Asson's forehead.

Slip scurried to the fallen mage and, bypassing chants and ritual, sent a flow of healing into him. Asson shivered, gave a ragged cough, and started breathing more regularly. Taslin looked at her, startled, but nodded in thanks.

Davoren groaned and rose. His face was shredded—three furrows ran from lip to brow. His eye had been spared by the space of a few lashes. "Don't all bow at once."

"What're you talking about?" Slip asked.

" 'Twas my power that saved you all," Davoren growled. "Have you forgotten?"

No reply arose from any of them.

Twilight stared at the fallen wight that had wounded Davoren. Her eyes went to its dropped battle-axe, then back to its agony-stricken face. She heard rasping—not like breathing, but more like growls through a shredded throat. Then the thing moved, she thought, itching one great hand toward its weapon. "Lie," it said. "Lie."

Twilight shook.

"Oh . . . look." Davoren grinned. He lifted one gray hand toward the ceiling and fire, red like blood, danced along his fingers. He snapped the hand down, and the wight's head exploded, spattering Twilight's face. She didn't flinch—just watched him die again.

" 'Light?" a hand closed on her elbow. "Are you well?"

"Away from me!" She threw Liet off. The youth staggered back, stunned.

Davoren smiled and gave her a look as pointed as his teeth.

<hr />

What seemed the length of a bell later, Twilight sat on one of the sarcophagi in the empty room, spinning Betrayal's hilt between her hands. The steel made a soft hiss against the stone. It was vaguely comforting.

Slip and Taslin had seen to healing the others. Gargan and Asson required the most attention, having taken grievous injuries. Asson had lost one of his feet and was coughing and retching horribly. For his part, Gargan had borne the brunt of the wights' fury, and though he said nothing, the goliath could barely stay upright from fatigue and weakness.

Taslin could heal wounds, but she did not have the magic to restore a damaged spirit—to wipe away the wights' touch. The halfling was remarkable in her healing, seeming able to cast any of the sacred spells she desired as she needed them. The others found this curious, but none questioned. They were just pleased to be alive.

Asson needed much healing, and his old body hadn't done well. Nothing could cure his stump of a leg. If he had limped and breathed heavily before, he would be a wreck to travel with in his current condition. Taslin bore him shakily to the wall, where he could rest, then knelt at his side for a long while, patting his hand.

Meekly, Liet crept up to sit with Twilight, his hands clenching and unclenching.

"The way you distracted that wight just by shouting," Twilight said without looking. "How did you manage that? Latent magical talent? Favored of a god?"

"I know not," Liet said with a shrug.

Twilight listened closely. It was not a lie.

"My thanks," said the youth after a moment.

"For what?"

"Saving my life," he said.

Twilight bristled. Whether it was resentment at the risk that saving him had brought her, or embarrassment that the others were watching, or annoyance because it was too easy to hear his gratitude, she couldn't say. Twilight looked at him venomously. "It's what you asked of me, isn't it?"

Liet's eyes widened and he stood up. Whether out of respect or hurt, he made no sign. After a breath, he padded away.

"You're hurt," came a soft, feminine voice, startling Twilight. She looked up and Taslin stood before her, her hands folded at her waist. Of course the sun would come to see if she needed healing.

The shadowdancer shook her arm. "A nick. Hardly worth worrying about."

"The wight's draining touch . . . Slip's power to heal a damaged spirit—"

"Save it for someone who needs it," Twilight said, interrupting her. Her eyes remained distant—staring at the object of her malice.

———◆◆◆———

Taslin saw, on the other side of the room, similarly isolated from the others, that Davoren sat glaring at Twilight. The girl returned the gaze in kind, spinning her sword with more conviction than before. Red-black blood still smeared her cheek. Perhaps she was not such a child after all.

The priestess glided cautiously to Davoren's side. The warlock sat slumped, his face still a flood of gore. He didn't look up as she approached.

"Davoren," she said. No reply. "I have come to heal you. Corellon's gifts . . ."

"Are neither required nor desired," the warlock said icily. He spat, and blood dripped from his lips. He shifted and winced in pain. "Be gone, and take your feeble tricks with you. I care nothing for the whimsy of a naïve, spoiled god or his whores."

The blasphemy rankled, but Taslin suppressed her anger. She turned on her heel and walked two steps, then stopped.

"I . . . I've also come to . . . thank you, Davoren," Taslin said. "You saved Asson and myself, and for that you have my grat—"

"I don't want your sniveling gratitude." He still stared at Twilight.

Taslin stiffened. A hand went to her sword, but it would be dishonorable to draw on a foe in such pitiable state. "What do you desire, then?" she asked.

"Your respect or your fear," Davoren said. "I don't much care which."

"You shall have neither," Taslin said. Her hand tightened on the hilt. "Ever."

There was a pause.

"Well, then," Davoren said. "Go back to your decrepit sack of bones, and leave me in peace from your whining. Have I earned that much?"

As Taslin walked away, she decided she hated him.

They made camp in the ruined mausoleum where they had fought the wights. They could have pushed on, but all were tired and Asson needed rest badly. He also begged for time to study his grimoire.

Leaving Taslin in charge, Twilight and Slip—the least

wounded and stealthiest of the bunch—searched the other rooms of the crypt, but found them cleared of any residents. They chose not to disturb any of the sarcophagi, lest they discover more defenders. Had Twilight been alone, she might have done just that to see what treasures she might find, but she had a band of squabblers to look out for. And after Arandon, her heart wasn't in it.

In their search of the crypt, the women found little more than dust and ash, a great many claw marks, and a series of runes carved on the walls and sarcophagi, filled in with something that looked like dried blood. They looked much like the symbol they had seen earlier on the stairs, but Twilight prevented Slip from springing any traps.

By the time they return, Twilight and Slip found the others engaged in a familiar activity: bickering. A part of her supposed it wasn't so bad—they couldn't be panicked and fearful if they were busy. Still, it grated.

"If not for me, none of you would be alive," growled Davoren. His face was still horribly cut, but the bleeding had subsided. It made him even uglier.

"And if not for Corellon's might," countered Taslin, "the first rush of those creatures would have overwhelmed us and slain you. Your art could hold only so many."

Davoren seized on the approaching elf and halfling for more bolts to loose. "If your accursed cave shrimp had paid attention, I would have destroyed them all." He clenched his fist. "If you blade swingers knew your role and served your purpose—"

"Hey," cried Slip. "I'm no one's accursed cave shrimp but my own!"

Twilight wasted no breath protesting the argument.

Instead, she walked into their midst and shoved Taslin bodily away. The sun elf staggered, dumbfounded. Twilight put a finger in her face. " 'Twas your insults that took us off our guard," she said. "Asson's injury is your fault. Take responsibility for your own actions, sun."

Taslin stared.

"And Davoren," Twilight said. "Try and focus, if your little mind can stand it, on the matter at hand, lest something more than scarring befalls you next time."

His gray face went red. "How dare you lecture me, you—"

She unsheathed her dusky blade in the blink of an eye and leveled it at Davoren's throat. The others flinched at her speed.

Twilight stared at him. "Care to finish that bit?"

The warlock backed down with a scowl.

"The next one of you who insults another of us loses a tongue," Twilight said sharply. "Then a nose, then an eye, then the other. Then I get creative. Understand?"

Davoren nodded, smirking.

Twilight drew the blade away and looked at Taslin. "And if anyone doubts I have the sand to do it, as we say in the Shining South, I'd be more than happy to demonstrate." She traced tiny circles through the air with her blade.

No one spoke. Oblivious to their camaraderie in it, Taslin and Davoren both stared at Twilight with shock and loathing. Slip looked horrified. Even Asson, who had struggled to his feet again with many coughs, fixed Twilight with an angry look.

"We survive together, or we die apart," said Twilight. "If those wights are any indication of what's waiting, we need everyone. Understand?" She stared hard at Davoren. "*Everyone.*"

Davoren sneered, but nodded curtly. He moved away, presumably to find a soft spot to rest. The other adventurers followed suit.

Twilight stood for another long moment, then sheathed her rapier. When no one spoke, she whirled away and padded off.

Before she had taken two steps, Taslin caught her by the arm. Twilight expected a rebuke, but instead the sun elf's eyes revealed shame.

"You were right," the priestess said. "I apologize for my foolishness."

Twilight eyed Liet, watching her surreptitiously from a distance, as she answered.

"I don't want you to apologize," she said evenly. "I want you to *obey.*"

Taslin gaped.

With that, Twilight shook herself free of the priestess's grip and sat down on one of the overturned sarcophagi. She pulled a knee up to her chin and rested her head on it, watching the others. Silence reigned. The others ignored her, except Gargan, who stared. Once again, that odd sense of eternity manifested in his eyes. She had seen that gleam of wisdom before, and knew enough not to trust it.

Twilight looked away for a time, then back. Gargan was still gazing at her. Was that esteem in his strange eyes, or disdain for her methods?

Either way, at least someone understands, Twilight thought.

Then she looked down at the cut on her arm. She tore a strip from her precious blouse and cleaned the wound. It would have to do. She wiped the blood from her cheeks and forehead as best she could.

She was the captain of this band, and damned if she would show any sign of weakness. They would absolutely follow her lead—they had no alternative. Twilight hated the responsibility, but she knew they had no choice.

Watching the disjointed band and ignoring her growling stomach, Twilight slowly drifted into reverie. At least, she hoped so. She did not think she could stand another night of the barbaric human sleep she had been finding so often lately.

For some reason, she couldn't keep a certain laugh out of the back of her mind.

<hr />

Gestal stood over the slumbering Twilight, watching the way her sweat-streaked face gleamed in the torchlight. Only one of them stood guard, running her fingers gently over the brow of a sleeping, withered man. She was completely oblivious.

It mattered little to Gestal. His gaze stayed upon Twilight, who slept apart from the others, where no guard could see her easily—or admire her, for that matter.

Twilight's eyes flickered under her lids, the eyes of a girl caught in violent nightmares. After a single candle's burn, she had dipped into true slumber. It surprised Gestal that the she-elf slept like a human, rather than lying in trance like most of her people.

How innocent she became when asleep, how frightened. Perhaps this was why she stayed away from the party—to keep such fragile, vulnerable beauty to herself.

Gestal, on the other hand, would have none of that. He bent down, fingers extended. Twilight shifted in her sleep, recoiling as though she sensed the hand coming.

Lord Divergence ran his fingers through her raven locks. She shivered. They stretched out their thoughts with the softest chant of magical power, and . . .

Nothing.

Gestal had expected as much. Through that sapphire amulet, he could not see into her mind. Nor could he divine her location or watch her from afar. Only through the eyes of others—or his own—could Gestal see her.

He could take it now, but why? He enjoyed her pretensions.

Gestal smiled. This trifle added to the game.

CHAPTER SIX

Twilight awoke in a groggy murk. Sometime during the night, she had slipped once again into the sleep of humans. In that unnatural chaos, she had experienced dreams as humans do—uncontrolled, nonsensical visions that would have frightened her to wakefulness had she not been used to them. Most of the dreams had been nightmares—as usual. She had wanted desperately to awaken, but as always, she had not. And some dreams, even stranger, had been the kind she hadn't *wanted* to wake from.

Many of those visions had centered on the young Liet Sagrin, of all folk.

She sniffed and rolled her eyes. Barbaric. Enjoyable, but simply *barbaric*.

Twilight dismissed the dreams as more of the unpleasantness she encountered with greater frequency than others in her profession. Most elves, she well knew, never slept more than twice or thrice in as many centuries, but Twilight was not like most elves.

Like most, though, she desired to eat at sunup—and, of course, to relieve herself.

As she made her careful way into a chamber removed from the huddled band in order to do just that, Twilight met Slip coming from the other direction. The little thief, wearing her mace and a dagger that she had apparently found somewhere, smiled when she saw the elf.

"Good morrow!" the halfling said brightly.

"Yes," Twilight managed. The halfling wandered alone? "What are you doing?"

"Oh, just a morning walk." Slip's smile didn't fade.

Twilight's suspicion did not fade either. "A morning walk," she repeated.

"Absolutely!" said Slip. "Nothing gets the vim and vigor flowing like a good jaunt around the meadow"—she looked around—"er, crypt. Anyway, we take them all the time back in Crimel. Gets the body ready for the day, and makes breakfast at the Tumbling Troll taste even better!"

"Crimel," said Twilight. "The village in Luiren?"

Slip blinked. "You've been there?"

Twilight's suspicion deepened. "I've heard of it," she said, truthfully. "I've passed through the Shining South."

Slip nodded. "Have you heard of Arvor Brightbrows?" she asked gleefully.

"No," said Twilight. "A relation?"

"He's me da—the march warden of Crimel," said Slip brightly. "And Denrin Lightstep Brightbrows? Revered Nurturer Hubin Sharpears?"

Twilight shrugged.

"Me brother, silly!" she exclaimed. "An' me second cousin, thrice removed! He's a priest o' the Matriarch."

Finally. Someone Twilight knew, of the divine variety. Yondalla, mother of the halflings. Slip's mistress.

"How about Nola Treestump?"

"Your mother?" Twilight guessed.

"The quirky druid who's spent too long in the woods!" Her eyes rolled and Slip scoffed. *"Obviously."*

"Obviously," Twilight said.

Something flickered across Slip's face. "Have you heard of Reeman Lightspinner?" she asked softly. "Though his full name would be Reethelmanath Ballufguts Bumper Lightspinner the twenty-sixth."

"Ah, no," said Twilight. "I've not." She raised a brow. "A halfling? With such a name?"

"A gnome," Slip said wistfully. "From Lantan. A magician—well, illusionist—brilliant. He and I were handfasted." Her face turned up at the ceiling and softened.

That caught Twilight by surprise—a halfling, bound to a gnome? She had heard of humans and elves mating—experienced it on more than one occasion, in fact—but the little folk? Curious.

"I see," said Twilight. "You 'were' handfasted?"

A cloud passed over Slip's eyes then. "It didn't work out."

"Oh." She ached suddenly for Lilten—his companionship, his wonderfully smothering embrace—and she shook her head to clear it.

Twilight realized Slip was still staring at her. She wondered if the little one could read her thoughts, so intently did she . . .

"Well, good morrow!" Slip said brightly.

With that, the halfling was off, scurrying toward the companions' camp as though she had never stopped. There was a story there, and Twilight's instincts told her it was important. She touched the Shroud about her neck, briefly.

Twilight watched, then went on her way, finding a good shadowed place and thanking providence she carried *thareea* cloths wrapped in her boot tops. Small comforts. From her belt of thieving supplies, she pulled out her hand mirror and looked at her face. Her eyes strained to hold up dark sacks and her features seemed shrunken—shallow.

She saw a smudge. A smear of blood across her cheek.

She looked closer, and there were two curls, almost like two snakes wrapped around each other.

Suppressing a shiver, Twilight wiped it away roughly.

◆━━━◆━◆━━━◆

The others were ready to go by the time Twilight returned. They ate a simple meal of white cheese and acorn wafers, along with a wine-colored jelly of mixed berries. When a spell of Taslin's filled up a set of waterskins, even Davoren grudgingly admitted the cleric's usefulness. Quietly.

The seven quickly found an exit. A set of stairs behind a half-collapsed wall led up to another level. Twilight wasn't sure why she hadn't noticed it earlier—perhaps she had just been distracted. As before, with caution, they crept up, Twilight and Slip in front, Gargan at the rear, the others in the middle. Asson hobbled, coughing. He made surprisingly little sound for one his age with such injuries, and Twilight respected that.

She could not dismiss a feeling of trepidation, as though they were being stalked. Something wriggled in the back of her mind: a frightening suspicion.

Halfling and elf passed through a half-open grate into a large, round chamber with corridors leading in six directions. Eerie light came from phosphorescent fungus that grew along the walls and ceiling. For a moment, she might have thought they were in the Underdark, but these tunnels were of human make.

Mad human, more like it. The room's architecture curved, dipped, and swayed. In its center and leading down the six corridors, the floor formed a trough that might once have held water but had long since gone dry. The channels' walls and gutters were stained brown and green, and not from paint.

"Sewers," Twilight said.

"Really old sewers," Slip corrected. "Even the stink's gone. Well"—she sniffed the air and coughed—"the stink of the living."

Indeed, a faint odor of old musk—more dust than rot—adulterated the stale air.

"True enough." Seeing no ambush or traps, Twilight waved up the others.

If these passages were truly sewers, then no one had used them for scores, if not hundreds of years. Mottled brownish stains striped the walls, as though a great battle had splashed up a river of putrescence. The ceiling was caked with stains as well. All liquid was gone, leaving no traces but the stains. The dust showed disturbances, as if someone had walked the rooms not long ago.

Twilight pursed her lips in thought, trying to derive clues

as to the nature of their prison. Either they had found an abandoned sector of sewers, cut off from the main system for a long period, or they had found imprisonment in a long abandoned city. A ghost city? But what manner of necropolis included a magically altered, yet very much alive troll guardian?

Taslin and the others examined the hexagonal layout. Six corridors branched from the room, one leading from each corner. Most of the tunnels were blocked by rubble, leaving only two remotely passable. The tunnels were more or less straight, compared to the curving architecture.

Gargan pointed and spoke a word in his deep-throated language.

"What is it?" Twilight asked.

"He means, I believe," said Taslin. "To point us north."

Twilight eyed her suspiciously. "How did you—?"

Davoren misinterpreted her question. "What difference does it make which direction is which?" he asked. "Or do you know which way to go, *leader?*"

"I never said I did," Twilight replied. "We go east." She gestured and headed in her chosen direction, moving quickly away from any possible protest.

"Why east?" Liet asked as she strode toward that tunnel.

"Ever onward," Twilight murmured. "Ever away."

The others followed, keeping guard. No horrors like the wights lunged from the shadows, but Twilight kept the band on the lookout for ambushes and roving dangers. They reached a second chamber where more tunnels branched out, continuing the bizarre layout of the sewers. Twilight split the group, taking Davoren and Slip while she sent the others under Taslin. Though Twilight was reluctant to show favoritism toward the priestess over the warlock, Taslin was the only one she trusted—and then only halfway.

Working together, stalking cautiously but quickly through the rooms in their immediate vicinity, the adventurers got more of a sense of their surroundings.

It took the entire day.

The sewer system seemed to stretch forever in all directions, and nowhere could they find a way up or out. Many times, a black disk of metal like a hatch was seen in the ceiling, but they saw no way through. Even Gargan, empowered with flight by Asson's spell, could not push open the strange panels. The one in the dungeon was likely loose and weak, as though it had been used many times before. Twilight did not doubt that somewhere in these sewers was a ladder to a trapdoor above, or an entrance to stairs, but that seemed less than comforting considering the size of the complex.

In a few places, they found claw and nail marks on the floor and walls, giving evidence that others had occupied this sewer before the seven companions. Twilight redoubled her wariness.

Further complicating matters, Twilight discovered a network of unfinished tunnels that wove in and out of the sewer system. The rough-hewn burrows, over forty hands in diameter, looked like a maze carved by some manner of insects—*giant* insects.

"Glory be! You could fit ten of me under this!" said Slip, looking up at the ceiling. Then she smiled at Gargan. "And four of him, even!"

"Only half as many," said Twilight. She winked at Slip. "Of both."

When the adventurers assembled again in the second main chamber, Twilight assigned Davoren to explain the situation while she lingered at the westernmost tunnel. The warlock enjoyed being in a position of superior knowledge so much that he didn't seem to notice Twilight was instructing him.

As she leaned against the wall, arms crossed, Liet came up behind her. She noticed that his boots gave a little squeak when he walked.

"Trying to surprise me again," she said without looking at him.

"I didn't try the first time—just looking for the pleasure of your company."

"My company." Twilight looked at him with her eyes slit. "Is that all?"

"Rule four," said Liet.

Twilight couldn't help but roll her eyes at that.

"So what's the matter, 'Light?" asked Liet. "Worried about Davoren and Taslin? You handled them quite well, I think—I didn't think either of them could avoid biting each other for more than five breaths."

"Maybe something's watching us," Twilight said.

Liet's brow furrowed. "Watching?" He wiggled his fingers. "By magic, aye?"

Twilight shook her head. She twirled her amulet on its chain. "Not through this," she said. The sapphire on its silver chain glittered in the torchlight. "With this trinket, I don't exist. Not here, not in the Realms, not anywhere."

"Fascinating," Liet whispered.

Something in his tone made the hairs perk up along Twilight's spine. There was more to this boy than met the eye. Once again, she wondered how he had frightened that wight. Did Liet have an untapped aptitude for the Weave, or something more?

"Regardless, it seems possible we're being watched," said Twilight. "Something or someone has set us up, as though we're being tested."

"Set us up?" Liet scrunched his face in confusion.

"Our weapons and equipment, kept in stockpile, behind a simple lock," said Twilight. "A perfectly balanced group— Davoren and Asson to sling spells, Gargan and you to swing steel, Taslin and Slip to mend wounds, and Slip and myself to scout and open locks. None of us alike, all of us necessary. We overcame the troll without difficulty. Even our escape was too easy. We're being set up."

"Aye," said Liet. "And I suppose the wights were waiting for us as well?"

Twilight nodded and traced her fingers through the dust on the wall. "I am no stranger to running a maze set by someone greater than myself."

Without realizing it, she had drawn a star on the wall. When she noticed it, she brushed it away.

"And this feels the same. Except." She touched the amulet again. "Except no wizard can be tracking us."

"So there must be—" Liet said.

Twilight laid a finger across his lips, silencing him. Her pale eyes flicked back and forth, making sure none of the others were watching or listening.

"Maybe," said Twilight, "maybe."

———◆———

The elf needn't have worried about the others. The warlock's muttering and the priestess's conjured food kept them more than occupied.

Rather, creatures not at all akin to the adventurers were listening, though they were not watching, exactly.

Had the pair looked up, elf and man might have been lucky enough to spot a pair of gray-skinned creatures pressed against the stone. They hung upside down, ears turned to listen to the conversation. Though they couldn't understand the words, they carefully memorized the sounds—a simple matter, since even their whispers sounded like obnoxious shouts. They recorded inflections of voice, scent, patterns of breathing, even the shape and texture of clothing from the movement of air, all from high above.

The creatures didn't note faces, not having eyes with which to do so.

The scouts memorized the characteristics of the things until the intruders continued into another series of sewer chambers. The seven had not yet invaded the sacred tunnels, but they had come close.

The sentries waited until the sounds stopped, then scurried back to report.

The Voice of the Great Slitherer would want to hear about this.

———◆———

The discussion yielded three resolutions. First, they would avoid the rough-hewn tunnels diligently. Second, Gargan would take Twilight's place at point—the goliath seemed to have a sharp eye. Twilight was not happy about giving up the lead, but she could stomach it if need be. And third, they would search the sewers again. Perhaps they had missed something.

As they marched through the sewers, following Gargan's lead, Twilight hung back. Eyes closed, torch shadows dancing about her like amorous flames, she padded along in silence and distraction. Had Taslin or one of the wiser adventurers looked upon her, they might have thought Twilight was praying reverently to a dark deity.

And they would have been wrong.

Damn you, Uncle Nemesis, she thought to him. *What is your game this time?*

As always, her patron did not answer. She figured he didn't care even to listen.

I do not know how you found me, or how you have managed all this, she continued mentally. *But I tire of it. Can you not give me a moment's peace, that I might live on my own without you watching over my shoulder? Did we part on terms that were the least bit ambiguous?*

Twilight thought she heard, somewhere in the back of her mind, a snicker.

Very well, you bastard, thought Twilight. *Have it your way.*

A sound came—a scoff—but this one turned out to be real.

Davoren scowled and gestured at the empty air. The others avoided his hideously scarred face. "Time passes, and we find nothing. Why *don't* we go down the corridor?"

"If you wish it so, go first," Taslin snapped. "We shall follow at a safe distance."

Weakly, Asson coughed and retched. It seemed he had not yet recovered from the wight's attack. Twilight felt a twinge of sympathy, which surprised her.

"What corridor?" Twilight asked.

In one of the sewer tunnels, they had stopped near a section of wall that had partly collapsed, revealing a tunnel that must have been added to the sewers after their creation. It was small, just too short for Gargan's twenty-three hands of height. The yawning darkness looked none too inviting.

Twilight froze. They were in a section of the tunnels she

had searched, and she had no memory of this corridor. It wasn't hidden—how had she overlooked it?

The others seemed oblivious to her pause.

"My reasoning," Davoren said, "says that the one who built this passage wouldn't have wanted to wander through these wretched sewers, so there must be a way out nearby." He sniffed. "And we've found nothing on this side, so we should search the other end. Besides"—he plucked the edge of his cloak from the ground—"I cannot abide another moment in this filth."

Twilight shrugged. "Sounds reasonable," she said. "Why the argument?"

"More traps than I could disarm at my best," said Slip. Her fingers shook. "And even more I couldn't find without my magic. Mostly pressure plates and trip wires, but wards, too. Traps within traps, meant to spring when you try to disarm one or the other. Resetting traps, as well—spring them once and they aren't done."

"So try harder," Davoren said, his voice dripping.

Slip shivered and hid behind Gargan, who looked from her to Davoren. The warlock fell silent. "Besides," Slip continued. "I . . . I don't think we're *supposed* to go that way. Maybe someone or other's meant to be kept in. On the other side, aye?"

"Whoever built that tunnel really, *really* didn't want us going down it," said Liet.

"All the more reason to go," Twilight said. When the others balked, she flashed a sly smile. "I've never been fond of doing another's will."

The irony in her voice caused more than one of the others to eye her suspiciously, Taslin in particular. "Your decision then," the priestess said. "Slip's skills are insufficient. I hope you know a few things about traps yourself."

Twilight's lips twitched up at the left side and she drew her blade. She knelt and studied the darkness for a hundred heartbeats.

"Come now," growled the warlock. "Are we going to wait in this stinking sewer all the day while you think about it? Just disarm them like a good sneakthief."

" 'Twould take two candles," said Twilight. "To be safe."

Davoren threw his hands in the air. "Wonderful," he said. "Waiting for two candles to burn down. We'd be a meal sitting here for some beast that comes along—like that troll—while our fearless leader takes her time for the sake of safety."

"What have I told you about insults?" Twilight said.

"It's an insult to call you 'fearless?' " Davoren feigned shock.

Twilight shook her head. "Very well," she said. "Follow and move as I do. But wait. A four-count should be right."

Brows furrowed. "Four?" Slip asked. "Why not five?"

"Why not six?" snapped Davoren.

Twilight shrugged. "Chameleon, I hope you're enjoying this," she murmured.

No response, as always.

The shadows coalesced around her. Then she ran.

A veritable firestorm of metal shards, swinging blades, and crossbow bolts filled the tunnel. Twilight lunged, danced, and dodged. She rolled under a blade that would have taken her head from her shoulders, sprang to the side between two chopping axes, and stopped short just in time to avoid a pair of darts shooting from either side.

Slip and Liet looked at one another, then charged after her. It took the others another breathless moment before they, too, followed the elf. They ran past as each trap reset itself.

Twilight ran, snaked, and dipped. Here she went low under darts, there she snapped a trip wire with Betrayal. Where she pulled up short, the others froze, and where she ran, the others dashed. More bolts fired out, and she twisted around them. Writing flared along the wall, and a fringe of flames shot out. She dived under the flames and rolled, scant feet from the end of the passage.

A sword swung down from the ceiling. Twilight dodged and hopped, but she sensed an attack from behind. Like a perfect pendulum, the blade scythed for her back.

Unlike a perfect pendulum, however, it wove from side to side. Then it veered to the right—directly at Twilight.

She managed to leap to the left, but not before the trap tore a gouge across her shoulder. She went down hard on her backside, and looked up to see the weapon streaking for her forehead. It would split her neatly in two—at least halfway. The sword probably didn't reach all the way to the floor.

Twilight found it amusing that she'd made it all the way through the corridor by sheer luck, only to fall to the last trap of all—and the most obvious.

"You're a bitch, Misfortune," Twilight cursed.

Then a ray of flame shot over her head and cut the sword blade from its swinging mechanism. The trap swung toward Twilight, but the blade's weight drove it into the stone floor a hair's breadth from her midsection.

"I take it back," she said.

Twilight was up with a start, taking Liet's hand. Carried by Gargan, Asson wiggled his fingers at Twilight, to show that he had fired the flame that had saved her.

Trailing smoke and dust, the seven emerged from the tunnel, leaving behind a wake of triggered traps and bolts studding the walls like porcupine quills.

Aside from sweat, hard breathing, and anxiety, none of the seven carried any marks to show for the experience, except Twilight's single shoulder wound.

"Let me see to that for you," Taslin offered.

Twilight flinched. " 'Tis nothing."

"It could fester," the priestess pressed. "That trap was very old."

Twilight was tempted to point out that lockjaw from old metal was a myth, or at least an incomplete notion, but instead she conceded and turned her head aside. The priestess cast the healing, and Twilight's torn shoulder knit itself without argument.

"Aye," said Slip. "I'm not sure we should've gone this way."

Twilight looked around at her surroundings for the first time and agreed.

They could see that the sewer did not extend far beyond the trapped corridor. Five paces from the tunnel, the carved floor gave way to natural stone. Beyond were two cave entrances, tunnels just large enough to admit the goliath if he stooped.

To complicate the scene, a five-pace diameter tunnel of stone also cut through the chamber, its smooth walls assuring Twilight that it came from the same source as the other perfect tunnels they had found.

"I don't know," Davoren said. "I find the change of scenery rather refreshing. Anything but more dismal, filthy tunnels."

"Everything's 'dismal,' 'wretched,' or 'filthy' with you, aye?" Slip asked. "Do you only *know* three adjectives?"

The warlock's burning eyes flicked to her. "I would advise silence, little one, before I think up a fourth—just for you."

The halfling shivered but held her tongue.

CHAPTER SEVEN

They rested from their exertion while Twilight decided which tunnel to take. She sent Gargan and Slip to investigate the cave entrances. In the meantime, Taslin conjured a simple meal of cakes and wine for them. They sat on fallen rock debris and ate.

For a time, no one spoke. Then the priestess broke the silence.

"What manner of sword is that you carry?" Taslin asked.

Twilight gave her a nonchalant look. "A rapier."

"It is shorter than any rapier I have seen," the priestess said.

"She's right," said Liet. Twilight flashed him a warning look, but the young man spoke before she could stop him. "I've learned a bit about swordplay, and there's an accepted length for a rapier. Yours is short by a full hand."

"The gods shine!" Twilight said wryly. "Creativity."

Slip bounded into the chamber just then. From the gleam in her eyes upon seeing the food, Twilight knew better than to ask her first what she had discovered.

"It looks more like a thinblade," said Taslin. "An elven weapon. But it is short even for that, and too long for a smallblade."

Asson decided to join the discussion. "And that material—I've never seen metal of that gray sheen. I saw what it did against those wights—the little lick of flame, the spark of electricity. What is it?"

"Hizagkuur," said Twilight, taking a drink of water.

"I've never heard of it," said the mage.

"Neither had the dwarf who discovered it," said Twilight. "So he did what dwarves usually do, and named it after himself."

"Who was that?" Slip asked excitedly.

Twilight looked at her with an absolutely blank face. "Hizagkuur," she said.

"Oh," said Slip. "That would have been my third guess."

"Dwarf craft?" Taslin did not bother to hide her curiosity.

"One of the first Hizagkuur weapons ever crafted in the Northland, long before the rise of Cormanthyr, in the days when elves and dwarves traded freely," said Twilight. " 'Twas a commission—and not by me."

If they were expecting more from her lips, they did not get it.

Someone cleared a throat. "Who taught you to dance the shadows?" Davoren asked mildly. "You do it so *well*."

"Careful, Davoren," Twilight said.

"We have some moments before Gargan returns," the warlock said. "Perhaps it's time to introduce ourselves better. For instance—what means that star on your naked back, she-elf? Why is your sword so named? 'Betrayal' is so charming. And I believe I heard you muttering a name in your sleep—Neveren, was it?"

Stunned, Twilight opened her mouth, but Taslin gave Davoren a warning glare, her hand falling to her own sword hilt. "She will tell you when she wishes," she said. "*If* she wishes. I suggest you respect her privacy else."

The warlock looked at her hand and scoffed. "Drawing steel against an unarmed man?" he asked. "Surely your petty Colonal would frown on such a dishonorable act."

Davoren's pronunciation sounded closer to a human military rank than to Corellon Larethian himself, Lord of the Seldarine. The wizard had not even bothered to disguise his provocation. Twilight might've taken his words as an insult, but she hated this whole bloody band far too much.

Taslin, on the other hand, went almost as pale as Twilight—remarkable, considering her complexion, which glowed like the setting sun. "How dare—?" she started, letting the words trail off into indignant snarling.

Asson took Taslin gently by the arm, and his touch startled her out of her wrath. She put her hand over his and stared coldly at Davoren.

"Still your vocal cords," she said, "before I cut them out for you, *mahri*."

"I apologize," Davoren said. "Is my pronunciation incorrect? Such a difficult tongue." He looked at Twilight. "And on the subject of tongues, weren't you meant to cut hers out by now? I believe she just insulted me. Or perhaps"—his eyes glittered—"you were going to be more creative?"

Twilight slit her eyes. "Both of you," she said. "Silence."

"What a pity." Davoren smiled wryly and took a drink from his wineskin. Twilight noticed at that moment that the gouges on his face seemed, inexplicably, to have healed to half their former size.

Twilight bid silent thanks to Asson. The old man looked frail and weak, but he was proving his worth at tempering Taslin's furies.

While he lasted, of course.

Gargan returned in a short time. The goliath revealed, in curt sentences, that he had found evidence of bipedal, barefoot creatures, but he had seen none of the creatures themselves. His cave had doubled back into the rounded tunnel.

Slip eventually finished stuffing herself with Taslin's food and described her own discoveries. She claimed to have caught sight of gray hides scuttling into the shadows—but she admitted she may have been seeing things. Her cave had led to a network of caverns and passageways, which she had chosen not to explore. On her way back, she spotted a tunnel leading upward, perhaps two spearcasts into the cave and to the right. That seized Twilight's attention.

"We go," she said. "I want to find the way out of these sewers by nightfall."

"How would you know when night is?" asked Davoren. "I've

seen no sun, and unless you can see through hundreds of paces of solid rock, neither have you."

"I have a sense of when the night is darkest," she said. "You acquire one when you steal for a living. And besides"—she added, lest she be tricked into talking about her past—"Taslin's *Coronal* grants spells at dawn, so she knows when the sun rises."

Taslin turned her chin up at Davoren.

The warlock shrugged. "I see," he said. He stood, flexing his skeletal fingers and cracking his joints with one hand. "I do not wish to sit here all 'day.' Let us go."

Twilight watched him carefully. She could feel eyes boring into her back, and she was surprised to realize they were not Taslin's. Rather, Gargan gazed at her. For some reason, she was pointedly aware of the crimson markings upon his gray skin.

Suppressing a shiver whose origin she did not understand, Twilight motioned for the others to follow the warlock.

As soon as the last of them stepped into Slip's cave, the attack came, and it came swiftly. A dozen dull gray man-shaped forms that had at first appeared to be rocks broke away from the walls, brandishing stone axes. Coils of greasy hair hung from their scalps, and huge cracked teeth dripped yellow spittle.

Twilight needed only to see the smooth, empty depressions where eye sockets should have been to know what the creatures were. "Grimlocks," she hissed, just before the ambushers were upon them.

Slip and Taslin were knocked down before they realized an attack was coming, swatted unconscious by the blind monsters. The others managed to draw steel, but barely in time to meet the attackers.

Davoren's hand blazed with crimson energy and a dangerous, almost maniacal smile spread across his face. He met the first grimlock with flame. The blast shattered the creature's chest and sent it flying back in an arc. Then the warlock moved his hands side to side, showering energy blasts all around to repel the creatures. As each blast struck a grimlock, the creature shrieked in pain and terror, halting in its rush. Davoren couldn't strike them all, so he dodged and fled when his fire flickered out, retreating to blast again.

Twilight ducked an axe swing and whipped out Betrayal. With her speed, she might have managed a riposte, but the grimlock charged in, bowling her over. The grimlock crushed the breath from Twilight's body against the wall, stunning her. The creature moved to maul her, but stepped into the path of a fiery blast. Davoren shattered the grimlock's back and its legs went limp. Twilight finished it with a thrust to the throat.

Asson managed to swing his staff in line to block an axe, which shattered the oak pole like dried firewood. The one-footed mage fell, and his attacker lunged forward, only to meet the point of Liet's sword. The boy sent the grimlock tumbling down, but couldn't pull his blade free in time to block a whistling axe. Abandoning his weapon, he leaped away, cursing and fleeing a stone blade.

The action gave Asson time to cast a spell from the ground. Noxious fumes roared into place around the advancing grimlocks, setting them to wheezing and sputtering. Within seconds, they hit the ground, overwhelmed by Asson's cloud. Then the mage broke into a coughing fit and writhed, just below the vapors.

Only Gargan held his ground. Two of the sightless beasts pressed him with their axes, but he spun his battle-axe faster, snapping it back and forth like a whip. He knocked aside two slashes, then smashed the blade across a grimlock's face, sending it toppling.

Two more leaped upon his back, holding the goliath's arms while another of the beasts drew back an axe.

"Gargan!" Twilight shouted. She leaped to aid, but couldn't avoid an outflung axe handle. Twilight took it in the belly and doubled over.

Beshaba, it was only a jest, she thought.

Then an axe came at her face, and she knew only darkness.

A ruby streak smashed the grimlock's face into a bloody mist as Liet's short sword tore its way through the nearest one. The grimlock still snarled, caught in its death throes. The Dalesman seized its throat and pushed the dying thing away as it sank to the floor. Its claws beat at him limply. Liet gasped and shuddered when it was dead.

The warlock snarled and threw out another blast, burning a fleeing grimlock. He scanned the room, searching for other breathing targets, but only two stood: the hulking Gargan, and the blood-spattered Liet. Noxious green smoke obscured half the room, but it was beginning to fade. As the cloud dissipated, Liet saw no grimlocks for Davoren to slaughter.

Davoren saw it too. "By the Nine," said the warlock. "What a disappointment."

"Everyone well?" Liet's head ached where an axe handle had struck it. "Asson?"

The mage coughed and shimmered into visibility where he sat on the floor. "This old heart's still beating."

"Gargan and Davoren, you're both well?"

"In a sense," said Davoren. "I believe my hair was mussed." He cracked his knuckles and smoothed the gray spikes back against his scalp. He didn't look injured. The goliath nodded silently.

Liet didn't see anyone else, so he called their names. "Taslin?"

No response.

"Slip?"

There came a groan. "By the Mother," the halfling's soft voice cracked.

Gargan bent down and prodded at a small body half hidden under a grimlock. He murmured something. The halfling shook her head and sat up. She looked up at the giant man, smiled weakly, and threw her arms around his leg. Gargan blinked at her.

" 'Light?" asked Liet.

No reply.

His voice shook. "Twilight?"

Tracing a semicircle over the room with his hand, Gargan growled something in his rough tongue, and while Liet did not understand, the meaning seemed clear.

"No bodies," Asson said, reflecting his thoughts. "Taken?"

Liet helped him up, and the old man leaned on his shoulder. Liet propped him against a wall and broke away to search the room. He saw nothing.

"Five or six escaped," Liet said. "The elves are light."

"My, my," said Davoren, "how unfortunate for them." He smiled at the halfling, who was still shaking her head. "Now, child—point us toward this upward tunnel."

Slip rubbed her brow, where a little blood trickled down. "What?"

"No." Asson turned to confront the warlock. Davoren's red eyes went to the mage's face, and he faltered but spoke up. "We can't just aban—"

"Abandon them?" Davoren proposed. "What an excellent idea. I think such a course is the optimal one. If Tymora smiles, they will keep the creatures occupied while we make good our escape. Wenches tend to be adept at such things. If they aren't dead already, that is." He cracked his knuckles. "Now. Where is the tunnel?"

The wide-eyed halfling pressed her face into Gargan's knee.

Ashen-faced, mouth open, Asson put one hand up as though to cast a spell. Davoren pointed two fingers at him. Red fire danced around his gauntlet. "Oh yes, whitebeard," he said. "Try me now, when your little love-slave isn't here to protect you." He looked down. "Or hold you up, even."

"I-I object," Liet said before he realized his mouth was open. When the warlock turned smug eyes on him, he stammered. "W-we have to save them. I think—"

"Truly?" Davoren shrugged. "Well, you're wrong. Now then."

"In the absence of our leader, we should put this to a vote," Asson said, drawing Davoren's gaze. Davoren kept one hand aimed at Asson and moved the other toward Liet. Fire arced between his arms. Liet could feel his body shaking.

As soon as those red eyes left him, Liet felt his tongue freed. "Aye. A vote."

With death pointed at Asson and Liet, the warlock burst out laughing. "A vote? Oh, please. We've gone over this before. We'll do what I say, because I am the strongest. Oh, but *do* object. By all means. I shan't need the two of you, anyway."

"No." Liet's eyes widened as Gargan put his hand on the back of Davoren's neck. How had he moved so stealthily, with such a huge body? "Vote."

The warlock glared up at the goliath for several long breaths, but it was unclear what he was thinking. Perhaps he realized the fragility of his position—a twist of Gargan's wrist would snap his neck—or perhaps he was considering whether he could press on without support.

The warlock finally shrugged. "Very well. I shall indulge your foolishness." He crossed his arms and Gargan released him. Davoren strode over to lean against the wall across the cavern from Asson. "This time."

"Good," Liet breathed. He wasn't quite up to words. He was glad of the goliath's support, though the emeralds in his gray face remained unreadable.

"I argue that we go back to save Taslin and Twilight," Asson said. "They have served us well, and it would be foolish not to rescue them."

"Of course you would," snapped Davoren. "One of the wenches shares your bed, so your judgment is clouded. Thus, your voice holds no sway here."

Asson's face went bright red. "But—" The word became coughing.

"If we must vote, at least let our discussion be rational," said Davoren. "I do not think you appreciate the dangers inherent, old man, in the proposal that we chase the grimlocks. I rather think you are considering with your—"

In the face of this intimidation, Liet felt angry rather than afraid. "Despite your lack of respect, Davoren—something I have come to expect from you . . ." That was Twilight talking, he realized, and it made his heart leap. "His vote must stand."

"No. He is highly emotional, incapable of real decisions. Look at his face."

Asson looked away.

"W-well then," Liet said. "His vote counts as an abstention. I vote aye. Even you cannot twist me into conceding an emotional state."

Davoren sneered. "Even your obvious affection for our erstwhile mistress, eh?"

Liet fought to keep his face from blushing. He hadn't been thinking anything of the sort, but somehow the words stung. Nevertheless, Liet spoke, his voice a little choppy. "She has struck me more often than any sane man needs as a deterrent," he said. Again, that was Twilight. "That should tell you of her affections."

Davoren considered, then shrugged. "Some day, you should ask her about her former lovers—and the fates to which she led them," he said. Liet shivered, and Davoren looked at the trembling Slip. "The halfling, then."

Asson smiled at Liet. "Perhaps you truly are the age you seem."

Liet blinked. "What?"

"I'd thought you but a child in a man's body," Asson said softly, "but you do have your moments of wisdom, do you not?"

"Uh."

Something happened at that moment—something that made Liet blink. The room grew colder, or perhaps hotter. Davoren—dark and frightening of appearance as he was, suddenly darkened, as though a devil had climbed into his skin. Or, more accurately, as though his soul had blackened and became even more intense. His eyes gleamed and his voice flowed like silk.

Liet knew he had invoked some fiendish abilities, but damned if he could recognize a word or gesture of casting. Even Asson looked at Davoren, stunned.

"Child," the warlock said. "You want to get out of this dark hole, do you not?"

Slip looked at Liet pointedly, as though awaiting some signal. She shivered, but her eyes were calm. What did she want? Why did she look to *him*, out of all of them?

Unanswered, she looked back at Davoren. "Uh . . . aye."

"And you do not want to waste precious time, or risk more attacks before you can escape, eh?" His smooth voice seemed infinitely persuasive.

Liet was speechless. He felt the sword in his hand, and wondered if it had any chance of injuring the warlock—the fiend.

"Uh, no. No, I don't w-want that," said Slip.

"And neither do you want to risk your life, or all of ours, just to assuage the lusts of fools, old or young."

Liet bristled, and this time he would have attacked had Asson not coughed. At least, such is what he told himself. The concept of making a move against Davoren struck him as being like suicide—only more certain.

Asson slowly shook his head. "This is her fight," he said. "Do not interfere."

Liet realized at that moment that Asson was afraid, too— even more afraid of Davoren than losing Taslin? The youth shuddered.

Slip shook her head.

"Then speak up," the warlock invited. "Speak against their fool crusade."

"B-but . . ." Slip said.

The warlock frowned. "You are strong of will, child," he said. "And you care about them more than you confess. If you will not speak against their rescue, at the least decide that you will not speak *for* it. Abstain."

"I-I will," Slip said finally. "I abstain."

Liet gasped. "You cheated! You forced that out of her!"

"No," Slip argued. "No. I just . . . I can't decide on this. I don't want to make up your minds for you. As Yondalla teaches, saving them is . . . the right thing, but killing us all to save them. . . ."

"Very well," said Davoren. "It looks like we're undecided. In that case . . ."

"Actually," Asson said. " 'Tis one vote left."

"Truly?" Davoren said, feigning astonishment. "Oh yes—there *is*." He sneered.

Liet realized he had played right into the warlock's hands. Gargan.

Of course, Davoren expected the goliath to vote nay—the hulking creature had shown no signs of attachment to Twilight and Taslin thus far. And Asson had planned this, too. All his hopes rested on the goliath.

They all turned toward Gargan, who until that moment had been silent.

CHAPTER EIGHT

I *thilnin karanok! Garum tellek!"*
    There was mud amid the darkness, dancing shadows, and a dull ache.

Throughout her long life, Twilight had spent enough time unconscious to know not to open her eyes immediately. That was a common mistake that had earned many a novice thief a solid punch in the mouth at best, a rusty knife in the gut at worst.

She used her other four senses first—the kind that weren't obvious, and wouldn't prompt such unpleasantness from her captors.

Around her, Twilight picked up the sounds of chanting in a language she could not understand. Regardless, her keen mind processed the growling, rough texture of the words. It might have shared common roots with Dwarvish, but it was otherwise unfamiliar.

"Ithilnin karanok! Garum tellek!" the chant proclaimed.

Doesn't sound good, whatever it is, she thought.

Twilight smelled a combination of moldering wood and old stone—a musty scent she sensed was that of the grimlocks—mixed with a kind of summer flower, very faint, whose source she could not even guess. Falling into awareness of her body, Twilight surmised that she was being carried upon some kind of platform, laid out lengthwise. And, most importantly, her hands and feet were tied.

That was *not* a good sign.

Slowly, Twilight opened her eyes. She was right—four grimlocks bore her, bound but not gagged, upon a wooden pallet, marching down an aisle formed by their chanting fellows. There were no torches, so she could see only with her darksight. On her right, Twilight saw Taslin similarly secured and carried by four more.

That would explain the flowery scent, thought Twilight. She could tell from the priestess's breathing that Taslin was awake, but feigning unconsciousness as well. Wise.

"Ithilnin karanok! Garum tellek!" the grimlocks chanted.

Twilight almost hoped Taslin wasn't merely pretending so that she might be spared what would come next. "Taslin," she said, since the sun couldn't see her.

Taslin's eyes opened slowly. *"They did not gag us,"* said the priestess in Elvish.

"The better to enjoy our screams, I would imagine," Twilight replied in kind. *"Try not to move."*

The nearest eyeless beast turned its attention to Twilight. Its sightless focus felt as keen as any knife. As open-minded as she had become in her travels, the empty gaze of the grimlocks still disturbed Twilight profoundly.

"Their senses extend only so far," Twilight said. *"They can see without eyes and can hear us, but it seems we can talk. You will only provoke them if you move. And no spellcasting. They have their own priests."*

Taslin looked about without moving her head. Her eyes flicked back to Twilight. *"This is a ritual,"* she said.

"Indeed."

"Ithilnin karanok! Garum tellek darakow!"

"And we're the ones to be sacrificed."

"I can only assume so."

"No," said Taslin. *"I can understand their words."*

Twilight raised a brow.

"My earring," she explained.

"Right."

"Ithilnin karanok! Garum tellek darakow!" the grimlocks roared. In Twilight's opinion, the chant was starting to grate.

"A chant about a god, a name—Ithilnin—and sacrificing us." Her face turned stormy. *"They think we're drow."*

"That would explain the yellow and white flesh, respectively."

"You could always be an albino drow," she said.

Twilight couldn't help but smile. Of all the things she had been called in her long life, she hadn't heard that one before.

Not, of course, that the grimlocks could distinguish color, she realized.

———◆———

Floating along that dark path, completely blind—the grimlocks had no need of torches, being able to "see" in perfect darkness—Taslin sighed. Her attempt at levity had been artifice. Unless the others came to rescue them in the next two dozen heartbeats. . . .

"Do you think the others survived?" she asked, hoping Twilight was still awake.

"No." A pause. *"And even if they did, they wouldn't come back for us. Davoren will control them—and he hates you almost as much as he hates me."*

"Why does he hate you so?"

Twilight did not reply.

"How do we escape?" Taslin asked.

"Occasionally, being polite works." Twilight said. *"So I'm told, anyway."*

"Then I shall speak to them," said Taslin. *"They may understand Common, at least."* The priestess addressed the nearest grimlock in the trade tongue. "We are not your enemies. Release us," she said. "Appease your vile god some other way."

Something warm and sticky struck her cheek, and the creature growled in its own guttural speech, which came through her earring as Elvish. *"Silence, drow."*

"I confess, my suggestion was something of a jest," said Twilight.

Taslin ignored the spittle running down her face. *"Come to think of it, they probably can't see color."*

"Ithilnin! Ithilnin karanok! Ithilnin!" The chant only redoubled in volume.

"That's it, then," Twilight said. *"Can't go wrong with pretty lasses on the altar."*

"You are so young." Taslin shook her head. *"Do you take nothing seriously?"*

"Not if I can help it." The tremor in her voice didn't display calm, though. *"In the face of inescapable death, if you haven't got your sense of humor, what have you got?"*

Taslin closed her eyes in silent acquiescence, and she forced an ironic smile, even though she felt like crying. She'd just learned something about her companion—not from her words, but form how she had spoken.

Fear. Twilight was afraid.

———◆———

During the silence that followed, Twilight took the opportunity to explore their surroundings, moving only her eyes.

The grimlocks carried them through a plain, if large, cavern. With closer scrutiny, however, Twilight realized it was some sort of settlement. The city—if such it could be called—was completely unlit. If not for her darksight, she would have observed none of it.

Three dozen or so houses carved out of the rock adorned the sides of the cavern, stacked two, three, even four high. A series of ladders led to each house, and grimlocks stood—dead silent—outside each door, their arms held aloft in recognition. Male and female they stood, Twilight guessed, along with children. She might have found it charming if the situation hadn't been so dire, and if they weren't so eyeless. The unnerving, empty gazes felt like death itself.

In front of the window or door of each house hung several rods on a rope that Twilight took for a crude wind chime, though there was no wind underground. She was proven wrong, however, when one of the creatures reached up and tapped the contraption. Its three reeds spun, producing a series of whistles that rippled through the air, perking up ears and turning heads.

A means of producing sound—thus making them able to find their way—without opening their mouths, Twilight thought. How practical.

The grimlock leading the ritual procession held his arms aloft and stopped. Silence fell and all eyes in the city—all four of them—went to his crude robes, horned headpiece, and gnarled staff. Twilight noted that the leader wore both of the elves' swords, though none of their other equipment had been taken.

She also couldn't help but note that he wore a particularly shiny ring on his finger, a plain gold band that looked rather familiar. Twilight's eyes narrowed. A coincidence?

Twilight felt the reassuring pressure of her hidden amulet against her collarbone. Its power would prevent anyone from noticing it who wasn't specifically looking. Ordinarily, Twilight would be comforted, but part of her wanted the amulet off so any searchers would see her peril and come to her aid. And of course, her hands were tied.

Ironic, she thought. How like her lord and master to trick her to her death.

Indicating the prisoners, the grimlock priest uttered a series of grunts and hoots, casting his staff back and forth as though fighting invisible attackers. When he was done, the grimlocks of the city hooted and growled in agreement.

"*What did he say?*" Twilight asked quietly.

"*Calling upon their god, Ithilnin,*" whispered Taslin, "*and a blessing over those the Great Slitherer shall consume.*"

"*Radiant,*" said Twilight. "*That sounds like something I'd look forward to.*"

The chorus of applause and hooting ended, and the column moved forward again.

Twilight saw Taslin's lips moving gently. She spoke silently. Not magic—the shadowdancer would have sensed that. Rather . . .

"Aillesel seldarie," Taslin prayed quietly. *"May the Seldarine preserve us."*

"You say that as if they would," said Twilight. Taslin's eyes flew open and a pained look came over her face, colorless in darksight. *"The gods hear what they choose to hear, and they don't need us telling them what prayers to answer."*

They reached an even greater cavern than the one that held the city. The rock walls were plain, and other than the massive size, the space was unremarkable. A perfectly rounded tunnel, much like the ones Twilight had seen earlier, opened from the floor in the center of the chamber. The sacrificial chasm, she imagined, out of which their god would emerge.

"But—"

"If your lord wanted to save us, he'd have done so," said Twilight. "Or maybe he yet will. Either way, he doesn't need you reminding him that we're about to die. Or—more accurately—be eaten by this Ithlin-ithnin thing."

One of the grimlocks snarled at her, recognizing the word as its god, and Twilight flinched despite herself. "Ith-*il*-nin," she spat. "My mistake."

<hr>

Silence reigned.

"You made it clear you will not talk about your past," Taslin whispered.

"Good," Twilight said in the Common tongue.

The blind creatures lifted both their pallets and set them up high—likely on an altar, Taslin thought. The priest's voice lessened, as though backing away. She imagined that she and Twilight were alone. Abruptly, some sort of light appeared in the darkness—bonfires lit by the grimlocks. Their heat fell upon Taslin's face, and she could see flickers and dancing shapes. The moon elf was lying straight and dead as a rod, looking around.

"If you're wanting a heart to heart now that we're about to die," she said, looking at Taslin sidelong, *"can't say I'm interested."*

"I have only one question I wish to ask," said Taslin.

Her companion sighed. *"I suppose it hardly matters now, since we're about to be eaten and all. Query, Taslin, and I'll answer."*

"You serve Erevan Ilesere—the trickster god—do you not?"

Twilight looked at her curiously for a heartbeat, then looked away. That told Taslin all she needed to know. *"I see,"* the priestess said softly.

The moon elf smiled with bemusement. "You got that idea from the mark?" she asked in Common, gesturing with her head toward her hips. "Or from the sword hilt? Or perhaps my charming personality?"

The world shuddered and the chanting increased in speed and intensity. The fires were blazing and the chamber was lit up as bright as day. The grimlocks' gray flesh glistened with sweat, drool, and other juices Taslin didn't care to identify.

"All of them," Taslin replied in kind. "My real question, though, is that if you are a fellow servant of the Seldarine, why do you not pray for aid, as I do? Why not supplicate your lord?"

"Because I would rather die," she said, "than talk to that scheming, lecherous, backstabbing old bastard ever again. He used me, and as you can see, he hates me."

Taslin realized that was a lie—or perhaps not the whole truth. She wasn't about to be deceived. "Why not beseech Lord Corellon, then? Surely the elf gods—"

"I want nothing to do with the elf gods," Twilight said. "I turned my back on the People long ago, for reasons that are my own, and I've no desire to turn again."

Why was Twilight lying to her?

The grimlocks' chanting rose in volume.

"No offense meant, of course."

Taslin nodded. The two fell into silence.

Perhaps her bravado was a lie, and she truly was a child.

❖

Twilight looked away from the priestess to hide her shock. Taslin didn't believe her, and that made her afraid—more afraid than all the grimlocks in all the Realms could have made her, sacrificial chants or no.

Only then did she realize that the cavern had fallen silent. The grimlocks had ceased their ecstatic chanting and stood rapt, their hands wide. Tremors shook the vast chamber. The creatures all turned toward the hole from which their god would emerge.

"What—" Taslin started, but a roar tore her words away, shattering the tranquility of the cavern. If the roar was loud to the elves, it was splitting to sensitive grimlock ears. The creatures fell to the ground, hands clasped to their heads.

A great serpentine form burst through the tunnel, its head letting out a mighty cry. Its purple carapace—smooth, thick, and solid as steel—creaked and twisted in the air high over their heads. Yellow-green spittle dripped from its jaws and dotted the floor, leaving the dark stone pitted and hissing as acid burned it.

A purple worm, Twilight thought. She'd never seen one this big.

The grimlocks, hearing and smelling their slithering god emerging from its tunnel, gave a great cry of "Ithilnin!" and supplicated themselves, putting their foreheads down on the stone. The high priest intoned a phrase in his tongue and laid himself prone.

Twilight nodded grimly and stared up, resolved to look death in the face. Taslin did the same, gave a slight smile, and fainted. Curious—not the faint, but the smile.

Then Twilight looked up, wondering as to the source of her mirth. The worm did nothing more than loom overhead, cast its gaze back and forth, and roar every so often. Then silence fell—absolute silence around them.

In the quiet, the worm was less frightening. In fact, she barely realized it was there. Twilight was about to express her confusion when she felt fumbling hands and her frown became a grin.

Working quickly, Slip and Liet severed the bonds that held Taslin and Twilight, while the worm distracted the grimlocks. Within a magical bubble of silence, they were as good as invisible. Slip mouthed instructions to follow her, then gestured—clearly the spell was set upon her—but Twilight knew the reach of such a spell.

She rolled off the pallet, dropped to the stone without a whisper, and padded over to the prostrate priest. The creature shook his head, but the silence kept him blind.

Just as her fingers were about to relieve the priest of her sword, Twilight felt Liet catch her arm to keep her within the magical silence. She wanted to struggle, but he was right—the spell did not extend over the priest, merely up to him.

Twilight realized her tricks at legerdemain would hardly work on a creature that sensed by nose and ear, rather than by eye. She loathed leaving Betrayal behind, but she understood necessity.

A shock rippled through the floor of the chamber, throwing a startled Twilight to the ground. She could hear nothing outside the silence, but one look at the scores of quavering grimlocks, blood running from their ears, told her enough.

Her eyes turned upward to the beast above them, and she saw not one, but *two* purple menaces.

The real Ithilnin had come.

CHAPTER NINE

The second purple worm loomed even larger than the first, its scaled carapace cracked and spiked with serrated spines. At its top, huge bone jaws like dozens of axes snapped wide enough to swallow a team of horses whole. At the other end of the worm sprang a stinger the size of an ogre's two-handed sword. Dark veins of greenish acid ran over its body, burning away the stone around its body.

But most astonishing, when the acid struck the first worm, the creature flickered and winked out of existence. Asson appeared, hovering in the air where the illusory worm's maw had been.

The grimlock high priest snarled—or so Twilight guessed, for no sound penetrated the aura of silence. He wove his hands through a counterspell.

Twilight leaped at him as he cast, scrabbling at his hands to ruin the spell, but she was too late. Sound rushed into her ears, including the mind-splitting roar of the grimlock's looming purple god.

Everything seemed to happen in a single moment. The huge worm lunged at Asson, who flew away, showering magical flame upon the creature in a vain attempt to drive it back. As Taslin shouted a warning, Liet and Slip drew out weapons to strike at the grimlocks around them who had risen, axes ready. The high priest began another chant even as Twilight yanked her rapier from his belt and ran the creature through. The words died in a gurgle, and the priest's bodyguards lunged at her. Twilight pulled at her weapon, but it had stuck in the high priest's ribcage.

Two of the grimlock honor guards spun to behead her with their stone axes, but seemingly from nowhere, Gargan leaped to her defense, bowling the eyeless creatures over. Twilight seized the opportunity to relieve the high priest of Taslin's sword, the familiar gold ring, and Betrayal, which was still caught in his ribs.

"Taslin!" Twilight shouted, and tossed the priestess's blade as she lunged to run a grimlock through with her own.

Already chanting, the priestess caught it, renewing her connection to Corellon in a heartbeat. Holy power burst from her hand and smashed aside four of the grimlocks who were rushing at the adventurers. Twilight flinched away—not anxious to get so close to holy power, which would burn the darkness out of a body. She didn't think Corellon would burn her, but better safe than dead. At least she was not *evil*.

Speaking of evil . . .

Sand and dark, she exclaimed silently, where's Davoren?

Had the warlock been slain? Twilight doubted that. More likely, Davoren had betrayed the others, leaving them all to perish at the hands of—

A flaming blast of dark power ripped through the cavern, blowing the grimlock facing her into a thousand bits. The power arced to a second eyeless brute, shattering his ribcage, then a third, sending the creature spinning to the ground. The shadowdancer looked up to see Davoren standing near the exit to the cavern, lashing out with his demonic powers.

Gargan stood with Twilight, his axe working furiously to fend off the eyeless monsters. They faced half a dozen foes each, and it was all Twilight could do to fend them off with her rapier and avoid being chopped in two. She couldn't block the axes with a rapier, and each time she parried a stone spear aside, sparks flew from the Hizagkuur blade.

Arcane syllables in Asson's aged voice rippled on high,

drawing Twilight's eyes. Flame shot from Asson's outstretched hand. The worm's jaws shut just in time and the fire burned its way down the beast's sides. The creature, undeterred, snapped at him, but the old mage flailed out of the way. The worm caught the fringe of his reddish robe, tearing a long strip of fabric free.

Launching a double parry to deflect spears sailing in from the right and left—just wide enough to escape their points—Twilight realized that as overmatched as she was, the mage knew worse straits. His foot didn't impede his flight, but he could not defeat a purple worm by himself.

"Davoren! Help Asson!" Twilight shouted.

She lunged forward, inside a grimlock's swing, twisting her arm back and around to reverse the blade. The stunned creature couldn't do more than blink as she slammed her back into his chest. Her blade shot under her arm and skewered the grimlock's heart. She ducked aside as he fell and sized up her next target.

She hadn't expected, however, that the creature would be so wide or fall so fast—she couldn't get out of the way fast enough. The limp grimlock toppled and pinned Twilight to the ground. Betrayal skittered away. A nearby grimlock raised his flint spear, and she could do nothing to defend herself.

" 'Light!" came a shout. The grimlock whirled and a blade impaled his belly.

Liet shoved at the corpse that held her down. Perhaps he was not quite a man in his head, but he wielded steel well. Unable to keep herself from flashing him a thankful smile as he worked, she looked up to assess how the others fared.

Gargan's axe and fist worked together to lay grimlocks low. Slip and Taslin, sword and mace singing, held off a dozen of the eyeless creatures. Though a hundred or more grimlocks had filled the chamber before the worm's appearance, many had fled the battle, leaving only the best warriors, perhaps two score of them.

The grimlocks, however, were the least of the band's worries. The hulking purple worm hissed, spat, and weaved, chasing after Asson. The mage was a mere darting insect to the serpentine colossus, and a single bite or spit of acid would destroy him.

Fortunately, the old man's magic bore him quickly enough to avoid the worm's lunges.

Meanwhile, Davoren sent ray after ray of ruby energy into the creature, timing his attacks to match Asson's magic. Twilight imagined that the unseeing worm, its senses based on hearing and touch, could not know that the pesky mage—of which it was well aware—was not the source of the stinging blasts.

The battle would remain at a standstill, Twilight realized, until Asson's magic expired or the others ran out of spells. Then that worm would turn its attention from the source of its pain and devour the others.

Seeing that Twilight would be free in a breath, Gargan sent another pair of grimlocks staggering back with a pulse of his powerful shoulders. He lunged across the cavern to join Slip and Taslin, who faced difficulties of their own.

With Liet's help, Twilight squirmed out from under the grimlock corpse, and not a moment too soon. A pair of grimlocks thrust spears at them. Liet managed to knock one aside, and expertly twisted it out of the grimlock's hands with a flick of his wrist.

Twilight dodged the other spear thrust, letting it slide harmlessly past her, and plucked up Betrayal with her toe. Then she danced inside the creature's guard and the grimlock through. Liet's foe whirled, and she put her rapier through the grimlock's face.

"Heh," Liet said. "I'm better at disarming than finishing, eh?"

"Retreat!" shouted Twilight. "Away from the—"

At that moment, instinct told Twilight to duck, and she never failed to trust instinct. A thrown spear glanced off her shoulder. It should have torn through her silk shirt, but the gold ring she had slipped onto her finger draped her body in magic as thick and protective as a suit of mail.

Someone caught her arm, and Twilight almost killed Liet. "Are you all right?" the youth shouted in her face.

Twilight cringed. "Easy, lad," she snapped, rubbing her ear. "I'm right here."

Back to back in a circle of bodies, the two batted away weapons and riposted. The creatures came from all directions but Twilight and Liet were only two, so they kept turning. Spears jabbed at them, and they deflected the points as best they could. One caught Liet's shoulder and the man gasped, but Twilight pushed him back off the flint tip.

A stout grimlock charged, spear low. Twilight swept her rapier down to turn it aside, and Liet stepped in her path before she could riposte. He smashed his fist into the creature's face. From the way he flinched and flexed his hand, Twilight was glad she hadn't tried that.

"That's what swords are for," said Twilight. She demonstrated by putting her dusky blade through the startled grimlock's throat, sending him to the floor.

"Point taken," Liet scowled. He sidestepped a chop, slapped the wielder's hands away from the grimlock the haft, and showed his newly acquired strategy by stabbing the grimlock in the side.

"Well done," Twilight said. He didn't fight very well, but he knew how to disarm.

"You never answered—" started Liet. He parried an axe high, his muscles straining against those of the grimlock and the flint sparking against his steel. Twilight stepped under his raised arms, twisted her wrist to shorten her grip, and thrust once, twice, thrice, skewering the creature each time.

"Hmm?" she asked idly as the grimlock fell.

"My question," Liet finished, panting. Blood flowed down his shield arm. "You never answered it."

"Because it was a foolish question," Twilight said simply. She turned back to the business of escaping. They'd broken the grimlocks' circle and she hauled Liet back. They fought a retreating battle toward the others, near what Twilight hoped was an exit tunnel.

Asson spun out of the way just in time to keep his head, and threw a lightning bolt into the worm's body. The worm jerked and whipped, caught in a fury of electricity, but only for a moment. The beast was as tough as a serpent of stone and as fast as a dragon. Twilight knew Asson could not flee to save himself, for he was the only thing distracting the beast.

The shadowdancer couldn't think about strategy; she fell fully into instinct and bladework. Over and over, she parried and retreated, parried and retreated. She deflected a blow meant for the staggering Liet and leaped back, wrenching the youth by his good shoulder. His shield went up to block spears, but weakly, slowly—barely.

The grimlocks pressed the two groups of foes—Twilight and Liet one, Gargan and Slip the other—into a circle around Taslin, who cast spells from the middle. Together, they backed toward the exit. Davoren stood aloof, off to the right. He blasted at the worm, and every so often, any grimlocks that dared to approach him.

"Asson!" A chopping axe stole away any other words Taslin might have screamed, and she fell into a chant, calling on Corellon's power as she parried and cut.

The old mage threw a ball of webbing directly into the purple worm's hiss. The sticky threads exploded into a wagon load of webs, coating its face and fangs, just as another ray of Davoren's power struck the creature ten feet below the maw. The creature spat and sputtered, trying to clear its mouth. Its acid was making progress slowly. Asson took the opportunity to fly backward, keeping as much distance as he could between himself and roaring, serpentine death. In its thrashings, the worm narrowly missed clubbing him down.

The tide seemed to be turning—the seven could escape. The worm's cries multiplied as the spellslingers inflicted blow after stinging blow upon it. The shrieks wreaked havoc upon the grimlocks' ears. Those that remained winced and moaned with every roar. Distracted as they were, the companions could defeat their numbers.

Facing the last grimlock she saw on his feet, Twilight ducked under a slashing sword blade and came up inside the creature's guard, wrist swinging. A grimlock with a sword—a steel one?

This grimlock must have seen her trick and caught on. It released one hand from the sword to keep his balance and put his right knee into Twilight's stomach, sending her reeling.

Liet darted in to strike, but the grimlock brought his blackened sword around and dealt his head a glancing blow with the flat of the blade. Liet fell helpless beside Twilight, who struggled madly to catch her breath. The grimlock rose over them and spun the sword over his head, the blade dripping with a green liquid that hissed like acid.

Then the creature stopped.

Twilight looked up, blinking, and saw Gargan holding the grimlock's arm in his powerful hands. The two strained against one another, exerting all the force of their tightly corded muscles, and barely budged. The eyeless creature looked to be some kind of royal guard, wearing strings of gems around his neck. The grimlock wielded a masterfully crafted sword of steel, surely taken from another sacrifice. A black lacquer crossbow—drow construction, perhaps—hung from his belt.

Hissing, the grimlock shot out a hand to catch Gargan by the throat. The goliath released one hand from the monster's sword arm to lock his stonelike fingers around the creature's wrist in an attempt to break his grip. Without both arms holding the sword back, Gargan could do little but watch as the grimlock slowly forced the keen edge toward his face. Acid dribbled on his chest.

Twilight cried out and lunged, blade stabbing. The grimlock stiffened and released a little hiss. The sword slipped from his fingers and clattered to the ground. Twilight's rapier speared his side, leaving a small hole that spurted gray-red blood.

Panting, a trickle of blood coming from the corner of her lip, Twilight stepped aside to let the grimlock fall. She relieved him of the crossbow almost unconsciously.

Gargan spoke words Twilight did not understand. *"Gol maula kae."*

The appreciation was clear enough, and the elf gave him a smile that was suitably winsome, considering the circumstances. Her belly ached in all sorts of ways. The goliath helped Liet to his feet, and without flinching, wiped the acid off his stony skin.

Unsettling strength, that.

Then Twilight remembered their surroundings. The grim-locks were dead, but the worm yet lived. "Away!" Twilight shouted up to Asson. Taslin, Gargan, Liet, and Slip dashed toward the exit. The old man threw another lightning bolt at the worm and swooped toward the tunnel.

Taslin hung back, gazing up at the old wizard with fear on her face. Twilight caught her arm and pulled her around. "We have to go. *Now.*"

The priestess struggled, but Twilight insisted. "He can fly—we can only run," she said. "Let him wait until the last—he has the best chance to escape of any of us."

From the furious, confused look Taslin burned into her face, Twilight gathered the priestess objected to Twilight's reasoning. Taslin shrugged her off and rushed at the worm, sword in hand.

"Taslin!" Twilight snapped, but it was too late.

Gargan was faster, however. He bounded in front of Twilight and caught up Taslin, slinging her over his shoulder like a sack of grain. The priestess screamed and beat at his back, but the goliath did not reply to her cries.

Together, they fled toward the others.

The shadowdancer let out a sigh of relief, just as Davoren's words rang out. "Fall, damn you!" the warlock shouted. Then, half a beat later, "Fall!"

Twilight heard something in his words that made her blood run cold—or perhaps it was something she felt—some bit of magic, a touch of compulsion.

Asson picked just that moment to plummet from the air. The wizard didn't even flail as his spell failed and his body slammed into the ground with shattering force.

Within a heartbeat, the hissing purple worm snaked forward and crushed the old wizard beneath its coils.

CHAPTER TEN

Taslin's heart shattered.

It all happened so fast. One moment, Asson had been flitting about, unscathed, borne on the wings of magic. Alive. In the next instant, he became little more than reddish paste spread along the ground under the worm. He couldn't have dodged—couldn't have escaped.

Silence reigned in the cavern for a split second.

Then the priestess let out a shriek. Having been dropped by the goliath, she threw Twilight sprawling and dashed toward the worm.

"Taslin!" Twilight shouted, but Taslin didn't listen. What would that child know of this?

Golden hair blazing around her, the priestess bore down on the purple worm like a wrathful goddess, her sword low at her side in a two-handed grip. It hissed along the stone. As if it sensed her coming, the monster hissed and snaked down, opening its acid-slavering jaws wide. Taslin ran, full out, directly for them.

Then the priestess did what no sane warrior would do: she leaped into its mouth.

And as she went, she slashed up and thrust through its upper palate. The keen elven steel bit a hand-length deep into the burning pink flesh. The worm jerked back, stung. Taslin almost lost her balance and fell, but she held to the sword and rose as the worm did, inside its mouth. Though acid ate at her boots and she could scarcely breathe amid the fumes, Taslin bent at the knees, centering her weight.

"Corellon!" she cried, and drove up with all her strength even as it bit down.

The elven blade gave a screeching wail as it drove through the creature's flesh.

The monster screamed and slammed its head blindly against the ceiling of the cavern and managed to dislodge Taslin, who tumbled free. She did not know how high she was, but she didn't care. One of the monster's fangs tore a gouge down her arm, but the priestess hadn't the breath to scream. Likely, it was for the best—her lungs would have filled with noxious fumes, enough to kill her.

The creature gave one last screech of pain and toppled, with ground splitting thunder, to earth. Taslin followed, wheeling like a leaf in the wind.

"For you, Asson," she whispered as she tumbled toward death.

<hr>

Twilight's mouth opened as the purple monster screamed and rasped, whipping back and forth like a headless snake in its death throes.

"Burn me," was all she said.

Gargan tossed Liet his axe and sprang forward to catch the priestess's acid-spattered body. Taslin, miraculously alive, coughed and sputtered in the goliath's arms. She had somehow kept hold of her sword—the half that still remained. The other half—a full two hands of steel—was lodged in the dying purple worm's head.

Again, silence settled over the cavern, and the exhausted adventurers stood rapt. Then a chorus of vengeful shrieks came from the exit tunnel. A score of grimlocks, all wielding stone axes, flooded in to avenge their fallen god.

Davoren cursed in single infernal syllables as the creatures swarmed toward him. He waved his hands, spreading dark power like slime. It struck the ground in the grimlocks' path and spread into a pool of impenetrable blackness, its gleaming surface reflecting the charging monsters. Then he fled.

As the first grimlocks stepped into the pool, a thousand tentacles of dark energy sprang from the black matter, wrapping the limbs and bodies of the eyeless creatures. Many were caught, and they screamed against the sucking blackness. Half the grimlocks charged through the tentacles, however, and they ran toward the intruders with slavering mouths and single-minded purpose.

Twilight saw Davoren running ahead of them, but only just.

"Run!" Twilight shouted to the others. "We can't fight them all!"

"We aren't to save Davoren?" asked Liet, drawing a startled look from the elf. "We need him—you said it yourself!"

"Sand," hissed Twilight. She had never hated being right this much. "Gargan! Slip! Take Taslin! Run!" She looked to the exit but shadows of grimlocks moved within. She cursed. "Another exit! Go!"

The goliath and halfling nodded. "Another tunnel," said Slip. "That way!" She pointed to a small opening halfway around the cavern from the exit. They ran for the tunnel, Gargan cradling the limp priestess like a child swathed in a wet blanket. Taslin moaned in the goliath's arms.

With a brutal nod, Twilight turned to Liet. "Lad, you're with me."

"Uh," said Liet, looking at the oncoming horde, "I didn't mean—"

"*Now!*" shouted Twilight, darting toward the grimlocks like an arrow.

Liet cursed and sprinted after her, huffing and puffing as he went.

Ahead of them, the warlock panted and fought to keep running. The grimlocks were still gaining. They would soon overtake him, or drop him with a spear throw. Unless Twilight had a chance to argue the point.

"Here!" she said, wrenching Liet to a halt.

"What is it?" Liet stopped and leaned over, hands on his knees, his bloody sword dangling. His shield was split and would hardly withstand more punishment.

Twilight closed her eyes. With a hiss of her will, she brought the shadows flickering about her body, ready to to cover their retreat. Then she paused, cursing. She had no energy left for a shadowdance, and little enough for manipulating the darkness. And the creatures had no eyes anyway—shadows could not save them.

Liet misunderstood. "It only *now* occurs to you that we're going to die?"

Twilight ignored that. "I guess we'll have to do this the energetic way," she said. She fell back into a fighting stance, awaiting the rushing grimlocks. Davoren came roaring past, running full out, and didn't even slow to help them.

"Typical," murmured Twilight.

At that moment, an ear-splitting roar came from the entrance tunnel, drawing all eyes and ears. There stood a distorted troll with limbs of various sizes and patchwork, greenish and reddish skin.

"Blind-dims!" roared Tlork, hefting his hammer. "They's mine!"

Only half a dozen paces from Liet and Twilight, the grimlocks skidded to a halt. They turned and charged Tlork, hissing with rage.

"Run!" Twilight snapped, snatching Liet's arm. "Come on!"

Together, they followed Davoren back to the side tunnel, fighting the exhaustion seeping into their limbs and the fire tearing at their lungs. Gargan waited there, the last grimlock's black sword in hand, ready to fend off any that pursued.

He needn't have bothered. Drawn to the troll by some unknown animosity, the grimlocks lunged at Tlork with flailing axes and the troll beat back at them. The troll outpowered the grimlocks—his muscles, fiendish body parts, and ferocity made him the perfect killing machine—but there were so many that Tlork would be long delayed.

"Poetic, really," said a voice at Twilight's shoulder. She turned to find Davoren watching the battle with more than passing interest. "Playing one foe against another. Amusing to watch so much death, isn't it?"

Twilight kept calm. She wiped Betrayal on her thigh and sheathed it. For now.

"Should we—ah—help?" asked Slip.

"Help who?" put in Liet. "I'm thinking we'd best flee before—"

A massive hand on his shoulder stopped the boy, and Twilight looked up to see Gargan there. The goliath, still holding the unconscious Taslin, did not speak, but his gaze conveyed volumes. His eyes fixed upon Tlork—analyzing, weighing, judging. He had looked at Twilight and Liet in the same way, as though sizing them up for a duel.

"Aye," said Twilight. "The longer we watch, the more we learn about the troll."

Tlork's massive warhammer appeared awkward in his ten-foot skeletal arm, but the troll wielded it with exceptional skill and balance. Each swing of the weapon knocked two or three monsters aside, and his fiendish stinger caught those the hammer missed. When a grimlock came inside his reach, Tlork would simply flatten the eyeless wretch with his elephantlike leg or eviscerate him with a snap of his claws.

Twilight had to wonder. Why had the grimlocks been drawn to the troll, if they could not defeat—nay, couldn't even *injure*—the creature?

As Twilight studied the foes, the assault made perfect sense. The grimlocks' world was one of sounds and smells. The troll had bellowed loudly enough to rival the purple worm, and his stench was so pungent Twilight could catch it even at her distance, a spear-cast away. Tlork was perceived as a much greater threat than the seven of them.

Six, Twilight corrected herself with an inward wince. She felt empty, as though something had been clawed out of her.

Then Tlork broke through the grimlock horde, shattering a monster's chest with a pulse of the mighty hammer. Those that did not lie dead had already fled in terror before the half-fiend, half-troll monstrosity. The path cleared, Tlork fixed his mad eyes on the six companions, and charged.

"Time to be going!" Liet hissed.

Twilight stayed him. "Wait."

Summoning her will, she wrenched the shadows to her and sent them forth. This was not the dance—it would not consume all her strength. The shadows coalesced and melted into scything blades—a wall of shadowy steel that flashed through the air—sweeping straight for Tlork and the few remaining grimlocks. She heard Liet gasp beside her, and knew it was because her gray eyes had flashed black.

Twilight was used to it. She preferred it to her other powers. The shadows were another aspect of Neveren's legacy, rather than part of her service to a god who hated her.

The fleeing grimlocks who yet lived ignored the shadowy wall of razors—the illusion was only visual, and they had no eyes—emerging unscathed and oblivious. The troll, however, immediately fell to the important business of knocking the blades out of the air and smashing them to splinters against the ground. Not surprisingly, the hammer passed through the swords like the shadows they were.

"Let us see how—" she started.

"Enough of this," Davoren snapped. With a flicker of will, he shot a pair of fiery bolts up at the ceiling. The power burst and sent a web of cracks through the stone.

"Ah," said Slip. "What—?" Twilight shoved the halfling down the tunnel and pulled Liet behind her as she ran. Gargan shot the warlock a glare but followed.

Not a heartbeat later, the ceiling cracked and collapsed, sealing off the tunnel with a shattering crash of stone.

<hr>

Tlork skidded short of crushing his body against the tons of stone piled up around the tunnel mouth.

Then a chunk of stone tumbled down from the top of the pile and smashed into the troll's face with enough force to snap his head back and shatter his spindly nose.

Tlork merely blinked, confused, as the carrot-shaped member straightened of its own accord and sucked in the blood dripping down his patchwork face. The troll's regeneration left very little that went uncured.

"Dumb them!" Tlork growled. "Dumb dims!" He hoped some of the dims had survived, so he could squish them.

The troll turned to see the floating blades coming again.

Those things wouldn't give up, even after Tlork made sure they were good and dead. Or had he just run past them? He couldn't remember.

Tlork hammered at the first one, but his weapon went through the blade like so much air. It wavered a bit, but kept slashing at his chest. Funny, it didn't make any noise—not even a good whistle through the air—and Tlork didn't feel the sting.

Any creature possessed of reason higher than that of an overripe turnip would have seen through the shadowy illusion, but Tlork had never been all that high in the garden hierarchy. Sun-baked green squash, slightly moldy, was about his level.

Tlork kept fighting the shadow swords until they faded from view—only a few breaths. Then, unnerved at how they disappeared, the troll set to work dispensing with the rocky barrier.

As the dust settled, the adventurers found themselves breathless and in silence. Gargan lowered Taslin to the ground and stood ready with his blade, just in case the troll burst through the rubble. Slip moved stiffly to the sun elf's side and murmured healing prayers. Liet put a hand on Twilight's shoulder, though whether it was to comfort her or himself, she did not know.

She shook him off. Why would she want to feel, right now, rather than think?

Twilight scanned the dark corridor. It was not a worm's corridor but one carved by hand and pick. Nor was it of the shabby, rough craftsmanship of the grimlock city. She ran her fingers along the walls, feeling the subtle symmetries and imperfections.

Not dwarf work, either. Nor was it rounded and curved like the sewers. Rather, the tunnel was straight and smooth, traveling perhaps twenty paces before it branched right and left.

A new section of the depths? The concept made her uneasy.

"Liet," she said.

His eyes glazed and he did not respond for a second, seemingly lost. Twilight clenched her hands and bit her lip, uncomfortable at being patient.

"Liet!" Twilight snapped.

The youth started and looked over at her.

"Did you come through these tunnels to rescue us, or another set?"

"Can—can you not give us but a moment?" His voice was plaintive and weak. "I mean, Taslin, and Asson—he's—well, he's—"

"Dead," Twilight finished. Liet recoiled as from a slap. "As we shall be, unless we make sure no grimlocks can come after us. Sentiment comes only when we're safe."

Twilight could feel them staring at her—hard. Good. It distracted her, and them.

She continued. "Now, do those tunnels lead back to where you came from, or—?"

The youth scratched his head. "These . . . are the same tunnels, I think . . . but they seem different." He shrugged, and his eyes were damp. "We only got through guided by Gargan, and . . . and . . ." He trailed off.

So that's how it would be. Well, she could play this game. Twilight was adept at eliciting attention. "A maze?" She scowled.

As though shaken, Liet looked at her. "What's wrong?"

"Bad experiences," she said, drawing his attention. "What do you find in mazes?"

"Ah," said Liet. "Twists and turns? Lots of dead ends?"

Twilight shook her head.

"Treasure at the center?"

"Minotaurs. And depending on the local wildlife, often *ravenous* ones."

"Oh. That." Liet's eyes were far away. It hadn't worked. "Just staying optimistic."

Twilight growled. "What?" she asked. "Are you all so stunned that you can't even hide to stay alive? Come on!"

No effect.

As though he heard and understood, Gargan thrust the sword through his belt and stepped to her side. The weapon shimmered in the torchlight. A row of emeralds met carvings of wind and flame along the back of the blade. The golden hilt depicted a coiled serpentine creature—its profile resembled a black dragon. Too lovely for a grimlock anvil, Twilight thought distantly. It must have been stolen.

The goliath rummaged through his rucksack and pulled forth a skull with two broken horns.

"That's a good sign—I guess others must have gotten here first." She ran her fingers across the skull. "Unless, of course, minotaurs eat their mates after season."

Liet gaped at her. "Th-that was a jest, aye?" he asked, trembling.

Twilight grinned at him.

"Ah." Liet's face scrunched. " 'Tisn't a matter I'd thought of—ah—overmuch."

Slip cast a final healing spell upon Taslin. The priestess coughed and awoke. Acid had eaten holes in her mail, ruined her boots, and burned red marks across her cheeks. The sizzling fluid had not ruined her fine features, but the scars remained apparent. Her sword had incurred the most damage—its blade broken and the crescent moon symbol pitted and scorched. Twilight hoped it was still usable.

"There, lass," the halfling said to the moaning priestess. "You're safe now."

If any of us are safe, Twilight thought.

The priestess said nothing, but looked at Slip in confusion, anguish, and thanks. Then her eyes fell on the warlock, and her face turned to anger. Slowly, she climbed to her knees, then with the aid of the halfling, to her feet.

An awkward silence fell.

"Now then," Davoren said to her, out of his dark hood. The wounds on his face had faded entirely, it seemed, his skin once again sallow and smooth. "Feel free to thank me for saving your life. I might even look upon you with favor—assuming, of course, sufficient groveling transpires."

Taslin's lips narrowed.

"Yes?" the warlock asked. "Did you want to say something?" He did not give her a chance to speak. "It was rather foolish of you to take such a risk. Your wounds were unnecessary and your weapon was destroyed. We could have easily escaped without either loss, and now we must waste healing. I hope your idiocy is a source of pride."

Silence hung. Twilight almost drew her rapier and ran the warlock through. The only thing stopping her was doubt; she was fairly certain that they would need the warlock's magic to survive, let alone escape.

Taslin had no such considerations to stop her.

Ruined sword gripped in both hands, the priestess lunged at Davoren, angry tears streaking her cheeks. "Monster!" she screamed. "You will pay for what you've done!"

Twilight stepped between the cleric and the warlock, but it was Taslin she restrained, twisting an arm back and wrenching the blade free. Davoren assumed his wicked smile, but the intrusion of Gargan's massive form kept him from saying anything else. The goliath made no move, but his thick hand was not far from his sword hilt.

"*Now is not the time,*" Twilight hissed in Elvish.

"*Away, child,*" growled Taslin. Then, outside the tongue of the People, she rounded on the warlock. "He murdered my Asson! He'll murder us all!"

"Perhaps I will, perhaps I won't," Davoren sneered. "Who's to stop me? You? Without your pet cripple?"

Twilight and Liet both blanched. Slip sobbed. Even Gargan scowled.

A hoarse, despairing cry came from Taslin's lips. "I know it was you! I know it!" She squirmed. "*Let me go, Twilight—let me go!*"

"We need him!" snapped Twilight. *"Control yourself!"*

Taslin struggled for a few tense heartbeats, but finally relented. She relaxed against Twilight, shuddering, and stared daggers at Davoren.

"I've said it before," said Twilight, "but I'll repeat. If any of us plans to make it out of here alive, we need to work together." Then she added, so only Taslin would hear and understand: *"We don't know if any of us helped or harmed Asson. Have your suspicions if you will, but don't let them jeopardize us all."*

"As you say," Taslin said. She turned to Davoren. "But as soon as we leave this place, human, I shall cut out your heart for this. Upon Corellon's bloody tears—"

"No!" Twilight hissed, trying to stop the cleric, but it was too late.

"—you will not see another sunrise," Taslin finished. "This I swear."

Twilight fought to stop a scowl. A blood oath was never taken lightly by either party. She knew then that the two might work side by side, but their mutual hatred would leave a crack in the band. And their survival relied upon cooperation.

The warlock only smiled. In his eyes was a bitter promise—he would see Taslin dead, for no other reason than because he could.

Twilight knew what she had to do—weakened thought she might be.

She handed Taslin over to the goliath. "Go," she said slowly and levelly to the others. "Follow Gargan. Skirt the labyrinth, find the sewers, set camp. Leave markings." She turned back and looked upon the warlock, who smiled. "Davoren and I shall join you presently."

"But 'Light, ah—" Liet started.

"No argument," she said. "Davoren and I have some words to share. Lead them, Gargan." She nodded to Liet without looking at him. "We shall join you."

Liet nodded slowly and began walking. Taslin kept her eyes on the warlock, but let Slip tug her along.

Gargan stared at Twilight hard, and she flicked a gaze to him. She was reminded once again of the keen intuition behind those emerald eyes. Without words, they conversed, and Gargan understood entirely what Twilight intended. He made her an offer, but she declined. She had to do this alone. He nodded and turned.

As the goliath joined the others, disappearing into the darkness, Twilight let a smile spread across her face. She took a deep breath and let it out slowly. Then she relaxed, and flashed Davoren a winsome look.

"Is anyone watching?" asked Davoren, flexing his fingers, around which little sparks danced.

"I think not," replied Twilight, hand on her rapier hilt. The shadows came to her.

Davoren's lip curled. "Good."

Twilight's rapier scraped out of its scabbard and she lunged, just as the warlock threw ruby flames at her.

CHAPTER ELEVEN

Twilight twisted in mid-dive and the blast scorched across her back. Only her ring's protective magic kept her skin intact. She landed lightly and kicked out. Davoren scowled and threw himself aside just in time to avoid the blow.

Feeling rather than seeing the miss, Twilight wasted no time reversing her momentum, spinning, and slamming an elbow into the warlock's chest. Davoren recoiled and fell back a step, but his eyes were already blazing with ruby light. The warlock snarled an infernal oath and jerked his hands apart.

"Damn and burn," Twilight snapped, throwing herself back, trusting instinct.

The elf maid somersaulted back as a fan of ruby fire cut over her chest. She flipped completely over, landing on her feet in a crouch. She rose halfway into a combat stance, keeping her eyes on Davoren. The man had backed away and was holding up burning, clawed hands, one forward, one at his ear.

"Come, fiend-spawn." Twilight hissed as she dipped and wove. "You can do better than that, eh?"

The warlock grinned as they both circled. "You think you can elude my power, do you?" he said. "You await a strike, thinking you will dodge and I will be open, eh?"

"How clever." Twilight never took her eyes off him. "And your solution?"

Davoren lifted his left arm. The diabolic face molded into his leather bracer chuckled for an instant. The air rippled and a chittering giggle floated forth that matched the gauntlet's mirth. A tiny winged creature with night black flesh—an imp, Twilight realized—appeared a few paces at her back, laughing and hissing.

Summoned aid, Twilight thought. How original.

Davoren threw his blasts of flame past her, and she understood. With a curse, she sprinted toward the warlock.

The flames consumed the imp before it had the chance to move or even squeak in protest, then the heat arced from its ashen remains to strike Twilight in the back, blowing her out of her charge and slamming her body against the wall.

Davoren laughed uproariously. "Fool!" he said. "You think you can outwit Hellsheart?" He fell into the grip of fiendish power once again.

Fighting against the pain that ripped through her, Twilight struggled to her feet. Little trails of smoke rose from her back. The ring's magic had absorbed much of the blast, but not all. Limping, she extended the rapier toward Davoren and bent low.

Davoren's right gauntlet shimmered with magic. A second imp, identical to the first, appeared at her back. Wonderful.

Twilight didn't give Davoren the chance. She straightened, pulling her rapier back to throw, and ran toward him. She might not cover the five or six paces between them in time, but her blade would. The warlock's eyes went wide and he shot flame at her. Had he blasted the imp, it would not have arced to Twilight in time.

Even in panic, though, he had not abandoned all aim. The ruby ray struck her rapier's hilt, superheating it in an instant and unleashing a tremor upon her hand with the kind of force that would have shattered bone had she not released the weapon to fly over her shoulder.

Cursing in pain and consternation, the shadowdancer watched as Betrayal skittered along the ground behind her. A thumb's breadth lower, and his blast would have destroyed her hand to the wrist. Davoren cursed his missed blast and danced back, power flickering in his eyes as he invoked his lord's gifts again.

"I will destroy you, whore!" Davoren sneered.

Always insults about my lovelife—or my profession, she mused as he threw fire that consumed his imp. It darted for Twilight.

This time, the elf managed to dodge, but only by leaping onto Davoren. The flames jetted over her head and slammed into the wall, sending chips of stone flying. The elf and the warlock went down in a heap of bodies, kicking and scrabbling.

Davoren slammed Twilight to the ground, but she hit his stomach with her knee. The warlock reeled, rolling away, and Twilight seized the chance to pounce atop him, hands going for his throat. He caught her wrist in both hands and pried at her grip.

They locked, pitting wiry muscles against each other. She had his throat in her right hand. Her left slapped her belt, searching for some weapon. She knew she didn't have the strength to choke the life from him or shatter his neck. One of her lockpicks would do; a quick thrust to the eye or temple would put the warlock down.

Then a thin blade appeared in Davoren's hand, snatched from a sheath inside one of his demon bracers, and it darted for Twilight's face. Her hand shot out and caught Davoren's wrist. The warlock spit and slavered, straining against Twilight, the point of his stiletto just a hair's breadth from her jugular.

The tip scratched her neck and a bright spot of blood welled up.

"Almost, *filliken*." Davoren hissed through clenched teeth. "Almost."

"Almost *nothing*," she said.

Twilight squeezed the tendon in his wrist just so, and Davoren squealed in pain. She slammed his hand against the ground once, twice, knocking the blade free. The warlock, to his credit, kicked Twilight off him, but she was already extricating herself. She rolled free, over the fallen stiletto, and went for Betrayal where it lay.

Davoren struggled up, aimed his fingers at her back, and spat dark words, taking his time to articulate the brutish syllables.

In mid-roll, Twilight reversed direction and came up in a crouch, her hand crossbow pointing at the warlock's face. Moving for the rapier had just been a distraction, meant to keep the warlock's eye on the steel while he ignored the real threat.

By the time he saw the crossbow, the bolt was streaking for his face. Davoren wasn't quick enough to flinch.

Or perhaps he had no reason to fear.

The crossbow bolt skipped off Davoren's cheek, causing less damage than it would have to a mountainside.

"Sand," Twilight swore. She had forgotten Davoren's fiendish skin.

The failed attack allowed Davoren to complete his invocation, and a curtain of black-laced fire appeared around Twilight, trapping her in a circle that measured no more than five paces across. Discarding the crossbow in favor of the rapier she had collected, she growled at her foolishness.

"Davoren!" she snapped. "Face me, coward! I have steel in hand. Face me!"

The only response she received was the roar of the infernal flames, growling and laughing around her.

Twilight realized that he could be preparing any number of deaths for her, so she switched tactics. "Why not face me, warlock?" she asked. "I stand here, shaking, and you hesitate? Surely you do not fear me—a weakling wench like myself, eh? You don't have the sand, perhaps—or maybe the sword?"

Davoren laughed derisively, a sound much louder than the fires. "Ah yes, the courageous Fox-at-Twilight, always so witty, always so much better than others," he said. "Is that why you chose us, I wonder, because you think yourself superior?"

Ducking below the smoke that was filling the chamber, Twilight opened her mouth to tell him exactly what she thought of that, but he was already rattling on.

"I wonder if Telketh and Arandon ever knew how little you thought of them. Or perhaps they were too distracted, having shared your bed. They were so eager to give their lives for you. I wonder if they ever realized you meant them as little more than monster feed. I wonder about Quelin, the sniveling paladin, or even that bitch Galandra. Did you seduce her too, I wonder?"

His voice came from all sides, as though he were stalking about her fiery prison. She loathed evil monologues, but they were a typical consequence of an assault on a spellslinger's pride.

"You disappoint me, Davoren," Twilight said. Without any stealth—knowing that he couldn't see her beyond the flames or through magic—she reached back with the warlock's stiletto and slid it, point-first, into a flask at her belt. "I would have thought one such as yourself would recognize the value of ruthlessness."

"Nevertheless," Davoren growled, but said no more. Twilight was grateful.

"I thought I was hiring a spellslinger worth a dozen gold a day in Westgate," she called, "but I see now you're nothing but a pathetic worm. You're too afraid to confront—what did you call me on the way to this expedition?—a 'two-copper trollop with a flimsy metal twig she calls a sword'?"

"I'm sure I was more imaginative, whore," came the warlock's reply. "But I wasn't far off the mark. Your meager skills and your pathetic powers are nothing compared to mine. Your sniveling changeling god is as nothing against the might of the Lord of Baator."

"Why not stand and face me, and show me this supposed might?" Twilight asked. "If you are truly as great as you claim, there is little a poor lass like me can do to defeat you." She stretched her back and grinned. "Unless, of course—you aren't."

Davoren strode through the flames, dark power licking at the fringe of his robe. His eyes pulsed with ruby energy and his face contorted with rage. Fire leaked from his fists as he bore down upon Twilight.

"Insolent, mongrel bitch!" he growled. "I shall see you beg!"

"Many have spoken thus," said Twilight. "All are dead."

"You'll join them!" Davoren lunged, power streaming from his hands and eyes.

Twilight put out the dusky rapier and dropped, a low stop thrust that would have spitted any sword-dancer foolish enough to charge thus. Davoren, however, merely sent the sword clattering aside with a pulse of his power and loomed over Twilight. She spun with the blow and buried the stiletto in his side.

The darkness abated and the wall of flames flickered out, leaving an eerie, vile smoke hanging at the edges of their vision.

Davoren, shaking off his surprise, gave her a mocking grin. He looked down at the little trickle of blood making its way down the stiletto's edge. "Not cold iron this time, eh?" the warlock asked. "I hardly feel it."

"Not the blade." Twilight smiled. "The poison."

The warlock blinked in confusion—once, then a second time slowly, then a third time, in which he fought to move his eyelids. He felt it then, a subtle chill that flowed through his veins. His eyes went wide and his mouth opened, but he could not move.

Twilight glared in his face. "My *nar'talas* venom. Locklimb, humans call it," she said. "Brewed from the juice of a rare breed of centipede native to Evermeet. Causes mild euphoria when inhaled and instant paralysis when introduced to the blood."

She yanked the dagger free. Davoren didn't flinch—couldn't, Twilight thought—and wiped it clean on the warlock's robe.

"Only a little bit flows in your veins, enough to keep you frozen a few moments—enough to silence your spit hole while I make a few things perfectly clear. Understand?"

She knew Davoren could not reply. His outraged eyes, though, said enough.

"Before we get to business, while I've got you transfixed, perhaps you can help me understand something I've always wondered about." She paused. "If you're the descendent of demons, how is it you serve Asmodeus?"

That got his attention, and Twilight saw a flicker of uncertainty in his eye.

"I wonder," she said. "The grandson of a demon prince, a

servant of archdevils, who takes his power from both the Hells and the Abyss? Which was it, by the way—Graz'zt or Orcus? I'm curious. The latter, I bet. You look like the son of a corpse."

Unsurprisingly, no reply was forthcoming.

Twilight knelt down to stare into Davoren's eyes. "Hear this now," she said. Her voice was soft. "You cannot comprehend what it would mean to cross me. Your master does not frighten me—I have spat in his eye myself."

Silence for a heartbeat. Twilight knew he believed her. The truth of that mattered not at all.

"And if you think for a single moment that your power frightens me, you are making a fatal mistake."

He offered no response but a hateful glare.

"Now then, to the real business at hand," she said. "I *know* you had something to do with Asson's fall. I heard the magic, the word of command. I could have been mistaken, perhaps, but if it were just me, I'd gut you right now and leave your entrails for the scavengers, just to err on the more pleasant side."

Twilight paused, allowing Davoren to drink in her entire meaning.

"But it's *not* just me. I have to think of us all, and if we're going to get out of here alive, we need to work together. We all need allies to survive this, and you've got none—not even your own tongue." Her eyes narrowed. "So let me make this clear—from here on, you're either with us, or you're dead. Savvy?"

Twilight could tell from the way the color began to bleed out of Davoren's face that the poison was starting to dilute through his blood, and he could feel his body once again. Soon, he could speak. "Ye-yes," he managed. "Yes, that's clear."

Twilight slammed him against the wall again. Though she was not a big woman, or a strong one, she knew exactly what angles to ply for sufficient leverage.

To further emphasize her point, she stabbed him again for good measure.

"Aack—" Davoren managed. Then he could only look at her, stung and furious.

"I wasn't finished," she said.

She wrenched the dagger out, causing Davoren's eyes to water, and raised it before his face. His dark blood mingled with an amber jelly smeared along the blade. Then she reached down and pulled out the vial of poison, to wave it in front of his face.

"I carry more of this than you might think. If you try something like that again—if you even *think* it—I'll pump you so full of venom you'll be able to do nothing but lie helpless while the vermin of this hellhole start with your eyes and work their way toward your brain." Her eyes bored holes into his face. "How does that sound, Lord Hellsheart, servant of Asmodeus?"

Davoren could do nothing but stare daggers at her. She saw a touch of pain in his eyes, and she took it for fear. So he was just a bully.

"Remember," she said. "You betray us again, and I *won't* bury you."

The warlock kept silent. He could speak again, but he could barely move, Twilight knew. She left him then, and Davoren could not follow.

"Twilight?" his voice floated after her. It was pained—broken. "Twilight!"

She rounded the corner, losing sight of the half-paralyzed warlock. Try as he might, Twilight knew that he could not catch up, not for a while. Long enough, hopefully, to make her point sink home, like a finely crafted blade between a certain pair of ribs.

Twilight shook her head to clear the image. One could dream.

Davoren's despairing cries echoed as she went farther down the tunnel, just loud enough for her to hear, but not for the others to do so.

"Twilight!" he shouted. "Come back here! Don't leave me alone like this! Help! Please! He—" Then the sound faded. He would catch up.

Probably.

Twilight's grin widened.

When Twilight found her, Taslin was sitting alone, in a chamber far from the others. Wrapped in a grimlock cloak, her acid-eaten armor removed, the priestess sat with knees pulled up to her chin. She was on the edge of a chasm in a great chamber where many sewer passages met. The place probably smelled foul centuries before, when waste flowed through the sewers, but the cool emptiness of the deep underground had replaced it. Only a slight mustiness hinted at the filth that filled these halls in an era long dead.

As though the priestess sensed her, Taslin spoke as Twilight crept up behind her. "You would have loved Asson as well, had you known him as I did—as he was once."

"He was not always such a noble old man?" Twilight sat and pulled her knees to her chest, as Taslin did.

"He was not always so old, as humans measure the years," said Taslin. "Asson lay in my arms for fifty summers and fifty winters. I knew that our parting would come one day. I have dreaded the moment of loss, but not the leave-taking itself."

"You did not fear to lose your lover, then," said Twilight.

"Not a fear that I would lose him—that fate I knew to be inevitable," the priestess said. "Rather an acceptance of the truth and a choice to see past it."

"See past death?" Twilight kicked a stone off the edge of the chasm, watching it disappear into the darkness. Hollowness spread through her. "You'd have to be dead."

"Endings and leave-takings are of this life, just as meetings and beginnings," said Taslin. "To fear losing what you love is to abandon loving it here and now. To fear losing one you *know* you will lose makes less sense still."

"Life to be lived in the moment . . . I've heard it before. The life of a human."

"The life of an *elf*," Taslin corrected. "You are young, and do not understand what it is to live as we do. To know the joy of every moment, to release love of the past and fear of the future."

Twilight looked at her. "No." She meant to be firm, but her voice betrayed the slightest tremble. What was this she felt? And what did Taslin know of her?

The priestess met her gaze. "Asson and I knew many years of happiness together. And while they endured, each of us loved to the fullest, knowing that our time together would end. And now those years have ended, and I can be content, knowing that he rests. It has been the same for the four lovers I have known—all of them human."

Twilight raised a brow at that. She looked into the chasm—its beckoning darkness comforted her. Or at least so she told herself.

"I lost a lover once," she said. "His name was Neveren. He died in my arms. I understand how you feel."

Taslin sighed. "You know what the greatest irony is? If we could recover his bones, by Corellon's grace, he could be restored to me."

Twilight's gaze snapped to her. "You have that power?" she said, stunned. "Why not use it? Would Asson not answer?"

"He would return if I called him," said Taslin. "But I would not call."

"You do not grieve for him?" Twilight reached out and laid her hand, ever so lightly, on Taslin's shoulder.

The priestess closed her eyes gently. "I do, in my heart," she said. "But I . . ." She trailed off, her eyes soft. Her hand reached for Twilight's.

Twilight eluded Taslin's touch and brushed a lock of her golden hair away. With techniques long practiced, Twilight ran her fingers through Taslin's golden hair and over her shoulders and neck. She felt the tension in the sun elf's body—sensed the vibrations in the priestess's bones that spoke of buried grief. Twilight shifted, leaning against Taslin's back, and stroked her hair gently. She told herself to stop, but that self didn't listen.

"Sometimes," whispered Twilight, knowing the words, "grief can—cannot . . ."

Then, inexplicably, she stumbled. She couldn't say it—couldn't speak that lie. Who was this priestess, who had such power over her? Was this Erevan's doing?

In a matter of heartbeats, tears began to fall down Taslin's cheeks, through the acid-etched furrows like streams of pain and sorrow. The priestess wept in Twilight's arms for a long time, her strength and endurance bleeding away into a fragility not even Twilight would have thought possible. It staggered her.

Twilight knew that Taslin did not weep as a champion of Corellon Larethian, or as a mighty priestess, or even as an elf who had seen more than three hundred winters. In that moment, Taslin was merely a woman, crying from her heart for the man she had loved—still loved, though he was gone.

And through it all, Twilight felt again the terrible pain and anger in her own heart, boiling and festering like a sore, a canker that would never heal.

Never would she let herself weep for love. She had known too much treachery for that. It was an aptly named sword she carried, Betrayal, its blade dyed the dusk of stone after the darkness that had bled from her pierced heart into its steel.

Twilight was so lost in her rage that she almost did not notice when Taslin turned in her arms. She did notice, though, when the sun elf bent in and pressed her lips to her own. For a single, stunned breath, Twilight did nothing but let Taslin kiss her.

Then hot blood flowed through her veins. She looked into green-gold eyes and saw there the light and hope she wanted—desperately needed. Her hands clasped both sides of the priestess's face and pulled her deeper into the embrace. As though Taslin suddenly realized what was happening, she tried to break the kiss, but Twilight clung to her, pulling her and throwing them both to the stone.

Then the priestess let out a muffled gasp and Twilight felt her surrender. Supple arms wrapped around her back, and she felt nails through her blouse but she was hardly aware of the world outside the kiss.

All of Taslin's fiery passions poured into that kiss—all her wrath and rage about Asson's death, all her determination and love. She kissed hard, violently. Her hands gripped Twilight's arms with white-knuckled force, the nails nearly drawing blood.

Then it was broken. Twilight rolled away to lie beside Taslin, both of them panting heavily in the murky torchlight. The two women looked at each other for many heartbeats, neither speaking. They merely breathed.

Twilight's heart raced so fast it scared her. No, she thought. No!

Then Taslin made a sound that made Twilight's heart fall back into shadow. It was a mere giggle at first, but soon it became an outright laugh.

She laughed alone.

How much the mirth stung startled her. Twilight felt like weeping, for she had been wrong about Taslin, but no—no tears. Instead, she bound that hurt deep inside.

While the priestess seemed capable of letting it pass, Erevan's servant was not so carefree. Perhaps the Maid was toying with her again, or even the Trickster himself. He had ruined everything else in her life, why not this?

"My thanks," the priestess said. "Perhaps there is more to wisdom than holding it all within the heart." Then she smiled innocently, and her eyes softened.

Twilight wanted to agree—she wanted to reassure Taslin, to tell her all would be well. She could see that Taslin needed only those words and her heart would be whole once more. It should have been so easy to give her those, to give her the comfort and love she needed. Even if Taslin did not want her as a lover, Twilight should have been able to take Taslin into her arms and let the sun elf weep on her shoulder, sharing the pain.

But it would've been a lie—an inward lie. She could not tell Taslin that grief had to be entrusted to others—she did not *believe* in trusting others. And the priestess, much as she possessed the warmth Twilight's cold heart craved, did trust, and that made her a fool. More than that, she was stupid enough to want Twilight for a friend.

Twilight believed in only three breeds of people in the world: lovers, enemies, and those who were both. That left no room for something so naïve as friendship.

All trust and friendship had earned her, in her young life, had been more than her years' worth of heartbreak and loss.

Without a word, Twilight stood and walked away. She didn't look back.

She thought she heard Taslin say something behind her, but the words hurt less than those pained eyes, stabbing into her back.

"May Corellon guide you," the sun elf said. "And may you accept his hand."

CHAPTER TWELVE

Liet breathed a sigh of relief when Davoren returned. His demeanor showed no aggression or wrath, surprisingly, and his eyes darted nervously. Liet wondered, with no small shiver, what could make the invincible warlock afraid.

A short time later, Liet saw Twilight gliding from the tunnel in the direction that Taslin had gone several bells earlier. "Take this night for mourning if you wish, rest if you do not." Her tone made it clear she addressed them all.

Taslin, nude but for the cloak they had found for her, followed not far behind, and Liet had to look at her twice. He glanced at Twilight, wide-eyed, but she didn't return it.

Twilight continued. Her voice sounded tired. "Tomorrow, we head south—circling back to the rising tunnel Slip found."

They nodded solemnly. Gargan was the only one who made a sound.

"*Goli lenamaka nae,*" he said. Then he separated from the others, hand on the hilt of the sword he had taken, and disappeared into the tunnels.

Slip blinked out of her doze and watched the receding goliath. "Hey!" she called. "Hey, wait!" She got up and ran after him into the darkness. Gargan paused and waited until Slip reached his side, and they disappeared together.

Twilight stared after them. Taslin crossed to her side and laid a hand on her elbow. "He goes to keep watch," she said, pointing to her earring.

Twilight seemed to accept the priestess's words, though she looked decidedly uncomfortable. She shrugged, took up her sword, and wandered toward a tunnel.

"Wait, 'Light," Liet said with a start, but the shadowdancer was already gone into darkness.

"Don't need you," Davoren murmured, huddled against the wall. Blood dripped from his mouth as though he had bit his lip. "Don't need *any* of you."

"Eh?" Liet said. "What did—?"

"Silence!" Davoren snapped, with more self-loathing than real anger. Still, it was enough to stun Liet. The warlock went back to muttering. "Don't need you—*any* of you."

The Dalesman bit his lip and suppressed a nervous shudder.

It occurred to him that Davoren was wrong. Each of them needed the others to survive, and not just for protection. They provided one another something else in the darkness: drive, or purpose, perhaps. Slip and Gargan had each other, it seemed, and Taslin had depended on Asson.

He looked at the scarred priestess, who meditated two paces distant. Would she die, now that she had no ally? No. Liet resolved that he would protect her. She had been kind to him, and he felt for her, with Asson gone.

Observing the shuddering warlock, Liet imagined that Davoren lived only because of Twilight's protection. They were not friends, certainly, but allies? The two of them had entered this dungeon together as companions at arms, but was there any true connection between them?

What of Twilight? Who was *her* protection? Certainly not Davoren, and all the fire seemed to have gone out of Taslin. Gargan was an enigma, and Slip had enough trouble watching out for herself. Perhaps . . .

A hand fell on his arm, and he jumped. It was Taslin. Her scarred face may have lost some of its beauty, but her eyes had lost none of their intensity. He felt calm, peaceful, in that gaze.

"Go to her," the priestess said. "She craves solitude, but she needs you. You and she are so alike—younger than this world demands."

"What?" Liet asked, dumbfounded.

"Do you not desire her?" Taslin asked. In the corner, Davoren was a thousand leagues away. "You stand close to her, and your hand reaches for hers. You laugh just a touch too loud, and stare a breath too long."

"I don't . . ."

"Have you never had a woman, young master Liet?"

"Well, ah, um—" She put a finger to his lips. She reminded him of Twilight.

"My heart will mend," she said. "Hers . . ." She gazed toward the corridor.

Liet hesitated. He wanted with all his being to go after Twilight. What he would say, he had no idea. But he couldn't leave Taslin and Davoren alone, he told himself. Couldn't face the monsters that could be out in the dark . . .

"Courage," Taslin whispered. "You are older than the boy you act—be the man you are." She kissed his cheek, softly.

He would do it.

Liet got to his feet. "I shall return," he said. "I'll bring her with me."

"Go," Taslin said peaceably. Her hand snaked out to caress bare stone beside her, though she didn't seem to notice. "I shall be well."

He looked from Taslin to Davoren, a bit nervous to leave them. But he pushed fear away. Liet wasn't convinced, but he didn't care—not more than he did about Twilight.

The passage yawned forbiddingly, but he was determined. He stole after Twilight, quiet without his boots, seeking where she might have gone. He heard the rapier scabbard clicking against the stone ahead, and followed the sounds.

He saw a flicker of movement. "Slip?" he asked, hesitantly. The figure froze, staring, then dashed around a corner. Hand on his sword, Liet hurried after.

He turned the corner and gasped, seeing a light glimmer

on the far wall. There was movement. He dropped his hand to his sword and stepped forward, cautiously, straining to see. He couldn't make it out clearly, but it looked like a black hand—he couldn't count the fingers—extending out of the wall itself. As he approached, the hand snaked around and extended its palm toward him. He saw an eye in its midst.

His own eyes widening, Liet hurled himself into the shadows and froze. He had no power, no magic of his own—at least, none that he could use. What could he do against . . . whatever this thing was?

The arm twisted back toward the wall and searched along its surface. Then, as Liet watched, it dipped its fingers into the stone as though into pudding and reshaped it. The hand simply tore a gash in the wall, revealing a new passage. The stone bled drops of black onto the floor. Liet's stomach rose. He looked back, fearful, wondering whether Taslin or Davoren could arrive soon enough to save him.

Clutching himself tightly, Liet massaged his arms and winced at the sudden burning pain. Why did they hurt now?

Then the hand was gone, snaking back into that shimmer, which winked out, leaving him in blackness—blackness that was complete except for the torchlight flickering from the new passage. He crept up to it, wary that the hand would reappear, and looked in. More sewers beckoned that they had never been in before.

" 'Light," Liet said. He needed to tell her of this. " 'Light!"

In the darkness—less than a pace from where the useless one hid—Gestal took careful note of the hand from the wall. It did not please Lord Divergence, being this far into the lower domain. Certain forces would not welcome his presence.

The eyes turned back down the passage whence the useless one had come. Yes.

Gestal had an appointment to keep.

He found her after only a few breaths—silent, still, in the middle of the corridor. Twilight's head was bowed as though she were praying. Liet's heart hammered in his throat. He opened his mouth but forgot whatever he had been about to say. As he tried to remember, his thought slipped away.

Liet was about to speak when Twilight's hand shot out and grasped his collar. Before he could say a word, she slammed him against the wall and put a thin, sharp knife to his throat. Liet squeaked, and she withdrew the blade and sighed.

"Torm's name!" he cried. "You can't just say 'well met'—like a *sane* lady?"

"You can't just approach from the light, spouting poetry, like a conventional suitor?" Twilight put the knife away.

Heat shot into his face. "I, ah, I guess I'm sneakier than I thought." His eyes widened. "I'm—I'm really not trying to sneak up on you!"

The elf smiled halfway. "A lass can never be too cautious," she said. "Strange men, creeping about dark corners, watching lasses from hiding, carrying sharp steel?"

"I see your aim," said Liet. "I'd have spoken, but I reasoned you'd hear . . ."

"And you were correct," said Twilight. "Just here to gawk as I take my rest, or do you have a purpose?" As she spoke, she slipped out of her breeches and blouse, shaking them out. Liet gulped, and though his mouth opened, he had no words, only shock.

After a moment, Twilight raised an eyebrow, and his flush only deepened. He finally thought to whirl around just as she wrapped a dark cloak around her bare body.

"Little point now," she said. "So speak. I have little enough time for wandering lads who fancy watching lasses more than a century their senior strip bare."

Liet turned about, hesitantly. "Ah," he said. "Well . . ."

"Now *there's* a deep thought," the elf observed.

"I need to tell you, ah . . ." Liet trailed off.

"Are all men of the Dales this eloquent?" Twilight's face contorted. "Out with it! Did you come to berate me for letting

Asson die? Or question my methods with Davoren and Taslin?" She eyed him fiercely. "Or perhaps just a quick tumble on the stone here? It's been a long day. I could certainly use some vigorous comforting, how about you?"

"I'd settle for a vigorous handclasp," murmured Liet, not thinking. Then he froze.

Twilight blinked. "What?"

In an instant, the angry gleam in her eyes took on a new tone.

"Uh, ah, that is, I—"

"What did you say?" she asked softly.

"Ah," Liet said. "I merely wanted to—make sure you're well, after ah, today."

Twilight looked at him as if no one had ever said such a thing to her before. "Why?" she asked finally.

It was Liet's turn to be speechless. "I just, ah—just concerned, that's all." Hadn't he wanted to tell her something? Something important?

"You're not breaking one of my rules, are you?" Twilight asked with a wry smile.

"Most maids would call me chivalrous," said Liet, "and not accuse me of—"

"Do you know how to please an elf, manling?" Twilight's eyes narrowed dangerously. "A kiss upon the tip of the ear or a lick on the palm of the hand is quite a thing."

"Uh, 'tisnt, ah, why I'm here," Liet managed.

"Really? You're certain you're"—she slid up to him and pressed herself against his chest, using her lithe curves to full effect—"not breaking"—Liet stiffened, but only from surprise, as she traced her fingers down many days' stubble—"rule number"—she finished, pressing her nose against his, caressing his lips with her own—"four?"

"And what—what if I am?" Liet was almost breathless.

With a little laugh, Twilight shoved him away.

"I could make an attempt at poetry," Liet said. "If that's what y—"

He instantly regretted it. In her face, in her stance, he saw that whatever fire had been lit had vanished. He felt like a child.

"Go to your rest, boy," she said. "I present far too wild a beast for you to tackle, this night or any night. You do not wish to try."

He sniffed. "Is that not my choice?"

When Twilight raised an eyebrow, he cursed inwardly again. Why must she be so clever?

"Ah, I mean, not whether I tackle you—uh, but whether I *wish* to, ah, try?"

"Go to your rest," she repeated. "And that's the end."

Liet turned away, defeated. Then he caught himself on the wall and looked back. He was tired of being treated like a child, so he decided to say something not boyish. Of course, as soon as it came out of his mouth, it sounded quite juvenile. "I'm not afraid of you, Twilight."

Her reception, however, was not what he expected. She stared at him, her skin white, as though he'd said something quite mature. "You're certain?"

"Aye," said the man Liet had suddenly become. "The question is, are you so certain *you're* not?"

She did not answer, but merely stared at him until—a little more confident—he went back to his blankets.

Twilight awoke the following morning to screams. Cursing, she fumbled out of her cloak and grabbed Betrayal. She ran down the tunnel to her companions.

Taslin sat in the middle of the room, screaming and moaning, rocking back and forth. There was something red on the floor in front of her. Gargan stood over Davoren, axe ready, and Slip huddled behind him. Liet had his short sword at the warlock's throat.

"Hold!" Twilight shouted. "What is this?"

"He . . . he did something," Liet stammered, "to Taslin."

"You saw him?" Twilight demanded. "What was it?"

"N-no," Liet said. "But he did something!"

"Not I," the warlock said. Liet put pressure on the sword and Davoren fell silent.

Wary, Twilight walked to Taslin. A rag-wrapped bundle lay beside her, the size of a loaf of bread, perhaps. The rags were simple roughspun, and were soaked red. "Taslin?"

The sun elf shook her head violently.

Twilight prodded the bundle with Betrayal. No reaction. She knelt to examine it, moving the swaddling aside with her steel. Then she flinched back with a curse.

A pair of red buttons stared out of a rag face. The doll wore rough, tattered robes dyed with what looked like blood. It was flattened, its stuffing leaking out from a hole in its chin. It looked like a scraggly beard.

"Someone has done this," Taslin said. "I will have blood." Taslin glared at her. "Someone . . ." Then she trailed off, staring at Twilight's face.

Twilight looked around, moving only her eyes. All of them looked far too horrified. Trying her best not to tremble, Twilight lifted her fingers and felt sticky wetness on her cheek. She did not need a mirror to know what must be there—a mark of some kind, traced in blood. She turned and wiped it away.

"From now on," Twilight said, slowly and calmly, "no one wanders away from the others. We stay together. Understood?"

Agreeing silence answered, but the eyes she felt on her back lost no suspicion.

<hr />

"Down!" Twilight hissed.

Liet fell behind a pile of rubble, landing hard. Gargan ducked with them, hiding Taslin and Davoren around the corner.

Liet rubbed his bottom. "What did—"

Fingers fell on his lips, silencing him. Twilight gestured over the rubble with her eyes. Liet's blood ran cold and he couldn't bring himself to look.

"Tsch," Davoren said from the corner. "Simple primitives, hardly worth a moment." He did not walk into the open, though.

"Agreed," hissed Taslin. She scared Liet—since that morning, her eyes had shone with troubling intensity. "Let us slay the rabble—they block our path." She did not move.

Twilight gestured to Liet to look. He peeked over the stone, as low as he could.

A score of creatures covered in black and red scales ambled about the wide cavern, illuminated by the torches on the walls. Their faces were slack-jawed and they wore simple dark loincloths for clothing, but there, the resemblance to primitives ended.

Adorning the creatures' necks and wrists were necklaces and bracers of silver and gold. They hefted swords of like metal and spears of obsidian. Liet wondered if the lizards had plundered ancient crypts and treasure rooms to secure the precious items. Beneath the finery, some of the lizards' eyes burned with unholy fire and their features twisted and curled wickedly. Small horns marred the crowns of their heads, and tiny limbs that might have been wings sprouted from shoulders.

Liet looked to Twilight for clues as to their next move, but her face was ashen. He understood intuitively, somehow, what she was thinking. Though the creatures had not detected their presence, they stood right in the path. No other tunnel through the sewer led around this central chamber—not unless they backtracked as far as their campsite, quite a distance back, and took a different direction.

Looking at Twilight's nervous face, Liet had the sinking sensation that somehow, the enemy had known exactly where to wait.

"Where's Slip?" Twilight asked.

"Here!" the halfling piped merrily at Liet's side, startling him with such proximity. He shushed her before Twilight could do so, and the elf smiled weakly.

Then one of the fiendish lizards gave a cry. Something big and invisible lifted it and smashed it against the ceiling. The rest scrambled to heft their weapons.

A hulking creature of gray appeared in the middle of the chamber, holding the crushed remains of a lizardthing. It resembled a statue of iron plate armor, twice the height of a man. Without a sound, it dashed two lizards to the ground with one mighty fist. The other dozen beasts fell on their attacker, spears and obsidian swords shattering against its iron carapace.

"What *is* that?" Liet asked. "What do we do?"

"A golem," Twilight breathed at his shoulder. "Right." She looked to Slip. "You and Gargan keep the others hidden. I will be right back." She moved.

"What?" Liet lost track of her within a heartbeat, as if the shadows had swallowed her whole, devouring her before his eyes.

The battle lasted less than twenty breaths. Methodical, brutal, and completely unemotional, the golem—as Twilight had labeled the iron monstrosity—smashed and trampled the lizards into the ground. They fought with indescribable wildness and inhuman ferocity, but they were as nothing against the golem. Its fists rose and fell with hideous speed and strength, powdering bones and sending webs of cracks through the stone. Every few swings, its helmet breathed out a cloud of vapor that melted skin and set the lizards flailing and gasping.

Finally, when half the fiendish creatures were slain, including two that seemed more demon than lizard, they admitted defeat and fled. All who could move scrambled away and ran down the narrow tunnels.

They went without pursuit. The golem, its work finished, gave the room a long gaze. Liet hunched behind the stone, praying that it wouldn't see him. After the space of a long, agonized breath, it shimmered and vanished. But it didn't seem to leave.

A moment of silence followed. Terrified, Liet looked around, trying vainly to find Twilight. She seemed to have vanished. Was her body amid the dead? He couldn't tell.

Liet rose, shivering. Even if the thing was still there, hidden from view, he felt better revealing himself than not knowing.

Then a hand caught his arm, and Twilight appeared out of the shadows at his side. "Going somewhere," she asked, "without me? I'm crushed."

" 'Light!" the swordsman exclaimed. He longed to throw his

arms around her, but he stopped himself. She'd confused him before, and now wasn't the time—not in front of Davoren, and especially not in front of Taslin, with Asson so lately slain.

Then he noticed the body she was dragging.

"*Thalea*," Gargan mused. Liet reasoned it must be his word for "lizard."

"Uh, Twilight?" he asked. "What—what's that?"

"A present," said Twilight.

It was an unconscious lizardman with black scales and fiendish features. Its body was completely frozen, even its eyes. It wore a rough loincloth and a black sash, upon which was embroidered a sigil of a sickly gray tentacle enwrapping a scimitar.

The only sign the creature lived was the madness in those reddish orbs. If anything, this imprisonment in its own body would drive the lizard even more insane.

"What's wrong with it?" asked Slip. "Is it—dead?"

"Paralyzed," Davoren said softly.

"How do you know?" the halfling asked.

The warlock scowled.

The fiendish lizard's eyes blinked, both sets of lids slicking over soft surfaces. The paralysis was fading, Liet realized. Then the beast recovered the use of its tongue, and it wasted no time using it. The words the creature spat were deep and violent, their texture broken and jagged. And though none but Taslin seemed to understand its words, the tone was clear enough.

"What tongue's that?" Slip asked.

"Infernal, wormling," said Davoren. "So garbled I cannot understand a word."

"That's because it's Abyssal," corrected Twilight.

As Davoren glared, bested, Slip brightened. "How many tongues *do* you speak?" she asked the elf.

"Irrelevant," the warlock snapped. "What's he saying?"

Twilight looked to Slip first. "Many enough," she said. Then she turned to Davoren. "And it's a she."

The warlock started to retort, but shut his mouth. Liet understood and agreed—he really didn't care to know how Twilight could tell.

"The same words over and over: *Takt der shar,*" Twilight pronounced, her silky voice curling perversely around the fiendish tongue. "The Mad Sharn." Taslin shrugged.

Hearing the words, the fiendish lizard spat at Twilight and said something dark and unfathomably vile. Liet saw his companions fall to the ground, writhing and moaning. Gargan and Twilight sank to one knee. Taslin fell as though dead. Slip blinked, then clasped her hands to her ears and sank to her knees. Only the warlock remained standing, staring hard at Liet, to whom the word was mere profanity.

Why did it not harm him? Was this some inner power, as with the wight?

The fiendish lizard didn't finish the phrase, though, choking off in the middle. It was as though the very words stopped its heart. The creature died with a dry rattle.

"I suppose that solves that problem," was all Davoren said.

Liet ran to Twilight and helped her up. The elf looked at him, uncertain of something. Then her eyes widened. "A sharn," she said. Liet could feel her shiver in his arms.

"Its master, I expect," Davoren said. Leave it to the warlock to know some of the darkest secrets of the Realms. "The madness of demons fits a creature born of chaos."

"Chaos?" Liet asked. "What—?"

"There are certain forces in this world you should not know about," Twilight said. "That no sane mortal would *want* to know about."

"But you do," Liet argued.

She conceded that with a nod. "A race that was old when the elves were young," said Twilight. "Mighty spellweavers before Corellon's tears conceived the first elves—children of the primal chaos that came before the gods themselves."

Her voice took on a mystical quality, as though she recounted the memories of a pleasant childhood or a beautiful, half-forgotten summer. Liet could almost fall asleep into dark dreams, listening to that lovely, haunting voice.

"Sharn is simply what men call them, though in truth that is only a fantasy. They are an ancient, mighty race, but not one that most would deal with lightly—not even gods." Her eyes darkened, and Liet heard a second meaning. "Which would be wise. A creature born of such disorder cannot be trusted."

Liet Sagrin shivered, and not just with fear.

CHAPTER THIRTEEN

W hy do you follow me?" Twilight asked later as she clicked open a lock. "I told you to stay with the others. You have a habit of disobedience."

"Why do we camp at a crossroads?" Liet asked.

The heavy door sighed when Twilight pressed on it. She gestured, and Liet helped her push it open. The door growled in protest but opened. The plain chamber within was empty but for refuse—shattered wood chips, broken ceramics, worn statuettes—and ancient dust. Footprints, distinctly those of a lizard's feet, traced a path through the chamber to an open portal across the room, but the prints were old. She wished she were a tracker, and might have known *how* old.

She pulled a torch from her pack. Liet grinned until she shoved it at him. No reason *she* had to carry it—she had darksight.

"I asked you first," she said.

"I'm sure 'tis the same answer."

"Guaranteed escape route?" Twilight asked simply.

"I thought you only, ah, appreciated the concept," he said sheepishly. "Of a crossroads, I mean. That's not—you know—the same answer, or anything."

"Well, we all derive our chuckles in some manner," Twilight said. "I enjoy frustrating young lads much, much more."

Liet let that one go. "But your reason doesn't make sense," he said. "Camping at a crossroads, that is. Foes can come from any direction, even from behind."

"Yes, but they would have to be quite organized to come at us from all three," she said. "Something I have a feeling might be beyond the average demon-touched."

"What of hiding?" Liet rubbed at his hidden arms, nervous.

"I've always ascribed to the 'fleeing' school of thought, rather than the 'hiding,' " Twilight said. "If someone's searching as determinedly as I'm used to being searched for, hiding doesn't do any good." She left it at that.

"I see." Liet looked around the dusty chamber, straining his eyes in the flickering torchlight. "Where are we, anyway?"

Though the place was empty of creatures, shelves, books, or anything besides the rubble along the walls, Twilight could detect traces of the magic that must have been used there. She imagined it must have been a library or laboratory, long defaced by lizardfolk, smashed by golems, or worse.

"Wizard's sanctum," said Twilight. "Long abandoned."

"How can you be—?"

"I'm sure," she said. "There's nothing here. Go back. I'll be along shortly."

Twilight inspected the yawning doorway. A series of runes lightly etched into the stone radiated magic. A stone barrier had once existed there, but it had long ago become rubble, though the ward remained. Likely, thanks were owed to the lizards. Beyond, the corridor stretched into empty darkness.

Twilight was disappointed, to be honest. After a day spent avoiding battle like a scourge, she dearly wished for the opportunity to bloody Betrayal. The companions hadn't engaged any of the roving lizardmen in the tunnels—it would have been a waste of resources. And they could ill afford to stumble upon a golem, so they'd been very cautious.

She looked again at the portal wards. Twilight considered dealing with them, but thought better of it. Any foe coming the other way would trigger them—no purpose making ambush easier for one's enemies. She could always disarm them the next day.

Twilight wondered if they would go this way, anyway.

During their exploration, she had found two unblocked passages—tunnels that went east and north from their resting chamber, both of which led up. One ended in an old, dust-covered stairs ascending—the same stairs that had led her to the wizard's sanctum. The other stopped at a trapdoor above, with the remains of an old ladder.

Typical, Twilight thought. To search an entire labyrinth for days on end for a way out, only to find not one but *two* exits in close proximity. It seemed like something *he* would do to her.

"Come to think of it," she whispered. "You probably *did*, eh, N'tanathil?"

"Huh?"

"Pay it no—" Twilight turned. "You're still here."

"Aye, indeed," said Liet, leaning against the wall.

Twilight bit her lip.

She crossed back to the entrance of the chamber and stalked down the corridor to their camp—or more accurately, to the place where she had chosen to rest. She would take Reverie—or the human sleep, as would likely be the case—ten paces up the passage from the others, around a corner. Here, she could find the privacy she craved. Unless, of course, the boy insisted on following her.

Which he did. When she stopped, he stopped as well. Liet's face told Twilight he wanted to speak, but an awkward silence hung between them.

She decided to break the tension. "Is there some way I can assist you?" She was unable—and unwilling—to keep the suggestiveness out of her tone.

"N-nothing like that," Liet said. "I just wanted to know what—"

"*N'tanathil* is, in the trade tongue, my old 'uncle nemesis,' " said Twilight. "And believe me, if you knew the dastard like I do, you'd agree with the sentiment." She stripped off her glove and began unlacing her boots. "But you didn't come to debate the subtleties of linguistics, I would guess. So what is it?"

Liet turned as she doffed her boots and went to work on her

breeches' strings. Her tendency to eschew modesty made him nervous, just as Twilight intended.

"I was just thinking," he said. "About Taslin."

"Pining for a lady, and not me? I'm shocked." She gave a grand sigh and put a hand to her forehead.

Liet whirled angrily. "No, no, 'tis not like . . ." His eyes widened at both her loosened clothes and her words, and he gaped.

Twilight finally snickered. "Well, boy," she said. "Speak, if you will."

Liet swallowed. " 'Tis about Asson. He . . . 'Twas he that persuaded us to come back for you. I wanted to, but I didn't have the courage to stand up to Davoren—not really, not without Asson. But that old man . . ."

Twilight wondered if that was the truth.

Soothed by the cold stone beneath her bare feet, she spoke without looking at Liet. "Don't take it so hard," she said as she unlaced her blouse. "We all fear death. Old Bones is a hard one to face—and an atrocious dancer besides."

After giving her an odd look—probably wondering what she could possibly mean—Liet turned halfway. "No, 'twas not that, either," he said. "I . . ." He paused and fidgeted. "My apologies. I should go." He started down the tunnel, heading toward the others.

Now it was Twilight's turn to gaze oddly. His words said one thing, his actions a second, and his eyes a third. She caught a glimmer in his face, as though through a crack in armor. Twilight's perception cut right through his humble, self-deprecating exterior, and what she found there startled and excited her.

He *understood*.

Twilight had always been too direct for her own good. "You really would have died for us."

The words caught Liet as surely as a hand on his arm. He stopped and turned. She expected him to look shocked, but he didn't blink.

"Nay," he said simply. "Not . . . not for *her.*"

Oh, no.

Twilight smiled slightly and stepped toward him. She could feel her heart in her throat. She let the collar of her silk blouse slip, revealing one pale, smooth shoulder. "For me?" she asked. "You'd have died for *me?*"

Liet fidgeted. Sweat appeared on his brow, and she heard his racing heartbeat and heavy breathing. On some level, Twilight knew she was being somewhat pitiful—he was such a boy—but she found his feelings deeply flattering. Twilight felt her own pulse pick up—an experience she knew all too well and loathed just the same.

Stop yourself, wench, she thought. Don't do this.

"Speak," she said, stepping forward. "Don't lie. I'll know." They were almost touching when Twilight stopped and looked into Liet's face. "Would you die for me?"

Silence hung between them for a long breath. Twilight read the youth's tells—every twitch of his cheek, the way his eyes purposefully avoided her, the shifting of his weight—while Liet paused. She could see his battle—a war of will against instinct. One told him to flee, another told him to catch up Twilight's lithe form in his arms and crush her to him.

Twilight wondered idly which she embodied: instinct or will. She almost always preferred the latter, but it was so rarely the case.

"Aye." Liet looked in her eyes, unflinching. "Aye, I would," he said.

She knew then that this was a victory over every—admittedly good—instinct that told Liet to flee, and she loved that, almost venerated it. Twilight was ever a creature who worshiped her own destruction.

"Oh, damn," she said to herself.

With a flick of her wrist and a foot behind his ankle, she had Liet falling to the ground in a breath. This time, she was not about to beat him. Instead, she pressed her lithe body into his young, muscular frame. He made startled sounds, but she silenced him with a long, all-consuming kiss.

By the time she pulled away, leaving his tongue free to move, it was obvious Liet had forgotten whatever it was he'd been about to say. He looked at her without thought, blissful, innocent.

Twilight went for his tunic, but Liet stopped her with a wince. She remembered his scarred arms, but she decided it didn't matter. She went for the breeches instead.

"Uh, 'Light . . ." he started, but she kissed him again to shut his mouth. It worked.

"I should warn you," Twilight said candidly as she tore at his laces. "You've got *some* boots to fill. I've known—"

Liet put his fingers to her lips. "Nay," he said, eyes soft, vulnerable.

Twilight stopped. She realized the tale would hurt him, but that was who she was. So many men, so many times. Didn't he see?

Of course he didn't see. No one had—no one but . . .

Damn you, Erevan, Twilight swore inwardly. You and Neveren and Lilten, and all your lackeys—even Nym. I don't need you—I don't need *any* of you. Not anyone!

" 'Light? Are you . . . well?"

Twilight looked into mismatched eyes full of hope and fear. She realized that this boy had never known a lover, but it didn't matter. He was ready to accept her, banish their loneliness—but at the same time, he was terrified of her. Or terrified *for* her?

"You're scared." She brushed his cheek with the back of her fingers.

"N-no . . ." Liet's body shook.

"You should be," Twilight said. "But not for the reason you think."

Liet's face broke into a tentative smile. It was the most beautiful thing she remembered seeing in a long, long time.

Oh no, she thought, just before will became instinct again and she devoured him. Twilight crushed his lips and levered her wiry body to keep his pinned.

"Now you have one more answer to give," she said between furious kisses. With each one, she thought the same word: damn, damn, damn. "And I want the truth."

Liet nodded frantically, his eyes terrified.

Leaning in close, Twilight ran her raven hair across his cheek, tickling his skin with its softness. "Silk?" she asked, "or . . ." she seized his ear and bit down just hard enough to secure a gasp. "Teeth?"

"Ah," said Liet. "Uh, I don't . . . this does not seem quite the way . . . ah, heh . . ."

"Very well, then," said Twilight. "I shall make that decision."

———◆◆◆———

Distantly, Gestal watched the two bodies entwined, delighting in one another, with something between absorbed curiosity and clinical dispassion.

"Perfect," he said to no one in particular. No one could hear him, after all. "I couldn't have planned this better—well, actually . . . hmm."

His ears caught something to which the lovers were oblivious, though the sense was more than simply aural. The walls were shifting again. The enemy was not idle.

"You thirst for attention like a puppy, always barking your nonsense," he said. "You hate others but you cannot live without them."

Gestal's eyes looked over the elf's writhing body with desire and disappointment.

"You are lying again, child—to us and to yourself."

Her sweaty face, locked in passion, turned toward him briefly, but she did not respond. She had not heard him speak. Gestal visualized running his claws down that soft spine.

"You expect this to end as all the tales do—with the villain dead and the heroes in bed." Gestal shook his head. "But not this story. Not this one."

Then it was over, and Gestal grinned as he faded into silence once more.

Now it would be easy—so easy—to drive her to the master.

———◆◆◆———

"Did you tell me about rule four in earnest, or so that I'd break it?" Liet asked as he traced the elf's—no, nymph's spine. The star on her lower back—asymmetrical, with many rays—gleamed, hot to the touch. He loved how she shivered when he touched it.

"Rules exist for a purpose," said Twilight. She lay on her belly at his side.

"Was that an aye, or a nay?"

"Neither," she said, "though if you were to fall in love with me, 'twould make you more pliable, and assure your loyalty."

"I've never known a woman," Liet said. "I mean, I *had* never—"

She laughed. "I had guessed."

Liet smiled. He found his mind drawn back to her other tattoo—the silver and black fox below her belly.

Then he saw a queer light in her eye. "What?" he asked.

"You must go now," said Twilight. She pulled her cloak from under him and wrapped it about her body.

Liet blinked. "What?" he asked. "B-but, we—"

"Enjoyable, I do confess. But now you have to go." Her face was utterly serious.

"Can I not . . . ah . . ." Liet reached toward her, to trace his fingers down one bare arm. "Can I not stay here with you?" Twilight twisted aside slightly and he touched only stone. "My love? My goddess?"

She put a finger to his lips. Then she shook her head, and he felt his heart stumble.

"Against my better instincts, I lead this traveling feast—er, *party*, and I can't be seen to favor one member over another."

Liet made to protest, and Twilight silenced him as she had before—with her lips.

"And that's why you have to go. Tell the others that we'll take the tunnel to the sanctum in the morning, as though I was merely discussing plans with you." She reclined against the corridor wall and stretched her arms. "And see if Taslin's conjured up some food—I'm famished."

Liet, adrift in confusion, could do nothing but stare at her. Then, when Twilight reached for his arm, he came back to his senses with a twinge. He pulled away, fighting his outrage down. He wouldn't get angry. He was better than that.

He wondered if she truly thought so little of him.

"But," he said, "but no one's seen us at—"

"No, but if you don't sleep in your own blankets, it'll have the same effect."

"B-but—" Liet started.

Twilight did nothing but stare into the dark corridor ahead. Liet studied her, long and hard. He perceived a miniscule wince at the edge of Twilight's left eye—the tiniest of flaws in her defenses. And underneath that cold exterior was an even darker chill. He wondered if she hadn't meant for him to see that.

Liet saw the truth of Twilight, then—one of many. One of her masks.

He became aware of how she had lied to him. He wondered about her outrageous stories, her flippant comments, her emotions and her coldness. He wondered about her name. He thought he'd known her love, but he hadn't touched her—not inside. He wondered if there was anything true about her.

"Good even," he said, though it made his heart hurt.

"Good-bye," Twilight said, still not looking at him.

CHAPTER FOURTEEN

"This isn't how I remember it," Twilight said softly the next morning. The six ascended the dusty steps and entered the first room of the wizard's chambers. The curved and undulating walls of stone were as her memory told her. Yet something was missing.

"Eh?" Slip asked.

To Twilight's eyes, the room was empty, and that was precisely her concern.

"Cast a scrying and see for yourself. This room's changed since last night."

Taslin lifted her hand to draw upon Corellon's blessing, but Davoren shoved it back down. "Save your power. The might of the Nine is infinite," he said.

He intoned a string of dark words. The others, excepting Twilight, flinched at the vile syllables. When Davoren had completed the chant, he cast his gaze about the room.

The sun elf favored him with a glare of pure murder. The death of Asson had changed her, and the doll seemed to have removed her last cache of serenity. Indeed, Twilight reflected—after that day and night, Taslin had been edgy, sharp, and quick to temper. Yet she was forgivable—Twilight understood heartbreak.

And as Taslin weakened, Davoren grew stronger. "Asmodeus's

might is with me. I see no wards active." Davoren laughed, and Twilight wondered if she needed to cow him again. "Yet you delay?"

"That's the very matter," she said. "There should be wards active on that door"—she pointed at the opposite exit—"and possibly beyond. Something's been here before us, and it tripped the wards." She bent and scanned the floor.

"The word of a thief," Davoren observed, "is worse than worthless."

"There's no sign?" asked Liet, hunkering down beside Twilight.

Twilight shook her head. "I don't see any new tracks, nor is the dust disturbed," she said. "But I know there were wards active on that door. I saw them."

"*Saw* them?" scoffed the warlock. "Magic is not so simple that a gutterkiss can 'see' it. Or is there some other power you hide, *filliken?*"

Twilight shot an angry look at him. She thought about threatening him again, but since she hadn't followed through the first time, her threats meant much less. She rose silently and stared down the dark hallway, standing close to Liet.

"We should go back," she whispered.

"Why?" the youth asked. "We explored this way yestereve."

"Was that *all* that transpired yestereve, I wonder?" Davoren asked.

She wouldn't let that nettle her. "Something's come this way and lies in wait."

"How can you know that?" Taslin asked.

"Truly," said Liet. That was a shock, but Twilight buried the twinge of hurt. Of course she couldn't look offended that he didn't take her side. She almost would have preferred his comment to be vindictive, but his eyes held nothing but cold logic.

"A feeling." Twilight paused. "But I know 'tis a true one."

Davoren chuckled at her "feeling," and broke into a full laugh. "Well, *we* don't know that. I say we press on."

"I see no reason to turn back," said Taslin. "We have only just begun the day."

"I don't know, she could be right!" Slip said. Davoren and Taslin both glared at her. "Or . . . not." She looked up at Gargan, but the goliath said nothing. Slip looked back and forth between the two opposing camps and followed his suit.

"Liet?" asked Twilight, not wanting to. "What say you?"

The youth looked at her for a long breath, rubbing at his sheathed arms. Finally, he shrugged. "If something tripped the wards and survived," he said, "logically, 'twould have attacked us as we slept, watch or no. At least we'd find a trace. Since it didn't do so, and we didn't find any sign, I say you could well be wrong. Perhaps the wards merely expired on their own and needed no help. Regardless, there's no reason to go back."

Twilight bit her lip. She shouldn't have cared, but it still hurt.

"Here!" exclaimed Slip from just beyond the once-enspelled doorway. She stood inside a narrow alcove off the corridor. "Look at this! Some manner of markings!"

Fighting the discomfort that came from being contradicted by Liet, Twilight knelt down beside the halfling. Sure enough, something had been etched into the inside of the doorway—four roughly vertical lines with dashes, crosshatches, and markings that rose parallel to one another, almost like tally marks.

"What are they?" asked the halfling.

"Qualith," said Twilight. "Illithid. Crude. Scratched with a talon, mayhap."

"A mind flayer wizard?" Davoren said doubtfully.

"Sorcerer, more likely." The warlock just shrugged as if to dismiss the distinction. "I've seen stranger things."

"You say that often," said Liet.

"And 'tis true every time," Twilight said, eliciting weighing looks. Mystery was comforting—he'd come just a little too close to her that night.

"Believe it or not, these are the marks of the Illithid language. They record emotions and thoughts." She ran her fingers over the markings.

"What need has a race of mind mages for written words?" Davoren scoffed.

"Telepathy has a limit," said Twilight. She laid her hand flat against the writing. "And this message was left for someone."

"Can you read it?" asked Liet.

"Qualith is amazingly complex, meant to be read by illithids themselves. It would take extraordinary talent or decades of study to decipher these markings," said Twilight.

"So which do you have?" asked Liet.

Twilight smiled. It was hard to stay angry at the youth. Perhaps she could forgive him his lack of support. Later, perhaps, once he had well—and fully—atoned.

Eyes shut, she traced her fingers down the four lines.

"Anything?" asked Slip, shifting anxiously.

"Resentment," said Twilight, "at being imprisoned. Rage, at the writer's captor. A touch of fear, at the power of those above. And a name." She scrunched her brow in thought. "This illithid was a prisoner of a place called Negarath."

From the way the warlock reacted, Davoren knew the name somehow.

"You recognize this word?" asked Twilight.

Davoren bared his teeth. Their battle had certainly made him less guarded in his contempt for everyone and everything.

"Never you mind," he snapped. "This prisoner is long gone, as is anything else in this wizard's sanctum. There is no danger."

Twilight cast a supplicating look back toward Liet, longing for support, but the youth merely shrugged. Twilight bristled.

"Very well, then," said Twilight. "We move forward, against my judgment. I want that noted."

The others nodded, and only Gargan looked at Twilight with something approaching uncertainty. Not that he acted on it.

What good are you if you don't speak up? Twilight cursed.

The corridor beyond the back chamber of the wizard's sanctum turned out to contain many such alcoves for holding prisoners—in magical stasis, Twilight reasoned. The alcoves were empty and appeared to have been so for some time. Twilight felt no magic active anywhere in the corridor. The dark pathway terminated in another portal, this one complete with a stout stone door.

Twilight could hear no sounds through the door, so she examined it. She found no hidden needles or pressure plates, and while the device used a dozen sliding bars in a complex design—a dragon grinning as though bemused—the actual lock seemed simple enough. She slipped out her picks and fell to work, springing the device in a few breaths.

"Sand. Something feels wrong," Twilight said as she stood and stepped back for Gargan to push the door open. The door cracked and creaked, then swung open on its own into darkness, lit only by dim candle flames. "I think—"

"What's the worry?" Slip asked. She smiled at Gargan. "It's just—" she gasped.

Twilight looked into the darkness, as did the others. In the chamber beyond, four startled lizardmen blinked at the companions, roused from their game of bones.

Not hesitating a heartbeat, the goliath leaped forward and split one from fangs to tail. His engraved sword hissed as it burned the lizardman's flesh away like boiling water through sugar. The steel itself bled greenish acid. The hapless creature's companions gave startled squeals. They drew obsidian weapons.

The goliath's rush overturned the dry rotted table at which they had been playing, which promptly shattered on the stone floor. Gargan kicked the remains aside and carved another lizard in two, but the distraction gave the third time to hurl a cracked stool in his face. As Gargan reeled, the fourth hissed a war cry and lunged forward with a scimitar.

Then smoking blood spattered Gargan's face as Davoren's ruby blast blew a lizardman's head into a black and red abyss. The creature flopped headless to the floor with a disconsolate plop, and the flame arced from it to burn a hole through the stool-hurler. Both twitched, smoking.

As Gargan, Liet, and Slip fanned out to search for more of the creatures, the warlock stifled a yawn with one hand. "That was interesting," he said to Twilight. "And you say you are afraid of an ambush?"

Twilight glared at him but said nothing.

The room was ten paces on a side, filled with the crumbling remains of furniture and decorated with filth. Arcane sigils in much worn and faded paint adorned the walls, though they were all defaced and defiled. It had likely been a casting chamber. The room was just as old and as strange of architecture as the corridor and first chamber, but smelled much fouler.

Twilight was glad the lizards had not bypassed the wards to enter the previous chamber—the smell had been contained.

No other fiendish lizards were found in the chamber, nor could they see any of the creatures down the next corridor.

"Must have left the main group," said Davoren, "for some rest and diversion." He grinned. "The rest theirs, the diversion ours."

"Scouts, testing us," said Twilight. "We should still go back."

The warlock groaned.

The door, however, ended that debate for them. With a scrape of stone on stone, the heavy portal swung back into place, despite their best efforts to restrain it. In place, it looked no different from the rest of the wall, and it had the appropriate lack of door handles, clasps, hooks, pulleys, and opening catches.

"I suppose you're all pleased," said Twilight. "I don't even know how to begin opening it. Probably a command phrase." A mechanical thunk and rasp from the other side struck her ears. "And that would be the locks sliding into place." She folded her arms and looked away.

"All's well," said Liet. He put a reassuring hand on Twilight's shoulder—an act no one but the oblivious halfling missed—and smiled gently. "Be not afraid."

"Only of those things that warrant it," Twilight snapped. She shook Liet off roughly, hoping it would be an action none of the others would miss.

Slip, alert halfling that she was, remained completely oblivious. "I know what'll lighten this up," she said. "Let's figure out the mystery!"

"Mystery?" Liet asked, turning from Twilight, who signaled that they might as well explore these rooms in greater detail.

"Of where we are, silly," the halfling explained. "Where lies this dungeon?"

"Please," Davoren said with a dismissive wave. "It's hardly a dungeon. Deserted ruins, more like it." He gestured at the sloping, twisting, curving walls. "The deserted ruins of some mad child's doll house."

The image of a blood-soaked doll flashed through Twilight's mind.

"Speak louder, and we shall see how deserted it is," promised Taslin.

"Can we not move on?" asked Twilight, tapping her foot nervously.

"Praise be to the Lord of the Hells," said Davoren. "The *filliken* offers a glorious suggestion." He grinned at Taslin. "We should listen, scarred one."

"I am curious as to Slip's thoughts," said Taslin. "Say on, noble small one."

It took Slip a moment to realize the priestess was addressing her. "Well," said Slip. "I'm trying to figure out . . ."

Ignored by the others, Twilight pressed ahead, examining the darkened corridor. An exceptionally stout portal had once closed off the casting chamber from the hallway, exactly opposite the hall of prisoners, but it had since fallen into rubble. Probably aided, Twilight thought as she glided carefully through the darkness, by the fiendish lizards.

She deemed traps unlikely, since the lizards had gotten through unscathed, but there was no such thing as being too careful. She sensed multiple auras of magic, so she crept onward slowly, searching. At the other end, having walked the hall untouched, she waved the others forward.

"We stepped through a portal near Longsaddle," Taslin was saying. "And it did not lead where we thought it would."

"Ah," said Slip. "Same with my band. Though not Longsaddle, but Dambrath."

"Band?" Taslin asked.

"Aye! Four, originally. Me, a blue-haired girl, a thick dwarf, and Liet, of course."

The youth squinted. "I'm sorry? What—?"

Even as he chuckled, Davoren narrowed his fiendish eyes in confusion.

Slip blinked. "Oh," she said finally. "I must be taking you for someone else."

Twilight did not flinch. "We should be silent," she said. "An ambush may await."

"Oh, Belial's pisspot," growled Davoren. "An ambush like that of the lizards, perhaps? Some leader you are, always overestimating the danger."

The shadowdancer narrowed her eyes but made no reply. She crossed into the next chamber, casting about for some foe, but she found nothing there to distract her.

The room in which they stood might once have been a monster's fighting arena, with stone floors that sloped gradually down to a pit at the center. The remains of sigils drawn in crimson paint around the pit indicated a ward of some kind, perhaps a summoning circle.

Four statues of rusted, broken armor stood at the corners of the room, two shattered beyond the faintest possibility of repair, and the others propped against the wall like inebriated knights set there by obedient squires and left to rust by those less loyal. Six doors led from this chamber.

"What do you suppose—?" Liet started.

In retrospect, Twilight should have seen it coming.

"Whee!" Slip exclaimed, sliding down the slope to the bottom of the shallow pit. She bounced and landed face down with a great "oof!" and moved no more.

"Are you well?" shouted Liet.

"Oh aye!" Slip called back. "My face broke my fall!"

"Pity," Davoren murmured.

He might have said more, but there was a sudden creak of metal too long left to mold and dust. The two statues that still resembled upright people shuddered into motion.

Too late, Twilight understood the significance of the statues. Too late, she realized what would trigger their purpose: a creature at the center of the circle when the runes of protection were not operating. Wizards sometimes kept guardians for just such an occasion, particularly when they summoned creatures strongly resistant to magic.

"Slip!" she shouted. "Run! The—!"

That was as far as she got before the first of the helmed horrors drew its rusty blade and lunged at her. The weapon burst into flames as the creature charged.

Everything seemed to happen at once, in that moment. Twilight rolled away from the one that swung at her, only to see Liet stumble into its path and be dashed to the ground. Gargan leaped upon one of the horrors as it loomed over Davoren and Taslin, his acid-coated sword smashing it. Slip blinked, transfixed by the statues' sudden movements, and screamed.

That doesn't help, thought Twilight as she dived between a pair of armored legs. With an upturned wrist and a dip, she thrust her rapier up through the monstrosity's breastplate, an angled strike that would have unmanned, disemboweled, and slain a living man, but had no such effect on the creature. Her sword did stab into the horror's essence, and a blue-white mist began to leak between the fringes of its armor.

The construct shuddered but did not slow. It swung down one rusty fist with not-so-rusty speed, which Twilight narrowly dodged. She danced back, keeping impeccable balance, until Liet sent her stumbling as he charged at the horror.

"Fool!" Twilight cursed in anger and fear.

Liet might have replied, but Twilight saw energy crackling around the horror and her eyes went wide. She hissed, and Liet dived just below a swath of flame that sliced the air overhead, erupting from its breastplate. She dodged, but just barely.

"Davoren!" Twilight shouted, gritting her teeth against the pain and the heat.

The warlock didn't need to be told twice. Crimson power erupted from his hands and dark tendrils appeared from the ground, surrounding the helmed horror, enwrapping and entangling it. The creature swung its deadly, flaming blade at Twilight and Liet, but it could not reach them—its sword cut just a hair too short. Twilight flinched away, putting as much distance between herself and that burning steel as she could, and the flames kissed her cheeks. As she did, she caught a glimpse of Gargan and his foe, and that stunned her.

The goliath faced his opponent in a sword duel that rivaled a tropical storm at sea. Swords flew and spun, cutting like scythes caught in a whirlwind.

The horror might have spent centuries moldering and rusting, but it moved as though it had been built a tenday past—like the deadly weapon it was meant to be. Its attacks left and right, up and down, flowed through continuous motion as though launched by an elf duelist with a mithral saber, rather than a suit of armor with an iron greatsword. All the while, the horror itself was the picture of mechanical calm, simply fulfilling its appointed task.

Its unruffled exterior, however, made for a poor reflection of Gargan. While many swordsmen fought with their muscles, backing fierce blows and counterstrokes with hot fury, and those trained in the fencing arts like Twilight fought with their heads, knowing every strategic attack, parry, and riposte through long practice, this was something far different. Gargan fought not by heart or mind, but by spirit.

Gargan's face was serenity itself, and no rage burned beneath its surface. The blade in his hand danced seemingly of its own accord, turning away strikes Twilight barely saw coming. The goliath never batted an eye as he parried steel a finger's breadth from his nose. He slapped the sword wide, reversed his grip as though spinning a baton, and slashed back in underhanded, tearing a burning gash across the creature's helm. The blade's acid took its toll upon the thing, impeding its flexibility and movements.

Davoren bellowed with fiendish laughter and threw blast after blast at the horror. Taslin summoned Corellon's power to melt away its armor, piece by piece. All the while, it slashed at Twilight and Liet, where they cowered, with the determination only the dead and the mindless possess.

"Corellon!" Taslin cried, throwing her melted sword-and-symbol skyward, where it stopped and hovered in the air just out of reach. White fire crackled around it, and the blade blazed suddenly whole. Twilight thought she saw something skitter out of the way above, but it fled her mind when she had to turn away to keep from being blinded.

A column of divine flame tore down through the ceiling, engulfing the monstrosity. The Lord of the Seldarine's wrath tore through the suit of armor with its flaming sword. A biting squeal of metal rose over the roar of the inferno. The smoking horror gave a disappointed hiss and crumbled to the floor, inert and useless. Its form fell with a solid thump, fused by the extreme heat of Taslin's spell.

A heartbeat later, Gargan slashed and ripped his foe to scrap. The horror gave a pitiful hiss as the goliath spun with his final backhand and lightly tapped the sword point to the floor. Behind him, it clattered into a pile of half-dissolved rubbish.

"Well," breathed Twilight.

"What a deep thought," Liet said with a grin.

CHAPTER FIFTEEN

S o . . ." Slip said in the resulting silence. Her demeanor could not have been more tranquil. If a battle had been fought, she seemed not to have noticed.

Liet decided to bite. "Aye?"

"So we all came from different places!" exclaimed Slip. "Through different portals!" Apparently, she truly hadn't noticed.

"Remarkable concentration," scoffed Davoren.

"Belt up, and give the little one a chance," Taslin shot back.

Slip continued undaunted. "Thus . . . thus!"

Liet thought the brainless halfling should get a third chance. "Thus?" he prodded.

"We all have different dirt upon our boots!" the halfling said excitedly.

The others rolled their eyes and Liet sighed. Twilight gestured to the floor.

Slip looked down at her bare feet. "Oh."

"You twit," growled the warlock. "It means we have come to this foul place by means of twisted Art. Someone is interfering with our portals, likely." His eyes fell on Twilight venomously. "I recall that the leader of *my* band led us through just such a conveying path, without regard to the consequences, of course."

Liet looked at Twilight as well, but the elf's face was blank. Her eyes, though, shifted back and forth uneasily. That struck Liet as odd. He felt perfectly calm, the thrill of combat fled. Hadn't the battle ended?

"So some force has drawn us here," said Taslin, standing amongst the group, "bringing us through various portals, all to the same place. The question is why."

Gargan said something then, in his strange goliath tongue. Deep and rough, yet noble. He had no idea what the words meant, but he could see the impact they left on Taslin, who could understand somehow, and Twilight, who seemed to have a sense of such things.

"You did not come through a portal," Twilight said softly.

"Eh? Wait a breath—" Slip started.

Gargan said something, and Taslin nodded her head.

"It seems he came upon a cavern while hunting a troll that had been spotted in the area," she said. "He followed the beast in and—"

"And there must be more of them," said Twilight.

"Why must—?" Liet asked. He was so confused.

"Goliaths are social creatures, even more so than humans," she said. She looked at Gargan sharply. "Where are the other goliaths?"

It took Gargan a breath to understand her question. He shook his head and spoke.

"He is an exile from his people," said Taslin. "Called . . . hmm. The closest word in the Common tongue is 'dispossessed.' "

Gargan nodded. "Dispossessed," he repeated.

"I see," Twilight said. "Second time I've heard such a name. The first wasn't so pleasant, as I recall."

Liet looked at her, expecting more, but she left it at that. He wondered if that was true—and what it all meant. She resumed pacing about the room.

Gargan continued speaking to Taslin, who translated for the others. Liet assumed it was magic of some kind. "The troll he was tracking—Tlork—ambushed him in the cave, and they fought. Blackwyrm, his acid-weeping sword—the one he carries now—was key, but the creature defeated him. When he awakened, he was in the dark cell."

"This begins to make sense," Twilight said. "The master of these depths—"

"The Mad Sharn," hissed Davoren.

"We don't know that for sure," said Twilight. "This labyrinth . . ."

"Whatever he calls it," Slip said. "Midden's more like it. A foul pit!"

Gargan eyed her curiously, but Twilight didn't know why. "It's not so foul, as dungeons go," the shadowdancer said. "I've seen—"

"Stranger?" filled in Liet.

"Fouler," Twilight corrected matter-of-factly. She turned to Gargan. "What land have you come from? Where do these caverns lie?"

Gargan looked away, something like sadness falling across his stony face.

With a shiver, Twilight understood somehow. "What awaits us above?"

"Death," said Gargan.

Taslin let out a hiss, her eyes narrowing. Her voice sounded upset, eager, and her face gleamed in frustration. "Death?" she asked. "Can you not be more specif—?"

Then a long cord slithered down from the ceiling, curled about Taslin's throat, and drew the priestess into the air with a quick jerk.

———◆◆◆———

Twilight was too shocked to do anything more than stare at the ceiling, from which hung the struggling Taslin and her attacker. The creature was vaguely humanoid, if twice the height of a man, fashioned out of slithering, whipping ropes of black silk. Two white orbs blazed where its face should be.

She ignored the sinking in her chest and yanked Betrayal free of its scabbard. As she did, she felt the choking herself, though nothing clutched her and fought it down. She knew Taslin was dead, and if she did not act, the others would soon be as well.

" 'Light, what *is* that?" Liet stammered.

The tendril from which the priestess twitched and kicked recoiled and the other appendage extended toward them, sending a dozen ropes to claim their next victim.

"Down!" Twilight shouted, pushing Liet to send him staggering.

The quick motion saved him from being caught up by the rope tendrils, which went for her instead. Flicking like silent snakes, they lunged for her arms, and Twilight almost screamed despite herself.

She settled for a startled hiss and invoked her powers. Dancing into the shadows, she vanished before the ropes could catch her and reappeared across the chamber near Slip. Liet, running toward that spot, gasped when he saw her appear.

"A simple matter," Davoren said calmly, preparing a blast of fiery energy to throw at the creature as it looked about for a new target.

"Wait!" Twilight shouted, but it was too late.

The warlock's burning power stabbed into the creature's chest but boiled away, fizzling to no effect. "What?" the warlock shouted furiously.

"As I thought," said Twilight, dropping one hand to her belt. "A golem."

"A rope golem?" asked Liet at her side. "What—?"

The creature, moving in absolute silence, snapped its tendrils, and Taslin jerked spasmodically. Her arms fell to her sides. It flung the sun elf to crunch against the wall, where she collapsed limply to the floor. Cowering behind Twilight, Slip screamed. Liet caught her and shielded her eyes in his chest.

With both limbs free, the hangman golem lunged at Davoren, who fled, and Gargan, who met its grasp with sword swinging. The ensorcelled steel, streaming its acid, caused only minor damage to the creature, scratching and nicking the rope limbs.

Davoren dashed to the wall and began searching it with his hands, as though he had detected something nearby. Twilight could not have sensed any magical emanations, not with such a huge magical creature attacking them.

"Get back here!" Twilight called to him, but the warlock did nothing of the sort. Soon enough, the wall opened and the warlock slipped through a hidden passage.

"What do we do?" shrieked Slip, tugging at Twilight's belt.

"Anything," she said, slapping the little hands away. She rummaged through the vials stuck through the laces of her belt. She retrieved one, which held a silvery liquid within. "You have power, aye?"

"B-but . . ." Slip said.

"Any spells of aid, cast them on Gargan," said Twilight. With that, she dashed toward the combat. As she stalked, she picked out a rope tendril and followed it with her eyes, focused, making it the center of her world.

The halfling sent a twinkling star of white trailing toward the golem, where it burst into a discordant roar. The sound jarred Twilight and Gargan alike, sending them reeling, but it did little to the hangman golem.

"Magic does nothing!" Liet cried.

"Sorry! Sorry!" yipped Slip. "I'll try harder!" She sprinted toward Gargan, tearing free of Liet's grasp.

Stunned by the sonic blast, Twilight almost caught a rope in the face, but the goliath stepped in the way. He caught the rope in one hand and yanked, pulling the creature with him. It slithered along the ceiling, diverted from the others.

"My thanks," shouted Twilight, but Gargan did not respond.

The goliath held the hangman golem in a toe-to-toe duel—a strange sight with the creature fighting upside down from the ceiling. His sword left dozens of rope pieces flopping like worms on the floor in its wake. This hardly slowed the golem, but the acid leaked by the black blade ate at the strands of its body hungrily. The creature sensed this damage and focused its attention on Gargan.

Mistake, Twilight thought. She saw her chance and jumped, rapier extended, and ran a single tendril through. The golem hardly noticed. What was one strand to a creature composed entirely of ropes? The rapier did not even sever the strand.

Holding tight to her blade with both hands, Twilight swung across the room on the rope and tossed a vial to the goliath in the same motion, praying that he understood. "Gargan!" she snapped.

As Twilight swung, her single rope slapped across dozens of seeking tendrils, tangling them all. The creature twisted and shook, thrown off balance and distracted.

Gargan spun and flung out a massive hand to catch the vial. In one smooth motion, he leaped away from the golem's tendrils and shattered the vial against his black blade, which suddenly gleamed with silvery-white radiance. At almost the same instant, Slip arrived at Gargan's side and touched his hip, completing her spell. The goliath's body showed no change, but his aura of strength grew.

Twilight dodged back and forth, twisting this way and that, avoiding the slapping ropes at all cost. She blocked ineffectually—the ropes simply whipped around her parries, regardless of how wide she held the blade. Here and there, her billowy blouse became stained with red, or open gashes appeared along her leather breeches.

Only reflex kept Twilight from being pummeled into a crimson stain on the stone. Even so, she screamed as the golem whipped her, desperate dodges or no.

"Strike it, Gargan!" Twilight shouted. "Stri—"

At that instant, a rope whipped under her high parry and struck her across the cheek. Twilight's head snapped back and she spun to the ground. She heard her head strike the stone with a loud crack, and darkness took her.

Liet almost cried out when Twilight went down, but he was too busy panting, trying to drag his sword back and forth. He ran to her side, slashing at the tendrils again and again, but to no avail. The ropes were too hard. Then they knocked him flailing.

Unhindered, the rope golem flowed along the ceiling,

soundless. It drew itself along the ropes that held it aloft and loomed over Twilight. If it had been a living thing, the golem would have hissed hungrily.

Liet knew Gargan could not have understood Twilight's words, but from his actions, he understood her plan intuitively and acted accordingly.

With a pulse of powerful legs and arms, the goliath hurled his huge sword, slathered with the alchemical concoction, into the air, where it spitted the hangman golem's chest. The creature reeled, though it made no sound.

Gargan wasn't done. He followed the sword with a mighty leap, his legs strengthened by Slip's divine magic, and caught the hilt in both hands at the apex of his jump. The goliath's momentum carried him past the golem and his firm grasp on the sword ripped the weapon through its innards.

Gargan's sword tore the creature in two in a way that was anything but tidy.

The golem reeled, pieces of itself flopping all over. The tendrils holding it precariously to the ceiling strained and snapped free of the stone, and the golem tumbled to the ground. It wheeled and writhed, trying to reform. Its tendrils slithered and whipped, caught in death throes.

Climbing to his feet, Liet breathed out in relief, but his eye fell on the fallen elf. " 'Light!" he shouted, taking a step toward her.

When Twilight's gloved hand moved, Liet's breath caught. Then her blood-streaked face turned up to him. He smiled, and the tiny twitch of her lips might have been an attempt to return it.

Slip was on her way, healing at the ready, a tremendous smile on her face. "We *got* it!" she squealed.

A tendril snaked up behind her.

"Down!" Twilight shouted, yanking the halfling off her feet and rolling over her.

Eyes wide, Liet saw what was about to happen and threw himself down.

The golem lashed out, its tendrils a whirlwind of whips that caught the three within. Liet cringed and jerked as his body felt dozens of kisses and slashes.

When it was over, he looked up to see a bruised and battered Twilight lying, unmoving, where she had collapsed limply over the halfling.

" 'Light?" Slip screamed, shaking her by the shoulder. "Wake up!"

The golem, its fury spent, collapsed into a quivering mass of tendrils.

Liet blinked at the two, then at the golem, then at the staggering Gargan. Then he realized that if he didn't act, no one would. Whether Twilight lived or not, the rest of them would certainly die if Liet did nothing.

"Now!" Liet shouted. "Burn the ropes!"

"But magic doesn't work, remem—?" the halfling said.

"Torches!" Liet said. "Flints! Anything!"

Slip looked confused, almost hesitant. Then she looked down at the limp Twilight, who had saved her life. She pulled out one of the flints they'd collected and struck a torch. Then she produced several vials of lantern oil from the small bag at her waist—why she had them, Liet had no clue, but he didn't care—and in heartbeats, the three had doused the quivering ropes. Liet threw his torch on the pile, and the hangman golem twitched and thrashed its way to motionless oblivion.

For a moment, all was terrible silence in the aftermath.

Then Twilight coughed where she lay. Liet rushed to her side to help her up, and she took his hand. She offered a kind of smile, marred by the blood trickling down her slashed cheek. Then, as though just realizing their proximity, she pushed at his chest.

Her finger had hurt like a punch—a two-handed punch. Nothing had struck him so hard—not the guardians, not the golem, not even Taslin . . .

Taslin.

Silently, Twilight limped from Liet's side to where Slip stood over the unmoving Taslin. Liet wanted to go to her, but he could only stare at Taslin's body. The golem had been destroyed, yes, but the toll was heavy. Even at this distance, Liet knew there was nothing to be done for the golden elf.

"Well then," said a voice, startling them. "Enjoyed ourselves, eh?"

Liet turned, numbly, to see Davoren walking toward them. He had not been injured—likely, he had spent the entire battle hidden, safe.

The words stabbed into Liet's numb, shocked ears. He looked at the sword in his hand, and almost ran over to ram it down Davoren's throat right then. It was illogical to blame Davoren for Taslin's death, but Liet wasn't feeling logical. He was afraid of the warlock, yes, but he could do it. He could . . .

Then he noted something new: a gold rod carved like a snarling dragon hanging from Davoren's belt. That must have been what he had collected during the battle. Rather than giving aid against the golem, he had gone instead for treasure. Liet couldn't sense magic the way Twilight seemingly could, but he guessed that Davoren had become a little stronger, while the rest of them had become weaker.

"At least the rest of the time we spend getting out of this wretched place will be quiet," said the warlock, prompting a roomful of horrified looks.

Liet couldn't reply in the face of such vitriol. He looked instead at Twilight, kneeling beside Taslin. She was shaking. "Are you well?" he asked.

Twilight did not respond. Her hand kept caressing the dead elf's hair.

"Of course she is," Davoren said behind him. "Spared of scar-cheeks, who wouldn't be?"

"Don't you care?" Slip cried. Her cheeks flushed, streaked with tears. "Don't you care that she's dead? Don't you care about anything?"

Davoren shrugged. "Of course I care." He nudged Taslin's corpse with his boot and looked down disdainfully. "Her magic was the source of our food."

Fighting outrage, Liet clenched his sword hilt with white knuckles. He had to suppress his anger—he had to. Then he looked at Taslin again and felt empty.

"That raises a point," Davoren asked. "Can your pitiful Yondalla conjure us up something more filling than unsweetened cakes and seeds? Else, this journey is liable to be a hungry one."

The halfling hissed at him with surprising vehemence and huddled against the staring priestess, sobbing.

———◆◆◆———

" 'Light?" It was Liet.

Twilight did not reply except to gaze down. She pulled her hand away from the ravaged face and hair. The elf's eyes bugged out at her, and her mouth hung open, tongue distended. What acid and heartache had not managed—ruining golden beauty—death seemed to have accomplished.

Unsurprising, that. Twilight knew all too well the power of death.

Twilight felt the constriction about her neck again, and almost wished it real—that she could die in Taslin's place.

She wondered what was going on behind her. She looked away from Taslin's body—that brute thing, no longer her companion—toward her comrades.

Face burning, Slip sobbed over the corpse, while Davoren smirked, tapping his fingers against a dragon-shaped scepter he wore at his belt. Liet stood aloof, hand on his sword; he didn't meet Twilight's gaze, and she appreciated that.

Gargan was saying something in the goliath tongue, and Twilight could not understand. Trembling, she bent down and gently took the ensorcelled earring from Taslin's ear and put the device in her left ear lobe. She heard an arcane hum, and suddenly she could understand everything Gargan said. She caught him in mid sentence, but he said enough.

"—*found no trace,*" said the goliath, pointing up, where the creature had clung to the ceiling. "Its trail was not on the floor."

Twilight ran—limping, but she ran.

" 'Light!" shouted Liet. "Where—?"

Sword in hand, feverish, Twilight darted back through the chambers, eyes raised. She followed their exact path, but she wasn't watching as the corridors flew past. Somewhere along the way, her hip smashed into a broken table and she stumbled, but her eyes never left the dusty ceiling. To an onlooker, she must have looked quite mad.

Finally she arrived back at the spellcasting chamber and searched above. With a wrenching wail, she collapsed to her knees in a pool of dried lizardfolk blood, clutched herself tightly, and fell to cursing.

"I was right," she gasped. "Oh, Erevan! I was right."

When the others came a breath or three later, staring at a madwoman, Twilight was still swearing incoherently and weeping angry tears, staring up.

There, the path of long coils—the path she had followed from the site of the ambush—terminated at the secret door.

CHAPTER SIXTEEN

W hat's the matter?" Liet asked as Twilight lay against him, a long while later.

"Is it not obvious?" she said, tracing her fingers idly down his chest. "I failed."

They lay out of sight of the others, but not as far as the previous night. She had chosen a side chamber off the main summoning chamber, which must once have been a wizard's bedchamber. The others camped near the wrecked horrors.

Their lovemaking had been fierce. Twilight could feel more than see Liet flinch as her fingers found a bruise here or a scratch there, but she did not care. She was furious, even as she took profound joy in him. Such conflict—the lay of her life.

Liet, half clothed, leaned against the wall. Twilight, her breeches and blouse flung carelessly aside, lay against him. Both were wrapped in his cloak. She'd wanted him to take his shirt off, but Liet had been adamant about his arms. Perhaps he found their sight too painful. Twilight understood a thing or two about pain.

After building Taslin a decent cairn and marking it with the remains of her sword, Slip locked the room as best she could. They spent the rest of the day exploring the sanctum listlessly. The magic had been long ransacked or ruined, either by passing tomb raiders, golems, or lizardfolk, and they found the place largely empty of anything of value.

The party found only a ratty pair of boots, to which the halfling had taken a liking. They were not magical by Twilight's estimation, though she did not have the heart to disappoint Slip. They also discovered a set of three rather dull steel rods now carried by Liet, which the shadowdancer knew to be magical but could not sense anything other than their general purpose—altering something.

She wished they could alter that day.

And there was Davoren's newly acquired scepter, and anything else the treacherous warlock had seized during the battle.

Half a dozen lizardmen had entered the sanctum at one point, and following Twilight's better judgment—against her bitter anger—the five had hidden, not fought. That concession to discretion had grated on Twilight. More than anything else, she felt helpless in this barren place, with her allies being slain one by one, without any real direction. She felt a failure as a leader.

And now there was Taslin's death, a death that could have been averted had she listened to her instincts.

" 'Tis not true," said Liet. He slid his soft fingers along her welts and scratches, caressing her. Twilight winced a little, but she did not stop him. "Not true."

It took Twilight a moment to realize what he meant—he was answering her last words. "Yes, it is," Twilight said. "I shouldn't have listened to you. Wanderer's sand! I should have followed my instinct and gone back."

"No one blames you," said Liet.

She looked him in the eye. "For all your vigor, dear boy, you're a terrible lover."

"Why so?" he asked, hurt.

"You simply cannot lie." She settled down with a sigh.

Liet smiled weakly. "Maybe, but you can, and you're doing it to yourself. 'Tis not your fault. 'Tis no one's fault," said Liet. "The hangman was merely passing—"

"Passing over us, through the door. It attacked us in the mage's chambers. Makes perfect sense." Twilight's voice was angry. "Whoever created that iron golem must have done it. Set it on us."

"Mayhap. But none of us could've known of that . . . thing."

Twilight let the silence linger. "Are you so sure?"

Liet fixed her with an odd look. "I don't understand, lass."

Twilight didn't correct him.

"Too many coincidences," she said. "The wights' ambush, the tunnel of traps, the grimlock attack, the golem in wait that the lizards stumbled across, the rope golem." She shifted. "We're being watched. Someone's luring us into ambush after ambush."

Liet laughed—a forced sound. "You're imagining this."

"And whatever watches us left this where I could find it." She fingered her star sapphire amulet. "Because it would make me believe it impossible."

"The amulet that—ah . . ."

"Blocks scrying," said Twilight. "Our keeper could watch directly, with magic—but the amulet protects me and anyone close by. Or it could watch indirectly, with a spy."

"You're jumping at shadows—thinking about this too much."

Twilight found that ironic. "That's why I told each of the others a different direction," she said. "This way, I can see which one it is."

"I'm dense," Liet said. "Which what is what?"

"The spy," said Twilight. "Think about it. How many weapons were in that chest? How much clothing? How many of us were there supposed to be?"

"Six sets of weapons, six sets of clothing, seven of us." Liet shrugged. "I suppose that makes sense, but would that not make it . . . I don't know, *obvious?*"

"We're supposed to think that," Twilight said. When Liet frowned, she sighed. "Whoever's watching us did it—the clothes, the equipment, my Shroud—purposefully, so that we'd wonder if there were a spy, and guess that there must not be, because it would be too obvious. What more perfect way to cover up a spy?"

Liet blinked at her and Twilight sighed. Her mind was simply faster than his.

"There were enough supplies for six, and the spy makes us seven. That's one." Twilight put up one finger. "The wards on the spell chamber were penetrated from our side, and that door was one-way." Two fingers. "And from the golem's tracks—whoever released it must have done so through magic, from under our very noses." Three. "Whoever the spy is, he or she is still with us." She eyed Liet pointedly.

"Are you accusing me, 'Light?" he asked carefully.

"It could be you," Twilight said. "Why such a reaction?"

Liet smiled and Twilight read him, as she had read so many in her century of life. She noted every tic of his body, every twitch of his fingers, every flick of his eyes. She could see the rising warmth in his cheeks and hear his heartbeat. Twilight would know if Liet lied to her.

"Well?" she asked.

"I'm no spy," said Liet. "Whether you believe me or not is your prerogative."

Twilight allowed the faintest of smiles to tickle her cheeks.

"We shall see." She knew, though, that he told the truth.

Another thought occurred to her. "Now. Back to your blankets."

Liet looked at her hard, as though searching desperately for a jest and finding none. Then he rose and walked stiffly away, hurt in his every step. Why didn't he fight?

"Liet," Twilight breathed. "Wait."

The youth turned back, arms crossed.

She wanted to apologize. She wanted to say that he was right, that she trusted him, that she needed him, but nothing of the sort came out. She couldn't lie now, but neither could she tell the truth.

Instead, all she managed was a question—a question she had no right to ask.

"Whence the scars on your arms?"

Liet bit his lip. "If you trusted me," he said. "If you'd share your scars with me, maybe I'd share mine with you." Turning purposefully, he walked away.

"It would make this all easier if you'd express your anger," Twilight whispered to the closing door.

She desperately wanted to tell Liet that she believed in him, that she knew he wasn't a spy and a traitor, but she resisted the impulse. The logical, reasoning side of her nature, by far the dominant facet of her being, knew that admitting such a thing to him would endanger the stability of the group.

How can equality be maintained, Twilight mused, if not by mutual antipathy?

With a shiver, she realized that it sounded like something *he* would say.

In that moment, she felt legacy stab like a thrust from Betrayal. And in that moment of defiance—despite all her emotional defenses, despite her rage and pain—Twilight almost called Liet back. She almost let her walls drop, almost let him in. She almost reached out to another. She almost loved him—or more appropriately, let *him* love *her*—in that moment.

But she did not.

Every one of Twilight's carefully cultivated fears and confirmed doubts came back in full force, and she was alone once more. She didn't need anyone. No one could hurt her—not again.

She found herself thinking of Taslin, of how noble the sun elf had been, and how close they had come, just as Twilight had with Liet. She remembered how Taslin had looked in the breath before the hangman's attack, beautiful in her anger.

Twilight scowled. The gods toyed with her—one in particular.

"Damn you, Erevan," she murmured as weariness claimed her. "Damn you."

The useless one paused outside her chamber, not quite within Gestal, where he stood watching. " 'Light?" he called through the open door.

No response.

Gestal waited, watching as she lay. He was certain she slept, but that was not all he awaited. The large one went off for watch, and the small one stirred in her blankets. She looked in his direction, eyes wide, then rolled back and huddled.

Satisfied, Lord Divergence entered, closed the door behind them, making sure it was locked, and stood over the one he wanted. She hadn't bothered to dress, but had fallen to slumber in clad only in her cloak. He knelt and traced the hands a hair above the soft, lithe body. He passed over her curves, made note of her scars. Their eyes lingered.

The elf's lip trembled and her face went white, but she did not wake.

"I could be your lover," he whispered. "I understand. I see."

No response.

"I see through your lies," Gestal said.

Gestal stayed, their eyes not an inch from her own. He wouldn't touch her—not any part of her body. No, Gestal would do far worse.

He bent low, their lips just a hair's breadth from her throat. The elf's hands shook and she sobbed in her sleep. "Lilten," she murmured.

"No," Lord Divergence said. "A better lover."

Twilight's eyes snapped open. It was dark and quiet—so still that she might have awakened in another world. Somehow, the tranquility was not tranquil, and she shivered. Something wet and cold was upon her, like sweat. She brushed idly at her face and her hand came away sticky.

She realized she had not dressed. Instead, she had fallen asleep wrapped in the roughspun cloak upon which she and Liet had held one another.

"Silly wench," she chided herself. "Don't you realize that's not safe?"

Then she looked at her hand and froze. Blood was on her fingers.

It wasn't her own blood, she knew. She immediately fell into awareness of her body—no injury, no soreness. Nothing had damaged her—not physically, anyway.

The room suddenly seemed much larger, and she was terribly aware of her solitude. "Liet . . ." she whispered. Her voice came soft and weak—vulnerable.

Hardly daring to move, Twilight looked at her bare chest and belly. Her eyes widened. Bloody handprints covered her—hands on her breast, hands on her stomach, hands on her arms, hands on her legs. She felt the stickiness on her throat and face. The prints were not violent—they were what might be left by the caress of a lover, but they were not Liet's hands. The blood she didn't know, but the hands . . .

The hands were Taslin's.

"No," Twilight said, searching her skin. "That can't . . . can't be . . ."

She thought she heard laughter, soft and hidden, behind her.

Twilight shrieked and scratched at herself, desperate to get it off, but it only smeared. She tore open the precious waterskin and splashed it over her. She scrubbed, furiously, with the sweaty cloak, cleansing herself as best she could. All the filth of days trapped in these caverns came back to her, and she moaned and cursed the cloak that it would not cleanse her—not fully. She looked to her tinderbox.

Then something slammed into the stout, locked door. She screamed again and scrubbed harder. Harder. Knuckles split, and the scratches drew blood.

She didn't stop, couldn't stop. She couldn't let them see. Couldn't let them . . .

———◆◆◆———

Gargan finally bashed the door open and Liet tumbled in, sword drawn, to defend Twilight from whatever could be attacking her. Slip danced in behind him, mace in one hand and obsidian dagger in the other. Even Davoren was there, scepter in hand.

Liet saw Twilight standing nude in the center of the room,

Betrayal in both hands. Scratches covered her body. Shaking, midnight hair wild, she stared at them with terrible vehemence. In the corner of the chamber, something burned smokily.

" 'Light?" He thought to sheathe the sword, but wasn't sure it was prudent.

"Stay away," Twilight snapped. "Stay back! Traitors! Liars!"

Liet stepped toward her. The rapier pointed at his face. "Back!" she screamed.

There was tense silence punctuated only by her heavy breathing.

"Davoren," Liet said quietly. "Davoren—give Slip your cloak."

For once, the warlock did what he was bid. Despite a weighing smile, he stripped off the black fabric, tattered as it had become, and handed it to the halfling.

"Slip," Liet said.

She hesitated, trembling.

"Slip, please."

The halfling looked up at Gargan for support, and the goliath nodded. Slip crept into Twilight's chamber and proffered the cloak. As Liet had thought, the elf did not attack her. She accepted the garment, looked at Slip with something like thanks, then collapsed like a discarded marionette.

They rushed to her side.

CHAPTER SEVENTEEN

In her own clothes, having had some water from Liet's skin, Twilight felt more herself, though the shudders hadn't quite passed. Of course she hadn't told the others what happened—a nightmare, she said. She wasn't even certain that had been a lie, though she suspected not; she smelled like blood. She worried they noticed.

Davoren stretched and moved about his tasks of the morning with a spring in his step that had nothing to do with the lack of food. "I halfway enjoy life in this labyrinth without the golden bitch constantly whining," said the warlock. "Ah, silence."

"You said that already," growled Slip from her cloak.

"Ah yes," Davoren replied with a smile. He bent down next to her and looked her in the eye. "I just wanted to make sure my point came across quite fully."

The halfling bristled but said nothing, prompting the warlock's grin to widen. Slip shoved the rest of her gear in her pack and scurried over to where Twilight sat against the wall, clasping her arms about herself. Twilight met the halfling with an easy smile.

"Good morn, little one," she said as Slip thumped down with a sigh. She reached over and put an arm around the halfling's shoulders, as one might a child. Since her horror of the night before—which might have been a dream, anyway—she had found nothing as comforting as the small one—not her clothes, not her sword, not Liet.

After a time, Slip spoke, quietly and hesitantly. " 'Light, I've a favor to ask." Her innocent voice sounded particularly meek in the dark cavern.

"I'm a great proponent of conversation. Say on."

"Well," the halfling started. She contemplated the dark spot she was busy scuffing on her boot. "If I paid you enough . . . would you . . . kill Davoren for me?"

Twilight bit her lip, not a little stunned. Slip was always so compassionate, so loyal, so . . . *good*, for lack of a better term. Twilight could hardly believe the little woman could ask such a question.

"What could you possibly have to pay me?" asked Twilight.

"I could save the strongest healing magics of me lord for you," the halfling said. The words sounded so blatantly strategic. "If you'd do this thing, I—"

"Firstly, there can be no alliances," Twilight said. "If any of the others perceive us as partners, or even as friends, it will spark a schism. I do not want to worry about the others plotting against me, or you, or both of us."

"But—"

"*No* alliances. If I'm wounded, it's just the same as if Gargan, Liet, or, aye, even Davoren were wounded." She clutched Slip's arm tightly. "I want your word on that."

Slip's eyes fell and she sniffed. "Fine," she said, defeated.

"Secondly, do I look like an assassin?" asked Twilight. "Gods, no. I'm a thief, just like you. I don't kill for coin. Might as well be a dinger, or a fen, for that matter, winning with brute force and manual labor what I couldn't get through finesse." That she slipped into cant, referring to a thug and a prostitute, should have told Slip something. From her blank eyes, it didn't, so Twilight stopped. "I have a little more self-respect than that."

It was difficult to tell if Slip was pleased or disappointed.

"And thirdly, the prime reason you can't pay me to kill Davoren," said Twilight, leaning in close. She adopted a cold tone. "I'd gladly do it for free."

Slip giggled and Twilight grinned, though she didn't laugh. Slip was more than she seemed, and something she'd said had struck Twilight as wrong, but damned if she could place it. She was too tired.

The events of the previous night had drained her and left her numb—empty. She knew, however, what the others expected of her, and she could use it to her advantage. She felt like her old self again—or one of them, anyway. Taslin's blood had been a shock. Things couldn't continue as they had. Something had to change.

She hugged the little halfling tightly. Nervous about Liet, Twilight was glad of Slip's companionship. Perhaps she had her mysteries, and perhaps she was less than stable, but at least Twilight could rely on her to be mysterious and less than stable. And if there was a spy, she would need someone she could trust.

"We go by the south door," Twilight announced when they were ready to depart.

The reactions were myriad and telling. Liet bit his lip. Davoren rolled his eyes. Gargan shrugged noncommittally, and Slip balked. Liet thought they were past this, but whatever had happened to her this morning must have changed that.

"B-but," Slip said. "You said . . ."

"It matters not what I said," replied Twilight. "But let us be more specific. You four shall take the route south of the sanctum, which I know leads up."

"How?" Davoren snapped.

Twilight flashed him a whimsical smile. "I wouldn't be much of a thief if I didn't scout ahead," she said. "The door, which I have unlocked, leads steadily upward until it arrives at a trapdoor hidden in the ceiling, inscribed with the inverted Netherese runes we saw before. There, you will find your way."

"What do you mean, 'you' will find?" asked Liet. "You're coming with us, aye?"

"I rather fancy a jaunt through the east passage."

"The east passage!" Slip exclaimed. "But why? And alone? 'Light!" She ran to Twilight and threw her little arms around her—or, rather, around her legs. " 'Tis too dangerous! You can't leave us!" Tears started to roll from Slip's eyes.

Liet opened his mouth, but he was too stunned to speak. Was she *mad*?

"Pitiful whining whelp," mused Davoren. "Let her go—and good riddance."

"Oh, worry not, little one," said Twilight kindly. "I'm *sure* nothing will be awaiting. My scouting of last night revealed simply a door I had yet to open, perhaps a chamber yet to be explored. No markings of lizards upon it. I doubt any of the creatures has opened it. I plan to stroll in, without taking any precautions." She gave Slip a thoughtless wink.

"Gods, 'Light—" Liet started, but Davoren laughed him to silence.

If the halfling had been afraid before, she was truly terrified at this news. She looked up with eyes wide as tureens. "You should come with us! Where 'tis safe—er, saf*er!*" She buried her head in the shadowdancer's belly. "I can't lose you, too!"

The elf beamed at her as though she had not a thought in her head. "Do not worry for my safety, little one. 'Tis but a morning stroll—like you took in Crimel, yes?"

"No!" The halfling's eyes flashed. "At least take one of us—take me, aye?"

"The half-wench raises a decent argument," said Davoren. "Perhaps you *should* take someone, to make sure you are not hunting treasure—or arranging to betray us."

"Don't be silly," said Twilight with a laugh. "Survival takes priority over gold. The simple acceptance of this fact is precisely what keeps the numbers of folk in my profession breathing steadily. And if I meant to slay you, you'd be quite dead."

Davoren would not be deterred, though he looked a little unsettled by her manic demeanor. "Yet, we have only the word of a thief and a liar. I insist you take another."

"Insistence noted!" Twilight said brightly. "Liet—"

"Oh, *very* well," said Davoren, rolling his eyes and turning away. He waved dismissively. "Take your handsome swain—this choice does not surprise me. And I'd be happy without his useless carcass slowing us."

"Liet," Twilight continued. "I place you in command."

"What?" Liet and Davoren exclaimed at once.

Twilight pinched Liet's cheek. "Listen to the lad's word as you would mine," she said. "As you have followed me, so you must follow him in my stead."

"I 'must' do nothing!" Davoren roared, ruby energy flickering around his hands and arms. His fingers twitched toward the snarling dragon scepter at his belt. "I have sworn no oath—certainly none that involves following a bare-faced boy! I refuse!"

"Well then," said Twilight, suddenly serious. "I shall simply have to kill you." Betrayal hissed out and she leaned back into a fighting stance. Her eyes brooked no debate, and she showed no sign of mirth.

After a long, motionless breath, Davoren laughed. "Very well," he said. "Play your game. I care not. I shall do as you ask, for now. Only know that mine shall be the last word, the last thrust, and the last smile."

"You just keep reassuring yourself of that, handsome," Twilight said as she sheathed the rapier. The warlock, it seemed, was successfully cowed.

As Gargan, Slip, and Davoren made the final preparations to move, Liet caught Twilight's arm. "Is this wise?" he asked. "I don't think—"

She touched his face with her fingers and traced down his stubbly cheek. "Nothing I do is wise," she said. She touched her lips against his. "Only prudent."

Then she kissed him, lightly at first, then harder, pressing her body against his. Not enough to warrant an outcry from the others, who stared.

Her farewell stunned Liet, remembering all the times Twilight had sent him from her side, so as to keep their affair a secret. Had she lost her mind? What was—

"Hmm," Twilight murmured. She nuzzled at his chin.

"Be wary," said Liet.

"I always am," said Twilight whimsically. With that, she was gone, vanishing into the shadows of the yawning east doorway.

"She . . . kissed you," Slip said, with awe, confusion, and something like jealousy. Liet wasn't sure who Slip was jealous over.

"For luck," said Liet. "Now, let's be going."

Stupid, stupid, stupid wench. Twilight berated herself as she made her way down the other path. *Are you falling in love, or are you falling apart?*

Both, she guessed.

She knew she shouldn't have kissed him. But she'd been mad, right—that's what they'd think, right?

Reality intruded, and Twilight was thankful for it.

Thirteen fiendish lizards, brandishing sickle blades and whips, crouched hissing and slavering in alcoves along a tight, winding corridor. They waited for a foolish creature to wander down that hall, the better to pounce and devour.

Crouching in the shadows around the corner from all that black, scaly flesh, Twilight considered stepping out to say well met. She decided against it, however, tending to avoid death and dismemberment on her part whenever possible.

So there *is* an ambush this way, she thought. And the same fiendish lizards.

As she let the implications bounce around in the back of her mind, Twilight judged the length of the corridor. Two dagger-casts. Perfect.

Twilight did not bother to leave her hiding place in the shadows. She flowed into them, dancing through the darkness. Silently, she emerged at the far end of the corridor with none the wiser. Once again, she thanked Neveren Darkdance. The dastard had given her a great gift, even if he *had* ruined her.

Having expended much of her power for the day—she could not dance that distance again—it dimly occurred to her that she should consider how she would get back, but that was a matter for another time.

Ignoring the fiendish lizards at her back, Twilight strolled to the open archway.

This area did not suffer from the same filth and defacement that the rest of the complex evidenced. These lizards had not been here long, though how they could get past a locked door, Twilight did not know. She shuddered to think of what she might be facing, if it could somehow teleport its minions into position. Perhaps there was something to this "Mad Sharn" business after all, in which case Twilight was in trouble deeper than her pointy ears.

A glyph ran the archway's length, and Twilight wished, not for the first time, that she had Asson beside her. The old man's tranquility and magic would have been useful, as would his understanding of Netherese.

She tapped the earring she wore. If the words were spoken, she would understand them. Slip's detection spell had set off the other warding, but Twilight did not . . .

Then an idea struck her.

She hated calling on her other powers, but sometimes blind curiosity got in the way of good grudges. Mouthing his name, she invoked a prayer he had taught her. It was not for detecting magic—thanks to Erevan's kiss, she saw mystic emanations as she wished—but rather a spell for locating a missing item. In this case, she chose the archway. Though she knew exactly where it was, casting any spell upon it should . . .

Sure enough, a sibilant voice, speaking in an odd tongue, came to her ears, and she understood every word.

"The taint of evil kept without, the power safe within," the ward said.

"Ah," said Twilight. "Helpful."

Just then, a horde burst into the chamber, screams of rage on their lips.

No choice, Twilight decided, and threw herself through the archway, hoping by Beshaba's bodice that her instincts told her true.

Sure enough, nothing happened to her, but such was not the case for a few unfortunate lizards.

Green and blue fire arced from the runes along the archway, tearing into fiendish lizards, searing flesh apart and blackening bones. The creatures put up pitiful wails, cut short by the furious wards that cut them to pieces with flame. The wards killed six before the remaining seven fiendish lizards panicked and trampled over one another in their haste to get away.

Twilight would have stood laughing but for the unpleasant odor of the destroyed lizards lying in a heap at her feet. Then she turned and strode though another archway, this one plain, and stopped dead, staring.

"Sand," she cursed.

As Twilight had promised, the four found no ambush awaiting them through the south door. This tunnel was of different design than the twisting, turning sewers. Rather, it was straight, two paces wide and thirty hands high, and rose gradually. Gargan led the way, with Liet and Davoren trailing at a few paces, and Slip taking the rear.

Liet wasn't sure he trusted the halfling entirely—certainly not enough to put her at his back—but keeping close to Davoren was sure, ironically, to keep him safe. No one watched his skin like the warlock.

Liet wondered when he had become so cold and calculating. When had he shed his youthful mentality, his naiveté? When had he ceased to trust others, and started thinking in matters of practicality, questioning the motives of all who surrounded him?

When had he become just like Twilight?

The day you broke rule four, he told himself with an inward sigh.

The corridor rose for forty paces before terminating in a space for a lifting mechanism, like the one they had used to escape the prison level of this labyrinth. The platform was down on the floor, and it would rise if someone stepped upon it—if the magic of the place yet operated.

The platform did not even tremble as they stood upon it, and Gargan boosted each of the others, one by one, before pulling himself up. The four moved down a tunnel toward a set of steps, and Gargan's long strides took him swiftly to the front rank. Davoren watched approvingly, but Liet suspected it was more in quiet consideration of what the goliath could do to Davoren's foes—his former allies—suitably armed and charmed. In all ways, the two seemed to be opposites.

Opposites . . . the thought bounced about in Liet's mind, reflecting off walls of indecision and longing. He and Twilight were so opposite one another, yet so close.

He no longer tried to tell himself that Twilight meant nothing to him. The first night they spent together had changed that, but the feeling grew more intense as time passed. He dared not mention it, for Twilight would certainly . . .

Gargan hissed a warning note, and Liet looked up.

They had ascended the stairs into open air, but there was no breeze in the darkness. Liet was suddenly aware that he stood upon something much like grass, though the sun was not to be seen. Great forms loomed out of the darkness, and Liet had to draw his sword and gasp before he realized they weren't moving.

All around them, the torchlight revealed huge bulks that looked, oddly, like flowers and vines of reds, oranges, and purples. Luminescence came from fungi on the walls, such as they had seen in the sewers below, and some plants shed light in many subdued colors. They felt as though they had come into some sage's arboretum.

Some plants were normal, most were strange and twisted, but all were gigantic. Something like a daisy was taller than Liet, and Slip had to brush away petals of violets the size of her face. Mountainous moonflowers and firedragons the size of their namesakes swelled around them. Liet had to stomp his way out of the clutches of a rose vine with thorns like daggers. Most of the plants he could hardly recognize—turgid buds and whorls coming out of green stalks, knobby trees like heaps of flatcakes that wove from side to side with budding pink flowers up every inch.

How they grew in perfect darkness was beyond Liet.

"What is this place?" Liet asked. He started away from his echoing voice.

"We have arrived," Davoren said. He held the scepter up and intoned deep, powerful words. A bolt of lightning arced from his hand, high into the air. It struck something like a steel rod and sizzled along it. In half a heartbeat, the bolt exploded out, illuminating the vast cavern in which the four found themselves. The great rod flickered, hissing at intervals like an unhappy dragon.

And occupying that cavern with them was a ruined, overgrown city.

"Negarath," Davoren said with a glint in his evil eyes.

If they had thought the architecture of the sewers odd, nothing could have prepared them for what lay before them.

Negarath was a city of madness.

Buildings spread wider as they reached upward, almost as though built upside down. All around them, sprouting from the sides of buildings, coming up from the streets, were the strange flowers, some growing large enough to dwarf Gargan. There was not a single perpendicular edge in the place; all was a mixture of curves, waves, and obtuse or acute angles. Windows hung upside down and horizontally, as though the interiors of the buildings did not match the exteriors.

Most of the doors to the varying buildings were of odd shapes—circular, triangular, hexagonal, octagonal—anything but rectangular. Only one building seemed even remotely normal—a central tower that narrowed toward the middle, like a pyramid, but widened again as it rose toward the cavern ceiling. There, the tower hooked and curled, spiraling under itself. It looked as though they could stand atop it.

"The designers of this place must have been madmen," said Davoren.

"Or geniuses." The others stared, and Liet laughed nervously. "Art—heh."

Gargan shook his head.

Slip beamed. "Magnificent," she said.

The others looked at her this time.

"Well, it *is*," she asserted with her hands on her hips.

The section of city in which they stood was markedly clear and empty, but such was not the case a few streets away. They saw something like a giant mound of clay, stretching from floor to ceiling—a calcified, golden-red web.

"What's that, I wonder?" Slip said.

The mass looked like red amber, with an eerie translucence. It glowed crimson from the inside, as though from a beating heart. Gold veins ran through it, like tunnels bored by a worm. The red substance ran over the buildings like glass, or perhaps ice that had frozen around them. It reached to the ceiling, holding fully half the city prisoner.

Then they became aware of a sound—a distinct humming, almost like buzzing, as though the air shuddered and crackled in expectation of a storm.

"Rain?" Slip asked.

"Magic?" Liet asked.

Gargan shook his head. He pointed.

Half a dozen black and yellow creatures swarmed out of holes in the mass of red amber and buzzed toward them. Flickering light twinkled off a hundred facets in their eyes, and gossamer wings zipped through the air. They might have been bees, if bees grew to the height of men and sported arms carrying spears, but these were abeil.

"Down!" Liet cried. A better command might have been "scatter," "ware," or even "run!" But he said the first thing that came to mind.

Liet did not know why he took one of the iron bars from his pack and placed it between himself and the diving creatures. Nor did he understand how he knew to press the end of the rod. Instinct, perhaps—or that odd power Twilight had spoken of. The rod gave a little hum but did nothing else.

A lightning bolt streaked into the sky and tore the wings from one of the bees, which plummeted to the street with a buzzing screech. Hefting his crackling scepter, Davoren scoffed. "Fear not. I shall defend you." He waved his hand and fire spread through the air.

Liet cursed himself. What had he been hoping for? A blast of fire, a protective shield? A flare of self-loathing came then, and he fought it back. Fury at himself, at Davoren. But he couldn't get angry—not now. Seeing the bees fly around the fire, Liet pulled up the rod and prepared to retreat.

Rather, he tried to retrieve the rod, for it could not be moved. No matter how much he strained, the rod floated in place. The bees were coming, so he abandoned it.

A bee-thing crashed face first into the immobile rod and crumpled around it, there to hang, broken. The rod did not twitch, as though a mountain held it still.

A hissing sound reached Liet's ears then. Now what?

A bouncing motion caught his eye—it was Slip, waving at him and whispering his name from an open, crescent-shaped doorway. Above it floated the flickering image of a hammer emblazoned with seven stars. The seven stars of Mystra?

Whatever the failing image betokened, Gargan was ducking in and Davoren was tearing through the underbrush toward the door, cursing the incoming bees. Then Gargan yanked Slip off her feet and slammed the door.

Bees swarmed past their crushed, hanging comrade, throwing themselves against the crescent-shaped door and oddly curved windows in a killing fury. In reply, Davoren invoked his powers, and a forest of black tendrils sprouted from the building, flailing. The bees swarmed away before he could conjure fire.

Liet and Davoren reached the door at the same moment. It popped open and the men tumbled in past Gargan. The goliath slammed it once again and they collapsed in the darkness.

The four huddled behind the door, Gargan holding it shut. Liet sat near the shivering Slip and looked around. The room in which they found themselves could have been a smithy of some sort. Hammers and chisels and many things he couldn't recognize lay scattered and shattered about them. In the center was something that looked like an anvil, or perhaps an altar—a simple block of jet black stone. Other doors were visible, all shaped like crescents, stars, and inverted triangles. In the center of the room was a black disk, like the trapdoor they had come through.

"I wonder if she sent us here intentionally," the warlock said.

He looked at Liet, panting heavily. "Come—what would your mistress say if she saw you cowering?"

Liet wanted to retort, "She would praise me for having the sense to stay alive under a surprise attack, but by all means, go play if you want. Try not to get yourself killed too messily," like Twilight would have. As it was, he said, "My mistress?"

Then a hissing sound came from below, as of metal grinding against metal. The inert disk gave a shudder and sank. They backed away and hefted weapons. When the disk returned, standing upon it was a familiar, dark-haired elf.

"You called?" she asked, wearily.

" 'Light!" said Liet, moving forward.

Twilight stopped him with a raised hand. Something had unnerved her, clearly.

"What is it?" demanded the warlock. "More foes, coming from below?" He spat.

"What did you find?" Liet asked.

Twilight shut her eyes. "A mythallar," she said.

Davoren scoffed. "And so? This is a Netherese city, and such was the magic of the empire of magic—"

Twilight shook her head. "It isn't that simple," she said. She gestured to the lifting disk that had just carried her up. "The mythallar I found—it's still active."

CHAPTER EIGHTEEN

S itting in a corner of what Liet had taken to calling the Forge
of the Seven Stars, Twilight blew out a long, troubled sigh.
Liet had called this a smithy, though there was no pit for fire or
water. Neither of these oversights surprised Twilight. If she *had*
seen them—meaning the owner hadn't used magic—that would
have surprised her.

Netheril.

That they were inside one of the fallen cities of that mighty
age was something Twilight could accept. That the city's
mythallar still functioned, however—at least partly—unnerved
her deeply.

The others hadn't seen the significance until Twilight
explained it. Aside from its own essence, she had sensed three
types of magic emanating from the mythallar—conjuration,
enchantment, and transmutation—which must reflect dweo-
mers that it maintained. That was its purpose, after all, to
maintain the function of magical devices—the question in this
case was what *sort* of devices?

Somehow, the mythallar maintained life in this cave, but
would that continue? Would Twilight and the others find the
limit of the mythallar's range, where the air would simply disappear and they would perish? Or, worse—would the mythallar
finally expire, and whatever life-supporting spells it maintained

vanish in an instant, killing them no matter where they were in the city?

These considerations fueled Twilight's desire to find a way out, and soon.

The bee-creatures Liet described had not reappeared, but Twilight had seen black forms moving in that strange amber substance. Was it a hive of some kind? That might explain the flowers. A veritable madman's garden bloomed outside, and in here as well. Moss and vines crept through cracks and empty windows.

Nature has conquered this city, Twilight thought.

She looked around at her companions. Davoren lounged against the wall, seeming to sleep but really watching them all. In contrast, Liet snored against the opposite wall. Gargan sat sharpening the band's blades—excepting Twilight's rapier and the stiletto she'd taken from Davoren.

Twilight saw the halfling sitting still—gathering her focus for healing, likely—her face nothing but tranquility. The group was hungry—they had eaten little since Taslin's death a day and a half before, rationing out the remaining food—but calm.

Curious. Even in such tense, dark circumstances, the little one could know peace.

"Slip," said Twilight. The halfling's ears perked up and her eyes opened. The shadowdancer slid to the floor beside her. The others weren't watching. "Tell me of yourself."

"I'm hungry," she said. "And thirsty. It's been near a tenday without food, aye?"

Twilight resisted the urge to chew on her lip. Water was worse—they had almost exhausted the last of the waterskins filled with Taslin's conjured water.

"No," Twilight said. "I mean of your life—where you come from."

Slip grinned. " 'Tisn't a riveting tale," she said. "Life in Crimel would bore woodpeckers to slumber faster than a Candlekeep sage's lecture on the life of the meadow cricket—even if there were crickets provided."

Twilight was not to be parried so easily. "Why did you leave?"

Slip shrugged. "The usual reasons—adventure, the open road, see the Realms, meet new faces, and . . ." She trailed off and her face went dark. "Reeman."

"Your sometime mate."

"A rascal if ever there *was* one!" Slip rolled her eyes. "He did say the nicest things, and he was ever so convincing." Her eyes closed, and a look came over her Twilight recognized only too well.

There was much to this story the halfling would not tell, and Twilight found no fault in the omitting. We all have our secrets, she thought.

"He was a kind lad, my Reeman—all of us loved him. Could talk a dwarf out of his beard or a dragon out of its hoard, then the both of them into leg wrestling. Which the dragon would win, of course." She smiled. "He had a trustworthy face, you understand."

"Perfectly." Twilight knew *exactly* what she meant, and it occurred to her that Slip possessed such a visage herself.

"And that's where the troubles began."

Slip sat silently for a moment, and Twilight did not press her.

"One night, Reeman convinced me to play at hiding with him, as a prank on my da—to get all of Crimel stirred up. I'd hide in the woods, and he'd tell everyone a mouther got me." She squinted. "You know what—"

"Yes," said Twilight. She knew the distorted abominations, with their four gangly limbs and tusks, by description if not by sight.

"Anyway," Slip said. "When everyone was gone looking, Reeman helped himself to all the gold at the temples and the warden's office, and set fire—accidentally, he said—to a few houses . . . while younglings were inside."

Twilight felt a chill creep through her body even as Slip hugged her arms tight about her own breast. This had stopped being an innocent tale.

"March wardens followed Reeman, and he came to me for help. I watched as h-he killed—*murdered!*—two of them with his magic, and tried to run. When he tried to take me too, I—I . . ." She looked down at her hand, as though a bloody knife had just appeared that only she could see.

Then she looked up at Twilight. "I had to do it, you see? 'Twas the—the right thing, and they cast me out for it!"

After a long moment, Twilight put out her arms.

Slip hesitated a few breaths, her lip trembling. Then her eyes softened with sudden tears, and she snuggled into Twilight's embrace. "Oh, 'Light!" she cried, as that of a child to a mother. "What else could I *do?* He killed two of my cousins afore my eyes and younglings besides!" Great sobs wracked her body.

Twilight closed her eyes in helpless sympathy and held Slip as she cried. She stroked the halfling's filthy hair—they were all filthy. Filthy, cold, tired, and heartsick.

How cruel she had been to suspect Slip—Billfora, Twilight remembered, for the story had allowed her to see the true halfling—how heartless. She knew all too well how easily a smile could conceal sadness, and how well tragedy could hide behind innocence.

Finally the tears stopped, and Slip breathed easier. Twilight made no move to release her.

"I was wed, too, once," she said, letting the words slide out. "Neveren. He—"

"Lilten, you mean?"

The world froze. Twilight blinked. "What?"

Slip blinked up at her. "What?"

There was a pause. Twilight looked at her very carefully. Ideas shot wildly through her mind—fears, anger, betrayal.

"Slip," she said slowly. "I've something important to do, and I need your help."

"Of course!" Slip said. "Anything, 'Light! You're my greatest friend!"

Twilight let that pass. "Can your magic recognize lies?"

"Aye. I know that spell! I can hear lies when others tell them." So it was magic, and nothing else. "How can I help?"

Twilight nodded, and explained. Slip listened. In conclusion, Twilight pointed to a back room, which must have been some kind of storage for tools. "Go into yon chamber and wait. I shall join you shortly." She brushed the back of her hand along Slip's cheek. "And you need not cry—all shall be well."

The halfling wiped the tears away and beamed at her as only a comforted daughter could. Then she scurried into the side chamber and shut the door behind her.

Twilight blew out a long sigh and rose. So that was it.

She touched the sapphire pendant. Was its magic fading?

"I need everyone else to wait here," she said as she dusted herself off. She gestured to the side room. "Davoren—come with me."

"What is it?" the warlock asked.

<hr>

Ten heartbeats later, Slip guarded the door and Twilight faced the mage from the other side of the room, arms crossed. Davoren had answered his own question.

"An outrage!" His hands gripped the back of a chair and they dripped with flame. The half-circles that formed the seat glowed red. "How dare you? I ought to . . ."

"Have peace, demon-spawn," Twilight said. "Just answer the question."

The warlock sneered at her and twisted his lip. He shoved aside the curious chair—all curves, no angles, like all this Netherese city. "I have suffered your humiliations long enough. You and your sniveling little rat—"

"That sniveling little rat can hear the truth in your words," said Twilight. "So if you just answer the question, we'll know of your innocence and you can be on your way, back to pray to your devil-god with a hand in—"

Slip blushed a fiery red and stared at her, horror-struck, so Twilight stopped. "Just answer," she repeated. "Are you a spy, or otherwise in league with our enemy, watching our movements so as to catch us in our weakness, or lay ambushes in our path?"

Davoren glared at her, and his eyes promised death. "Nay, I am no spy."

"He speaks true," Slip said behind Twilight.

Davoren sniffed. "Satisfied? I do not need trickery to slay *you, filliken*."

"Not there, however," the halfling said with a shrug.

The warlock gaped at her and his lips curled into a snarl. "How dare—?"

"Ah," Twilight said. Betrayal's dusky point tapped at Davoren's groin. "Careful. You had better not say something you might regret." She winked at him. "Now. Pass through yon portal." She waved at a rear door with Betrayal. "And wait outside."

" 'Wait outside'? That's meant to be safe?" he asked. "Or do you wish merely to kill me with those foul insect-men?"

"That's why I called you first. You are, after all, the most powerful."

The warlock hesitated for a moment before grumbling an agreement. He spat at the shadowdancer's feet, then stomped off, cursing to himself in Infernal.

Slip grinned at Twilight. "I was halfway hoping he would be the one," the halfling said. "I would've liked to see that fight."

"Yes," Twilight agreed, and from Slip's expression, she knew it was not a lie.

———◆◆◆———

Gargan was next, pacing in with his arms crossed, and Twilight shifted uneasily. The goliath wore the great black sword on his back—a weapon he could wield in one hand—but he could easily powder Twilight's skull and shatter Slip's delicate bones with just those fists. She did not grip Betrayal's hilt, but her fingers were not far from it.

"I come," the goliath said in the Common tongue. He looked to Twilight and spoke in his own gruff language, which she understood by virtue of Taslin's earring. *"Why have you brought me?"*

"I have questions," she replied in Common, the only way to be understood.

"I have answers."

"Let us see if they fit."

There was a breath's pause as he contemplated what that might mean. Then he nodded. "Blades in scabbards," the goliath agreed in Common.

That would have to do. "Are you Gargan Kaugathal, called the Dispossessed?"

"So I am called." Slip frowned at his words—she didn't understand them.

Twilight tensed. "In the trade tongue," she said. "Are you our enemy?"

The goliath did not seem surprised. "No," he said.

A quick glance at Slip told her it was true. "Are you a spy, or otherwise in league with our foe?" Gargan shook his head, but Twilight cut him short. "You must speak it."

He did, and Slip nodded.

"You may go." Twilight pointed. "And take my thanks."

The goliath nodded once, then walked away to join Davoren in the alley behind the smithy. The shadowdancer blew out a long sigh.

"One left," the halfling said.

"Yes," Twilight said, shivering. "One left."

Twilight held her breath as Liet came in. She had been dreading this, but she knew it had to be done. Of course she knew Liet was innocent, but she had to ask. It had to look convincing.

The youth gave her that familiar smile, as much to reassure Twilight as himself.

"A private audience." He eyed both Slip and Twilight. "Can I be of aid, lovelies?"

His comfortable manner—increasingly suave, she noted, and fancied she had something to do with that—put her at ease, but Twilight hesitated to show it. Her investment was likely common knowledge by now—their kiss had made that obvious—but it would not do to show favoritism.

"Just questions," she finally said.

"Pity," Liet said. He sat down, none too comfortable on the strange chair. It had nearly cooled since Davoren had heated the metal, for which Twilight was glad. A seat made answering thinly concealed accusations much easier.

"Are you Liet Sagrin, son of Harrowdale, and sometime swordsman?"

"And are you Fox-at-Twilight, daughter of mystery, and sometime thief?"

"This is no game," Twilight said. "You must answer my questions. Billfora has cast a spell that detects lies, and so she must hear your truths—and falsehoods."

Liet's eyes widened and his mouth trembled, pained. "You doubt m—" he paused, then finished the question another way. "You doubt your own ears?"

"Let us simply say," Twilight replied, "that I need a second opinion."

Liet's shoulders slumped. He was defeated. "Very well. Ask."

"Are you a loyal member of our band?" She raised a hand to cut off his objection. "Loyal to our well-being, and to the success of our venture."

"As best I'm able." She frowned. "Aye. I serve."

"But serve who, Liet?" She took a step toward him.

"But surely I serve you, Twilight," said Liet, rising toward her, "if I'm loyal to our well-being and the success of this venture of ours."

"Unless you think me mad or wrong." She stepped up to him.

"Unless that." He faltered for a heartbeat. "Though I don't think either."

They stared at each other, eyes not a pace apart. Theirs was a battle of will, rather than of words or swords. The world fell silent around them and they existed alone.

"Ahem?"

Twilight tore her eyes from Liet and looked at Slip. The halfling fidgeted.

"I . . ." Twilight trailed off. Asking the question should have been a simple matter, and yet it was not.

"Ask, Twilight," Liet said, and her eyes snapped back to him. He caught up her hand, and she could feel the warmth pass into her like a spark of power. The youth brought her fingers up to his lips. His next words were a whisper. "I'm not afraid."

Twilight could not say the same.

"Very well," she said. "Are you, Liet Sagrin, a spy?"

"Nay." He was telling the truth, as Slip confirmed with a nod. Twilight looked back, locking Liet's mismatched eyes—one blue, one green—with her own stare. She wondered what color her eyes seemed. They changed like her face—like herself.

"Are you in league with our enemy?"

"Davoren? Nay."

"The force that is attempting to slay us," Twilight said. "That Mad Sharn, perhaps, or whatever dark lord is responsible for the deaths of our friends—the murderers of Asson and Taslin . . . whoever our enemy is. Are you a servant of our foe?"

Liet's eyes searched her own. "Nay," he said.

Not a lie. Did she detect the hint of a smile? Just her imagination.

"Are *you* our enemy?" Twilight asked, inspiration striking. "Have you deceived us all this time, hiding your true identity in an effort to slay us and drive us mad?"

Liet stared, perfectly calm. "I suppose . . ." He shrugged. "Aye."

Twilight's eyes widened. His voice had not wavered; his heart had not palpitated. All the subconscious signs were absent. Her senses had not found any falsehood. Liet stared at her with absolute sincerity and, she thought, contempt.

"Lady Doom!" Twilight leaped back and snapping out Betrayal. How . . .?

Liet's mismatched eyes blazed, and she knew it was true.

"Oh!" Slip screamed. "Oh, gods! 'Twas a lie!"

Twilight flicked her eyes to the halfling, who was panting, terrified. Liet grinned.

"What?" Twilight asked.

" 'Twas a lie, of course." He gave an awkward, insufferable smile. "I've been taking your lessons."

"Slip?"

The little woman stared at her intently. "I swear, by all the gods I know, that he tells a lie," she said. "I mean, that's the truth—that 'tis a lie . . . I mean . . . he . . ."

"No." Twilight let out a sigh and turned back.

" 'Light—" the Dalesman started, but her slap cut him off.

"You think this is a game, boy?" she snarled. "Get out of my sight."

"But—" Liet started. He stopped when Twilight half-drew Betrayal and gave him a look no yet-living foe had ever seen on her delicate features. Liet stiffened and suppressed a sound that was much like a strangled cough. The mirth had gone out of his eyes, replaced by sheer horror. "Oh, 'Light, I'm so—"

"I won't say it again," Twilight said, her voice flat.

The young swordsman's face went ashen and his eyes gleamed with tears. "Sorry!" he cried, and fled.

A long while passed, the silence filled with heavy, angry breathing. Twilight was hardly aware of Slip's searching gaze, her frightened features.

All she could see were those horrible eyes, Liet's eyes, laughing at her—mocking her hard-trained abilities, her confidence to tell truth from falsehood by ear. Laughing . . . always laughing . . . what was he doing, trying to drive her mad?

From behind her, Slip shifted nervously—loud enough for Twilight to hear. "Ah," she said. "Are—are you well?"

"Oh, indeed." Twilight closed her eyes and forced an easy smile onto her pale face. "Friend." She turned and favored the halfling with her most dazzling grin. "How sure are you that none of them is a spy?"

Slip brightened considerably, smiling back as though nothing were the matter. "Absolutely certain," she replied. "Why?"

CHAPTER NINETEEN

When the screech came from the Forge, Liet bolted up from where he had slumped, his hands on his knees, against the wall of the alley. Gargan similarly unfolded himself from the shadows and laid his hand on his sword. Even Davoren paused where he had been pacing.

The rear door flew open and Slip staggered out. The halfling immediately whirled and drew her little dagger, but a dusky blade sent it whirling from her hand with a deft flick. The gray-white point of Betrayal hissed under Slip's chin.

"Help me!" Slip cried. "She's gone *mad!*"

"What's going on?" Liet asked, hand going to his sword.

"Back," was all Twilight said, but the fire in her pale eyes—almost red in the ruby light of Davoren's pulsing energies—told him much more.

"Do you not see?" The warlock sneered. "She has eliminated the options—me, you, the giant—and has but one left. The only one who could have lied—the half-witch." Darkness passed over his eyes and his arms pulsed with flame.

Slip, with Twilight distracted, stammered out the words to a spell, but Davoren chanted along with her, invoking harsh and vile names and deeds better spoken of in a tongue of pure evil. The halfling's magic faltered, defeated by the warlock's vora-cious powers, and tears ran down her cheeks. Twilight dealt Slip a savage kick to the stomach, stifling further magic. She pulled Betrayal back, lining it up with the little one's back.

Hissing black steel knocked it aside when she thrust. Gargan was there, sword drawn, and he and the elf locked blades and stares, waging a private battle. Their swords sparked against each other, bubbling acid hissing on the hot steel. The light flickering above her, like a hissing sun, plunged her face into light and shadow.

Liet shivered. From their stares, it was clear a life would be lost should it come to blows, and knowing Gargan's strength, it would likely be hers. The goliath didn't try to break her parry, only hold her sword back. If he attacked, maybe she could dodge, then riposte, perhaps, and . . .

What was he thinking? Had the world gone mad?

"Please!" Slip moaned. "Don't let this happen! Please!"

"Silence, traitor," hissed Twilight without taking her eyes off Gargan.

"Come, Twilight," said Davoren. As he spoke, he inched his way toward Slip, lying huddled and helpless. "Together we can slay them. We no longer need their aid."

The elf should have retorted but she did not, causing Liet to gape. Was she *considering* it?

Liet looked at Davoren. Lightning crackled around the warlock's scepter and flames licked his hands. Liet realized that if he did nothing, one of his friends would die.

And with that realization, something snapped inside him.

All the times he had watched Twilight confront the warlock fearlessly, all the wry smiles, throwing herself over Slip, all the memories of Twilight's courage came back to him in a single white-hot moment of bravery, and swelled into something inside that Liet had never imagined.

"No," he commanded. He stepped in Davoren's way.

All other sound in the cavern withered into silence. Twilight stared at him.

The warlock snickered, but Liet stayed firm. "I won't say it again."

"I see." Davoren slit his eyes. "The boy thinks he's pretty

enough and wily enough to split our fearsome leader, so that makes him worthwhile, eh? Allow me to explain how that isn't—"

"Enough talk," said Liet. He drew his battered, chipped sword and pointed it at Davoren's face. "You want to kill us, do you? Then do it now."

"Suddenly he's become brave," Davoren said, irritation in his eyes.

"Only braver than a coward," said Liet.

The warlock's eyes burned at him and his face contorted. Flames licked about fingers curled into talons. Davoren's face promised swift death and—

And went pale. The warlock's eyes widened, he backed away, and his gaze slid from Liet, as though he saw something that genuinely frightened him. He backed away and those red eyes showed real terror, and . . . something else. Pain. Hurt.

Liet felt a tingle in the back of his mind. Was this ability to frighten the warlock, whose unholy power dwarfed Liet's mediocre swordsmanship, a manifestation of that potential Twilight saw in him? Did he have a sorcerer's potential? Was he a hero?

He realized it didn't matter. All that mattered was that he had stood between Davoren and Slip, and the warlock backed down. Now he posed no threat to . . .

"Twilight!" Liet said suddenly. She spun where she stood, facing both halfling and goliath with sword drawn, murderous fury in her eyes. "Don't do this! Slip's innocent! We all are! There's no spy! You're being ridiculous!"

"Lies," Twilight growled. "You all passed the test. She's the only one who could have escaped—the only one whose word wasn't tested. She's a liar and a traitor! She's the only one it could be! The only *one!*"

No, Twilight, she's not, Liet thought suddenly. She's the only one except—

"Except yourself, *filliken,*" Davoren said. Liet glared and the warlock receded as before, but he kept a hand on the scepter at his waist.

A trifle unnerved but more worried for Twilight, Liet turned back only to see that the damage had been done. Twilight had gone paler than usual and her lip trembled, fighting against a cruel thought—a grave doubt. Liet felt his heart clench in his chest, torn between love and not a little fear that maybe, just maybe, the warlock was right.

Perhaps she saw it in Liet's eyes, or perhaps she thought the same. Her shoulders slumped and all emotion vanished from her face. She appraised Liet more as a dull blade than a companion, or even a living thing, and his stomach knotted.

"Very well," she said slowly. "The halfling may indeed be innocent, but—"

"Thank you, Mistress!" Slip threw herself down and kissed Twilight's ragged boots. "Thank—"

Twilight shoved the halfling away with a foot, eyeing her. "But I won't trust her."

"I'll watch her," Liet volunteered.

"No." Twilight shook her head.

"I," Gargan rumbled, drawing gazes from the other four. "I watch."

The silence lasted a long breath before Twilight finally nodded. "Very well," she said. "But you will watch her close, blade to hand."

"Blade to hand," Gargan repeated.

She turned away, casting Liet an angry glare, and slipped into the smithy. That gaze both thanked and warned him.

Unable to stand it, he looked away and thought he saw another of those black hands—with the eye in its palm—reaching out of a wall opposite the smithy. When he looked hard, it was gone.

Liet suppressed a chill.

———◆━━◆◆◆◆━━◆———

The length of a candle later, Twilight sat naked, alone, and crying.

They had moved from the Forge into a larger complex, nearer the center of the city. With Twilight's talents at stealth leading them, they had evaded the bees who came to investigate the shouts. This new building—a mansion, by comparison—might well have belonged to Nega himself, the high arcanist. Twilight didn't really care. It may as well have been hers now. Its wards and defenses had failed (clearly not the mythallar's priorities) and possession of the manse, as in all things, passed to the strong and alive.

Twilight had found an ancient bedchamber for herself—complete with an eerie floating bed of withered velvet, powered by the mythallar. She had stripped off her worn, ochre-stained garments, feeling filthy in them, and flung herself on the blankets, daring them to crack and disintegrate. They had not, and there she remained.

Though the room was far from the others, she did not mind. In fact, it suited her, for here she could scream and curse in privacy, without any of them thinking her mad.

Not that she did so. The day was more one for weeping than for expressions of fury.

Her tears had formed a damp spot on the bed cover nearly the size of a buckler when the door opened of its own accord—magic, of course. She wondered what manner of monster had come to slay her. Fiendish lizards, perhaps, or one of the bees. Maybe even the troll, though she imagined she would have smelled Tlork's approach. Perhaps even whatever beast had attacked her in the night, unless that had been a nightmare. She didn't know—she didn't know anything anymore.

" 'Light?" came a soft, hurt voice.

A sigh. It was far worse than any of the possibilities she had considered.

"Why do you frown, love?" Liet stepped forward, undeterred by her discontent—yet another aspect of him she loved and loathed. "It makes you too pretty."

She wouldn't take the bait. Twilight just looked away. He stepped closer, seating himself on the edge of the bed. She let him disrobe, stripping to his smallclothes, and his shirt, of course. He reached to embrace her.

"Surely this incident has told you—"

Twilight shoved him and he tumbled out of the free-floating

bed. Liet landed on his bottom with an unceremonious thump. He looked so adorable—and pounceable—but she ignored that observation.

"There are three possibilities," said Twilight, as though nothing out of the ordinary had occurred. "One, that it is Slip."

"That's out," said Liet. He rose, winced, and dusted himself off. The stone must have been cold under his bare feet. Twilight couldn't say she objected to the view, and for that reason she cursed him again.

"Two," she continued. "One among us can defeat her spell and my sense."

"Certainly not," Liet said. "No one can tell lies from truths better than you, love."

Twilight didn't bother to correct him. "And the third . . ."

"That there *is* no spy," the youth said.

Twilight bit her lip, then her eyes narrowed. "Have I been acting strangely of late?"

Liet gaped. "You can't be serious," he said. His surprise was a lie.

"It could be me," said Twilight. Her voice came out calm, a lie to the turmoil within. "How long was I unconscious without the Shroud? Any of my foes could have done this. I could be acting under magical compulsion—a spell I'm not even—"

Liet caught the shadowdancer by the shoulders and shook her. "Nonsense!"

No one did that to her. *No one.*

She formed a rebuke, but he laid two fingers across her lips. "This has been hard on us all—you especially, as our leader."

With effort, Twilight calmed herself. She'd hurt him without steel. "I have seen you lie once, well enough to deceive me."

Liet grinned. "I've watched you with open eyes and ears." He climbed onto the bed on hands and knees, aiming for her lips. "I lie in your bed. I don't *lie* in it."

"I'm no stranger to enemies lying to me," she said. "In my bed, to my face, or otherwise." Twilight stared at him levelly. "You're just one more."

She watched his face fall, then a surge of anger. "Like your Uncle Nemesis, eh?"

Twilight felt cold. "Fair even, Liet." She dismissed him with a wave.

The youth's face went pale. He realized once again that he had just said the wrong thing. "I—I didn't mean it," he said, suddenly sad. "It just—ah—"

Twilight slapped him. "Aren't you angry? Do you have a spine, or do you just apologize for everything?" She fended off his damnably comforting hands.

"Why don't you scream at me, or beat me if you want—at least *something*. Aren't you going to fight for me?" She shoved him off the bed. "Why don't you *say* something, damn you?"

Liet stared at her, shocked. "I—I'm sorry, I . . ."

Twilight sighed, the fire in her blood dying down. It was pathetic, but it was endearing. A soft smile came over her face, and she hated herself for it.

"I know," she said. "I'm the one who should be sorry." She felt that way, too.

She reached down to help him up, and her fingers scraped his wrist. Liet gave a shiver but didn't pull away. He looked at her, his eyes so sad and longing . . .

She pulled away. "I just—" she said. She was shivering. "I just can't do this."

The youth looked at her for a long time. Then he nodded. "I understand." He gave a knight's bow. "Fair eve, for a fair maid."

"Sweet water," she whispered, "and light laughter."

Then he walked away, and Twilight turned to weep as quietly as she could against the wall. No tears came—her eyes were dry.

After a ten-count, she sprang up and pushed the table against the door. No one would intrude—not companion, nor monster, nor nightmare. Not her mysterious attacker, if it even existed. And if it did after all, well, she could die.

That would be all right. Without Liet.

She knew, somehow, that they were done. Some things are not forgivable.

The youth walked away, but he didn't leave.

Sinking against the door, Liet thought about Twilight's drawn, haggard face. Nearly two days without food, and little water, and that mysterious incident that morning had taken their toll on the lovely elf. But her nerves hurt her far worse than that.

The tragedies of the last days, especially the deaths of Asson and Taslin, had struck them all, but none harder than Twilight, who seemed to take full responsibility. And now that her suspicions about the spy had come out, and she had been proven so wrong in an incident that might have condemned their friend . . .

Liet tried not to think about Twilight going mad before his eyes. He contemplated the others. The way Gargan had stared at Twilight, murderously, still chilled Liet. And Slip—clearly she had been a bit unhinged from the beginning. Ironically, Liet thought the sanest, safest of his companions was the power-hungry, blood-thirsty Davoren.

His hands clenched open and closed. He couldn't get angry, but how could he do anything if he . . .

It only took the thought of her tears, her shoulders shuddering with repressed strain to stir up pain in his heart and push the anger aside.

Liet promised himself he wouldn't give up—not on her.

CHAPTER TWENTY

"Are we sure this'll work?" Slip asked, for perhaps the eightieth time.

" 'Twas your plan," Twilight sighed, for perhaps the eightieth time.

"Oh." Slip considered. "Right."

Twilight could tell by the way Davoren's lips moved that he prayed to Asmodeus, perhaps for strength. Having an archdevil on one's side wasn't all bad, she decided. She wouldn't pray to Erevan. What was the point?

The five had risen after a reasonable amount of sleep. Day was night in the cavern, though Twilight knew it to be several bells after midnight on the surface, from her "gift." They could not have been imprisoned by Tlork long, but it seemed years had passed. Had her entire life until this point been an illusion, and the notions of "bells" and "midnight" just dreams? Perhaps Erevan did not really exist, and she truly was free—if freedom existed in a place like this.

That terrified her.

Twilight suppressed a shiver and shoved the thoughts violently aside. Liet had attempted to convince her of her sanity the previous night, but her own mind seemed Hells-bent on proving him wrong.

"If we climb that tower," Slip repeated, "we should be able to get out, right? I mean, we're underground, and going up takes us aboveground, aye?"

Twilight didn't have the heart to bring up complications like cave ceilings or the inability to fly. "If only it were that simple," she muttered.

"Aye, love?" Liet whispered at her side.

Twilight just shook her head. She wished he wouldn't call her that.

The High Tower—Davoren had assured them it must be the High Arcanist's Tower, if this had truly been a floating enclave, but Twilight was not comfortable so naming it—was free of the hive but not the garden. The Nocturnal Garden, he'd called it, and that name, Twilight did not dispute.

They wandered through a nightmare landscape of twisted, alien stalks and blossoms of myriad, disturbingly vibrant colors. Fumes and spores that could only come in dreams threatened to send them dizzily to the ground, but Gargan seemed able to guide them around the more dangerous plants. When they saw one giant snapping beast indistinguishable from the surrounding ferns lash out with its tentacles to pull a passing bee-creature down its pod-gullet, Twilight was glad she wasn't leading the way.

They made their way slowly, in relative silence, avoiding carnivorous flowers and attention from the bees. Several times, they ducked and hid in the shadows of Negarath to avoid a flight of three or four. Most of the time, the creatures stopped to harvest nectar from the various unearthly plants, and Twilight understood the purpose of the garden. The necter-dependent bees would be hard pressed for a for a food source if anything were to happen to their garden.

Within a bell's time, they entered the overgrown, moss-ridden High Tower.

The rooms had long since faded into a dizzying array of vast, empty affairs that must have held opulence beyond reckoning in the days of Netheril. Tapestries remained, but they had withered to blank sheets of cloth canvas. Most of the rooms and the curled furniture were entirely of some sort of metal—iron or steel—coated with cracked marble, sandstone, or obsidian, while some—the dangerous ones—were but broken glass.

The stairs that led up through the many stories snaked treacherously and madly, inside and outside the building, over and under balconies. A dozen times, steps crumbled underfoot, and a companion leaped to solid ground with a curse. Some sections of stair twisted upside down, unsettlingly, and these the five climbed over awkwardly.

Several times, they had trouble mounting inverted stairs—which had no support but magic—until Slip demonstrated that they needed to climb them upside down. That only increased Twilight's unease.

Having not eaten or had more than a few swallows of water in over two days, they were all weak and growing weaker, even the mighty goliath. As Twilight watched, Davoren fumbled and tripped over broken rock. She saw the lack of strength in his movements—the lessened energy.

"A morning meal would have helped, eh?" she asked once as she held him steady after a step crumbled.

Davoren glared at her. "We could've eaten the halfling, you and I," he said. "But oh, yes—you rejected that opportunity. Mark my words—you will regret it."

Twilight decided then that she wouldn't have minded seeing Davoren topple to his doom, were she not certain the fiend would blast them as he fell. She never got the chance to see if she guessed rightly.

Twilight exercised additional caution in those places where unbroken stairs flared outside—Liet had warned her that the bee-creatures might be scouting. No pursuit made itself apparent, though they had to duck and hide once when a trio of the humanoid insects buzzed by. Twilight noted their spears, helms, and shields distantly.

On the tenth floor of the soaring building, they came to a room without stairs. It was like a grand atrium, though the glass ceiling had long ago shattered. Blue trees with bright orange flowers filled the place, along with thorny bushes that might have been giant roses. Vines the thickness of human arms hung all about. The garden spiraled around a grand circle with a black disk in the center that was probably large enough for eight humans at a time.

"Thank the All-Mother!" Slip exclaimed through her gasps and wheezes. "I've had enough stairs to last me two tendays."

"Our thanks for that," Davoren said, "but we are all, not just you, still far short."

"Huh?" Slip looked at the warlock as though he'd sprouted a second head.

On a whim, Twilight checked to see if he had. He hadn't.

"In case you're oblivious, which isn't surprising," Davoren said, gesturing up through the absent glass ceiling, "we are only halfway to our goal."

It was true. The atrium seemed to be the top level of the High Tower, except for the spires that stood around it like tines on a crown. Several were broken off. The central spire leaned over precariously and curled under itself. There was no way into it, though it looked hollow, from windows in its surface above.

"Easy!" Slip said. "We just fly up there!"

"Asson was the only one who could fly," Twilight reminded her in a soft voice.

"Oh. Ah, well . . . we climb?"

"That far?" Davoren raised an eyebrow. "You *can't* be serious." He mimicked the halfling's accent with considerable skill. Slip bit her lip.

"Options?" Twilight sighed. She'd grown weary of the whole affair, and almost wished some great foe would fall upon them. She'd had too much heartache. Twilight longed for battle.

"This." Liet walked onto the black disk at the center of the garden.

"What?" Davoren hissed.

"This." Liet tapped one of his silvery transmutation rods to the black surface beneath his feet. Magic sizzled, and the black disk shuddered. Immediately, it rose as a disk-shaped platform, powered by Negarath's aging mythallar.

"How did you know to do that?" she asked.

"I saw you," Liet said. "Back in the Forge . . ."

Twilight almost smiled. The boy was becoming useful, even if they had had a falling out. She stepped up and Gargan immediately joined her—whether out of loyalty or because he still watched her suspiciously, she did not care.

"Is it—safe?" Davoren asked.

"Since when is the 'everything is wretched and dismal and filthy' warlock afraid?" Slip asked, mocking his voice perfectly.

Grumbling, Davoren climbed on. "Now what?"

Liet shrugged. "Now, we—" And suddenly they were shooting up, borne aloft on the flying disk. Twilight reached out to catch the startled human back from the edge. Liet had nothing but awe on his face as she held his hand. Then he came to his senses and squeezed her hand. Reassured, Twilight managed to tear her eyes away from him.

The disk bore them in a rising spiral around the garden, then up through what must have been, in ancient times, a hole in the ceiling, and carried them streaking out over the city.

Slip gasped. "Beautiful!" Then, eyes darting, she added, "And strange—very strange."

Twilight could not disagree. While Negarath showed a primal chaos, the purest of eccentricity in the works of madmen, it was difficult to resist the awe.

The disk twisted and turned its way around the spires, offering a silent tour of what must have been a glorious city in its day. And indeed, despite the oddity of its architecture, the ancient towers and statues whose features were worn away still held a sort of demented beauty. Towers curled downward, and stairs sprouted like teeth on the underside of arches. Spires twisted this way and that like needles thrust into huge stone cushions. Great facades with dozens of statues shrouded nothing, or they concealed great buildings in the shapes of flower gardens, blossoming wings of rooms that curved upward. A huge cathedral to the goddess of magic—Mystryl, Twilight finally remembered, as opposed to her successors, the Mystras—rose high into the cavern, its face looking like nothing so much as syrup poured over a mountain of melting cakes.

Past the cathedral, she saw a curious building shaped like a sun, which seemed to be turning, so slowly she almost did not realize it. It radiated some sort of golden light through cracks in the stone, as though it were the sun itself. Then the disk whipped them away, circling the city faster and faster, higher and higher.

"Wonderful!" Slip cried.

"Yes," Twilight agreed. She pulled the halfling closer, away from the edge. "Wonderful until you fall."

Looking upon that city of wonder, Twilight could not help a spot of pity. Surely this view would have been stunning centuries ago, when all the people within had lived, cried and laughed, hated and loved . . .

"Look!" Slip shouted, and Twilight did.

The disk circled about the buildings, making its way back to the leaning central tower—the High Tower. Twilight couldn't suppress a twinge of uncertainty—after all, the mythallar could fail at any moment and send them plunging down.

"Are you controlling this?" she asked Liet.

"I don't—" Liet's brow furrowed. "Maybe. I did *think* about the tower."

"Well, by all means, carry on. Thinking never hurts." The faster the better.

Whether or not the youth controlled the disk, they did indeed float to the tower. Approaching from a new angle, Twilight saw more accurately its fate. It bent against and away from the ceiling of the cavern like a tree growing under a rock, and about thirty hands—about twice Twilight's height—from where it met was a flat space. The disk hovered near and did not move.

Relieved, Twilight took a step onto the curled tower, observed that it was stable, and motioned for the others to join her. Whatever enchantments held up the strange structure must have still operated, for though the tower was bent and curled, it held firm.

Better, they were well within reach of the cavern ceiling.

"Davoren, Gargan," Twilight said. "Find us a way out."

The goliath drew out a great maul he had found in the Netherese smithy. For once, the warlock did not argue. He simply raised his hands and sent burning blast after burning blast into the stone, cracking and chipping the hard earth for Gargan to knock free with the hammer. He looked just as tired of this place as any of the others. Twilight did not like the way he fingered that blasting scepter at his belt, though. What was he planning?

Though the work must have taken nearly a bell's length to accomplish, it felt like a moment, so anxious were they. Davoren's blasts heated the rock, and Gargan hammered the stone again and again. Slowly, bit by bit, they burrowed up, and up, and . . .

There came a great crack, like the splitting of a thousand crossbeams of great wood, and the stone split apart. Twilight looked up.

Then she dived to avoid the blinding avalanche that showered down. It struck her back, burying her as it poured, and poured, and poured. All went dark, and she was buried alive.

Erevan! she shouted in her mind—by reflex, unintentionally. She supposed she should be thankful she hadn't done it aloud, for her mouth would have filled with sand.

There was, of course, no response.

Blast you, wretch, Twilight thought. *You're going to pass up the moment the impossible happens—when I call upon you for aid?*

But there came nothing, not even what she expected: the tiny laughter of a wild elf who found himself entirely too amusing. She really was alone.

Typical, Twilight mused. She knew she was about to die, but that was all she thought. *Typical.*

Then it set in—blindness. She saw neither light nor dark, just white.

She was lost. Alone.

Then Twilight *did* scream—and choked. She thrashed, swimming in sand, dying, abandoned. Out of control—out of her mind. Lost.

A breath later, a hand grasped Twilight's wrist. Liet, she thought.

She latched onto it like a line tossed over the rail of a storm-swept galley.

------◆-◆-◆------

Worriedly, Liet watched Gargan haul Twilight from the pile of yellow-white. She looked up, bright-eyed, but blinked in confusion at the goliath, as though she expected someone else. Then she nodded, and he returned it. Liet felt a little stab of jealousy. Ridiculous, he told himself.

He shook the snowy stuff out of his hair. "Sand?" he asked, perplexed.

The sand that had been trapped above ceased pouring out, leaving an open bubble of air. On the other side of this bubble lay another layer of sand. White grains hissed along its circumference as though along the inside of a great balloon.

Twilight furrowed her brow. " 'Twas what I was about to say."

"I don't understand," Liet said.

She plucked up a loose stone from the tower and hurled it upward with all of her might. It slowed as it rose, slowed, slowed even more, and almost seemed to hover as it reached a particular spot in the air—halfway between the tower and the sand. Then it accelerated up and up, and thumped into the sand as though it had fallen.

"What does this mean?" Liet asked.

Then there came a buzzing. From somewhere behind, Davoren shouted, and crackling lightning filled the air. The bee-men were upon them.

A stinger hissed straight for Liet. Crying out, he warded it off with his hands. Twilight leaped to his aid, her hand going to her rapier, but one of the creatures hit her from the side. Her head struck the stone with a crack, and her body went limp. Unconscious, she toppled, rolled, spun to the edge, and fell from the leaning tower.

" 'Light!" he shouted, agonized.

Then a dozen bodies slammed him down, spears gouging, and Liet screamed.

———◆◈◆———

Gestal watched as she fell, reflecting how like a discarded doll she was. He especially enjoyed the helpless cry filled with mortal pain. But as Twilight fell toward her death, he felt nothing but bemusement and a slight twinge of disappointment.

Then a pair of black hands snaked out of shimmering distortions in the air to catch the falling body, and the eyes narrowed. The foe. The hands dropped her, redirecting her fall, and Gestal saw abeil—the bee-creatures—catch her. How frustrating.

Abeil swarmed the four from every direction, spears thrusting and multiple khopesh blades whistling. In spite of a veritable storm of lightning bolts from the warlock's scepter, the creatures quickly overwhelmed them with blade and sting. A pile grew around the four, but the fools were outnumbered twenty to one.

The stingers penetrated their bodies, and Gestal shivered at the lovely agony even as they fell. How sweet he found those stings. In the meantime, he enjoyed the screams of pain and distress as slowly each went down, inevitably. The gray-faced warlock lasted the longest, with his demon's blood. He killed at least a score, but it would not be enough.

As Gestal watched slaying power pour from that scepter, he grinned. 'Twas only a matter of. . . .

Predictably, the scepter reached its limit, coughed when the warlock attempted to summon more killing bolts, and exploded in his hand, blowing the limb to nothingness. The warlock screamed, clutching his stump, and the abeil swarmed him.

The fiendish skin helped repel some of the stingers' force, but not the poison.

Well.

With the will of the Demon Prince, Gestal ripped into the other's mind and became *himself*. The other vanished into the darkness once more. The abeil hesitated but continued the assault, wondering why this one had risen, and why it looked so different.

Gestal smiled with lips that were his again. Their mistake.

He spoke a single word—a piece of pure chaos, born of the roiling madness that had reigned before the upstart gods had come. It was not an exclamation, nor was it even louder than a whisper. Gestal merely breathed, releasing the magical power of the master, and the spell soared out in every direction.

In a sphere centered on Gestal, scores of abeil simply stopped, their hearts or brains obliterated, and fell from the sky. The less fortunate ones screamed blood and splattered against the stone tower like raindrops, to lie writhing and screaming in buzzes and hisses. A hundred beelike voices rose in protest, and abeil streamed out of half the towers and windows of Negarath.

"Your time comes," Gestal said softly. "Our old foe."

Gestal looked down to where Twilight had vanished into the darkness. Then he was gone, fading into the form of a wraith and vanishing into the stone.

CHAPTER TWENTY-ONE

She had vague memories of golden walls—passing through tunnels sculpted of amber, or perhaps honey. Light pulsed and flickered. Hands held her, dozens of insect hands, and the buzzing as they carried her along ripped through her ears. Was she being taken to her death? To be encased in that comb, to be starved of air?

She didn't care. She'd failed, and all because she hadn't relied on herself.

Her price, for trusting others, was death, and she would pay it.

Liet, she thought. Liet, I'm coming.

Twilight awoke to terror and blackness so thick she could not see through it.

"Liet!" she shrieked. She started up, only to fall back when pain exploded in her head and forced her down. There was no reply.

No reply, that is, but for a pair of emerald eyes that opened and regarded her. The shifting of muscles like stones gave away his identity.

"He is gone," Gargan rumbled in his native tongue. That she could understand him meant she still wore Taslin's earring. *"But we are not alone."*

Twilight's hand shot to her throat. The star sapphire pendant still hung there. She breathed a sigh of relief without thinking.

Slowly, Twilight's eyes adjusted and her darksight returned to her. With it, she could see a few paces in the darkness, but no farther. Gargan, sword still sheathed on his back, knelt over her with concern written across his face. Twilight's eyes darted side to side, but she saw no one else—just cold stone. She sensed magic all over—the darkness itself seemed magical, though she expected it was simply radiation from something powerful, hidden within.

Then the pain came back, and she fell flat again. "The bees?"

"They left us and went back to their hive," the goliath said. *"Whatever holds us now is not their master."*

Gargan knelt beside her and laid his heavy hands on her temples. It struck Twilight as the second time he had touched her (the first, she'd thought he was Liet), and she was surprised at how gently his massive fingers caressed her skin.

Healing power flowed into her like pure water from a mountain stream. Twilight inhaled sharply, stabbed with ecstasy, and looked up at the goliath. Truly, there was more to this creature than met the eye.

She slowly sat, her hand on her head. She found that her clothing and weapons were in place. Even Betrayal was sheathed at her belt. "The others?"

Silence.

She turned to the goliath, who eyed her with dismay. "What is the matter?"

Gargan shook his head. *"You remember nothing,"* he said, to which Twilight slowly nodded. The goliath's face grew grim. *"The abeil attacked, and you fell from the tower. They must have caught you, but we thought you dead for certain."*

"Fate is not so kind," Twilight said.

She accepted his arm and rose to a kneeling position, where she might speak with him closely. Their voices sounded discordantly loud in the dark stillness. She found herself weak, though, and leaned against his strong chest for support and warmth in the chilly darkness. He did not flinch or object.

"What—what of the others?" Gargan's eyes grew cold.

"All fell," he said. *"I was buried under many bodies and watched Davoren, the last standing, cut down."*

"They're . . . they're all dead?" Twilight's pulse pounded in her head.

"I saw none escape."

"I . . . I cannot accept that," Twilight said.

"You need not," came a trio of voices, shouting in unison, seemingly from different corners of the room, "for they are not sssslain."

Twilight was fast to rise, but Gargan was faster. The speed with which he leaped up and drew his black sword made her look as clumsy as a feeble goblin. Light flooded the chamber, revealing four massive statues that stood around them at twenty paces.

One was a solid ruby, carved as a soldier in ancient armor, carrying a mighty axe of the same precious stone. One was clay, a hugely muscular dwarf of thirty hands with a mace. Another was iron—the same creature they had seen slaughtering the lizards what seemed tendays ago—an unstoppable knight with a sword longer than Gargan was tall. The fourth stood even taller and dark as night, shaped as a mighty sorceress with four great arms, each of which held a hooked dagger. Spiderstone, Twilight realized.

The creatures looked at them, then lifted their respective weapons.

"Gargan," she murmured. "Slowly . . . put the sword . . . down . . ."

The goliath seemed to understand, and he lowered his black blade. He put a hand on Twilight's shoulder and stepped in front of her, protectively. It was a gesture she hadn't expected but appreciated nonetheless, as ludicrous as it might have been.

It was a great and spacious hall. Pillars wider than four dwarves standing shoulder to shoulder held up a tall dome whose belly was decorated with mosaics depicting suns and flames. In the center of the room, lying before an altar, a vast slab of black metal rested, looking like nothing so much as a great hatch. A sun with a grim face hung at an angle above the altar. A faded sun mapped the floor, a withered candelabra at the tip of each of its twenty rays. It reminded her of the symbol of Erevan.

A strange golden moss marred the formerly beautiful architecture, and it was only when she looked away that Twilight realized it was moving, pulsing slightly. She fell into magic sense. The walls exploded with light, and she dismissed the sense with a wince.

Something Lilten had told her came back—a bit of knowledge that she shouldn't have, yet did. She'd thought it a lie, but she realized what she was seeing. Her face went pale. "Oh, gods," she murmured, finding breath hard to come by.

"Fox-at-Twilight?" Gargan's hand clutched her shoulder.

"Heavy magic," she breathed. "The walls . . . the walls are covered in it."

Indeed, the golden stuff dripped from the stone, caking it as mud on the soles of a boot. It covered the interior of the cathedral almost completely. No magic could penetrate the barrier that surrounded the cathedral, and only the strongest archmage could even *think* of the Art within its walls.

And, as though to address that point, Twilight saw a silvery window open in the air before a section of wall. A black mass reached through—she recognized it after a breath as a muscular arm—and pushed the gold jelly back into place as though caressing the flesh of a yielding lover. Twilight trembled as she watched the arm snake back through the shimmering window, and another window opened across the room, then another just a few paces from them. Gargan leaped back with a growl, his sword hissing from its scabbard.

Then a portal of light, reflecting the back of the cathedral upside down, appeared before them, and through it came a creature of such power and majesty Twilight found herself forced to her knees. All her tales of seducing archmages and staring down archdevils fled her mind and she was emptied. In short, she was terrified.

For Twilight, who had never had the gift of verse, its form was almost indescribable. The best she could manage was brute analogy. Its body was that of a bulbous tree with three limbs that split into six branches, each a muscular arm thicker than Gargan's chest. These arms ended in clawed fists that contained an eye in each palm. The arms constantly shifted location, as though the flesh were jelly. Sprouting from its body came three fanged, and nosed, but otherwise featureless heads amongst the arms, all of which spoke at once, making for a nigh incomprehensible cacophony.

"Welcome to my realm, dussssstlingssss," it said, echoing itself. The sheer majesty of the sharn, understandable or not, was enough to make Twilight want to bow down and worship, but she couldn't move.

Then the mouths began alternating syllables, but spoke them all at once, so three beats became one. "Sssshort lived racessss go by like dussssst in the wind. But you have not died thussss far." Then it ceased speaking, glaring down with eyeless faces and eyes dotting its six hands.

Twilight realized it was probably the closest the creature would come to complimenting them.

She could not see the details of its body well, even with eyes so attuned to darkness. It was a shapeless bulk of black and silver flesh constantly shifting in a way simultaneously sensual and discordant. Tiny sparks of magic burst and squeaked into being around it constantly—if anything about it could be said to be constant. Its heads and mouths twitched, as though it skipped through time and space every few heartbeats, the number varying as time passed. The six empty hands waved about, casting blank gazes this way and that.

"Chaos embodied," she whispered in a tone both bleak and awed.

Even though she had never seen one, nor wanted to, Twilight could tell at a glance that something was the matter with this sharn. Multicolored veins stood out along its sinuous frame, and here and there, tightly clustered matrices of light gleamed through its skin like radiant bones. Its mouths constantly oozed green-white fluid, and half its eyes had gone white, as though blinded, or burst entirely, leaving dripping sores.

"My-my lord Sharn," Twilight said with a bow.

"Ruukthalmuramaxamin," it corrected in two syllables, not looking at her. "Elf ssssings like bird on the wing."

From its display of Art and the presence of its guardians, Twilight realized that this creature controlled the golems they had seen. And that meant . . . Taslin.

"Not I. The hangman not mine, the death of thine not mine."

"What do you . . . ?"

"Ssssilence!" it shouted thrice, its voice shaking the temple. She heard the scream in her mind louder than outside it, a vice that crushed her head.

Twilight fell to her knees. Doom was upon her—how dare she speak, or even think. The sharn could snuff out her existence with a thought. She had no right to . . .

Liet.

She knew she was mad to show spine to a sharn. But Twilight was simply too tired and heartbroken—too worn—to care. She struggled onto one knee, looked it in the eye—an eye, anyway—and said, in a tone that would brook no argument, "What have you done with my friends?"

Silence reigned in the chamber.

One warm afternoon, Lilten had told her a legend of a sharn who turned a cabal of mighty sorcerers to toadstools and fed them to a gibbering mound—which it had summoned with a gesture much like what mortals use to stifle a sneeze. This was simply for pausing, confused, when the sharn asked for goblin pelt tea. Then it annihilated an unseen servant that delivered the noxious brew, on the grounds that it tasted bad.

In short, questioning a sharn was madness.

The sharn laughed. Rather, its central head laughed. The head on the right muttered homicidal promises in a long forgotten language Twilight only understood with the talisman. The third serenaded her with an ode to a desert posy in some ancient dialect of Elvish that predated the Crown Wars.

"Very well," it said. "Prisonerssss."

"Release them," she said, then quickly amended it to, "such I desire. Name—"

The sharn just laughed. "You dessssire, detessssst, dessserve nothing!"

The declaration rippled through the air, and the golden ooze caked on the ceiling hissed with a thousand spells and memories flooding through it.

Twilight found herself prostrate on the ground. Betrayal lay beneath paralyzed fingers. "Test me, then," she said.

The sharn did not pause, as though it expected this, and immediately shouted at her again, this time in a sort of half-mad, half-ordered poem. "Child of liessss, liar in love, lover of children," the sharn's three heads said, each beginning at the last's final word, eerily like a roundsong. "Do you know your mother, father, daughter?"

"My lord Sharn, this is not what I ask," Twilight said, rising to her feet.

For the first time, Ruukthalmuramaxamin turned all of its eyes upon the shadowdancer, and Twilight sank to her knees with a cry. Her head burst into flame within and she screamed, pressing her palms to her temples. This wasn't the mind-scream. It was reading her thoughts, tearing deep down into her memories. It took all her willpower not to tear out her own eyes to get at the agony or crush her own skull, much less resist. Tears poured down her face and she whimpered. She could do nothing else.

"He emptiessss you firssssst and fillsssss you after," Ruuk continued unabated. "Chokessss with blood and ssssoaksssss with laughter, but give him up you will, leading him to the kill."

"My lord, I do not under—" Her head felt as though it would rip itself free if her hands didn't tear it off first.

"Are the applessss in sssseasssson? Issss your esssssence broken, asssss is mine? Hasssss the inquissssitor come? Where issss the ssssword that wassss sssstolen, the life it took, the life it killed, the life it definessss?"

"My lor—"

"For whom would you fall, child? Who would feel the blade meant for your breassssst? Who puts a sssssword in your heart?

Whosssse kisss would you sssswallow and whosssse betrayal you lament?"

In her agony, Twilight opened her mouth to cry that she did not understand, but then she went pale. She knew the answer, though she'd never heard the question.

"For whom would you fall?"

Ruuk's gazes crushed her even further. It took all her furious determination—her rage at her betrayals, her hatred of those who had loved and wronged her—to resist the crushing hands that sought to annihilate her mind, the claws that shredded her soul, and the ever-tightening chain that grasped her heart.

How could it know? Did its eyeless gaze penetrate so deep? How could it know what *she* didn't even know?

"For whom would you fall, daughter of foxessss?"

Twilight's lip trembled and her body screamed, but she said it anyway. "All of them!" she moaned.

The sharn paused, considering. Twilight knew that upon its whim lay her life, that of Gargan, and those of her allies. She had been a fool, trusting in chaos . . .

Then the agony vanished and she fell breathless to the ground. If Gargan had not darted forward to catch her, Twilight might well have split her face on the burning stones.

As the goliath cradled the limp elf, Ruuk loomed over them, its three heads gleaming hungrily. Its hands traced patterns in the air—whether meaningless or slaying spells, she knew not. Then it spoke, and Twilight could hardly believe her ears.

"Two livessss for a death, two deathssss for a life," the sharn said. "Sssslay him, and your companions I-I-I . . ." It coughed, hissing ochre magic that flowed to the ground like blood. Veins like metal ribbons stood out on its black carapace. "I free will."

"Who?" Twilight croaked. "Who must I slay, my lord?"

The sharn coiled in upon itself, hissing madly, both in pain and in hatred.

"Gessstal!" Three throats screamed in unison.

Lord Divergence gazed down into the blood, scanning the overgrown city. Their scrying swept into the great hive, as far as the sharn's defenses would allow. As before, they could see only the borders of Amaunator's temple. That was far enough.

Yes, mayhap the heavy magic Ruukthalmuramaxamin kept in place would shield against farseeing. It would probably burn their eyes from their sockets or fry Gestal's mind to a blackened husk. But the way the sharn boomed—well, heavy magic did not keep sound from traveling.

Gestal heard their plan. Not that he expected anything different. For Ruukthalmuramaxamin was mad, and what lovelier madness could there be to a Sharn but predictability?

The eyes turned to a lifeless husk propped in the corner. "Time to go," they said.

CHAPTER TWENTY-TWO

"Gestal?" Twilight dared speak back. "Who is . . . ?"

Ruukthalmuramaxamin screamed in her mind and the world went fuzzy.

"Sssilence!" the sharn shouted with enough force to drive even Gargan to his knees. The thing lunged, mouths slavering, and the elf's heart skipped.

But death did not fall upon her. Instead, a new sound assailed her ears and a heavy mist struck her skin. Ruuk drew back, issuing an involuntary assortment of sounds ranging from growls to crows to outright coughs. Fluid trickled between the jaws of one head, which slumped down for just an instant, then shot up and leaned over its back, as though to hide itself.

"Then," Ruuk said. "We have a foe, you and I. He dwellssss above, in cavernsssss dark, there deceivessss, demon sssservessss."

Twilight opened her mouth but wisely did not speak. Instead, she reached up at the black fluid coating her face, and realized it felt like blood—blood mixed with bile and tears, but blood nonetheless.

The sharn spoke more softly then, though its voice was no less powerful.

"Long ago," the sharn said. "Before the elf ssssang, before the human dreamed, my and mine came, out of the formlessss darknessss from which had arissssen moon and her dark sssssissssster.

Chaosssss had ever been our sssstrength . . ."

Ruuk hissed with one mouth, screeched with another, and whined with the third.

"Now dying," he said. "Killed by antihessssissss, buried by logic. Ssssoul-ssssstuff becomessss bane, madnessss issss death to him-her-it. Trapped!" The last was a shout, with all three voices. "Now demon-fiend-prince'ssss power waxessss and wanessss that of my people."

Twilight was uncertain whether he was talking about the race or himself. That Ruuk might be dying, Twilight had not realized, but once that thought occurred, she accepted it as a possibility—an unsettling one. What could kill a sharn?

A buzzing warned her. She cleared her mind as best she could.

The sharn gave a gesture with its three heads that might have been a nod. "Sssssink to rise, do the deed. Kill Gessssstal, your friendssss be freed."

Though Twilight's blood raced at the suggestion, she had negotiated too often to be fooled. "What if we refuse?" she asked, having no intention of doing so.

Gargan blinked at her in shock. As she could separate truth from falsehood as easily as an angel might, so could she lie with the best devils.

"Ruukthalmuramxamin issss not cruel," the sharn said. "You and he remain here, my guessssstssss until you go."

So those are the stakes, Twilight thought. She did not know how long a sharn could live, but fancied it would prove much longer than her own span.

"What if Gestal kills us? Will you release them, or keep them as prisoners?"

The sharn answered instantly, having already considered that. "No use for them," it said. "They go free."

"Your word?" she asked. Gargan looked at Twilight as though she had lost her mind, but she did not react.

The sharn growled, hissed, and spat at her, all at once with three heads. A spasm shook its body, and rune-shaped veins stood out on its black torso. It wrenched its heads toward her and bowed. "My word bindsss," it said. "My word given."

"All of them go free?" she asked, her heart speeding up.

"Both them."

A weight pressed upon Twilight's chest, then, and she would have fallen had not Gargan reached out strong arms to steady her. In one three-pronged syllable, the sharn had told her that Liet might live, yet his chance was only two in three.

"Which?"

"Those whom order definessss," said the sharn. It spat the word "order" with another gob of the blackish blood.

Twilight's mind raced. Surely that included Davoren—he was vile, yes, but predictably vile, to a fault. And devils had created the most rigid hierarchy in the multiverse outside the planes of law and clockwork. So that was one. One other . . .

Was it Slip or Liet?

Twilight closed her eyes and swore inwardly. What did it matter? She owed it to both of them, and if she might save one . . . she preferred Liet.

It was not that she felt remorse. Twilight had never had much use for morality. Foolish concepts like right and wrong fell before necessity, in every instance. Two things she understood, though, were weakness and shame, and her cheeks colored in both.

What kind of monster could have wished the sweet halfling dead in that moment? One with black hair, pale skin, and eyes that seemed gold-red in the light of heavy magic.

Oh, Liet.

"Release one of them now," Twilight said.

The sharn glared at her with something much like surprise, mingled with a goodly amount of outrage. "Who, why, what?"

"The one called Liet Sagrin. If you release him, we will—"

Ruukthalmuramaxamin's mouths curled downward, and she would have fancied it confused. "No and no."

"Why not?" She cursed the desperation in her voice.

"No and no," the sharn warned.

Heedless of the pain she knew was coming, Twilight opened her mouth to argue, but Gargan caught her arm in a hard grip.

She hissed at him, but the goliath ignored her.

"What is Gestal?" he rumbled.

"Powerful priesssst," said Ruuk. "Demon-priesssst."

A demon thrall. Twilight's eyes narrowed. A servant of chaos in darkness, then, even as Davoren had been a servant of order, of a fiendish sort. But was not the sharn born of chaos? Did he not possess the very powers this Gestal worshipped? Why . . . ?

"Why do you not face him yourself?" asked Twilight. "He must be mighty indeed, for surely you—"

Then the sharn eyed her with a look that stole more of her breath than when he had nearly killed her at a glance. Not only did her head explode in agony, but her throat closed of its own accord and she staggered. Gargan reached out and caught her, and she didn't have the strength to fight him off.

"Do not quessssstion!" Ruuk roared. "Agree! Agree or die!"

Barely able to breathe, Twilight coughed. "Well," she said. "Then we . . . agree."

The sharn hissed, spat, and clucked in what must have been approval. Twilight assumed it must, for she was still alive a breath later.

"Here." Its mood changed utterly. "Take," the sharn said most amiably, as though offering them tea.

One of its arms stabbed into the air, through reality, to extend through a silvery portal before them. In the palm was a pair of crimson boots, which appeared to be sized for a human.

Completely inexplicable, Twilight thought as she put them on. It didn't occur to her to refuse. The boots adjusted themselves to fit her feet.

"And thissss." A silvery window opened in reality and a black hand extended through it. It dropped a sack that smelled glorious to her.

Twilight yanked open the pouch. It was filled with dried strips of meat and bread that smelled of corn. Also inside was an oiled paper packet with some sort of honey—Twilight wondered if it came from the abeil. She took a hunk of bread and two pieces of meat for herself, then offered the food to Gargan, who accepted it silently.

Another of Ruuk's hands offered a wineskin filled with a drink that tasted sweet, like some manner of fruit, with a distinctive, odd taste Twilight recognized as a sort of mushroom. Rarely had she tasted the wine of the Underdark, and unlike most elves, she enjoyed it. Gargan refused it, but the sharn offered him a waterskin instead.

Emboldened by the sharn's hospitality, she spoke up. "One question," she said. "If it please you, great lord."

There was a long pause. She reasoned she could take their continued existence for a yes.

"Why don't you . . . destroy him?" she asked. "You are so much . . . more powerful than us. Why *us?*"

"Hissss issss magic chaossss," Ruuk said. "Centuriessss millennia agessss ago, Ruukthalmuramaxamin wassss curssssed. Musssst ssssstay. Power mine."

For the first time, it didn't occur to Twilight to respond. She sat, rapt.

"Negarath wassss a city of the mad," Ruuk said. "Inverted, floating upsssside down, buildingssss of curvessss, archessss, twissssstssss, with dissssstorted creaturessss on dissssplay. Flayed mind flayerssss, ghossssstssss of elementalssss, demonssss of celessssstia, angelssss of outer darknessss."

"And a mad prisoner," Twilight stammered. "A sharn cursed to order."

"And dying!" Ruuk said. The sound was so loud that the temple shook. "Body failing, order rotting. Godssss of chaossss have turned away, abhorrent."

"Then help us," Twilight said. "Break free—" Her head burst and she sank again.

Even as her senses fled in pain, her half-mad mind perceived a certain kind of logic in the sharn's gift. It had threatened them, made them used to being threatened, then thrown them off balance. Its "random" actions apparently followed a set order.

The three heads spoke at once, but said three things. "Not free. No cure. No help." Then they joined together. "Sssssink to rissssse. Kill Gessssstal or die!"

Hands lifted her and her feet scrabbled across the stone.

She looked up, and it was Gargan lifting her. *"We go,"* the goliath said.

The sharn's hands blazed with golden magic, and arms reached from portals around them. Then the world shuddered to a halt, burned away as though scribed on parchment. They felt a sensation of falling, and then they were elsewhere.

Gods-only-knew how long later, Twilight stirred. Darkness had become her world, but that was easily remedied. She opened her eyes and perceived flickering torchlight. She saw the prison where they had left Tlork.

"We've arrived, it seems," Twilight said.

She was glad when Gargan, completely unexpectedly, broke the silence. He was kneeling at her side. Twilight felt weary and inexplicably old. She took his hand.

"How mighty is this creature?" Gargan asked. *"This . . . sharn?"*

Twilight shrugged in a fatalistic way. "What little I know, I shall put by analogy," she said. "You have heard of the Seven Sisters, or the Sage of Shadowdale?"

Gargan shook his head.

"Thay, perhaps," she said. "All the red wizards?"

Again.

"The empire of Shade?"

That got a nod. Curious.

"Well, then," said Twilight. "All the princes of Shade would jump to do a sharn's bidding, for if they didn't, it would likely destroy a city out of whim before resuming its morning meal of the stillborn children of gods."

"Ah." Gargan nodded hesitantly.

There was a pause. They both sat silent, listening for any sign of an occupant other than themselves. The dungeon was still.

"There must be another way down," she said. "If we must sink to rise, that is."

The goliath nodded, and they stole about the prison together, hands on hilts. They plied their senses at their keenest, followed every instinct, and explored every tiny crack and crevice in the floor and walls with their fingers. Dust, bits of bone, scraps of metal, and flecks of refuse Twilight didn't want to identify obscured the cold, damp stone.

They made their way into Tlork's chambers. The troll was not at home. All they found was a destroyed onyx griffin. Twilight resolved not to forget their hunter's strength.

"Why did you argue?" Gargan asked suddenly, making Twilight jump.

She slowed her heart with the exercises Neveren had taught her. "What?"

"You argued for his 'word,'" Gargan said. *"What means this?"*

"A promise. Not that I suppose it matters much to a sharn, but I would not break my word, once given." She managed to smile. "That's why I never give it."

Gargan did not find that amusing. *"You argued for something you knew to be false?"* he asked. *"Why?"*

"I was hoping to get him to release Liet." She hated herself for her feelings, but she was past such considerations now. "Then we could flee this place, the three of us."

"Davoren and Slip? Would the sharn think Gestal had killed us and free them?"

Twilight shrugged. It truly did not matter. "Wouldn't miss him," Twilight said. Then she sighed. "And she'd be regrettable. But for all we know, they're . . ."

She did not finish the thought. For all they knew, Liet was dead.

"You would shirk our duty to them?" Gargan said. *"Our companions."*

Twilight waved. "Duty is overrated," she said. "I am a creature of chaos, as is the sharn. We both know this—there would be no surprise." That wasn't strictly true, but it might as well have been. She had never dealt with a sharn before, but the fact that this one was cursed made the situation even less predictable.

At that moment, Twilight brushed away dust and some old

bones and found a crease in the floor. She traced the outline of a door cut into the stone. Through the bones, fur, and filth that littered the floor, she found an old brass ring attached to the stone. Twilight twisted the ring. The stone gave a lurch and sank downward, then to the side, revealing darkness below.

There came a sound of scuffling on stone, and Twilight looked down the hall, toward the levitating disk they had used to ascend to the crypt above. She thought she saw a flicker of movement.

"Who?" Gargan asked, drawing his sword.

Twilight shrugged. "We've no shortage of enemies," she said. "The sharn, or its golems. Gestal. The fiendish lizards."

"Tlork," Gargan added grimly.

"Darkness, don't forget the grimlocks," said Twilight. "We didn't part on the most amiable of terms."

Nothing moved for many long breaths. Twilight left Gargan watching the darkness and looked down into the new passage. It smelled foul and radiated humidity like a tropical swamp. Where the tunnels above had been dry and dead, this new level seemed the opposite.

A world built on opposites, Twilight thought.

Twilight wondered why they were going down. Had not the sharn spoken of Gestal dwelling "above?" Sink to rise, she reflected.

She put her leg down into the darkness and froze.

With a mighty heave that broke more than a few bones, Tlork finally wrenched himself out of the sewers. As he stood in the forested street, letting limbs pop back into place and torn flesh flow back together, he cast his stitched face about, searching, just in time for the swarm of abeil to descend with spears, halberds, and stingers.

Snarling, the troll whipped hammer and claw through the air in fury to drive off the swarm. Bee-creatures fell crushed, killed at the very touch of Tlork's weapons, but there were hundreds, and three replaced every one that fell.

Soon, the battle was like stirring mud, trying to swat them away while they rained pain and torment all over Tlork. Abeil speared his skin, stinging and stinging like mad, and soon he could hardly focus on anything but the stabbing and cutting. His body throbbed as though a thousand hearts beat just under his skin.

Slave, came a voice in the back of his head. Like all thoughts, his own or another's, it caused Tlork pain. *Come, slave.*

As he batted another abeil out of the air to smash like a ripe plum against a distorted building, Tlork whined like a dog. "But I come so far!" he argued. "I close!"

Come, the thought came again, *to the chapel.*

Unfair. Tlork didn't like the up-down room. It always made his stomach knot. The fiend-troll gave a great, strangling cry, turned, and ran. He dived through the hole into the sewer, ignoring the pain that came when his arm splintered against the edge.

That elf—she would pay for this. Not the pain, which Tlork had long since stopped minding, but the indecency of making him trek all the way back, even past the up-down room.

CHAPTER TWENTY-THREE

Twilight stared into the dark hole. Much of this world was inverted, she mused. It was a sharn's idea of order, curves where buildings should have corners, towers that sloped downward, even upside-down stairs on the underside of ledges. She had thought herself prepared for any shift of paradigm imaginable.

This, though, far exceeded any reasonable anticipation.

Gargan, seeing her hesitation, crawled over the edge, holding the lip, and let go. He didn't fall. Instead, he stood on the underside of the floor, looking down at her past his feet. It was as though Twilight stood on a mirror that reflected a world not her own.

"Come," Gargan said. *"Sink to rise."*

The implications struck Twilight like a thunder blow. Damned Netherese.

Now she knew why she had felt unsettled going into the dungeon, almost like falling. The gravity was in flux here, so close to the limits of the mythallar's field.

That was why the ceiling of the sewer had been as stained as the floor.

That was why half the architecture was upside down, why all the symbols of Mystra—or whatever the goddess of magic in ancient Netheril had been called—had been inverted.

Now she knew why the sand had not fallen in from the "ceiling" of the cavern, settling instead as though along the bottom of a bowl. Gravity was reversed in Negarath, all pulling down toward the dungeon, and below it . . .

All that time they thought they had been rising, they had been descending.

Gargan watched her uncertainly, but at last Twilight swung a leg down and pushed off, climbing to her feet on the ceiling of the chamber below. She passed through an invisible barrier that made her stomach go limp before she emerged in another world, one where gravity was opposite.

They stood in a crude tunnel sloping up from where they stood, down from the dungeon. Gone was the fine, if eccentric, carving and stonework of Negarath. The air was musty, and a faint, foul odor wafted through the tunnel. Rough steps led up.

"Gestal should be somewhere up there—or down . . ." Twilight could not help feeling a touch disoriented, but she did her best to dismiss it. "Up. Definitely *up*, if Negarath is upside down, below us." Twilight's head ached.

She noticed Gargan kneeling by the trapdoor, hand out, and narrowed her eyes. "What are you about?"

He drew his hand back and she saw that he had placed a stone in the air. It dipped back toward the dungeon, then up toward them, then merely floated, caught in that space where gravity pulled both ways. At the innocent fascination the goliath showed in the phenomenon, Twilight smiled despite herself. *"Come."*

Gargan—ever a man of few words—nodded and went with her.

They had not gone ten paces up the tunnel when they heard a scuttling from behind, as of a rock falling to the floor. Something had disturbed Gargan's floating stone.

The goliath was already charging back by the time Twilight had her weapon out and was pursuing him. Though her reflexes might have been the faster, he had keener ears. With the boots from the sharn, she ran as fast as he did. They fell upon their pursuer at almost the same instant.

There it was, five steps from the trapdoor. The shadow yelped and danced back, startled. Gargan's black sword swept aside a hastily raised mace, even as his other hand shot out and shoved its wielder over. Even as the intruder fell, Twilight lunged the intervening four paces—she loved these boots already—and rode it to earth, Betrayal at its throat.

The shadowy figure froze and put its hands up. "Stop! Stop!" she screamed. " 'Tis me! 'Tis me!" Twilight almost drove her blade in anyway, but Gargan caught her arm and saved Billfora Brightbrows's life.

"Slip?" Twilight asked, brow furrowing. "What are you doing here? Didn't they capture you? How did you escape?"

The halfling stared with terror-stricken eyes. "I-I-I . . ." she tried, but couldn't speak with the elf pressing her lungs, and a blade lying a thumb's breadth from her jugular.

Twilight straddled the little woman and bent low, keeping the blade still and putting her free hand on the halfling's shoulder. It would take hardly any force to push it through Slip's unarmored neck—in case it wasn't really the halfling, but a trick.

"Speak," she commanded, and Slip did.

"I-I got away," she said. "When those bee-things came, one o' them knocked me cold. When I woke up, I was under a toadstool. It must have broke my fall, and I was . . ."

"You weren't a prisoner?" Twilight asked, her heart suddenly racing. That would mean only Davoren and Liet were Ruuk's prisoners, and that meant . . .

"Uh," said Slip. Twilight heard her only distantly. "No. No, I wasn't."

"Did you see anyone else?" Twilight asked. "Where's Liet?"

Slip shook her head. "I didn't . . ."

"Why so quick?" Gargan asked, his voice dark. There was no pain in his words, only suspicion about the one who had been his friend.

It struck her that the earring was not translating his words to Elvish, as it must have for Taslin. Somehow, Twilight had become less than an elf—but she accepted that.

Slip blinked at the goliath and she smiled widely. "Eh?"

"Why are you here?" Twilight asked, clarifying. "How could you get here so fast? The sharn teleported us. What of you?"

The joy went out of Slip's face. "Well, I . . . I . . ." Gargan was staring at her, and her lip shook. "I've been coming this way for a day. I didn't . . . know where you were, so I came this way, because . . ." She blinked. "I'm afraid of bees."

No matter how heavy the moment or how deathly serious the look that had passed between Slip and Gargan, Twilight could not help but grin at that.

"Very well," she said, and got off the halfling. "My apologies. We reacted as we had to." She sheathed Betrayal and started up the stairs.

The halfling got to her knees, rubbing her temples. "Ah, r-right," Slip said, smiling blankly as though she had tried her best and largely failed. "Uh . . ."

"Come along," Twilight said. "We've a demon priest to slay."

"Aye, that," Slip said. She hurried to catch up with the shadowdancer—no mean feat with her short legs, and hugged Twilight about the waist, stopping her.

By reflex, Twilight put an arm up to drape it around the halfling's shoulders, as one might show affection to a child, but she stopped herself.

"Just . . ." Slip said, shifting awkwardly.

"Yes?"

The halfling's voice wavered and her eyes were very round as they fell upon the pouch of food that hung from Twilight's belt. Her stomach growled as though she hadn't eaten for days—which, of course, was the case. "Can . . . can I have something to eat?"

Smiling, Twilight extended the sack to Slip, who fell to it like a ravenous beast.

Gargan watched, doubtless thinking himself hidden in the darkness, but if Twilight had learned one thing in half a century in service to a god of deception, it was to watch the shadows carefully. She had never seen Gargan's face so dark and grim.

The air became even heavier and warmer as the tunnel led the three upward, and the smell from above grew in intensity. It was salty and sickly sweet, a combination of rotting vegetation and the acrid scent of blood. In this new, unknown place, Twilight forbade torches. She could lead the others with her darksight. From where she crept along, Slip made a face that was barely visible, reflecting her own feelings on the matter. Gargan hardly seemed to notice.

The tunnel was largely natural, but for a few spots along walls and floor that had been crudely carved as though by stone axes and picks. Their path rose to the edge of a rough, circular chamber from which led yet more passages. In the chamber, they found light—luminescence from green and blue fungi that grew from the walls, ceiling, and floor. Stalagmites jabbed out of the ground to loom above even the seven-foot Gargan's head. They twisted and curled in a way that reminded Twilight of Negarath.

They saw none of the lizards, but they could smell them. Husky and gangrenous, their odor lurked over hollows in which foulness lay pooled.

"Two sewers." Twilight wrinkled her nose. " 'Tis Westgate all over again."

"Westgate?" Slip asked, and Twilight smiled ruefully.

"A long story," she said. "One day, perhaps."

"You have lots of stories," Slip said excitedly. "I enjoy collecting stories—'tis like collecting lives, aye?"

A trifle unsettled by that comment, Twilight looked at Gargan, whose disapproving expression gave her all the excuse she needed. "We should be silent," she said. "One never knows what may be awaiting."

Slip, suitably chastened but undiminished, grinned innocently.

The next chamber they entered, following Twilight's direction, was not as vacant as the first. Nearly a dozen of the man-lizards occupied the cavern, milling about as if waiting for something. Eight devoured something rather bloody, while the other four stood apart, spears clenched in distorted claws, and scanned the shadows with bloodshot eyes.

"Oh, very well," Slip whispered. "I told you we should've taken the other path."

Twilight frowned. "We follow my lead," she said. Until she figured out who to trust, she would trust no one but herself—and that only so far. Even with the goliath's superior tracking abilities, and Slip's magic. Neither objected verbally to her words, so Twilight left it at that.

That still left the problem of the lizards blocking their way.

"You have spells that will assist us? Invisibility?"

The halfling shook her head. "I can hide us only to the walking dead," she said. "The best I can do is darkness." She grinned. "I fight better without my eyes, a'times!"

Twilight hardly wondered why Slip might know such a spell—likely, it had something to do with her larcenous tendencies. Slow tendays at the house of Yondalla, she imagined with a smile, when the tithes were not meeting expectations.

"Do we circle back, or sneak 'round?" Slip asked. "Either would take time."

The goliath slowly shook his head. "Attack," he said. Then he added something in the goliath tongue that Twilight understood with the earring. *"Ambush is not dishonorable."*

The shadowdancer was starting to like the gray-skinned warrior, with the intricate red designs that ran across his muscular chest. If only she could be sure he wasn't a traitor . . .

Her mind raced. They did not want to spoil their surprise, but neither could they delay. Slip's return brought limited healing magic, but without more food, they would weaken. Also, the longer they delayed, the longer Gestal had to learn of their coming. Their strength would wane, while his would remain high. They had to kill him as soon as they could.

"We'll go around," Twilight said. "That's the only . . ."

Then there came—whether real or imagined—an anguished wail that froze her heart in her chest. A woman's cry. She made out the color of the flesh the lizards were eating.

"No," she said. "No . . ."

Gargan was shaking her shoulder, Slip tugging at her blouse. Twilight looked at them, sharp as a knife.

"We kill them," Twilight said. "Surprise and speed. Now."

"You can't be—"

"Now!" And Twilight ran toward the lizards.

"What? What are you doing?" Slip asked Gargan behind her back. "Put me d—" Then her voice fell to chanting.

Twilight didn't notice. She just ran toward the lizards, Betrayal leading.

S'zgul perceived the darkness before it fell upon them, and that only startled her more.

The black swooped in as though hurled, rather than suddenly bathing them. She watched as the darkness swallowed her fellows, shrouding torches and stealing even her fiendish sight. Her allies recoiled instinctively from the wave of black, but it did not harm them.

The darkness did not, but what came within the darkness did.

A warrior screeched as a projectile struck his back and a blade jabbed into his stomach, ripping a hole for entrails to leak out. He would have clawed at his attacker, but the blade slashed across his throat, ending his roar in a gurgle.

S'zgul bellowed in consternation, demanding calm and reason, but to no avail. The others roared and scrambled, either groping for the edge of the darkness or slashing at random with claw and rusty blade. Two fell to their own companions, and thrice as many still hacked at one another and squealed.

The survivors tried to escape, but the darkness seemed endless. Finally, one broke free of the dark, only to find death at the end of two swords—one black and one gray. As he belched and flopped to the ground, his killers plunged into the globe of darkness.

With an oath to her father, the great Demogorgon, S'zgul snarled out a few syllables. With the power of the demon prince, the darkness vanished—

—just in time for her to duck the acid-smeared sword streaking for her neck.

Her bodyguard's scaly head flew into the air, and another warrior jerked and spat as a rapier slit his heart in two. The giant and elf spun into the midst of the creatures. The gigantic black sword slashed in a great arc, beheading one lizard and disarming another—the hard way. If the cavern had been disorderly before, it exploded in lethal madness when the darkness vanished.

The priestess watched her servants fall, one after another, fast as flowing water. The speed with which the three moved amazed her, especially the white elf: the female lunged and sprang like a tiger, wounding and dispatching with unflinching brutality. What was more, the shadows swirled around her and danced about her crackling, burning blade as though to lap at the blood she spilled. A pair of warriors jabbed at her from either side with obsidian spears, but she twisted around one thrust, letting it stab into the foe at her back, and rolled between the other's legs. She stabbed up and her blade went in along a weak spot beneath the spine and burst out beside the warrior's throat.

S'zgul, who had fought countless hulking males and fierce females for leadership in the tribe, and mated with as many demons as she had slaughtered, was intimidated.

So she turned from the furious shadowdancer toward the weakest foe she could see—a half-sized creature, tiny and delicate. S'zgul could break the half-female in two with her talons. She hardly needed the three-headed, barbed flail spinning in her hand.

The halfling didn't see her coming—so intent was she on slitting a warrior's throat. S'zgul hissed like a desert cobra, lashed the tiny creature about the legs, and yanked her down.

"Gark katulu!" she growled at the halfling.

The little creature rolled over, gazing up at S'zgul in confusion, fear, and . . .

S'zgul hesitated, startled. *"Daltyrex—naka!"*

Then the halfling smiled—a hideous expression to the lizard priestess—and showed her empty hands. A knife slid out of her sleeve and she opened S'zgul's throat in a flash of pain.

The priestess reeled until a dusty gray rapier split open her back, carved her heart, and brought only painful blackness and the hiss of her father, master, and lover.

———————◆————◆———————

Twilight took a moment to wipe the blood off Betrayal with the aid of the fiendish lizard's half cape. It marked the creature as a spellcaster, likely, or a shaman. Probably the one who had dispelled Slip's conjured darkness, though it didn't really matter. All the lizards were dead, and they had killed them before an alarm could be raised. Good enough.

It was good to fight, as well. Having to evade band after band of these lizards had caused trepidation and nervousness, and nothing wiped away such feelings like a good, bloody slaughter. Twilight's muscles felt loose and her blood was pumping—hunger was a thing of the past.

Had she been thinking rationally, she might have been disturbed that dealing death made her feel alive.

"You're fast," she said to the halfling, still panting in glorious abandon.

"All in the wrist—where the blood is." Slip held out her hand. Her little dagger had disappeared.

"That snake said something to you," Twilight said as she helped the tiny woman up. "I didn't hear. What was it?"

The halfling blinked, gazing up at her with those blissful brown eyes, and shrugged. "I don't speak fiend."

Gargan's eye twitched.

Twilight was no longer listening. She looked to the center of the chamber, where the lizards had been feeding. There, lying on the floor, was their meal. She recognized the pale golden flesh, the ravaged hair. Even the face, with its bugging eyes, one still present, the other a bloody hole.

"Gods," Slip said. "Is that . . ."

"Not possible," Twilight said. "Not—"

Then the emerald eye opened and it lunged for her, gasping and moaning. Two bloody stumps where hands should have been scrabbled at her chest.

"Taslin?" Slip gasped.

Twilight hit the forehead with Betrayal's hilt. The body fell back to the ground, writhing, and she hit again. And again. And again, beating that head into paste. Dark blood splattered the floor, and she could feel her teeth go through her tongue, but she didn't care. She pounded until those limbs stopped battering her.

When the animate priestess was finally stilled once more, Twilight could stand. She'd watched Taslin die, and she'd killed her again. She tried not to think about the implications of her wrists, severed as though by a knife and not by any lizard's claw.

"We keep moving," said Twilight.

The others were too busy staring to argue.

CHAPTER TWENTY-FOUR

From the chamber of the slaughtered lizards, they went north where the tunnel arched up. It was widely traveled, as evidenced by the smoother floor and walls where feet and hands had worn the stone. The tempo of Twilight's heart and the frequency of events were increasing, and she felt driven, hurried. She had to stop herself from running.

"Stay alert," she said. "An ambush could be around any curve. Swift and silent."

Gargan and Slip nodded—they both understood exactly what she meant.

They ascended into a series of caverns that spread like a disordered honeycomb around them, walls painted with dried lizard filth and old blood. Bones littered every passage, all picked clean, as though gnawed bare and tossed heedlessly. The fiendish lizards were plentiful here—scores, even hundreds of the creatures swarmed the warrenlike catacombs.

Twilight's blood was hot and Betrayal tingled when she touched the hilt, but discretion overcame bloodlust or courage. Erevan's servant had many flaws, it was true, but no friend or foe had ever labeled her excessively valiant.

Erevan. Damn you. This is all *your* doing.

At that moment, Twilight remembered the powers granted by her erstwhile patron. She had been so distracted that she hadn't given them much thought.

Thanks to Erevan's blessing, she had a keen sense for items of value, and could meditate to find the location of a chosen object—or person. She considered using this talent to find Liet. It would not be a judicious use of her power—revealing him in the captivity of the sharn would not aid her. And it might fail entirely if he were dead. Either way, Twilight couldn't bear to know.

Davoren, though . . . if Slip had escaped, why not the warlock?

Twilight decided, on a whim, to search for Davoren. Focusing her mind in the way Neveren had taught her, she reached out with her senses to find—

Davoren was not a prisoner of the sharn. In fact, he was only a little way ahead of them, ascending the caverns as they were. As her thoughts lingered upon the warlock, she sensed him moving, shadowing them from ahead.

Twilight's eyes widened as she realized the only possible explanation. Davoren. Gestal.

"What is it?" Slip asked, turning worried eyes toward Twilight.

"Silence," Twilight said.

———◆◆◆———

They passed through the warrens, subtle as shadows. Had any of the others been with them, their progress would have been hindered, but these three were the stealthiest of the seven. The halfling was a thief, the goliath a hunter, and she herself, after all, was the Fox-at-Twilight. The fiendish lizards on guard were not oblivious, but the three could pass them. They stole through the lizards' den, their eyes always moving.

The individual cells of the warrens epitomized wretchedness. Tattered straw mats rotted next to broken urns that must have been beautiful a thousand years ago, and now contained only mud and bones. Misshapen shamans shouted vile praises to a demon while hideous fiendish lizards crouched about cook fires, telling bawdy and violent jests in their clicking and hissing tongue. Twilight understood, by virtue of the earring, but did not wish to listen. She didn't want to think about what might be in those cook pots.

It was not difficult to find a tunnel that rose from the warrens, but it was increasingly difficult to pass by the scores of fiendish lizards that milled around the place. Dozens of times, the three ducked into the shadows or behind boulders to avoid detection as bands of the creatures appeared around a corner or lunged from a natural archway. For all their clumsiness and ugliness, the creatures were damnably silent when they moved.

Still, Twilight was determined. She kept the others hidden and, more importantly, moving. Her hand was never far from Betrayal's hilt, but she knew they could not risk a fight—not when a hundred or more of the creatures could swarm them from all sides and still summon others.

Twilight had watched Tlork fight, and though she had not seen Gestal, she knew he must be a powerful priest indeed for a sharn to fear his power. The only way they would win such a battle was if they could fight it on their terms, on ground of their choosing. They bided their time seeking a way past the fiendish lizards, making slow progress, shadow to shadow, dodging small clusters along the tunnels.

Until a commotion disturbed the barbaric tranquility.

The buzzing hiss that went through the hallway was their only warning. Twilight managed to duck and pull Slip behind cover just in time to avoid Tlork, who came rumbling around a corner. The troll's elephantine leg pounded down not a hand's breadth from her taut ankle, but Twilight knew better than to flinch.

Bellowing incoherently, the thing that had been a troll smashed a lizard out of the way and stomped down the passage. They scattered before him like ants after syrup, fleeing into passages and holes even she hadn't seen.

The only one who did not flee was the goliath, who slipped out of the shadows behind Tlork and padded behind him, sword sheathed. They had crossed twenty paces of tunnel before Twilight even registered it. Surely he was not thinking of taking on the troll alone, particularly without a ready blade. What could he . . .

Twilight's heart pounded in her throat. "Gargan!"

Tlork skidded to a halt, but the goliath was already gone, having faded into the shadows. Amazing, Twilight thought, the great camouflage his stony flesh gave him against the tunnel wall.

The fiend-stitched troll glared about the chamber, its mismatched eyes—one red, one violet—searching for the source of the sound. Then it snuffled, but that didn't seem to help. Finally, it rumbled on.

A sea of fiendish lizards poured out of bolt holes, cutting the three in two groups. The creatures had not seen them, but they made just as sure a barrier for their ignorance.

"What do we do?" Slip asked in a whisper.

Twilight wanted to conserve her power, but she had no choice. She wrapped Slip in an embrace and danced into the shadows.

They passed briefly through the dull, lifeless world of Shadow, where the fiendish lizards became blurs of inky blackness and their eyes became nightmare spots of blood. With a little gasp, the halfling stiffened in her arms, but Twilight cradled her closer. It wouldn't do to lose her companion in Shadow—after all, she needed Slip when they fought Gestal. And Twilight wouldn't deny having become fond of the halfling—though that was where it ended. No ties, no love.

She pushed thoughts of Liet aside.

Twilight and her terrified burden rematerialized next to Gargan, and one stony hand shot for her throat. The elf flinched and the goliath caught her shoulder instead. There was no malice in his movement. He merely guided them into hiding.

"What by the Lady's love life are you about, goliath?" she whispered.

The stony head shook. "I apologize," he said. "Instinct. Forgive."

Twilight pursed her lips. She did not disparage instinct—it had kept her alive over the decades whenever wits failed. Still . . .

"Forget it," she said. "But you move on my order, and mine alone."

The goliath nodded. *"Yes, Foxdaughter,"* he said.

Twilight blinked. "Good," she managed.

"One thing," Gargan said. *"I kill troll."*

"Well then." Twilight turned to Slip, whose mind was far away. "We go."

They followed the troll up the tunnel, which opened into a wide chamber, roughly circular, where the stalagmites and other cover had been broken away, leaving only jagged stalactites like fangs. They kept to the shadows and watched.

If the fiendish lizards' warrens had stunk of death and decay, the stained hall absolutely reeked of corruption. Crude murals of human-shaped and snakelike figures engaging in acts of violence, cruelty, and depravity adorned the walls, painted in blood, excrement, and fouler substances. Gooseflesh rose all over Twilight at the mere sight.

"Let's go!" Slip said brightly. The shadowdancer and the goliath hissed. "What?"

Tlork paced about the chamber, hefting the huge warhammer in his bony hand. Perhaps he was guarding something, but Twilight could not see any other occupant or another door. The chamber was wide and open, and Twilight had spent her shadowdance for the time being. There was no way around him.

"This could be a trap," Twilight said.

"You mean luring us into attacking the vulnerable troll?" Slip nodded. "Brilliant!"

Startled at the uncharacteristic sarcasm, Twilight looked but found only earnestness in her face.

"Right," she said. "If Gestal's not here, then he's likely trying to scry for us." She fingered her amulet. "We go quick and quiet, and put the troll down without alarm, to save the surprise. Gargan first, me second, Slip as reserve. Agreed?"

The others nodded silently.

"If this goes wrong and we face Gestal, get in close," Twilight said. "He'll be weak hand-to-hand, all his skill bound up in attacks from a distance."

Gargan furrowed his brow and Slip blinked. "You know this?" she asked.

Twilight's eyes narrowed. That damned warlock. She'd been a fool to trust him and it had cost her two friends, perhaps a lover as well. No more.

Her jaw clenched, like her heart. " 'Tis a death I should have dealt long ago, but I was blind." She grasped Betrayal. "No longer."

The goliath nodded gravely and drew his great black sword. The halfling stared at Twilight, then giggled through a hand. This disturbed her, but Twilight let it pass. After Gestal was dead, she would interrogate the little one. But for now . . .

She felt the hilt of her rapier, sheathed at her waist, took out her crossbow, and remembered the stiletto in her glove. They were as prepared as they could be.

Unable to shake a twinge of trepidation, Twilight gestured Gargan forward and rose from the shadows herself. The goliath darted into the chamber, sword out, and bore down upon the troll. Twilight came behind, ready to fire.

The gnarled troll gave a roar as Gargan's acid-sheathed sword hacked into his slim hip. The greenish liquid burned the flesh like parchment.

Twilight fired and the quarrel stabbed into Tlork's red eye, wrenching another cry of pain. This was going well. She darted toward them, dropping a hand to her rapier. If she could get behind the troll, she and Gargan could make short work—

"Well met," came a cold rasp, echoing around the chamber. "You've arrived just in time for the evening banquet—mine."

CHAPTER TWENTY-FIVE

Twilight's hand went to the quarrels at her belt, but Gestal's magic was faster. Dark power blazed from his fingers and struck her full in the stomach. She flinched and her body erupted in pain. The magic forced a spasm that consumed her with agony. Within the span of a heartbeat, her muscles strained and locked, cutting off a squeal of shock. The crossbow clattered to the ground.

Gestal stepped from the shadows, cloaked in tattered gray robes. Rot and corruption spread up the folds of fabric, as though it had never been cleaned. A pair of human hands emerged from the sleeves, wrists scarred and covered in swaths of black flesh that spread like a cancer up the forearms. Madness bled from the gaps in the robe like leaking ink.

"Fox-at-Twilight," he said, his voice disturbingly hungry. "I've been waiting."

Twilight remained calm. She suppressed a twinge of confusion. Davoren had never shown the power to freeze foes by pain, but he could have hidden it. She had been under spells like this before, and knew it was only a matter of time. All she could do for a few breaths was watch.

Tlork kicked, and Gargan, staggering over the uneven ground, took the troll's bony foot full in the chest. The goliath hit the broken stone hard but instantly reversed his momentum, rolling back the way he had come. He lunged to avoid Tlork's elephant leg. Rising behind the troll, Gargan slashed acid across Tlork's inner thigh, wrenching a fiendish screech from the troll. The goliath had no time for a lethal blow, however, having to duck a whirring warhammer that splintered a long stalactite.

Twilight told herself the pain was only in her head, and the demon power clenched her mind more tightly. This confirmed it, and her mind worked to slip out of the spell. It would take time, though, and it might be time they did not have.

Then she watched Slip materialize and scurry at the cloaked demonist with the grace of a black cat. She paused and gazed at Twilight, perhaps uncertain whether to help her friend or attack her foe.

"Kill . . . him . . ." Twilight tried to say. She was freeing herself, she hoped.

As though she had heard, Slip whispered toward Gestal, who was just finishing a chant. Dark, edifying power swirled around the troll. Unhindered, Slip drew her mace and dagger.

Then, in those cowl-shadows Twilight's eyes could barely pierce, Gestal smiled. His lips were moving. He could cast two spells at once?

"No," Twilight tried to scream, but she couldn't hear if she succeeded. "No!"

Then the halfling was upon Gestal, and the demonist turned.

He hissed the last word of his spell, a syllable in Abyssal that wrenched Twilight's heart and made her ears want to bleed. Vile darkness gathered and flared.

Slip screamed as her eyes exploded in a red spray. The fluid hissed onto Twilight's leg, where it burned like acid. The eyeless halfling collapsed, sobbing and weeping black. The demonist doubled over and quivered as though the spell's depravity had sapped his body's stability.

Then, reeling, Gestal burst into laughter. He could have been doubled over in mirth. "Daltyrex," he said. He clucked his tongue as though chiding a child.

The earring did not translate, but he could have spoken

the a spell for all she knew. Would the earring translate such a thing?

Spurred on by outrage, Twilight's wriggling mind finally slipped the spell's shackles. She leaped to shaking feet. She took a running step, only to be thrown to the floor when the world shuddered at Gestal's cry. A great tremor ripped through the cavern, tearing it asunder. Stalactites rained and moonlight from the desert above streamed down from a broken ceiling fifty feet up. The stars hid behind a cloud of dust. Gestal's mad laughter boomed across the screaming stone.

Twilight grit her teeth. How could he cast so quickly? Spells seemed to flow through him at random, all without pause, all deadly.

The quake dug a wide furrow between the combatants and the demonist. Twilight realized she could not jump it, even with the boots. As Slip collapsed into a moaning heap, the demonist smirked in the depths of his cowl and began another spell.

Twilight bit her lip. She couldn't give in to fear. She had to end this, and end it quickly. She shook off the last of her pain, extended Betrayal, and ran.

"Gargan!" she screamed as she barreled toward his back.

Gargan glanced and nodded. He hacked at the troll, driving it back, and whirled even as she jumped, tossing his axe in the air. His trailing hand caught Twilight's arm and heaved her over the crevasse. Her leap became a flying lunge. Then he spun back to the troll and caught his axe as it fell, just in time to block the troll's hammer with both weapons, the force driving him back toward the pit.

As she flew toward the shivering, chanting demonist, Twilight screamed with as much wrath and hatred as she could muster. All the tears that she'd shed for fallen comrades, her heartache at not knowing if Liet lived, and her crushing fear rose out of her in a roar.

Gestal turned and threw back his hood.

At the scream, Gargan rolled between the troll's mismatched legs and glanced after the elf. Gestal had drawn a blade—a cleaverlike dagger—and he used it to parry her lunge aside. She landed, staggered, and dropped her rapier.

"No," she said. She looked as though she were choking. "It can't be!"

Gargan knew the time had come to run.

Using instincts and reflexes honed against giants, the goliath eluded Tlork's claws and dodged the crushing hammer by a hand's breadth. With a mighty roar, the goliath dropped his axe and swung his huge sword down in two hands. The acid-laden edge slashed Tlork's thin arm in two, and the great hammer did not rise.

The troll staggered, but the goliath turned. His chance had come for a deathblow, but he ran for the chasm instead, hoping he would make it to Foxdaughter in time.

* * *

Twilight struck the waiting cleaver, but it would not budge. The blades screamed and she tumbled over the demonist's head, landing flat on her back. She tried to rise, but her legs failed her. Betrayal clattered to the stone and slid against the wall.

"What's the matter?" he asked, his voice husky. "Do you not recognize me?"

Gestal dropped his blade and threw off his cloak, revealing his bare arms and chest. Grotesque scars crisscrossed the black, scaly flesh over his biceps and forearms, stopping at his shoulders and hands. As she watched, rapt, blackness rippled across his body, painting the bronzed flesh with inky corruption. In a heartbeat, it spread to all parts of him, half shrouding his face in putrid sores. Clean on one side, oozing on the other, it was as though he had two faces.

As the scaly, festering skin covered his left cheek, a scorching brand depicting a two-headed snake wrapped around a serrated blade lit upon his right face—a face that remained hideously recognizable.

"No . . . " said Twilight. "It—it can't be."

"I'm afraid it can," said Liet in a perverse rasp, "my love."

Then his distorted arms extended like putty and clawed at her, one hand glowing with blood, the other with ink.

Twilight could not bring herself to dodge.

<hr>

Gargan ran for the crevasse lip, pushing his legs as he had in races with his clan brothers and sisters. Tlork swung his claws wildly and Gargan's shoulder opened in its wake. He realized his axe was gone, but it was irrelevant. He hit the edge and jumped, his mighty legs pulsing. A weightless heartbeat later, he slammed down on the other side.

His weight and the strength of his jump were too much for the brittle edge, however. The stone broke under his feet, and he began a groaning, inevitable slide into the jagged abyss.

Gargan leaped again and again, dancing across falling stones toward Gestal. The priest wore the face of Liet, but the goliath ignored the implications. He saw only the Foxdaughter, frozen in terror, and the demon priest's impossibly long arms reaching for her. He also saw Slip, seeping pits of black and red where her eyes had once been, crawling feebly away.

The distance between them was slowly increasing, so he couldn't reach them both. But he could save one of them, perhaps. Slip, his friend, or . . . He might have cried out, but it would do no good, he sensed. He just had to get there in time.

In time, horribly, to watch Gestal jab a red-glowing hand into the elf's breast while his black hand went for her face. She arched and screamed, blood and vomit gushing from her mouth. Horrid as her reaction was, it probably saved her from a worse fate. The black hand only brushed her shoulder instead of her cheek.

The world froze for an instant and reality shifted. Gargan thought he heard a faint mirthful sound, as of a mocking wind. It unnerved him. He had heard tales of travelers wandering leagues in the desert, following just such whispers.

Then the world flowed as normal, and Twilight went white as a corpse. She collapsed to the ground, limp as an empty cloak.

Gargan made no sound, but Gestal sensed him anyway and spun, bringing up his burning claws. The hunter plied his training against giants, with their exceptional reach, and rolled under the deadly claws, still arrowing straight for the limp elf.

Unlike the arms of any real creature, however, Gestal's hands twisted back, still bearing down on the goliath. Gargan thought himself lost.

The priest had miscalculated, though, and the elongated arms jerked to a halt, a finger's breadth from Gargan's foot. Both priest and goliath looked in the same instant, only to find Gestal's distorted arms hooked at the elbows. The priest cursed foully and snapped a word of pure chaos. Gargan felt power flare, but his soul went unscathed. Was this why the sharn had chosen them? Gestal's magic seemed to have little effect on the goliath.

Gargan dived for his prize: the still form beside the sputtering demonist. He stooped over her and his hands went to her feet. At his touch, the elf made a gurgling, gasping noise. Gestal was in the midst of another spell and the goliath knew his time was short. He had one boot off, then the other, and yanked them on.

Sure enough, they fit him perfectly, as their magic allowed. Another goliath might have thought this witchcraft, but Gargan had seen enough of the world to know good from evil.

He stood over Twilight then, clad in her boots, and hefted her limp form under one arm. In the other hand, he raised the giant sword and turned to face his attacker.

"No escape!" screamed Gestal, and fanned out his hand, from which sprang five darts of blackness—darts that had been his fingers. Somehow, the goliath ducked all but two, which wriggled and tore, locking his muscles and freezing his flesh.

Then the demonist charged him, his remaining fingers glowing green.

The eyeless Slip whimpered.

CHAPTER TWENTY-SIX

Her eyes flicked open.

The tent was silent. The air tasted rough and dry, like bone worn hollow by the wind. And flowers—she smelled something sweet. An herbal tang.

Twilight looked around. Vertical black hides bounded her dry world, and leather tapestries adorned with reds, greens, and blues. Skulls and various bones hung around the tent, on chains that would have clattered had there been a breeze.

She lay on a heap of soft animal skins, most of which still had fur on one side. Twilight ran her fingers slowly through the coarse hair and wondered, dimly, what could make her think rothé hide soft. She also wondered if she had always existed, in this place of supreme comfort. She had the sense that something terrible had happened, but her memory seemed more a series of dreams, not events.

Just about the time she became thirsty, Twilight noticed a clay bowl on the sandy floor beside her, containing what she soon found to be the most delicious water she had ever tasted. She drank it all without pause. Her stomach felt hollow and tight.

She stood from the bed and a chill breeze raised gooseflesh over her back. Only then did she notice her nakedness. For warmth more than modesty, she found a blanket of sackcloth and drew it over her shoulders before she pushed her way out of the tent flap.

Twilight emerged in a land that was mercilessly bright, but discomfort was far away. She stopped, and her eyes fell to the cliff edge just under her bare toes. Flecks of sand hissed down through empty air, falling what seemed a league. She vaguely noticed a circle of runes drawn in salt below the sole of her foot, smudged by her movement.

Her tent stood on the edge of a plateau that rose out of a gray-white desert like a graveyard. She looked out over the vastness of dusty death before her. Then, drawn by sounds from behind, she looked the other way, across the plateau.

Atop the crags, life bloomed like a garden. Tents of many colors stood before her, and muscular forms moved amongst them, fleshed in tones of grays and browns, oranges and purples. These were shades of stone, both exotic and mundane. The figures wore almost no clothing—the better to reveal the zigzagging patterns of color that crisscrossed their stony skin. Goliaths, she realized.

Parents and children worked in the shade of tents and boulders, while brawny youths carved arrows and spears for hunting. The tiny community bustled with daily business, yet a certain serenity enveloped all. Incomprehensible jests and bawdy laughs echoed from below, where males and females alike engaged in work and sport. She saw feats of strength, comparisons of skill at archery or rock flinging, and even a singing contest that was foreign to her elf's ears—deep and rhythmic and powerful. Other elves might have disdained it, but she found the music beautiful.

Below her, on mounds and spires of stone that rose up from a shallow, mist-filled depression in the plateau, a score or so young goliaths leaped and danced, hooted and jeered. They played some game, hurling what looked like a stuffed camel's hump back and forth. Occasionally, one of the goliaths would knock over an opposing player who was trying to make a catch, or the ball itself would lay one out. The downed goliath would sometimes sprawl onto the stone and sometimes fall off the mound, into the mists. This frightened Twilight the first time it occurred, but soon after, the goliath stood up and growled in their thick tongue. She didn't understand—she wore no earring to translate.

The simple peace of the goliath village set her at ease, and the sight of the game gave her an overwhelming sense of vibrancy. When had she forgotten the simple pleasure of breathing? Watching the young, muscular goliaths at their play reminded her of the sanctity and power of life. In that moment, the world seemed complete.

Complete except . . .

Twilight looked around for her companions. She didn't remember their names, but she knew there had been others.

Then she recognized one of them—seated alone not far from her own tent. He was markedly different: where the others wore simple tunics or loincloths, he wore a black cloak that hid his gray skin and red markings. And where they laughed and jeered one another, brimming over with vitality, he merely sat, a cold statue.

Gargan—that was his name.

Twilight wondered why he was not with the others—why they seemed not to notice him. Were they cruel, these goliaths? She opened her mouth to call out.

Then she felt something tingling in the back of her mind, as though a gentle lover were kissing the back of her neck, though no one was there. She stood, eyes half-shut, relaxing in the peace, and allowed the phantom fingers to trace down her neck, along her bare back, down, down . . . to the starburst mark at the base of her spine.

It was only a thought in her head, but it sounded like words. *Lover.*

"Liet?" she asked, her heart fluttering.

Perhaps, came the mental reply. *But not just now.*

Then she saw demons emerging out of the corners of her world, and she pressed her palms against her temples. Maniacal laughter filled her, consumed her, and she screamed her way down into darkness.

Gargan stood amid pots bubbling over fires. He watched the elf writhe, claw, and moan in the sick tent.

Her neck and face stood taut beyond reason, veins bulging all along her body. Blood seeped from her mouth and nose, and her eyes rolled in their sockets. She wore nothing but sweat, her tangled hair, and staining poultices where her ivory skin had broken open under the pressure of muscles spasms.

It took three goliaths to hold Foxdaughter still enough for Mehvenne Starseeker Kalgatan, the clan druid, to administer healing magic and balms, all to no avail. Blood stained her fingers from wrists, throat, and face, and from those who restrained her now.

"*There is a demon,*" the withered crone said. She reached to one of the simmering pots and drew out the long wooden spoon with a substantial helping of the ruddy orange mixture. "*A demon inside. She has brought evil into our camp.*"

Gargan nodded. By necessity, he knew, that was the closest she would come to addressing him. He wanted to assuage the fears of the goliaths, and tell them of Foxdaughter's strength, but they would hear and not listen. It was forbidden.

The elf screamed and babbled incoherently. He could tell the depth of her agony, from her tone. Delirious, she delivered stunning kicks and cruel gouges to those who held her, fighting them off as though they were attackers rather than healers.

The frail druid—the oldest goliath Gargan had ever known—knelt beside her, without fear as ever, and seized the Foxdaughter's jaw. The elf clawed, but Mehvenne pushed her fingers away firmly but gently, as one might discipline a wayward wolf pup.

The elf gagged on the liquid the druid forced down her throat. It worked quickly, and her struggles slackened. Finally, the tent was silent and she slept peacefully.

Gargan had learned his herbcraft at Mehvenne's feet, and even the rudiments of healing from her, but he was still impressed at the power of her potions and poultices.

"*Demons of the flesh,*" Mehvenne said, still not looking at Gargan, "*and demons of the blood or heart. We can fight these. But demons of the mind and soul, we cannot."*

Gargan did not pretend to understand the minds and spirits of elves, but he knew what she had endured in those depths. She had been right about a traitor in their midst. Gargan had never trusted any of the companions, but he'd given Liet the most faith.

Liet and Slip.

Gargan felt a twinge of regret for the little one, but the demands of fate outweighed those of friendship. He reminded himself of that looking at the shuddering, moaning elf who lay in agony on the furs and hides.

He stepped forward and the attending goliaths turned away. He did not blame them. If they acknowledged his silent existence, they would soon share it. As he took the elf's hand, only Mehvenne's eyes traced his square features—a tribute to her station in the tribe—but even she said nothing.

"Come back, little fox," he said in Common. "Wake."

Then the tent filled with a new sound, one that prompted hands to dart to crude hilts of stone weapons. Laughter.

The elf's lips curled back. "We have found her, monster," her voice said, with words that were not hers. "She will be ours soon."

An unholy chill flared from beneath her pale skin, shaking Gargan like a jolt of lightning. He fell, stunned, listening as maniacal laughter filled the tent for a long, painful breath. Then Twilight arched, her muscles snapping, and collapsed limply.

Finally shaking the shock out of his head, Gargan looked at the star sapphire in Mehvenne's ochre hands. "The Shroud," he said, realizing. "Gestal."

Then he thought he heard a soft little laugh, but it was not that of Foxdaughter, nor was it that of Gestal. Gargan looked around, but no one was there.

⬥

" 'Light!" Liet screamed. "Help me! 'Light!"

Demons pulled him down into an abyss from which flames

arose. Putrid corruption spread over his body, slowly at first, but faster as the fiends bore him away.

She cried out, but could not hear herself over the cacophony.

Snarling lizardlike demons surged around Liet's receding body, clawing and pawing at their new foe, barbed tongues licking and rending the putrid air.

Betrayal drawn, the elf-without-a-name slashed and stabbed, cut and lunged, all to no avail. The eldritch steel, its gray burned to white, bit into demon after demon, felling them as a scythe cuts wheat, but they kept coming—hordes of the fiends. She sensed them all around her and danced and dodged, trying to fight them all off.

She could not. "No!" she tried to scream, but she had no voice.

Then a single serpentine form rose from the darkness, towering over the other fiends. Its two baboon heads loomed over her, snickering and yowling at one another. The nameless elf cowered, her body locked in place by the awesome power that dripped from the demon lord. "Demogorgon!" shouted the fiends. "Demogorgon!"

Then the two heads had faces, and they were the same scarred, twisted, beautiful visage: Gestal.

"I see you," he rasped. "You cannot hide."

The nameless elf tore her gaze away, but everywhere she looked, there he was. Every demon wore Gestal's laughing face, Gestal's burning eyes, Gestal's broken grin.

"Shadows cannot hide you," the faces said. "We know your lies."

Gestal surrounded her, his madness beating at every corner of her will.

"No," she growled. "No!" The demons surged around her, and she slashed, tore, and cut, but there were so many—too many. She slashed at them and ran them through again and again, but they kept coming. Claws tore and rent her clothes.

"You fear," they all said, out of bleeding mouths and broken jaws. "You fear being stripped of your shadows—fear being nothing—fear knowing your lies for lies."

"They're not lies!" she lied. The claws and fire tore at her clothes—her flesh froze, even though the flames rose and rose around her.

Claws wrenched the gray rapier from her hand and they caught fire. Their blackness burned away before her eyes, stripped and peeled like thick paint on a flawed canvas. White gleamed underneath—white like bone—and she screamed and shut her eyes. The darkness was not an escape—the demons followed her.

"You're alone," they said. "A lonely child—a fool child. A *child*."

"I'm not a child!" she lied. She staggered and finally knelt, exhausted, naked, and surrounded. "I'm telling the truth!"

"No, you're not," a familiar voice said. "You are nothing alone—without your steel, without your lies. Nothing."

Then a loving, gentle hand—Liet's hand, she thought—reached out of the chaos.

Against all her instincts, against the demand of her will, gods help her, she wanted to take it—needed desperately to take it. She needed to let her mind go, let her heart take her fully, let the dream become her world.

"Come with me," Liet's voice whispered. He was there, welcoming, inviting. "Run—leave your pain and your lies. Accept what you are."

They were all gone. Every man or woman she had loved. Her father, Nymlin, Neveren—all of the hundred or so creatures she had loved were dead. Lilten had abandoned her. Liet was gone. She had no one to call upon.

"Where are you wandering?" Liet smiled so sweetly. "Come. Walk with me."

She reached out to take Liet's hand.

Then there was a sound, from somewhere in the depths of madness roiling around them, somewhere beyond the gray emptiness that stretched forever.

A child's laugh.

Reality shifted, the nameless elf hesitated, and an olive-skinned hand reached out and slapped his hands away.

And Ilira, for she remembered that Ilira was her name, screamed.

———————◆—◆—◆———————

The elf woke, lying on her stomach, into silence.

There was nothing in the world but stillness and herself. It was a pregnant silence, so tangible a sharp knife could shave off a bit to keep locked in a box, and so inexplicably sad that it could only live in a lady's heart. One arm pillowed her chin, the other hung at her side. A whisper of breath tickled the small hairs across her exposed back. She did not know if the dream had ended, or if it endured.

Twilight felt a presence and she froze. Slowly, as though any tiny shift would lead to horror or pain, she looked at the plain-faced elf she somehow knew knelt there.

Any *Tel'Quessir* who looked upon him would see a face like a reflection, but an elflord's face all the same. A moon elf would see pale skin and midnight hair, a sun elf bronze flesh and a golden mane. The skin would seem copper to a wood elf, aquamarine to a sea elf, deep brown to a wild elf. He would be so unremarkable as to be extraordinary—neither handsome nor ugly, old nor young.

But Twilight saw something different. She saw herself, stripped of her lies and fabrications—naked, alone, and helpless—and she saw *him*.

Fingers traced the sunburst tattoo at the base of her spine in a way that sent chills through her body. Whether it was a sensitive spot or something else, she did not know. In the other hand, he dangled her amulet—the Shroud.

He smiled, and she felt something like courage.

"I . . ." Twilight pursed her lips. "Are you . . . are you who I think you are?"

No reply.

"You are."

The smile widened a little, as though its owner laughed at a jest she had made.

"I see." Twilight shifted. She realized that the touch on her back was much more soothing than she imagined it could be. "I . . . I'm sorry for all the . . . all the lies I've told . . . about you." She bit her lip. "About me."

Then his eyes danced with laughter and turned away. His face slipped so subtly the elf barely noticed. His fingers tapped a rhythm on her spine and he rose to leave.

"One . . . one question?"

He paused and the eyes went to hers. The irises shifted, like a rainbow—red and blue and green and gold.

"When I wake . . . will those lies be true?" she asked. "Are you *you*, or just me?"

He grinned and held up two fingers, which he used to close her eyes. In that darkness, he kissed her on the throat, and the world turned only for her.

Breathless, Twilight opened her eyes, but he was gone. The star sapphire gleamed against the pale skin of her breastbone.

She let blessed darkness come, and wondered if she would find Reverie.

It occurred to Twilight that she might have asked if he loved her.

———————◆◆◆———————

Foxdaughter lay unmoving on her back, eyes wide but empty. The black blanket contrasted sharply with skin paler than the whitest Gargan had ever seen on a living being. The amulet sparkling on her chest did not seem to rise and fall.

"*I wonder why it sits by her,*" Mehvenne said to the tent walls. "*She is not dead, but neither does she live. She is lost.*"

"She dreams," Gargan said. He could not speak the tongue of the goliaths in that place, for a watcher might think he broke the laws.

Mehvenne inspected the back of her hand. "*It fools itself,*" she said. "*All my herbs and potions are for naught. The elf-child will die.*"

Gargan shook his head. There was nothing that would dissuade him.

"*I did not agree with the tribe's decision,*" Mehvenne said to her pots as she stirred two at once. Her emerald stripes sparkled in the half light of the rothé candles.

"Not their decision," Gargan whispered, inaudible outside the tent. "Mine."

That caught Mehvenne's attention, and she turned ruby eyes on him. Gargan felt something in the air strain, as though it would break.

Then she looked away and it returned. The distance between them that would always remain—would remain between Gargan and any goliath—until the day he died.

"*The Stoneslayer lost his way, and thus he became the Dispossessed,*" Mehvenne said. "*He is blind. This is not his destiny, no matter what he believes. Not this doe.*"

"Fox," Gargan corrected. "She is the fox."

Then the elf squeezed his hand.

Gargan looked at the soft skin stretched over delicate features. Her eyes blinked—red-rimmed, shot with blood, oozing tears, but alive. Mehvenne took a step back, startled and ready with a spell should she need to fight a demon.

But the next sound Foxdaughter emitted was a simple sigh.

"*Gys sa salen,*" she murmured, bringing one dainty hand to her forehead.

Gargan hardly spoke the Common tongue, much less Elvish. He wondered if his heavy mouth could even form such dainty syllables. But he, like all goliaths, was a student of body language and expression. Even though he did not catch the exact meaning of her words, he understood her basic desire.

As did Mehvenne, who knelt and offered the water bowl to Foxdaughter.

"No, my good lady," she sighed. "Not *that* kind of drink."

The druid furrowed her brow, almost looking at Gargan before she caught herself. Gargan could only blink and look down at Foxdaughter blankly.

"What was"—the elf paused—"that game . . . I saw?"

Gargan felt a smile tugging at his mouth. He squeezed her hand. "*Kukanath kuth,*" he said. Then he remembered that she wore no earring, so he exercised the few words he knew in the trade tongue. "Goat ball."

The elf smiled, and it was the most reassuring thing Gargan had ever seen.

CHAPTER TWENTY-SEVEN

As their escorts led the pair into the desert, the sheer size of the goliaths struck Twilight once more. Even standing at about seven feet tall, Gargan seemed stunted and short beside his clan brothers. There was a certain feral strength and speed about him, though—rage tempered by the wisdom that shone in his emerald eyes, and it was this that convinced Twilight he was the most dangerous of all.

And it was part of what had led her to doubt the goliath, Twilight remembered with a pang of guilt.

Well, no more of that.

They had stayed at the goliath camp for six days—three that Twilight had slept, three more that she had taken to recover. The poultices and chants had done wonders for her damaged bones and bruised hide, though she could not shake the soreness, regardless of how much walking and stretching she had done. She had spent those days as an observer in the goliath camp, watching the simple joys they took in boasts and tales, the artisans at their trade, and racers leaping the crags. She'd sat with storytellers, weaved necklaces and baskets, and learned some of the songs. She wore several goliath earrings, now, and they'd bound her hair with bone combs.

The goliaths knew peace, and Twilight wished she could be part of it, perhaps forever. But she had left many tasks undone in her life, and it was her lot—her purpose in this world—to see them done. There were many wrongs to be righted, many friends to be avenged. Asson, Taslin, Slip, Liet . . .

Gestal.

During her time in the encampment—after the dreams—Gargan had scarcely left Twilight's bedside, nor had the Shroud left her neck. The farthest he had gone from her had been to the tent flap, to sit cross-legged without, keeping watch. After that, he had been as her shadow, staying beside her at all times.

Twilight did not know if he had remained so near because of some sense of companionship, or if he was simply trying to remain within the protection of her amulet. She figured it was the latter. After all, the goliath had showed no real warmth toward her—they were as survivors of a shipwreck, joined by fate rather than blood or desire.

Why was he following her back into the depths? She had to go, but why him?

On the other hand, what proof did she have that he wasn't a traitor, like Liet had been—unknowingly, even? Perhaps her old suspicions of the goliath was true.

Ultimately, it did not matter.

Twilight hardly cared whether her suspicion was true, or whether her mistrust hurt Gargan. It was cruel, but all she could think of were Liet and Gestal—two very different people in her mind, though they were the same man. She would give them peace, though she wondered if her current path was madness as deep as theirs.

Not that it matters, she thought, though she wondered if she lied.

As though he sensed her uncertainty, Gargan laid a stony hand on Twilight's shoulder. Some of the tension flowed from her.

"We go," one of the four escorts said to Twilight.

Taslin's earring, dangling from her left lobe alongside three new silver rings with colored stones, translated the words, though she fancied that the few days she had spent among the goliaths had taught her enough to understand. That this was cursed ground went unsaid, but she caught hints of it in their bodies. There was regret in their voices, but only a touch.

The goliaths purposefully ignored Gargan, bowed to Twilight, and turned, never to look back. Twilight knew the goliath would not talk to his clan brothers—ever. The escorts walked one way, toward the desert mountains, and the elf and her companion went the other, into a wide expanse edged with rock pillars and broken crags.

"Why do they treat you so?" she asked as the escorts vanished over a dune.

"Exile," Gargan said. His syntax was simple: declarative and efficient. "I am dead."

That made Twilight smile in helpless sympathy. Perhaps she and the goliath had more in common than she had thought.

She gestured to the red markings that patterned his flesh. "What do they mean?"

"My destiny," Gargan said. *"My flesh is the parchment."*

That made Twilight blink. "You have tried to read it?"

Gargan shrugged. *"That is why—part of the why, not the whole why."*

"But you know what they say."

The goliath nodded. "Follow the fox with the white claw," he said. "My destiny."

Twilight had nothing to say to that.

She spent some time within herself. Her hip felt light without a sword. Betrayal lay somewhere in those caves—lost in the confrontation. She had to get in, elude discovery long enough to recover the weapon, find Liet, then somehow defeat Gestal.

She wondered, abstractly, how she would do all these things. She wondered about Gargan. She wondered what had become of Slip. She wondered about her dreams.

The one thing she knew for certain was what she had to do.

"We arrive," Gargan said at last.

They had come to the center of a grove of stone trees two spearcasts in width—the Plain of Standing Stones, Twilight recalled, if her geography was correct. Gargan knelt in the sand

and put his ear to the ground as though listening for approaching pursuit. Twilight knew better than to disturb him.

"His magic covered the hole," Gargan said. *"I will find the cave I entered first."*

The elf agreed, though she knew it could not fail to be a trap.

"There," Gargan said. *"This sand is shallow. Whispers."*

Twilight shivered. Whispers beneath the ground.

He pointed.

They walked to the nearest of the stone pillars and searched its base. Sure enough, between two boulders they found an opening just large enough for a goliath to squeeze through—or a fiend-stitched troll, perhaps.

"You are the stronger in a fair fight, but we will not fight fairly," she said.

He growled in his throat. *"We fight without honor?"*

"Best to eschew honor, when our foe can defeat both of us at once."

Gargan finally nodded. He put a hand to his sword hilt.

"Wait," said Twilight, motioning Gargan to stop. "I have a plan."

The goliath eyed her with uncertainty but obeyed.

Closing her eyes and falling into the shadow, Twilight reflected on the stakes. She hated using this power, as it meant letting part of herself go. She hesitated to let any part of herself out, but somehow, after her dreams, she felt calm. She wasn't so alone.

"This will only take a breath."

She began the ritual.

———◆◆◆———

The elf padded through the tunnel to the catacombs, her hand on the rapier hilt. She cast her eyes one way, then the other, then proceeded, as though certain she was safe. She moved on, stealthy and hidden to all sight.

All sight except the sight that comes with a demon prince's power.

A massive form fell out of the darkness above, crashing down like a falling wall. There was no way she could dodge, no way she could evade impending death.

Tlork was stunned when his hulking maul passed right through her, to smash into the stone, and he landed with a roar on nothing. The elf danced in front of the troll, whipping her blade out of its sheath.

Meanwhile, a hand reached out of the shadows and plucked up a certain rapier, which had been lying against the stone.

He'd missed? How? He'd clung to the stalactites, waiting, then fallen when there had been no chance.

Only then—when the blade darted in—did Tlork realize he'd been tricked.

Twilight thrust the Hizagkuur rapier deep into the troll's side without a hiss or cry—only a grim frown that bespoke firm purpose. The keen gray-white steel laid aside hard sinew and muscle like warm pudding and speared one lung, then a heart, then the other lung. Electricity and fire burned along its length, searing the tissue before it could regenerate—at least, so the elf hoped.

Twilight's knuckles slammed painfully into the basket hilt as the blade abruptly halted against Tlork's far ribs, and she pushed harder, with all her strength. The hilt buried itself against the troll's nearer ribs. She felt that if she were any stronger, she might end up with her elbows inside him.

"Try fighting with that wound," Twilight dared Tlork.

To her disappointment, that was exactly what the troll did. With a mighty roar, he whirled and writhed, shaking her furiously.

If Betrayal had been strapped to her wrist, likely Tlork would have wrenched her arm from her body. As it was, the tension snapped her arm back and she shrieked. She thought she heard bones snap before Tlork finally flung her away like so much refuse. And if even she hadn't, then she certainly did when her ribs crunched against the stone.

Twilight sank, broken, to the ground with a breathless sob.

Still burning, Betrayal stayed inside the troll, but the flesh kept regenerating. Why hadn't she considered that the demonflesh might resist flame, as did that of true demons?

The troll barreled toward her, his hammer held high.

Without a sound, the second Twilight danced in and stabbed its own Betrayal into Tlork's back. The sword wasn't real, but neither was it illusion. Its chilling darkness sapped the troll's strength at a touch. Tlork faltered and the hammer dipped in a pace-wide circle whose edge was a thumb's length from the real Twilight's head. The troll spun and growled in confusion at its attacker, and Twilight dared to breathe.

After that breath, though, pain overwhelmed the elf, and the illusion wrapping her shadow faltered. The false Twilight's skin shivered and vanished into ephemeral black—features bled away, leaving only darkness. The elf-shadow did not fade, though, and slashed at Tlork with unnaturally stretching fingers. The troll tried to smash it with his hammer, but the weapon passed through harmlessly, giving Twilight hope.

Then a gem embedded in Tlork's chest flared golden, and the shadow recoiled soundlessly. It cowered, as though rapt, then fled. Twilight knew only one thing that could scare a member of the living dead: the power of a god or, in this case, a demon.

Tlork spun back, slavering.

Then Gargan was there, catching Tlork's hammer haft in two mighty hands. He locked his muscles, holding the deadly weapon perhaps a pace from Twilight.

As Twilight had planned, Gargan attacked from hiding, but why did he not deal a deathblow with his sword? Was he a fool, thinking to save her and sacrifice his chance?

No, Twilight realized with a shudder. He must have seen Betrayal's failure, and surmised that Blackwyrm would fail as well. Neither could slay Tlork. And instead of running, as he should have, he had killed himself in a vain play to save her.

Twilight wanted to scream, but a hand came out of the darkness and covered her mouth. Another arm encircled her torso, under the shoulders, and she could do nothing but watch Tlork and Gargan struggle, heavy muscles one against the other, as her limp form was dragged back through the shadows. She saw the troll and goliath approaching the edge of the chasm Gestal's spell had torn, pushing and pulling . . .

Then Gargan's foot slipped, his leg crunched into the stone, and he went over, pulling Tlork with him. Twilight could do nothing but gasp, tasting leather pressed against her lips, as she watched her last ally plummet to his death.

"Foxdaughter!" he shouted as he fell. Twilight saw Betrayal, its gray edge burning, spinning, end over end, up from the chasm. It clattered, sparking, to the floor. With his last act, Gargan had thrown her the sword.

Then something struck her head sharply, she felt wetness, and darkness fell.

———————◆·◆·◆———————

Gestal watched Tlork fall in to the depths of his blood pool. The troll and the goliath still fought, wrestling and punching, all the way into the darkness.

He didn't bother to watch their inevitable demise. Gestal was much more interested in Twilight. The pool couldn't find her—she had her Shroud—but Gestal knew she had returned. Somewhere.

Well enough, he decided. She shall be along presently.

With a hand that had only three and a half fingers—the others were still growing—he swirled the bowl of blood. The image died.

———————◆·◆·◆———————

Her senses returned soon after the hands released her to rest and recover against the stone wall. Twilight coughed, pointedly aware of the trickle of salty blood that ran over her split chin. Broken ribs. She hoped nothing bled inside . . . much. Her right arm was useless, splintered by the troll's fury. She needed to catch her breath.

"Thank you, Davoren," she murmured. "I never expected *you* to save me."

The warlock, scanning the darkness they had just left with

his fiendish eyes, grunted. The sounds of Tlork's roars and squeals had vanished, presumably down the pit, but he would return. They both knew it.

Slowly, as she panted and groaned, Twilight climbed to her feet with Davoren's help. She leaned against the wall, her head still aching and the respective agonies in her stomach and breast biting at one another. Her fingers itched for Betrayal; it lay just visible a dagger's cast distant, at the end of the tiny crawl tunnel through which the warlock had dragged her. She started that way. She had to save Gargan—she had to . . .

"It's appropriate how you word your thanksgiving," Davoren said behind her, the chill of his words freezing her in mid limp. "I did save you—for myself."

As Twilight turned, Davoren's shoulder slammed beneath her breast, crunching the broken ribs and crushing her against the wall, and the warlock rammed the poisoned stiletto into her side.

Twilight had time only to gasp before she felt the freezing venom course through her blood. Her eyes widened—and stayed that way.

"A taste of your own trickery, then," Davoren said. "I couldn't let some brute kill you—not when I have blessed you with my oh-so exquisite hatred for so long."

Twilight's mouth hung open as though to scream. His wound had not been a fatal stroke, but a stab in the gut. It would take painful hours to expire. Especially . . .

Especially with that milky potion Davoren dangled teasingly before her eyes—exactly the same way she had dangled her poison vial what seemed so long ago.

"Death is yet a ways off," he said redundantly. "We shall enjoy its process, no?"

He must have misinterpreted the undying rage in her eyes as terror—Davoren had never been good at reading others—for he continued. "Do not fear, *filliken*—it isn't for your flesh I have reserved you, but for a higher purpose." His eyes roved her body. "Though, if my will overcame your decrepitude, I might reconsider . . ."

Silently, Twilight wondered if she truly looked so old and decayed, or Davoren meant something different. Somehow, it didn't seem like something she should point out.

"You always thought yourself better than me, but no more," the warlock said. "Perhaps I will leave you, as you would have left me—food or prey, or worse. Perhaps you'll be lucky—perhaps the troll won't be the first to find you."

Twilight's throat contorted with fury.

"How does it feel now, Shrew-at-Twilight? To be helpless before me? To know that there is nothing—absolutely nothing you can do to stay my hand?"

The edge of Twilight's lip twitched. Then she brought her good knee up between his legs. Hard.

"Except that," she said.

With a soprano moan, Davoren crumpled into a quivering heap. Twilight fell on him, unable to stand on her broken leg. She slapped away his feeble hands and took the healing potion he had taunted her with. She jabbed an elbow into his face, stunning him once more.

Twilight crawled away and uncorked the flask. She drained the sweet liquor, letting it spread to her broken limbs and ribs. It did not heal her entirely, but the pain receded. With a little exertion, she could stand again.

And as soon as she did, she kicked the warlock in the gut, just to stifle any spells, curses, or whatever else he might have mustered.

"H-how?" Davoren managed as he pawed at her without strength.

"Typical Davoren," Twilight said brokenly. "You may be strong . . . you may be crafty, and you may be powerful . . . but you don't know the first rule of poison. Never carry one that can harm you."

The warlock's face twisted in a mixture of agony and fury. Dark, perverse words started to form on his lips.

Twilight put a stop to that with her boot. "You'd be surprised the tolerance a wench can build with a century on her hands."

In reply, Davoren spat a pair of incisors.

"What biting wit," Twilight noted. Then she coughed and almost fell. The healing helped, but there was little enough a single potion could do for ribs as broken as hers.

Without the fear of the warlock striking her down from behind, she limped toward Betrayal. Where it lay, shadows flickered along its edge, and she remembered its former wielder. Her eyes grew bleary for a heartbeat, but only for a heartbeat.

"Thtop!" Davoren commanded, with Asmodeus's authority.

But Twilight was unmoved. Of her own will, she stopped and turned halfway to look.

"You neeth me," he said through blood and spittle, his voice slurred without some of his teeth. "My power—to ethcape thith plathe. You'll never make it witho'w help!"

"A good point." She pulled the amulet over her head—so *it* could find her. "Ruukthalmuramaxamin!" she called. "Hear me! I have a new bargain for you."

As gold energy began to circle around her, Davoren's face sank. "Whore!" he spat. "You had beth watch over your thoulder—my mathter never forgeth a foe! I'll take pleathure in watching you die, like I did with that gold weathel and her corpth of a mate."

Twilight paused. "Hold, Ruuk," she said, dropping the chain back to her neck. The magic faded, and Davoren chuckled—with a cough.

As the elf limped to where Davoren's stiletto lay, gripping her bleeding side, she listened to Davoren laying out his plans for her humiliating demise. She was amused.

As she crossed into the hall, her shadow broke from its spell and hissed back around her, its touch like a chilling caress. Twilight almost took comfort in it.

"*Filliken!* Trollop! Thuccubuth!" he roared. "I'll thow you! I'll burn a hole in your thull—an keep you alive, begging! Athmodeuth will have hith due tribute by my hand! Your trickery ith nothing to my art!"

Twilight slipped the bloody stiletto up the sleeve of her good arm. Then she tipped up Betrayal with her toe. Tilted, it sparkled hotly in the torchlight. She thought about running him through, but every way she looked at it, it just seemed too honorable.

She settled for stabbing him in the gut.

Davoren's jabbering turned frantic. "Juth like them. Juth like them all! I'm better than you!" Twilight heard the madness in his voice. Blood poured from his lips and his arm reached for her. "I'll kill you—I'll kill you—*kill* you!"

Then she bent, not without effort, and selected a nice, heavy rock. She smiled. "Not if I crush all your fingers first."

———◆———

Surrounded by candles of human fat, kneeling on blankets of skin, Lord Divergence prayed to the demon prince. He demanded power rather than begged. Demogorgon would give nothing to the weak.

And the fiend was pleased with its servant, granting greater powers than it had before. A new skill, a new talent came into Gestal's mind, and his jaw dropped. It was a complex ritual, calling upon his patron in a lengthy invocation, but when it was done . . .

If Twilight did not respond as he wished by her own will, certain powers could be brought into play from which not even her trivial trickster god could save her.

———◆———

Some time later, sharn magic deposited Twilight just outside the temple of Amauntor, Netherese god of the sun. Once Twilight had found it odd that a sharn would make its home in such a place—in order and in the dark—but now she found it fitting.

Golden light sparked and hissed around her, matrices and lattices of Art that served their purpose, then were gone. She felt the touch of order, so foreign to her free spirit, sliding away from her. The light flickered off the sapphire pendant hanging from her fist, then left her in darkness—not a barrier to her darksight.

She slipped her amulet back on, settling into its false security.

Twilight shivered, but would not allow something tiny like discomfort to stay her. Too many had died—too many friends had left her, stolen by Gestal.

And yet within that murderer, that horrible monster, she had glimpsed a spirit like hers. Abused, hated, and confused, surviving by lies. Like her, and like Davoren, too.

Seemingly of one mind, the doors to the temple ground open, scraping against the cavern floor as over bones. They thundered against the walls like the tolling of doom. As hesitant as if she were signing a death warrant, Twilight walked through that mighty portal.

As she did, she casually wiped Davoren's blood from Betrayal. A gleam of white shone through the gray, as though the troll's burning blood had eaten away a casing of rust, revealing a pure heart.

Twilight found that amusing. It certainly would not describe her.

Chapter Twenty-Eight

Twilight went quickly through the caverns, her only companion the shadow she had summoned. They moved as one, silent as death, fleeting as the darkness itself.

To avoid the fiendish lizards and other perils of the depths, Twilight did not hesitate to call upon the powers Erevan granted. With his power to silence her moves and keep herself shrouded, she descended to Tlork's dungeon, then ascended past the limits of the mythallar.

"I see, Chameleon," she said. "You know what I want, and you are with me—whether I ask for your aid or not. Guide me through this, and I won't curse you again. I might even speak well of you—only in private, of course."

No response came, and though Twilight had never expected one in the past, now she wondered.

Her shadow could not speak, but its eyeless gaze could convey emotions and thoughts just as well as words. It sent Twilight a wry, bemused glance, then flitted off into the darkness ahead. Twilight could only see it thanks to the darksight Neveren had taught her.

Darkness ahead and darkness behind, Twilight thought. No light to cast a shadow. She wondered if the absence of light meant the absence of hope—not that it mattered.

Life for Twilight had never been a matter of hope.

Twilight reached the hall with the perverse murals, at the peak of Gestal's domain. The tunnel she and Gargan had come through from the surface beckoned just a few paces to her right, cunningly hidden behind stalagmites just so, where one could find it only if one knew where to look.

She saw no one in the chamber so she went in, her shadow flickering at her feet. The crevasse into which Gargan and Tlork had fallen tore the chamber in two, leaving a small ledge on the far end. A little trickle of red light, from flames, bled from a crease in the wall—a door.

Twilight assumed this was the entrance to Gestal's chapel. Now she just had to get there. She kept to the walls of the chamber and edged close to the crevasse. Moonlight filtered in through the crack overhead, and sand trickled down.

Gestal's magic had split the hall from wall to wall, and the gap was near to two long dagger casts in width. Perhaps Gargan could have jumped the distance, but Twilight could do nothing of the sort, even with the leaping boots.

A twinge. Gargan . . .

A simple matter, Twilight reasoned. The other side wasn't far—she could simply shadowjump across. Except, of course, that the chamber was black as pitch. She could see only with the darksight. Other than the opening where she and Gargan had come down, there were no shadows—not here, not on the other side.

Twilight sighed. "Radiant."

She sent her animate shadow across to keep watch, then searched along the wall. Indeed, there were handholds and footholds, and a small section of rock still connected the two parts of the chamber. The crevasse had torn its way into the wall as well, and most of the rock Twilight could have climbed across had disintegrated and fallen off into darkness. To her right, the gap extended thirty hands up before coming together for about the length of Twilight's forearm and ending at the ceiling.

"*Quite* radiant," Twilight mused as she unbuckled her sword belt. No use complaining about fate. Unless she wanted to turn back now, that span of rock was her only chance.

Twilight tossed Betrayal across the crevasse. It clattered and rolled to a rest against the wall. Then she took off her leather glove and boots, which she sent over as well. The crossbow was too fragile to toss, so she looped its sling around her neck. She thought to throw Davoren's stiletto across as well, but a better use occurred to her. She wiped it on her bloody blouse and put it between her teeth. Then she retrieved some dust from the floor and ground it between her hands.

Ready.

With skills that predated her service to Erevan, predated her apprenticeship—and affair—with Neveren, and even predated her name, Twilight made her way up the wall as deftly as a spider. Her barely healed arm hurt, but she could stand it. Climbing up was easy. Getting across would be more complicated.

She reached the top of the wall and looked for a handhold on the narrow pass below the broken ceiling. She found one, wedged her fingers in, and looked for another handhold. There. She jammed her left hand in, ignoring the pain. That was nothing. She looked at the next handhold—a pace and a half distant. This was *really* going to hurt.

She took a deep breath, bit the stiletto, and let go with her right hand.

Screaming around the knife, Twilight swung, held aloft only by her ravaged arm, and grabbed for the handhold. If she missed . . .

But she didn't miss. She caught the crack and jammed her fingers in. They split, and blood ran, but she held.

Wiry muscles stood out on her arms as Twilight hung backward from the piece of wall, friezelike with its filthy scrawls, nearly at the broken ceiling. Her bent legs dangled over a chasm into which even her penetrating darksight found nothing.

If an attacker had come upon her dangling from the stone, she would have been unable to defend herself. Her shadow, still detached, kept watch, but it was unlikely Gestal, or those fiendish lizards with spears, would have had trouble knocking her to her death. But no such foe came upon her, and she swung along to her next handhold.

Hand over hand, Twilight made her way across the gap. Eleven or twelve handholds would get her to the end, she guessed.

Three, four, five.

She panted, trying not to think about the burning in her arms.

Six, seven, eight.

Gods, so tired. Almost there.

Nine, ten—

There was a crack, her hand slipped, and Twilight's heart stopped.

She caught herself, fingers of her left hand holding her aloft in the frieze. Her shadow flicked its gaze to her, but it could do nothing. It was just a shadow, after all, and had no body.

Twilight looked at the handhold she had fumbled. The rock had cracked and slid away, leaving nothing to grab. The other edge of the floor lay not more than a pace away, but she couldn't swing past it from where she hung.

Her arm was growing weary—at least it wasn't the half-broken one—and she couldn't quite touch the previous handhold. This was the smoothest part of the stone, and she couldn't see any other spots nearby to clutch. She wasn't sure her right arm could support her, even if she could have reached.

Could she have come so far, only to fail now?

Doubt closed around Twilight. What was she doing? She was here to attack a demon priest who couldn't help but know she was coming, and who would surely slay her with his superior powers. Where was necessity—her beloved pragmatism?

She had led so many to misery—companions like Taslin and Gargan, innocents like Slip and Asson, even villains like Davoren. By which of Beshaba's cruel whims was it that Twilight lived, when they did not?

It would be so simple to let go. What did she have left to hold onto? Everything she had ever loved had deserted or betrayed her. What seemed years of brutish darkness had hammered her already-jaded spirit into real despair.

Liet, Twilight thought, and resolve returned.

She started to swing back and forth, pumping her legs. As a child on a rope swing builds momentum, so did Twilight move, agonizingly slowly. Her arm screamed in protest, but she gritted her teeth and pushed the pain from her mind.

As she swung back and forth, visions came to her, reasons not to give up. She felt again the peace of the goliath village, saw the passionate Taslin leaping into the worm's jaws to avenge her beloved, and she basked again in Slip's ceaseless smile.

Images from deeper in her past returned. She saw the men and women she had loved and watched die—saw their living faces rather than their skulls. She saw Neveren sacrificing himself for her, and watched Nymlin's eyes as he plunged to his death for her. Memories from the near past. She saw Gestal's mocking grin and heard the way he laughed at her murdered companions. She felt Liet's loving gaze and remembered the way he leaped into danger to save her.

She saw her own face then, but the eyes were not hers. Those eyes she had glimpsed only in dreams—those of her lord, the being she had just met and had known all along. The face she saw was both the beings she served—herself and Erevan—though only one of those two served her in return.

Twilight realized, then, that she *had* something to hold. She had so much more.

She swung and swung, building up speed back and forth until . . .

The force became too much for her arm and she pushed off.

A weightless heartbeat later, she slammed into the stone, her legs jarred as though by a lightning strike. Twilight suppressed a gasp of pain and toppled—forward, not backward, she made certain—onto the ledge.

There she lay, stunned, blood seeping from her mouth. Her legs hadn't liked the landing, but her tender ribs had hated it, and she spent entirely too many breaths wheezing on the stone.

Get up, you mad wench, she told herself. Get. Up.

She did.

She knelt before a painted archway, and her senses picked up the passage of heat through the stone. Gestal's door. A door for her to . . .

Scout first.

With a gesture, Twilight sent her shadow slipping into the archway. It needed no words—only the flicker of the elf's will—to know it was to search and return in the span of five breaths. Meanwhile, she recovered Betrayal, her boots, and glove. No sense facing Gestal unprepared.

Twilight waited ten breaths for the shadow to return, but it did not. She sneaked forward, as quietly as she could move.

It turned out to be unnecessary. As if by command, the door ground open before her, and she looked in upon a chamber of cut stone lit by roiling flames. She let her eyes shift out of darksight and into her own keen vision. In the center of the chapel burned twin charnel pits—the throats of Demogorgan, she realized—from which rose flickering orange and red flames like dancing fiends. Beside them was a tilted copper basin with something like water trickling from its edge.

It was certainly a trap, but that didn't matter. Twilight had come this far; she couldn't stop now. She stalked in slowly, keeping to the dancing shadows that flickered against the walls.

The chapel was marred with perversity. Symbols and scenes of violence and depravity plastered the smooth walls, drawn with blood and offal. Bloody bones and discarded bits of flesh, as left from a meal, lay scattered about the place, and skins of varying shades of gray—Twilight did not want to think about their origin—hung from the ceiling. The place reeked of decay, corruption, and rot.

At her feet, Twilight found several hunks of flesh she guessed had come from fiendish lizards. There were also broken stingers as of abeil, black and gray scalps that could only be grimlock in origin, and heads, some of which Twilight could barely identify, and some she almost recognized before she looked away, sickened.

A shadow moved toward her, and Twilight almost drew Betrayal before she realized it was her own. "Where—?" she began. Then her shadow fled into her. She felt a deathly chill embrace her for just a heartbeat before it was part of her again, trailing from her feet instead of dancing freely.

A cloaked head rose from the rubbish and skins hanging about the room. "Well met, lover," Gestal said. His cowled eyes reflected the flames, and the snake tattoo smoldered on his demonfleshed cheek.

"Liet," Twilight whispered. Her hand eased, slowly, toward the hilt of her rapier.

"One of us," the demon priest said in a bemused tone.

Twilight did not respond, only extended her sword and took a step forward.

Demonic magic flared and the steel became white-hot. Twilight took three steps forward, gritting her teeth against the pain. The agony multiplied with every step, and the eldritch steel burst into flame until she could no longer hold it. With a cry, she let Betrayal clatter to the ground. Twilight pulled her hand back, wincing.

Her left hand brought up the crossbow and she grasped it in both hands to steady her aim. The quarrel streaked out and struck Gestal in the shoulder. He looked down at it, idly, and finished his second spell. Shadow blasted the crossbow from her fingers.

Now Twilight drew Davoren's stiletto, palming it under her arm as before, but Gestal finished his third spell. Every inch of her flesh ignited with abyssal pain. The thin knife clattered from her nerveless fingers, and Twilight staggered to a halt. It wasn't the binding magic, this time—Gestal wasn't so kind. Phantom pain wracked her. Her bones shivered, tearing at the inside of her flesh, and she gasped and sobbed despite herself.

With a cry, she fell to her knees, eyes staring down helplessly at her fallen sword. The flames had burned away the last of the gray film over its steel. It was a white sword now, for all the good it did her. She would not have the strength to lift it.

"To come against me alone, wounded, weak . . ." The demon priest grinned. Light and flame roiled in his eyes, which darted back and forth wildly. "I had thought more highly of you." He gestured upward. "Stand."

His voice carried the same compulsion Davoren had used to slay Asson, except with many times the power. Twilight's body jerked upright, grinding her broken bones, and she could not move. Tears trickled down her cheeks and she grit her teeth. Twilight found that her voice worked, with great effort.

"You'd have . . . killed me anyway," she managed. She marshaled her strength of will, and attempted to slide around his enchantment, as she had before.

"How fatalistic. How like you," he said. "And have no fear—your mind won't slip out of this enchantment."

Even as he said it, Twilight felt hope fading as the spell bound her mind with greater force—strength that was supple and flexible, with the adaptability of the mad. "Come . . . closer . . ." she said. "I . . . have something . . . to say . . ."

The priest took a step closer, and Twilight lashed out, clawing for his eyes.

And fell short.

Her cracked nails snapped within a thumb's breadth of his nose. Her hands twisted into claws, and Twilight strained, her teeth clenched, and veins stood out on her temples and forehead. If she could only break his will, she could free herself of his magic and gouge out his distorted features. She scratched desperately, praying, but she couldn't reach that wide stare.

Gestal hissed a single laugh. "You amuse me."

She let the hands fall. "I amuse you, you disgust me," she said, somehow finding the strength for a quip. "A fair trade, I suppose."

Gestal smiled—a sickening expression, because it lit flames in her heart even as it made her want to retch—which she could not do.

"I have an offer to make you."

"No," Twilight said.

"You have the choice, moonflower," he said. "The choice that is offered only to those strong enough to seize destiny in their teeth and wrestle it bleeding to the ground."

"Like you?"

Gestal's snarl was more like that of a hyena than of a man.

"Like my master," he corrected. "And those who serve him well." He stepped away from her and spread his arms wide, indicating the walls with their old bloodstains and perverse murals as though they were something grand.

"What choice?" Twilight asked. She could work through this enchantment, given time. Just keep him talking, just keep concentrating . . .

"I have controlled these depths for many years, seeking and searching for a companion—a powerful swordswoman, or a sorceress, perhaps, to serve my master. For the glory of Demogorgon. And now, I have found one."

Twilight blinked and her concentration went away. Her body jerked itself erect again and she stared. "What?"

"Join us," Gestal said.

Hope fled Twilight along with her will, fighting the spell. So that was his play—she had thought it merely part of her dream, to lure her to death and madness. But she saw now.

And she was tempted.

"My prince is the storm and the fury, Twilight of the Fox, the bloodstained hurricane," the demonist said in his emotionless, calm voice. "Demogorgon offers power beyond imagining, strength of sinew and will to control and ruin." He held out his scarred arms. "Stand at my side—serve him with me. With *us.*"

A thought occurred to her, along with the will to pit her mind against the spell once more. Not for the first time, she thanked the gods for her wit.

"You run this bedlam . . ." Twilight managed. "Just to find . . . love?" She forced a smile. "That's pathetic, or just sick."

Gestal shrugged. "Some search taverns, some festhalls," he said. "Some wander for gold and prestige to impress lovers. Some go to war for love, some shatter decades of peace for love." He lowered her hands. "Do any of these make more sense?"

"Correction," Twilight said. "That's pathetic *and* sick."

He looked at her hard where she stood, back arched.

"We are beyond your lies," he said. "Erevan Ilesere, prankster of the decadent Seldarine, is your scapegoat—the name upon which you blame all of your pain. I shall not begrudge you this, but it is a false path you walk. And what does it bring you?" He shrugged. "Suffering. Blindness. Emptiness masked by brief illusions like joy and purpose in a world without them. Your way of avoiding the inevitable—the truth."

"Purpose," the elf repeated.

"A delusion," said Gestal. "Desire, will, and consequence—these are the only truths. You must choose. You hide from this, and that is weakness."

"Weakness is in my heart." Just a little more. She could feel the magic eroding.

"What is the heart?" Gestal asked. "A muscle—a muscle that tastes just like rothé meat." He appeared to take Twilight's nauseated silence as an avowal. "It feels nothing but the blade that parts it."

"You are wrong. I don't run—I *have* chosen."

"Perhaps," Gestal said, inclining his head to that irrelevance. "But he—Erevan—is the wrong choice. You seek a way to define yourself, and he is not it. He is an illusion. Whether he exists or not, he is nothing but illusion to you. A lie. A deceit. You, only."

Like Liet, she realized.

"Who is real?" Twilight snuffled blood back into her nose. "Liet . . . or you?"

Gestal looked taken aback. "Why both," he said, "but I was the first. Liet is but a lost, love-lorn boy—a pathetic child."

No, Twilight thought. He's more than that.

"Are there others?" she asked, though she wasn't sure why.

Gestal furrowed his brow, as if searching his mind. "No," he said. "None of consequence—merely me, and my tool, Liet. I am his strength, and he is my weakness."

"Yes," she murmured.

Gestal grinned—hideously. "And yours." His skin swam and ran like butter slopping over a pail, and Liet stood before Twilight once more—Liet with Gestal's bastard eyes. "You choose devotion to a lie over your lover?"

Twilight realized he was mistaken. Firstly, Gestal was wrong—or rather, he was right, but he had just slipped and given her the truth. Secondly, his power was failing. The spell was fading, slipping from her mind. Twilight might have smiled.

"What do you choose?"

Twilight *did* smile. "I choose myself," she said.

Then the demonflesh flowed back. Gestal looked at her for a long time, his breathing increasing in rapidity until he panted, then dissolved into mirth. "You choose death, then?" he asked lightly. "Very well. All is desire, will, and consequence, as I say. And there are consequences for denying our desires." His hand came up, glowing black.

"One plea," Twilight said tightly.

That putrid grin returned. He pointed at the yawning pits— two holes in the stone, from which flames arose. "You want to go into the pits, instead?" He sighed. The blackness died around his hand. "I shall enjoy watching the climax of your fall, as I have watched its course these last days."

"Liet," Twilight said. "I have something to tell him."

The name struck Gestal's ears like a heavy curse, and he recoiled as though stung. He contemplated the floor for several shuddering breaths. Then, gradually, his panting became chuckling, and his chuckling became laughter. When finally he looked up, Gestal's face gleamed and twisted with amusement.

"I shall tell him," he said. "Perhaps I'll let him wake up to see your heart lying on a platter before us. Perhaps I'll even let him taste it."

"He's not watching." Twilight felt doubt. "He knows nothing of you."

Gestal grinned. "Perhaps," he said. Then he reached toward her and intoned a series of harsh abyssal syllables to his foul patron.

"No!" the elf begged. She forced tears—painfully easy. "I must tell him myself. Let me speak to him—your magic binds me. You need not fear. One breath."

"Why?" Gestal asked. "You do not trust me. I cannot blame you. We all lie to ourselves, what's to stop me lying to you . . . or to him, for that matter?"

"I . . ." Twilight did not need to lie, but she didn't know if she should say it.

She did it without thinking. "I love him."

Then Gestal's eyes froze, shuddered, and softened. As she watched, the hideous black flesh receded like water across him, and the demon brand hissed and vanished beneath the skin.

Liet awoke, standing opposite a shuddering Twilight. He wore bulky robes that felt heavy and sodden, and his hands were covered in a sticky liquid. He wasted only that heartbeat examining himself, though—his eyes balked over Twilight.

His lover looked horrible. She stood as though stretched by an unseen rack, her blouse and breeches shredded and soaked with red. Blood—there was so much blood—ran from wounds, nose, and mouth. Her right arm hung limply at her side, burned red and black, and her legs looked none too steady. Her black hair had become a tangled jungle of smeared, caked curls.

Light rippled around him, and he could perceive, out of the corners of his eyes, beams and latticework, as though something was peeling back the walls of reality, unveiling true order. The world seemed to fall into perfect balance—symmetry. Liet couldn't explain the feeling any other way.

" 'Light?" he asked. "Are . . ."

As he looked upon the pale, streaked face, his heart roiled in a mixture of bewilderment, confusion, and tragic, hopeless love.

Anger was coming—why was he angry? Oh, gods—why . . .

He stared unwittingly into the face of his betrayer.

Twilight could not manage words before the air between them shimmered and the room exploded in edifying golden light. The spell binding Twilight's body abruptly failed, dropping her unceremoniously to the floor.

"No!" she shouted. "I've changed my mind! No!"

Liet flew backward in a tangle of flailing limbs as the golden distortion shifted into a hulking black body with three heads and six massive arms, a gigantic sword clutched in each hand. Ruukthalmuramaxamin was already in the midst of a spell, one that would devour Gestal's body as he stood, and the swords darted out to rend the demon priest's flesh.

"Twi—!" Liet screamed. His voice, halfway through her name, was suddenly that of Gestal once more. "—light," it finished. The change swept through him almost instantly, the demonflesh hissing across his skin like blood. His eyes were bathed, once more, in chaos.

Ruuk's swords cut into Gestal and blood flew. The demon thrall cursed and sputtered and dodged back. A slaying spell came from the sharn, bearing down upon the demon thrall, and struck him solidly in the chest. In a heartbeat, he started to fall apart.

But even as the sharn's spell ruined him, Gestal screamed a single word of power. It was a word of absolute anarchy and madness, a word sprung from the depths of the primordial chaos that had existed before the Realms had ever known light. Even as the moisture evaporated from his body, his flesh withered, and the blood running from his lips hardened before it touched the ground, Gestal uttered the word of chaos.

To Twilight, it was merely a discordant cacophony of sound and fury in a set of twisting syllables. It signified nothing more than a crude limerick, a foul jest, or a random distortion of a tale told by an idiot.

To Ruukthalmuramaxamin, cursed as it was, it was doom.

Had any mortal spoken a parallel word of dictum in the presence of a sane sharn, it might have shrugged off the effects. But the curse that the High Arcanist Nega had left Ruuk, which chained its alien soul tightly within the bonds of law and order, had caused a single weakness: pure, unadulterated chaos.

The sharn screamed, bubbled, and shifted colors. It became a tree; a three-limbed dog; a tiny elf girl with angelic features; a shattered, crackling sword; an apple; and a hangman's scaffold. Then it exploded in a burst of burning power and brackish gore.

The room was silent for a heartbeat. Twilight gaped at the

remnants of Ruuk drenching her body and at Gestal, staring with murder in his mad gaze.

"You," he said, voice like weathered rock, stealing Twilight's focus.

The spell had ravaged his body, sucking the blood and juices from it like a century in the desert condensed in a single heartbeat. The flesh on his bones lay withered and black, drier than white sand. He coughed and gagged, though nothing would come, and struggled to his knees.

"*You*," he cursed.

Though he looked weak, Twilight made no move toward him. The power she had just witnessed rendered her speechless and paralyzed with fear, more firmly than any compulsion Gestal could have cast. If he had struck down a sharn—mad as it might be—with a single word, Twilight could do nothing.

What a fool she was to face him. Gestal was far beyond her—far beyond anyone.

Then he raised his hands, intoning the words to a new, fouler ritual, demanding Demogorgon to strike down this hateful traitor who knelt before him.

Twilight tried to lever herself up, but she slipped on the sharn's blood and went down hard. Wincing with agony from her wounds, Twilight climbed to her feet and took up her sword, shakily. Betrayal hardly seemed hers any longer, not with its gray surface burned away to white. The handle was slick and scalding; she dropped it with a curse.

She tried to pick it up again, but when she bent down, her legs crumpled, her feet lost their grip, and she fell, face first, to the floor.

Gestal continued his long, complex invocation to Demogorgon, and Twilight knew beyond a doubt that its conclusion would mean her death. From the flames of his scrying bowl and the twin pits, his shadow loomed out, long and fierce.

"What do I do?" she sobbed, calling upon Erevan, demanding that he help her, cursing his name when he was silent. She could shadowjump away, but not far. She was in no position to flee—she could hardly walk. "How do I—?"

Then her right hand brushed something hard on the floor and her heart almost stopped. The answer had come to her. Not from Erevan, not from experience or instinct, but from her own mind. She rose slowly, her fingers white-knuckled.

"No," she cried. "No!"

She ran, limping, toward Gestal, trying to get to him as fast as she could.

The demon priest pronounced the final syllables of his spell just as Twilight ran, brokenly, toward him. Burning, fiendish power filled the room as the magic took hold, and black fire burned between Gestal's hands. It shot forth in a line of red toward her heart, and Twilight felt more than heard the very air vanishing, destroyed, and the surrounding humidity rushing into the blast's wake. Briefly, Gestal's shadow vanished, but reappeared when the flame came at her.

Running at approaching death, Twilight did not even attempt to dodge.

Instead, she danced into the disintegrating shadows barely a pace from the roaring, slaying spell and reappeared in Gestal's own shadow. She threw herself into his arms, hideous and desiccated as his demonfleshed body had become, caught his face in her left hand, and locked her lips to his. His spell tore into the cavern wall, boring a hole more than two paces wide and ten deep.

His hands, warped and withered into claws, flexed impotently for a heartbeat, then closed, tenderly, around her waist. Twilight clung to him and kissed with all her strength, spending herself entirely in that exchange, as though her existence would cease the instant she broke away.

The stillness stretched. They stood in the eye of a magical storm, the wrath of the Abyss raging about them, but neither looked away. Gestal's power faltered and faded, and they heard two dimly audible hisses echoing around them—hisses that became roars.

Liet pulled away from Twilight's lips then, and his blue eye shone like the rising sun in the sky after a storm at dawn, the green like the seas of the west. His flesh might have been blasted, his health stripped and torn away, but there was more love in those eyes than Twilight had ever known or dreamed. And when he reached up and caressed her face, his touch was soft despite his petrified skin.

Twilight knew she had saved him—that he was free of Gestal forever—that he understood, and more than that, accepted all. And for a heartbeat, all was perfect.

For a heartbeat.

His eyes shifted to confusion, then to pain. He looked at Twilight, his lips forming a question that would never come. He coughed, and blood splashed from his desiccated lips to strike Twilight's face. Then, with a sigh, he staggered and fell, his fingers whispering down her cheek and leaving a scarlet trail.

"Daltyrex," he murmured as he slumped to the floor. "Why?"

Twilight could not move her left hand, which had been touching his face, nor her right, until the man she had known alternately as Liet and Gestal lay crumpled at her feet.

Then, as though a bolt of lightning struck her, the elf raised her scarlet-drenched right hand. Holding Davoren's stiletto up to her face, she collapsed to her knees.

She smeared Liet's blood across her cheek and sobbed. Then she hurled the deadly blade aside, cradled his body in her arms, and wept into his chest.

CHAPTER TWENTY-NINE

She sat there for a long time.

Then, after what seemed days, or years, a shadow loomed at the door, making panting and wheezing sounds.

If the elf heard the shadow, she made no sign. She merely sat there, cradling her friend in silence. The blood had ceased to flow, and the places where it had drenched the elf's garments had hardened into a firm hold. They might have been bound together, she and the corpse, their blood and flesh and hearts linked.

Not that it would matter to the creature stalking her.

It was ravaged: battered, bruised, broken in arm, leg, and rib. A withered left arm, formerly muscular and sleek, flopped uselessly at its side. The cracked and poorly mended legs propelled it at a ponderous gait, half-limping, half-sliding. The once smooth body had been ruined beyond repair.

The thing loomed over Twilight where she sat, near the pit full of dying flames and beneath menacing, stained spikes. It reached for her shoulder with one arm.

"Gargan . . ." she murmured.

It growled low. She turned her head and looked up without comprehension.

"Kill you! Kill you, pretty elf!" the troll spat, showering the elf's face with ribbons of bile and spittle. His mad eyes streamed tears and blood in equal measure. The troll raised the splintered warhammer high in his spindly arm. "You no kill Tlork! Tlork kill you! Tlork kill *you!*"

A black blade burst from his chest and Tlork froze. For a heartbeat, nothing happened. Then blood and acid leaked from the wound, hissing down to the ground, where they spattered only a thumb's breadth from the elf's bare feet. She seemed not to notice.

Then, without a word, Tlork stumbled back, wrenched away.

The troll gave a shriek as he went, his slowly reknitting limbs flailing on all sides, but to no avail. The blade ripped free and scythed about, cutting Tlork's torso in two. Over the edge the halved troll went, shrugged from the blade, into the twin pits of Demogorgon's throats. The troll screamed and roared and babbled all the way down, until the beast thudded to a rest, shaking the chamber. There he lay coughing and retching, impaled on a dozen man-high spikes.

Foxdaughter blinked up at her savior.

"Should not," said Gargan, fighting for breath, *"gloat."*

———◆◆◆———

At the lip of the tunnel that led out of Demogorgon's depths, Twilight shut her eyes against the fearsome desert wind. Gargan, bruised and bleeding from dozens of wounds, limped at her side, his arm wrapped protectively around her slim shoulders. His face, despite a single eye that had swollen shut, shone with serenity, as always.

How Twilight envied that, and always would.

"You pause," the goliath said, looking away. *"Come."*

"Where?" Twilight asked softly, tonelessly.

"I do not know," said Gargan. *"But we must go."*

Twilight's eyes closed. "Ever onward," she whispered. "Ever away."

Even when they had climbed the stones and stood at the edge of the desert, with nothing around them for as far as they could see, the elf could still feel him—still taste his lips, sense his fingers tracing her spine, hear his loving whisper. Twilight wanted to struggle, to break away from Gargan's grasp and run back down that tunnel.

"You set him free, Foxdaughter," said Gargan, as he embraced her tightly.

Twilight bit her lip, uncertain.

"Why did you come for me?" She looked at him. "Your pattern? Your fate?"

Gargan shrugged. *"You are the Fox."*

Then he began to hum—a song of goliaths, she realized—and sing. His voice carried her away, far from darkness and blood, toward the distant, white horizon.

He put out his hand.

She smiled.

EPILOGUE

At the bottom of the deepest shaft, broken into thousands of pieces, impaled on dozens of gnarled spikes, the fiend-stitched troll slowly, painfully regenerated.

Yes, it would take days before the bits of torn, greenish flesh could find their way back to each other and grow together once more, but as Tlork lay neither in acid nor in flame, he would eventually be reborn. Only a few universes of pain awaited him in the meantime, but Tlork was used to it. With stoic, brute will, the troll would endure.

For when it was done, Tlork would find that gray-faced thing and his little elf pet and smash them both. Yes, that's what he would do.

If only he could remember what they looked like.

———◆◆◆———

Standing at the top of that shaft, the new master watched the agonizing process, his thoughts dwelling upon this labyrinth built over the fallen Negarath—the halls Demogorgon blessed, the darkness in which vileness dwelt, the depths of madness.

"The Depths of Madness," he said, his voice no longer slurred from missing teeth—teeth that had regrown, thanks to his fiendish powers. "A fitting name, perhaps."

His crimson and black robes were torn, but his wounds

had largely healed. His fingers had grown back, too. Even his hair, formerly wild and tangled beyond the hope of redress, lay slicked back about his temples, except for a few stubborn spikes that hung over his eyebrows. His hands ached, but they would function fully with time, thanks to the potions he had found in Gestal's chambers.

More important was the red-purple flame that brewed around his fist—a reminder of enduring power. The gift of a devil, bought at the price of a soul.

Davoren Hellsheart allowed a tiny smile to play across his gray face. He could still hear the brute Gargan and the cruel Twilight shuffling, leaving the Depths of Madness behind them for the desert. Well, he was rid of them; they had served their purpose by destroying not one, but both of the Depths' former masters.

"I don't need them," he said to himself. "I don't need anyone."

Despite his faith in his lord Asmodeus—his confidence in success—Davoren was a bit relieved at the demise of both Gestal and Ruukthalmuramaxamin. He had thought for certain that he would have to challenge one or the other—preferably Gestal, he had thought until he had seen the powers of chaos triumph over the sharn. But the murderess and her thrall had secured for him a victory beyond his expectations. Somehow, he convinced himself that it had been his victory—that he'd manipulated them. He had won the spoils, had he not? This dungeon—the Depths.

As for Twilight and Gargan, he hoped the desert would kill them—he did not relish facing either again. Not because they could beat him—oh no—but because he hated them both so much.

"They are weak," he assured himself. He did not need them. "Let them die if they will. They shall not return." He had other concerns.

Asmodeus demanded power, influence, and worship, and he intended to give the devil lord all that and more. His first sacrifices would be the servitors of Demogorgon that had survived

Lord Gestal's fall—the lizardmen. Then he would enslave the golems that had survived the sharn. They would make excellent servants. The grimlocks, as well, even if they did not understand order. As for the abeil—sacrifices.

And by the time he used up all the eligible sacrifices, Davoren intended to have reasoned out the magical operation of the portals that led into this place. Why waste good slaves when innocent, naïve, goodly treasure hunters could so easily be had?

They deserved this. They all did, for what they and their kind had done to him.

"M-M-Master?" an echoing voice came from the shaft.

The troll had pulled himself together sufficiently to speak, though Davoren found that unpleasant. Soon enough, Tlork would be whining for food.

Davoren thought. Food was not a small matter. He was not about to stoop to the sludge the lizardfolk ate. The abeil, he doubted, would do any better. But Gestal had survived in this place, so there had to be some source of food and water. Davoren hoped he would not be forced into cannibalism. That turned his stomach. Perhaps the strange mushrooms he had glimpsed deeper in the city, with Twilight . . .

Davoren winced. Twilight. His groin still ached where she had kneed him.

How cruel she had been. She'd always thought herself better than him, never recognizing his talents, never even admitting his usefulness. Instead, she'd used him, like the spiteful bitch she was. And there had been nothing he could do about it. Nothing.

They would have laughed at him. All of them. His mother, his sisters, the other children, but Davoren didn't fear that. He'd made sure they would never laugh again. All of them. The stilettos he carried in his gauntlets still smelled of that blood—the one he had left, anyway. The other . . .

"Come to think of it," the warlock mused, "what happened to that knife? Shouldn't leave something like that lying around where . . ."

Then it occurred to him. Davoren had always possessed a quick and powerful mind, and it was a credit to the depth of this mystery that he hadn't reasoned it out.

It all made sense to him then, following a single key: Twilight's Shroud.

If Liet had been Gestal, it would have been a simple matter to arrange ambushes as they walked, but Gestal had vanished when the sharn's forces attacked—surely escaped to await Ruukthalmuramaxamin's next move. But if he had been gone, how had Gestal known when and where Twilight approached from the Depths to challenge him?

He could not have scried Twilight through her amulet. How had he still followed their every move after "Liet" had disappeared?

For that matter, how had he defeated Slip's truth scrying? It did not seem that Gestal had been able to cast his spells through the miserable Liet.

There was only one answer, only one possible solution: the only one who remained unaccounted for.

He knew who had left the bloody Asson doll for Taslin. He knew who had attacked Twilight—the only one who could have opened that locked door.

He thought Gestal had spared her in their confrontation, but he had been wrong. He knew now why, when they had first met, she had seemed to recognize "Liet," if only for an instant, before pretending they had never met.

And he knew then his greatest, final mistake.

He heard a little squishing sound, as of a frog hopping on stone. Davoren looked down and saw a pair of severed hands rocking next to his feet. Their slender fingers and golden skin left no question as to their origin. His eyes widened and his fingers blazed.

Then he felt something cold in his side and a growing wetness soaking his tunic. Irritated that perhaps he had brushed something damp, he moved reflexively to touch the spot but found that his hands would not obey. They shuddered, deprived of strength. Then they froze, as the locklimb venom seized his muscles.

"Master?" the demon-troll asked again. "Master, me hungry."

Davoren Hellsheart could reply only with the blood that leaked down his chin. Then his balance was gone and he pitched forward, only to tumble down the shaft into darkness and the gullet of a regenerating troll.

Through the darkness, he heard words. "Thank Master," Tlork murmured.

"Welcome," said a soft, high-pitched voice.

Tlork started to eat.

Paralyzed, Davoren could not even scream.

<hr />

"Thank Master."

"Welcome," she said.

It wasn't true, after all. She wasn't the creature's master, or rather, she was, now that *her* master—the lord of Divergence, first servant of the Prince of Demons—was dead.

She had betrayed him, of course, but well did it serve, for he had taken her eyes—eyes he had used so many times, just as he had used her body. And now, with the mad sharn out of the way, she ruled the Depths alone, and she'd make some changes.

Soon, she would root out all the allies of the sharn—enslave the golems that had served him, and poison and burn the abeil colony that protected his temple.

She would not limit the purification to Negarath: the grimlocks, deprived of their god, neared the end of their usefulness. If they would not convert to the worship of the Fanged Lord, she would have them destroyed, to make way for greater, stronger servants.

It was she who had been meant to rule all, she who had led countless adventurers to their deaths. Now she alone survived—always survived. She could make it alone.

Alone, alone, alone.

She might have kept the warlock at least. He'd have been fun, but ultimately unfulfilling. Too self-absorbed, always thinking about his parents, and the children laughing, and the blood.

She'd read him easily, just like the fox before she'd recovered the shrouding pendant.

That time had been brief, but she'd been able to unlock the elf's mind and all her secrets had opened to the mistress, even some Gestal had never known.

Ah, Ilira. Barking like a dog, begging for attention, terrified unto death of her own insignificance. What lovely things she could have . . .

Well, can't have all the dolls you want, she supposed.

She'd get lonely, but she'd get over it. Plenty of playmates remained to lure here, more lives to collect, and now that she had the blood pool and the portals . . .

It was she who had fled the wrath of her people, she who had shifted the blame for her actions onto that innocent gnome's shoulders, she who had fled Crimel as the guards' arrows had pierced his body and their skiprocks shattered his bones.

She had never felt whole. There had always been something missing, something that one of the naïve priests of the Halfling Bitch-Mother might have called justice, if such a vain and outdated concept could be formulated. Perhaps now, though, listening to those crunching, slurping sounds from below, she understood justice, or better—*rightness*.

Then she turned the bloody holes in her face toward the lip of the shaft, down to where the troll—loyal and strong, if dim and slow-witted—feasted upon the torn, shuddering carcass of the hateful disciple of the Devil King. She could not see, but by the blessings of the master, she could read minds without eyes. She felt Davoren, and Tlork, and loved it.

A smile curled onto her acid-burned features—a slight satisfaction, really.

For the first time in her life, Daltyrex Blacksoul—Mistress of the Depths of Madness and favored thrall of the Demon Prince, sometimes called Slip—had done something right.

LISA SMEDMAN

The New York Times best-selling author of *Extinction* follows up on the War of the Spider Queen with a new trilogy that brings the Chosen of Lolth out of the Demonweb Pits and on a bloody rampage across Faerûn.

THE LADY PENITENT

BOOK I
SACRIFICE OF THE WIDOW
Halisstra Melarn has been a priestess of Lolth, a repentant follower of Eilistraee, and a would-be killer of gods, but now she's been transformed into the monstrous Lady Penitent, and those she once called friends will feel the sting of her venom.

February 2007

BOOK II
STORM OF THE DEAD
As the followers of Eilistraee fall one by one to Halisstra's wrath, Lolth turns her attention to the other gods.

September 2007

BOOK III
ASCENDANCY OF THE LAST
The dark elves of Faerûn must finally choose between a goddess that offers redemption and peace, or a goddess that demands sacrifice and blood. We know what a human would choose, but what about a drow?

June 2008

RICHARD LEE BYERS

The author of *Dissolution* and The Year of Rogue Dragons sets his sights on the realm of Thay in a new trilogy that no FORGOTTEN REALMS fan can afford to miss.

THE HAUNTED LAND

BOOK I
UNCLEAN
Szass Tam has never been content to be one of the many powerful wizards who hold Thay in their control, and when a necromancer who is himself a lich goes to war, it will be at the head of an army of undead.

April 2007

BOOK II
UNDEAD
The dead walk in Thay, and as the rest of Faerûn looks on in stunned horror, the very nature of this mysterious, dangerous realm begins to change.

March 2008

BOOK III
UNHOLY
Forces undreamed of even by Szass Tam have brought havoc and death to Thay, but the lich's true intentions remain a mystery—a mystery that could spell doom for the entire world.

Early 2009

Anthology
REALMS OF THE DEAD
A collection of new short stories by some of the Realms' most popular authors sheds new light on the horrible nature of the undead of Faerûn. Prepare yourself for the terror of the *Realms of the Dead*.

Early 2010

THOMAS M. REID

The author of *Insurrection* and The Scions of Arrabar Trilogy
rescues Aliisza and Kaanyr Vhok from the tattered remnants
of their assault on Menzoberranzan, and sends them off on
a quest across the multiverse that will leave
FORGOTTEN REALMS fans reeling!

THE EMPYREAN ODYSSEY

BOOK I
THE GOSSAMER PLAIN

Kaanyr Vhok, fresh from his defeat against the drow, turns to hated Sundabar for the
victory his demonic forces demand, but there's more to his ambitions than just one
human city. In his quest for arcane power, he sends the alu-fiend Aliisza on a mission
that will challenge her in ways she never dreamed of.

May 2007

BOOK II
THE FRACTURED SKY

A demon surrounded by angels in a universe of righteousness? How did that
become Aliisza's life?

November 2008

BOOK III
THE CRYSTAL MOUNTAIN

What Aliisza has witnessed has changed her forever, but that's nothing compared
to what has happened to the multiverse itself. The startling climax will change the
nature of the cosmos forever.

Mid-2009

*"Reid is proving himself to be one of the best up and coming authors
in the FORGOTTEN REALMS universe."*
—fantasy-fan.org

PAUL S. KEMP

"I would rank Kemp among WotC's most talented authors, past and present, such as R. A. Salvatore, Elaine Cunningham, and Troy Denning."
—Fantasy Hotlist

The New York Times best-selling author of *Resurrection* and The Erevis Cale Trilogy plunges ever deeper into the shadows that surround the FORGOTTEN REALMS world in this Realms-shaking new trilogy.

THE TWILIGHT WAR

BOOK I
SHADOWBRED
It takes a shade to know a shade, but will take more than a shade to stand against the Twelve Princes of Shade Enclave. All of the realm of Sembia may not be enough.

BOOK II
SHADOWSTORM
Civil war rends Sembia, and the ancient archwizards of Shade offer to help. But with friends like these . . .
September 2007

BOOK III
SHADOWREALM
No longer content to stay within the bounds of their magnificent floating city, the Shadovar promise a new era, and a new empire, for the future of Faerûn.
May 2008

Anthology
REALMS OF WAR
A collection of all new stories by your favorite FORGOTTEN REALMS authors digs deep into the bloody history of Faerûn.
January 2008